A LOVE THIS GRIM

ELORA MORGAN

A Love This Grim

Copyright © 2025 by Elora Morgan

All rights reserved.

The characters and events portrayed in this book are fictitious. Any similarity to real persons, living or dead, is coincidental and not intended by the author.

No part of this book may be reproduced, or stored in a retrieval system, or transmitted in any form or by any means, electronic, mechanical, photocopying, recording, or otherwise, without express written permission of the publisher. No part of this book may be utilized in an artificial intelligence program of any kind, including but not limited to, training any software or program with the contents of this book.

Bound & Crowned Press

ISBN: 979-8-9882794-8-8

Printed in the United States of America

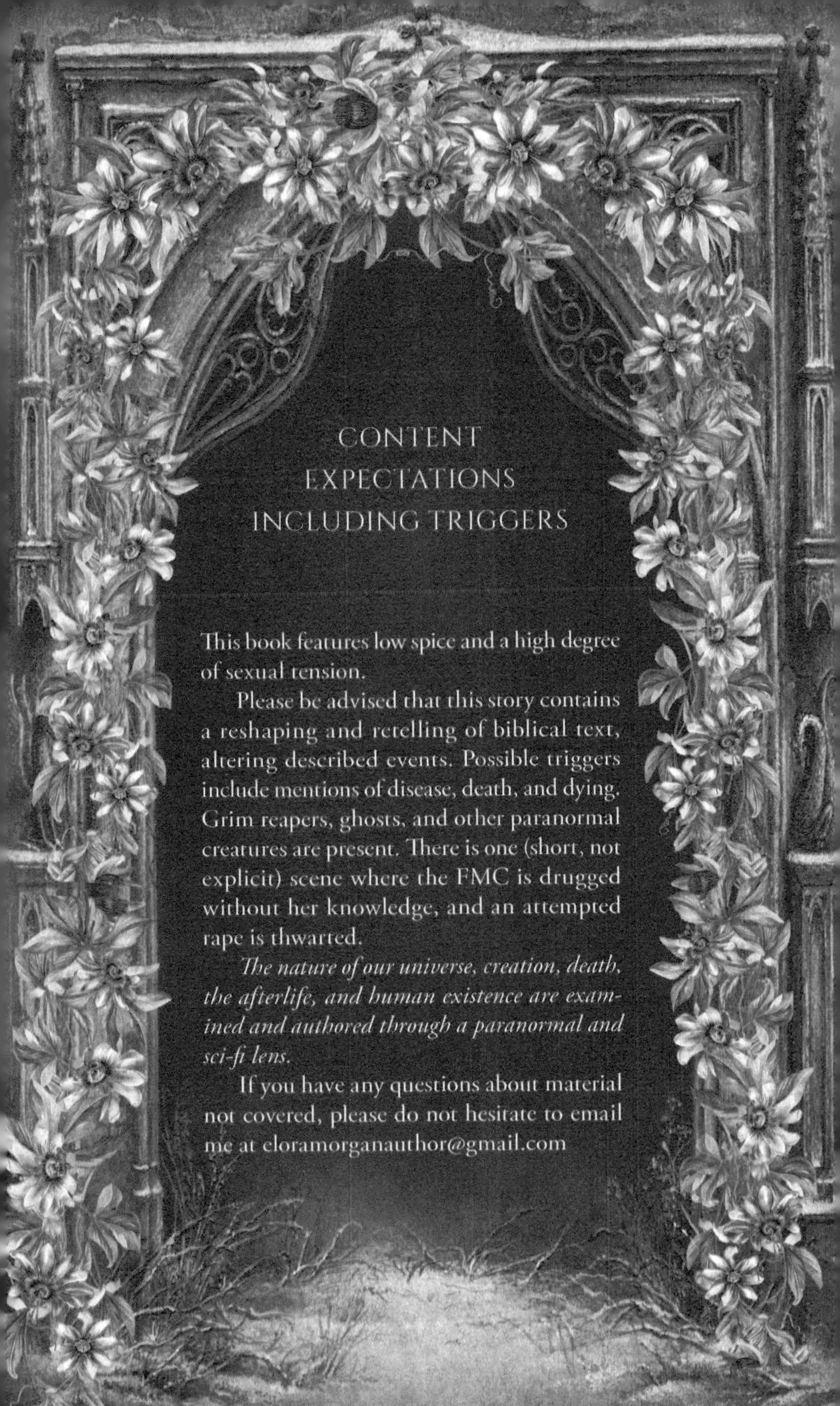

CONTENT
EXPECTATIONS
INCLUDING TRIGGERS

This book features low spice and a high degree of sexual tension.

Please be advised that this story contains a reshaping and retelling of biblical text, altering described events. Possible triggers include mentions of disease, death, and dying. Grim reapers, ghosts, and other paranormal creatures are present. There is one (short, not explicit) scene where the FMC is drugged without her knowledge, and an attempted rape is thwarted.

The nature of our universe, creation, death, the afterlife, and human existence are examined and authored through a paranormal and sci-fi lens.

If you have any questions about material not covered, please do not hesitate to email me at eloramorganauthor@gmail.com

A Dream within a Dream

BY EDGAR ALLEN POE

Take this kiss upon the brow!
And, in parting from you now,
Thus much let me avow—
You are not wrong, who deem
That my days have been a dream;
Yet if hope has flown away
In a night, or in a day,
In a vision, or in none,
Is it therefore the less gone?
All that we see or seem
Is but a dream within a dream.

I stand amid the roar
Of a surf-tormented shore,
And I hold within my hand
Grains of the golden sand—
How few! yet how they creep
Through my fingers to the deep,
While I weep- while I weep!
O God! can I not grasp
Them with a tighter clasp?
O God! can I not save
One from the pitiless wave?
Is all that we see or seem
But a dream within a dream?

PROLOGUE

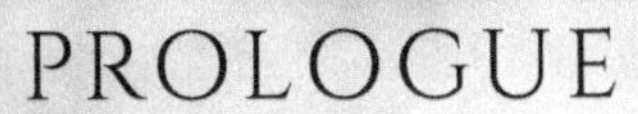

I FEEL TIME DIFFERENTLY THAN NORMAL PEOPLE. Endings.

Beginnings. Unlike most mortals, I remember mine, because life didn't start when I was born.

My real life began when I turned four and looked up into the abyss of my father's black eyes, two coals plucked straight from the fire and set upon his pale skin. He smelled vaguely of fire as well, and old books. Two things that beautifully complement one another but would be disastrous if brought together too closely. Perhaps that should have been a warning about my compelling and combustible future desire.

My biological mother and father lay on the uneven, splintery floor by the bed. If I thought about it, I could still hear the floorboards creaking today. We'd spent the month in an abandoned cabin in the northern forests of Slovenia. *Hippies,* Eligius would later call my parents. A long coat resembling a duster, from another time and place, covered a strikingly slight, but firm, frame. He waved his hand over their bodies, collecting the spark of life and secreting it beneath his overcoat.

I was not frightened, even then. The discarded needles on the floor scared me more than Death's bony hand, reaching out, offering. When he drew near, the promise of secret knowledge and unimaginable adventure caressed my face like a cool, mountain breeze.

I never saw my human mother or father again.

But I saw so much more than any mortal would.

PART I
TO CRAVE
A REAPER

CHAPTER 1

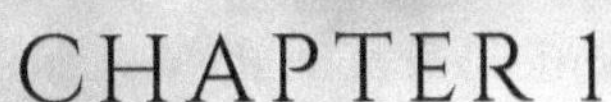

THIS WAS EXACTLY WHY I AVOIDED FUNERALS.
Heightened emotions inevitably led to drama.
Besides, father's work—*our work*—was with the dying. Not the living.

Bang, bang, bang.

"Let me in, please," the voice behind the door wailed.

As an expert in the realm beyond, I knew for a fact that the corpse could not hear his lover's insistent pounding on the other side of the thick, oak door. Much to the embarrassment of the funeral guests, however, his widow certainly could.

I clucked my tongue. People would gossip about this for years. Generations, maybe, in a village this small.

Unless… I relaxed my eyes and let them fall slightly unfocused, searching the room for a ghost. Spectres could never resist the temptation of attending their own funerals. Ask a phantom what anchored them to the Earth and they might wistfully sigh *"love,"* but I swore it was vanity. I never met a ghost—even those I considered family—who didn't have a touch more conceit than most.

Cramped rows of grievers nervously shifted their weight, threatening to break the spindly legs of old, rickety chairs. Faces looked to one another asking the same questions. *Should I do something? Will you do something? Certainly,* someone *should do* something.

I let my eyes settle back upon the sleek, dark casket atop the dais, disappointed I'd observed no ghosts anywhere in the room.

It would have been nice to have someone to talk to.

The vegetal odor of so many aging, sweaty bodies cramped in one space passed over and into my nose. But there was something else too, almost as if my work had keyed me into a base note of fear tinging the scent, of everyone wondering if they'd be next… and what awaited on the other side.

I wished I could tell them what I knew of the afterlife. I wished they'd believe me.

Despite winter's icy fingers finding ingress in the many cracks of the medieval stone walls, most of the musty antechamber was hot. I sat on the edge of the tightly packed rows, so that the chill of a wet, Northumberland spring pressed against my right side, while the heat of the crowd warmed my left.

The metaphor was not lost on me. I sat halfway between here and there, the living and the dead.

Boom, boom, boom, came the pounding once more, so loud that it ripped me out of my thoughts and, to my annoyance, I jumped a little in my seat.

Out of the countless deaths I'd assisted, I had to pick this *one* wake to attend.

"There was little dignity in the man's life. You'd think we could find some in his death," the widow whispered to her sister, a frown creasing her gently weathered face.

Her late husband wasn't the lucky recipient of a dignified death, however, so the current scene didn't surprise me. When Eligius and I arrived, he lay, trousers 'round his ankles and sprawled on the bathroom floor of neither the wife, *nor* this door-banging mistress but within a third lover's flat.

"Cause of death?" Eligius had quizzed, more out of routine than challenge. With the remnants of a greasy chicken wing spewed onto the tile beside his mouth, this was an easy one.

Gross. I'd wrinkled my nose and replied, "Choking. Chicken bone."

The only real question was why he ate poultry in the bathroom in the first place?

Bang, bang, bang.

"Let me in!" came the mistress's muffled cry once more. I rolled my eyes but resisted the urge to groan. The woman on the other side of that door would probably mourn for years, and for what? *The lie of true love.* It didn't exist; I'd witnessed too many scandals like this one to believe in such a fantasy. The only couple I knew who might have found it were Archibald and Yvette, and they weren't even corporeal so that didn't count.

A tall, bald man at the back of the room shot out of his chair and opened the thick door ajar, just enough to slide out.

Finally.

I turned, caught a glimpse of the girl, and silently fumed at the deceased. *What could she be twenty, twenty-one?* Somewhere around my own age. The bald man half-dragged the girl away, muttering promises she could pay her respects later, once the guests had departed.

A collective sigh of relief sounded as somber order was restored. Bored once more, I studied the people around me. Having dismounted from my Time Strider upon entering, I'd relinquished invisibility, and some faces stared at me in return. I ducked down in my chair. Did I stick out, too informal in my riding habit? Too young amongst those assembled? Did they think me... another young lover?

Preposterous. I snorted and instantly regretted it. The scrape of chairs echoed as guests turned in their seats to look. Quickly, I bowed my head and studied my lap, feeling their stares burn into my forehead.

Mercifully, a throat cleared somewhere ahead, and the procession of grievers continued past the casket. I watched them pass, if only curious to spy the other mistress, but that lover did not present herself at today's viewing.

Yet here I sat. A first.

I couldn't say the chicken-wing-in-the-toilet scene counted as the most interesting death out of the thousands I'd witnessed, nor the most tragic. But the widow, Lady Joyce Broomall, had a reputation as the finest pastry chef north of the channel.

I was here for the Banbury cakes.

DELIGHTFUL SPICES MELTED on my tongue, making me moan audibly. No one from the funeral stood outside in the biting cold, so I gave myself up to another soft, *"mmm,"* this time closing my eyes.

Just as I'd thought—worth the unconventional trip.

I inserted one foot into the stirrup and hoisted myself onto the back of my Time Strider. From my perch atop the hill, the fields of this northernmost county in England gently sloped down to the village in patches of brown and green, dotted with lines of bare trees. Inviting plumes of smoke rose from a few chimney stacks, grayer than the white cloud of breath that puffed from my mouth as I exhaled.

Surveying the town, boredom washed over me once more. It always rose like this, an unwelcome tide I couldn't stop. Everyday activities were just a distraction between the two things I most enjoyed—dancing and reaping. Of course, I could never personally reap souls, but I accompanied Death as much as my father would allow.

I sighed and stroked Orsha's neck, trying to think up amusing diversions. Perhaps I could spend the afternoon peeking into those shop windows, or maybe warm up with a cup of Earl Gray beside the fire in a cozy, old pub? I'd already veered off course in attending the viewing…

"Lee Lee," My father's voice, alarmingly urgent, jarred me out of my thoughts. It carried on the wind, over the hill, and straight into my head. I was taken aback both by his tone and the unusual mental invasion. Gently pressing my heels into my Strider's side, I steered her around. With their wings, Time Striders were more akin to Pegasus than horses, although they didn't resemble any Pegasus I'd seen in a book. All Striders possessed inky black coats, and their massive wings weren't feathered, but leathered. They also bore two long, curved horns atop their heads, gently angling backward in a more aerodynamic fashion.

Their most amazing feature, of course, was their ability to defy the laws of the mortal realm and fly great distances in a short time.

"Lee Lee," my father called again, more frantically. I tensed once more at his unusual tone and a sharp worry pricked my stomach.

What has happened?

Eligius sent his location to me telepathically and I whispered it to Orsha, who immediately took off.

My father rarely used his powers to enter my mind, as he knew I didn't like it. And going back through the years to the day he'd adopted me, I didn't think I'd ever seen Eligius so much as flustered. What in the world could ever rattle Death himself? Unless…

I swallowed and took off into the air.

I hadn't been named to die, had I?

CHAPTER 2

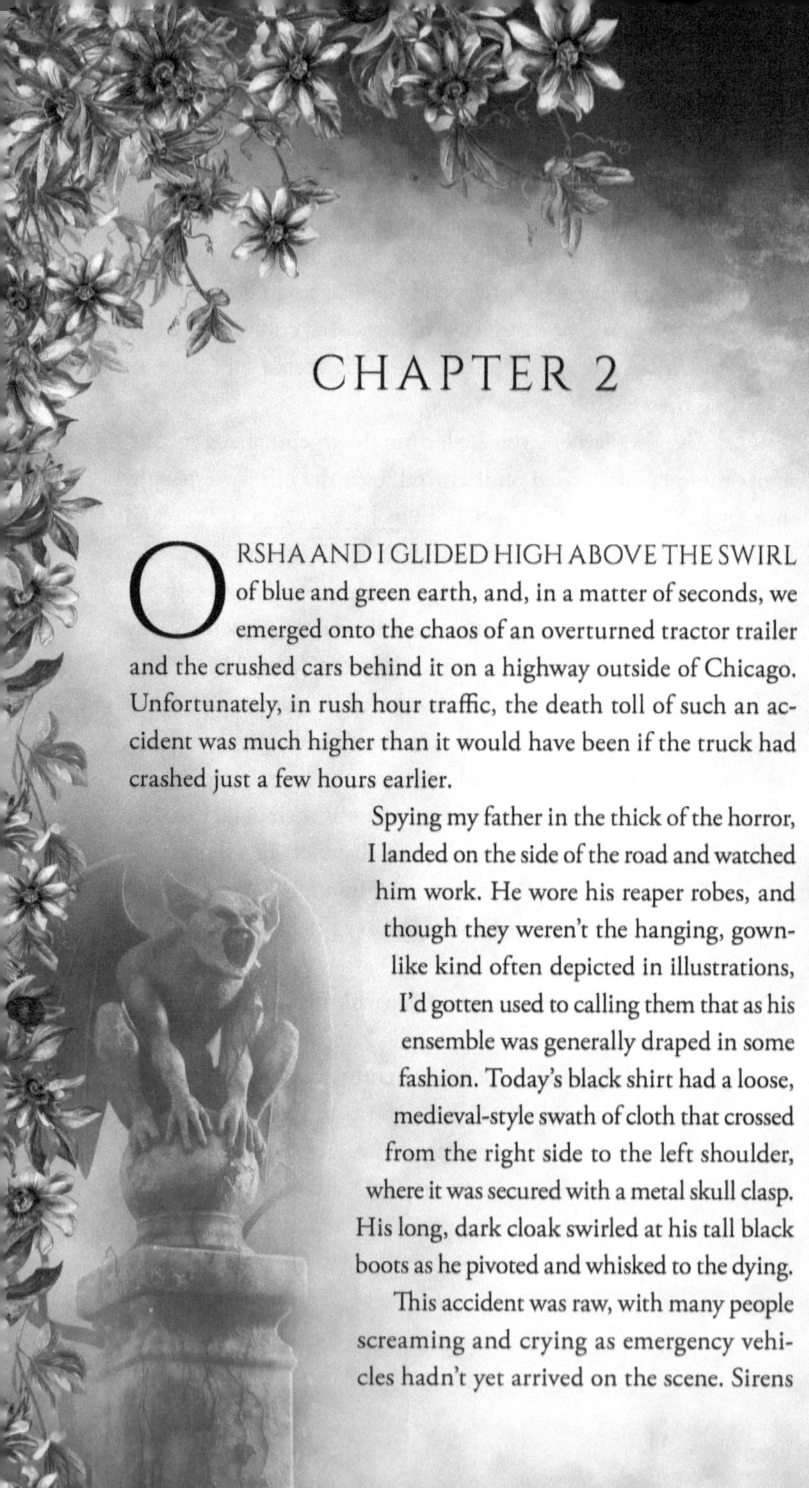

ORSHA AND I GLIDED HIGH ABOVE THE SWIRL of blue and green earth, and, in a matter of seconds, we emerged onto the chaos of an overturned tractor trailer and the crushed cars behind it on a highway outside of Chicago. Unfortunately, in rush hour traffic, the death toll of such an accident was much higher than it would have been if the truck had crashed just a few hours earlier.

Spying my father in the thick of the horror, I landed on the side of the road and watched him work. He wore his reaper robes, and though they weren't the hanging, gown-like kind often depicted in illustrations, I'd gotten used to calling them that as his ensemble was generally draped in some fashion. Today's black shirt had a loose, medieval-style swath of cloth that crossed from the right side to the left shoulder, where it was secured with a metal skull clasp. His long, dark cloak swirled at his tall black boots as he pivoted and whisked to the dying.

This accident was raw, with many people screaming and crying as emergency vehicles hadn't yet arrived on the scene. Sirens wailed in the distance as they tried to push through the tangle of morning commuters.

Eligius moved from the truck driver to those in their cars. One touch of his hand or his scythe delivered death, severed the soul from the body, and channeled it directly up to Elysia, to eternal peace.

Was I to be one of them? I wondered, holding my lurching stomach. *Had my name appeared in the Book? If so, how much time did I have?*

Sensing my arrival, Death whirled to face me and the dark hair that kissed his shoulders ruffled slightly as he turned. One of the veishkas flying around settled upon his left shoulder. Eligius's familiars, small creatures resembling a cross between a bat and a miniature demon, helped him reap the thousands of souls simultaneously needing assistance across the world. Twice as large as normal bats, veishkas possessed a long, thin tail, and bore two short, devilish horns upon their bat-like heads.

Eligius's black eyes were wide and worried, but he visibly calmed upon seeing me, which helped me to relax a little.

"Avalia," he said my name with relief, finishing his highway culling and crossing over to where I waited.

"What's wrong?" I asked. It would have been a ridiculous question for any normal human standing in the middle of a horrific accident, but a life of death was the only one familiar to me.

My father took my head in his hands, patting me as if to ensure I was real.

"It's nothing," Eligius said. "This event was unscheduled and I wanted to handle it personally. We've been having an increased number of last-minute cullings. As you're aware."

I frowned. Deaths were almost always scheduled in advance and spontaneous events were rare, but there had been a surge in hasty additions lately. I supposed Eligius worried that I might be one of them.

"Come. Let us walk," he said, leading me away from the grief and noise.

I shrugged my agreement and followed, still uneasy but relieved to know I wasn't likely to die today.

"You are not yet twenty-one," my father announced.

"No," I agreed, frowning again at the obvious statement. I had turned twenty ten months ago. As a birthday gift, I'd asked for an end to the ridiculous parade of governesses. I'd had sixteen thus far—one for each year since I'd been adopted. The last, procured in a hurry, was by far the worst. Cleaning up after the dishes she left all over the house and turning down the volume on the television after she fell asleep made me feel like I had my own ward to look after, instead of the other way around. The final straw was when she nearly choked to death laughing at a cat video on her phone while sucking on a butterscotch candy. Only my quick-thinking and application of the Heimlich Maneuver had saved her life.

Choking deaths seemed to be in fashion this year. Too much haste in a busy world, I supposed… or one of the gods had a particular penchant. It was impossible to tell which.

Eligius said the governess wasn't in any danger of dying; her name hadn't appeared in the Reclamation of Souls book. Or, she had been in danger, but I was always meant to save her. Things got murky around what was meant to happen and what was not, and it was always best to trust what was in the book of death.

Specifically, your name and the day. It was the end of your story, writ in black and white. Or, I supposed, in whatever color ink the writing appeared. I'd never actually seen the Book myself, being strictly forbidden to fly to the Rotunda. Not that I hadn't tried to coax Orsha to take me to its hidden location, somewhere in the sky. But Eligius had used the power of dissuasion on all our Time Striders to refuse that particular command.

Oh no.

In the midst of my musing, I suddenly had a sinking feeling I knew what this was about.

While the old-fashioned governesses were banished, I hadn't been granted similar amnesty from the growing pressure to do something with my life—something other than riding shotgun to reap souls.

What mundane mortal career compared to *that,* I couldn't fathom.

Chewing my lip and scrutinizing my father, I wondered if I should brace for another work lecture, or worse, an ultimatum to apply to college.

"I had planned… but… circumstances have dictated otherwise," Eligius said with a sigh.

My stomach tightened at his unusual hesitancy. Death wasn't one to waver.

"Well," Eligius continued, more resolute, "you'll be meeting the horsemen tonight. They are to come to Grimsmere for dinner."

My mouth dropped at the unexpected turn this conversation had taken. The horsemen?

"Why now?" I asked, disbelief cracking my voice.

Don't look a gift horse in the mouth.

Bad joke.

Eligius shook his head and, perched upon his shoulder, his veishka's tail twitched. "I'll explain… another time."

It was a promise, both genuine and dismissive. There would be no arguing when my father took that tone. It was clear he wasn't being fully honest, but since the outcome was something I'd always wanted, I bit my tongue.

And anyway, who cared about the reason? My heart beat faster at the news.

I was finally going to meet the horsemen.

Not, *of the apocalypse.* Religion really mucked that up. Horsemen didn't usher in any apocalypse at all, except your own.

Father's Four Horsemen were his reapers, his next-in-command. I liked to think of it this way—if my father were president of Death

Inc., they would be his vice presidents, gathering souls from New Jersey to New Delhi.

And always, *always* up until now, shrouded. Strictly forbidden.

Were they hideous, half-human beasts, with hooved feet and snout-like faces? Grotesque, rotting corpses, with eyeballs falling out of sockets?

Considering I had seen more obliteration than any human in the history of mankind—dozens screaming in fires, hundreds hollowed by disease, and thousands of mortals bedside, clasping the hands of departing loved ones… why then, did Eligius hide his horsemen from me? I'd witnessed more horror and loss before breakfast than any normal girl would ever see in a lifetime, so hadn't I been hardened already?

My whole life, Eligius had steadfastly refused to entertain *any* discussion on his reapers, shutting down my questions with a hard stare of his black eyes. What possible reason could he have for hiding them from me?

Until now.

CHAPTER 3

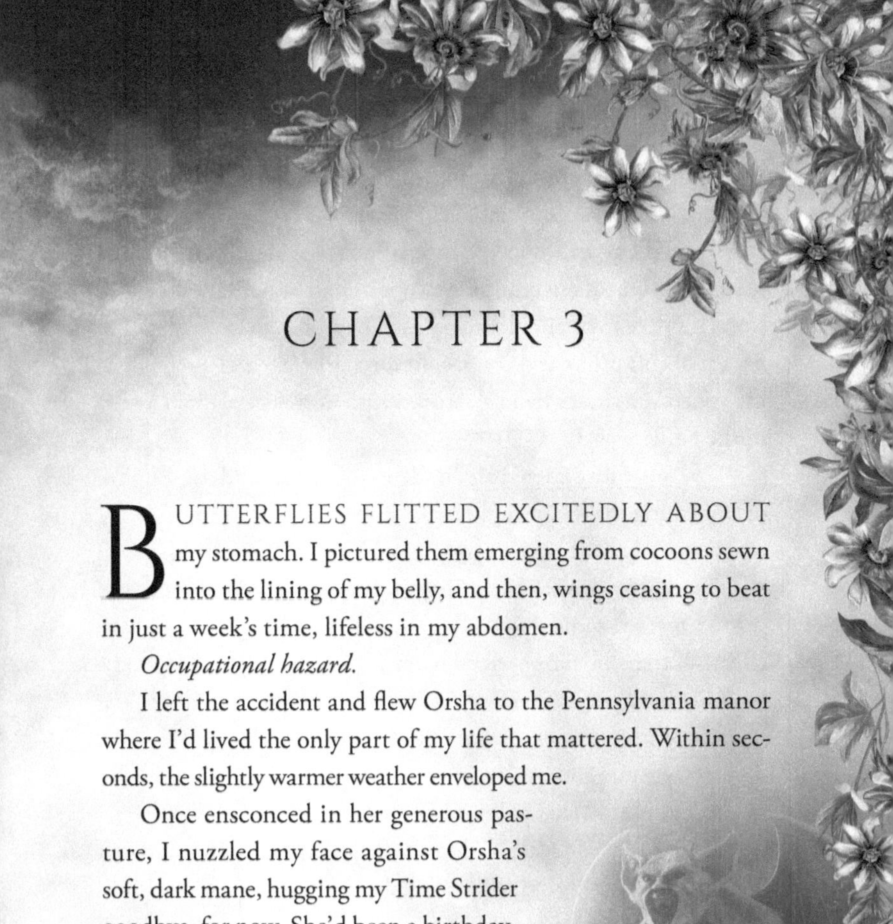

BUTTERFLIES FLITTED EXCITEDLY ABOUT my stomach. I pictured them emerging from cocoons sewn into the lining of my belly, and then, wings ceasing to beat in just a week's time, lifeless in my abdomen.

Occupational hazard.

I left the accident and flew Orsha to the Pennsylvania manor where I'd lived the only part of my life that mattered. Within seconds, the slightly warmer weather enveloped me.

Once ensconced in her generous pasture, I nuzzled my face against Orsha's soft, dark mane, hugging my Time Strider goodbye, for now. She'd been a birthday present when I'd turned eighteen—far better than any car.

Even better than an airplane.

I crossed the grounds of our estate and inhaled the sweet, familiar air of Solebury. It was the pastoral township we called home, with the bustling town of New Hope just a short walk down by the river. Our towering, gothic estate stood alone on the hillside of this region steeped in history… and more magic than anyone knew. If

Eligius hadn't glamoured most of our house, people would drive by to gawk. Even amongst the many mansions tucked away on large lots, our estate was unusual for its size and eclectic style.

Once in my bedroom, I stripped out of my riding habit and tossed the bundle over a pale slipper chair. The dark clothing stood out like my hair, black against a bedroom that was a dainty dream of soft pinks and creams, fit for a princess and a relic from my youth… a time when I'd danced with both feet planted firmly in the ballet world.

Why now? I wondered again, debating if I should ask Eligius, or if pushing the issue would make him change his mind.

Across my bedroom, I eyed the soaking tub beneath the deep window in my private bath. It would do me good to scrub and warm up at the same time. After all, *I* wasn't a horseman, and the effects of the Northumberland wind still chilled my mortal body.

Maybe Eligius's horsemen had snakes slithering out of skeletal nostrils, or wriggling maggots in the shape of hands?

I couldn't understand why we were to meet now, but, chewing my lip I admitted that at least I felt *something.*

Growing up as Death's adopted daughter, I'd often wondered if I'd been numbed to the mortal realm and all that came with it. The few attempts I'd made in a traditional school had bored me, compared to the forensic lessons at Eligius's side. Save dancing, most careers seemed meaningless. And when it came to relationships, they were too complicated to sustain in my life. What was the point of forming attachments when everything was fleeting anyway?

As I soaked in the tub with this new, curious mixture of anxiety and excitement, I couldn't decide if I liked the feeling. In every situation in the mortal realm, *I* was always the one who knew more than anyone else around me. But tonight, for the first time since I'd been adopted, I would be out of my depth.

After drying off, I grabbed a silky red dress at the back of my closet, hung it up, and decided to pass the time until dinner by reading. I lit a fire in my bedroom hearth and settled into my oversized chair. Each of Grimsmere's thirteen bedrooms possessed a fireplace, and another dozen were scattered throughout the manor. Several of these structures were large and looming, stacked with gray stones scavenged from old European estates and rising up to high ceilings. Others were polished marble with gilded, antique mirrors inlaid above. And some of my favorites were small and cozy, constructed by modest brick.

Our house was a curious hodgepodge, suiting an immortal who'd lived through every time period and in many places all over the world.

Concentrating proved a problem, as I realized I'd read a page of my book and retained nothing. The rest of day didn't fare much better. Repeatedly, I'd huff, throw the book down, and look out into our Grim Gardens. Little was blooming this early in April, however, save a few precocious dandelions on the hillside.

Over and over I repeated the same question.

Why was I suddenly meeting the horsemen now, when they'd been forbidden my whole life?

"THAT DRESS IS too mature for you," Eligius sighed. I glanced up as he—she—entered my bedroom.

I knew I shouldn't have left the door ajar.

I locked eyes with her reflection in the vanity's mirror where I sat, unmoving. "And the decapitated head rolling towards my feet last week wasn't? He practically looked up at me as he came to a stop, just a hint of a smile on those stiff lips. If I can handle that, I think I can handle the unforgiving drape of Alfonso's silk."

I blinked and smirked. It was a smug look, but I was increasingly on edge as time passed and the dress made me feel more prepared for the dinner. The scarlet fabric shone like a river of blood over my body and the boldness emboldened *me*. My ballerina build, all sinewy muscle and bone, was a source of pride on the parquet, but it did make me a little self-conscious when it came to social events, or intimacy.

Not that I'd had many or either in my life.

"Lee Lee," Death protested.

I laid my hands flat against the shiny lacquer tabletop. "Just because you're in a female form, do we have to resort to mother-daughter stereotypes of bickering?"

A glimmer rippled over her body and my father's most common form stood before me, shoulders widening, jawline squaring, and, of course, an Adam's apple appeared. Eligius must have been assisting a crossover today and felt a motherly figure best to ease the transition for this particular human.

Lucky mortal. It was rare to receive a personal escort from *any* reaper, let alone Eligius.

"The dress is too mature for you," my father repeated, this time in a voice a few octaves lower.

"I'm twenty," I reminded, tiredly. Even Death wasn't immune to a parent's inability to accept their child had grown. Eligius was probably worse than most, due to all the time we stayed apart. Closeness with a mortal increased the craving to cull that particular human, so my father regularly spent prolonged periods of time away for work. As a consequence, he seemed to forget that I continued to grow in that time.

"I'm quite an adult," I stated. "I believe there's government documentation of the fact somewhere."

No reaction from Eligius.

"I'm old enough to meet the horsemen," I pointed out.

"All the more reason..." my father touched his fingertips to his forehead.

"I heard need of a mother?" Yvette's voice came from the doorway, though no reflection shone in the mirror before me. I turned and blinked before relaxing my eyes, letting her spectral image come into focus. Yvette's hair was twisted and tied with periwinkle ribbons crossing the length of her head—I didn't think I'd ever seen Yvette without something in her hair—and her tousled curls framed her round face. The dress she wore kept with the style of her day, drop-waisted and falling a few inches above the knee.

Seeing a ghost was almost like viewing an autosterogram, popularized by cheap mall art in the 1990s. It was a trick of the eye involving depth perception. Most people could do it if they tried, and if they happened to be looking in the right place at the right time. Some people were especially talented, though they often believed their ability to perceive spectres as having something to do with an uncanny commune with the spirit world, and not just the luck of the draw in ocular aptitude.

Or bad luck, as it might be, since the observation required an almost cross-eyed gaze.

"I've asked you not to smoke in front of Avalia," my father stated in a clipped tone.

"She knows better. Don't you Ava?" Yvette asked.

I took in the long, slender tube of her cigarette holder and the ghostly smoke rising from one end. I hadn't even really paid attention, at first. Watching Yvette was more like watching an old black-and-white movie. I didn't translate her behaviors into today's world.

At my nod, Yvette said, "See? Good. You can smoke when you're dead. Which I am." She smiled and clamped her mouth on the end of the holder.

"You don't have to worry," I groaned to Eligius. "Really. You've taken me to witness enough smoke-related fatalities to steer me clear of the habit. I won't do anything stupid."

"The doorstep to the temple of wisdom is knowledge of our own ignorance," Archibald's deep baritone voice lectured as he appeared in the air beside Yvette.

She rolled her eyes but smiled good-naturedly. "He's been quoting Benjamin Franklin lately."

"Fine chap, fine chap," Archibald said.

Spying the lit cigar Archibald twirled in his hands, my father threw up his, then shook his head as if fending off a headache.

Archie glided over to my slipper chair and took a seat, brown eyes still on his spectral wife. He unbuttoned his black frock, revealing more of the double-breasted waistcoat underneath. Having broken away from his ghostly anchor in Victorian London to find Yvette, after only glimpsing one picture a relative carried of the dead woman's face, I considered their love story to be one of the rare, true ones. Not many people could remain in the mortal realm as ghosts, and even less could accomplish such a feat as moving so far from their anchor.

"What are we discussing?" Archibald asked, eyeing his cigar.

"Ava's gown," Yvette offered, fluffing her short curls in the mirror. "Eligius is being such a bluenose. Look how you've grown, child! Come, stand up, dear. Shoulders back. What's the occasion?"

Eligius remained very still. "The horsemen are coming for dinner tonight."

Yvette and Archibald exchanged a meaningful glance.

"Oh, it's the construction, darling," Yvette said, examining my dress and changing the subject. "I don't care whose name is on the label, it's not very well made."

"Are your reapers perverts or something?" I asked, setting my expression into mock-shock and clutching my chest with exaggerated primness. "Is that why you've forbidden me from meeting them for so long? Do they lack restraint, and you think they'll reap me the moment they see me? Because this life-long secrecy makes no sense, nor does the fact that as of today you've suddenly changed your mind."

I pursed my lips, hoping my outburst wouldn't tempt Eligius into reversing his decision.

"Really, Lee Lee? This is where your head goes? Corrupted flesh or corrupted minds?" Eligius asked, rhetorically. "I keep telling you that it's nothing of that nature, yet you continue to disbelieve me."

"You continue to evade. Just explain," I demanded.

"Okay, fine. I don't want them corrupting you."

I groaned. Eligius had not only completely pivoted, he'd said it in such a manner that I didn't know if he was just telling me what I wanted to hear or admitting the truth. His horsemen were really just bad influences? But after a lifetime of reaping souls, how could I possibly be corrupted in any way?

Seeing my father scrutinizing my gown again, I pointed out, "Very little skin is exposed."

"You are being quite old-fashioned about all this," Yvette agreed, relieved at the change in subject.

"Says the hundred-year-old ghost," Eligius replied wryly.

Archibald winked and Yvette crossed the room to sit on his lap. She whispered something in his ear and his eyes twinkled.

I looked away, not wanting to imagine her provocative promises because Archie and Yvette were family to me. They had been married—or as legally bound as phantoms could be—for longer than I'd been alive, but their honeymoon phase never ceased.

"Fine," my father said, rubbing his head again. Turning to me, he added, "Make haste, our guests will arrive within the hour."

As he departed, I cocked a brow at his own antiquated speech.

"What jewelry are you considering?" Yvette asked, rising and casually running her spectral hands over my antique boxes. The way she could choose to pass through or to touch items fascinated me, although the touching part was difficult to achieve and never prolonged. "Diamonds are a lady's swords, my dear, and pearls her shields. You should wear both."

"Am I preparing for war?" I laughed. "It's a meal, not a mêlée."

"It never hurts to present a strong first impression," Yvette instructed.

"Come," Archibald told his wife as he reached for Yvette's hand. "Let her finish in peace."

Yvette waved before disappearing and said, "Have a wonderful time, dearie. It's a shame we won't be here tonight, we'll be inn-hopping down by the river."

What else was new?

The fact that my ghostly elders partied more than I did—and that they had more friends than I did—always made me feel a bit ashamed. Like I was failing at life.

But it's okay, I reminded myself sternly. *Because you alone are so accomplished in death.*

CHAPTER 4

EXITING MY BEDROOM, I immediately spied my father's note upon the circular hallway table. Atop the thick card stock, his favored image of a winged skull was embossed.

I turned the note over, but he'd written nothing more.

I'm meeting the horsemen alone?

My stomach flipped at this sudden and unusual change of events. Something was wrong with this day, yet I didn't want to ask too many questions since I was getting what I'd always wanted.

Archibald and Yvette had left for yet another spectral soirée and likely wouldn't return until long after I'd gone to sleep, if at all. I released a breathy laugh because, should my ghostly family drink enough, those human guests were in for a frightening night they'd tell in stories for the rest of their lives.

Not that anyone would believe them.

But that left me utterly alone for something I'd been forbidden to do my whole life. It made no sense.

Turning the note over, I looked for more information but found it blank. For a moment, I stood frozen with indecision, then I paced to the wall and back. After a lifetime of waiting, why would I now meet the reapers alone? My theories of hideous, flesh-torn faces and leering perverts evaporated into thin air.

Eligius is lying to me.

Though I wanted to plop down, I sat carefully into a chair because my silk dress wouldn't allow such freedom of movement.

He's evading at best and outright lying at worst.

Of course, Death had business I couldn't or shouldn't always know, I reasoned. But what could be so important as to take him away at this moment?

Maybe it was another last-minute culling he wanted to handle personally—though why the powers that be were increasing the number of unscheduled reapings was an equal mystery. Maybe that's what Eligius wanted to find out.

Not that he ever got much information from the overlords.

The gods could talk to Death, sending messages through wis-pingers—little balls of firefly-like light—but he could not reply back. It was all wildly unfair, though I reasoned it was more com-munication than mortals had.

I glanced at the window, scrutinizing the sky. Unlike a reaper, I didn't come with a built-in celestial clock and didn't know the specific time of sunset. Hurrying into the study where my father kept his laptop, my heels clicked across the marble floor on the second story of our four-story manor.

I pulled up the sky reports on Eligius's laptop, not having a place to stash my phone on my slip dress.

Sunset at 7:28 PM, Eastern Daylight Time.

Glancing at the little clock on the bottom of the screen, my stomach jumped.

I had two minutes.

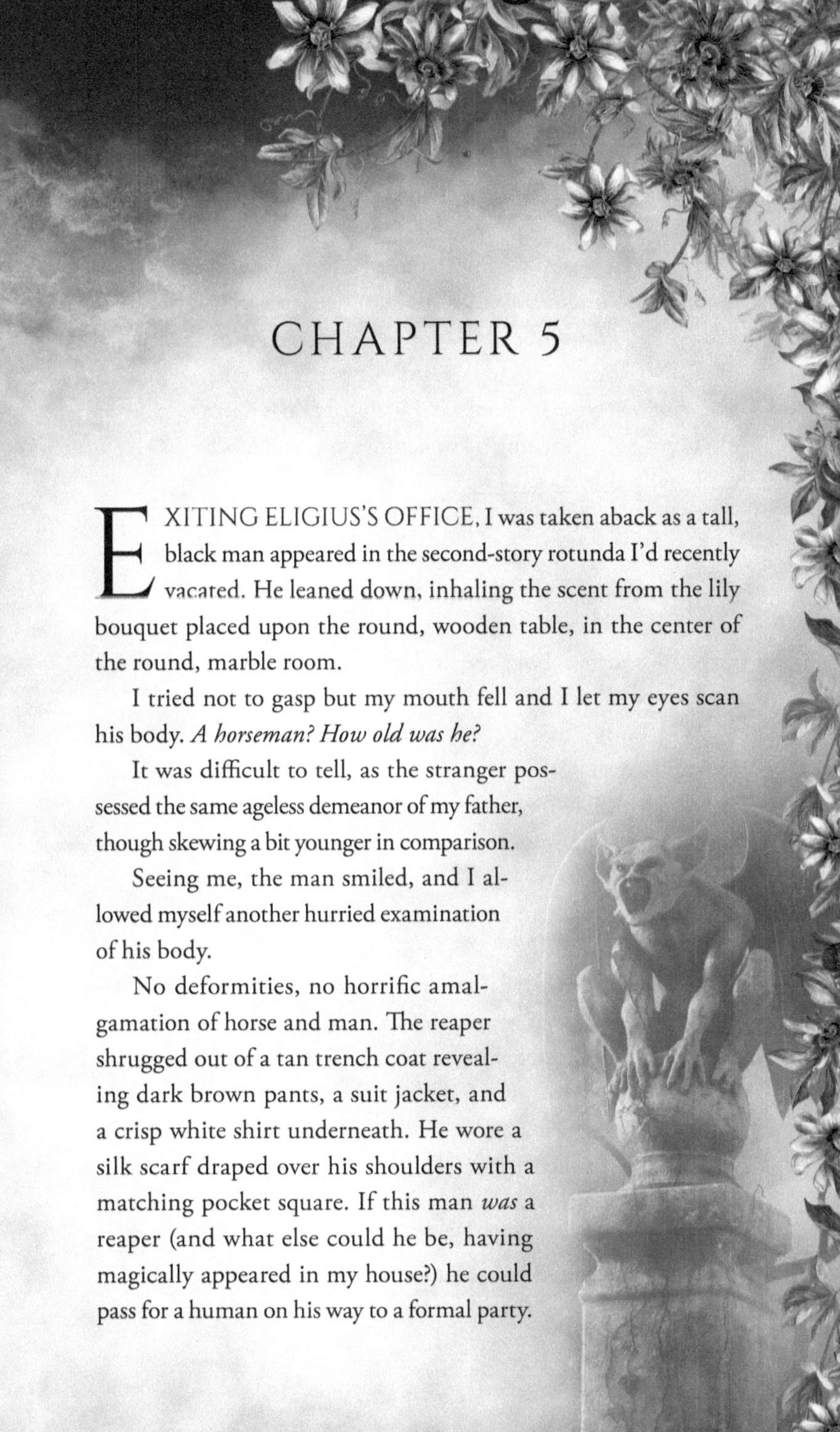

CHAPTER 5

EXITING ELIGIUS'S OFFICE, I was taken aback as a tall, black man appeared in the second-story rotunda I'd recently vacated. He leaned down, inhaling the scent from the lily bouquet placed upon the round, wooden table, in the center of the round, marble room.

I tried not to gasp but my mouth fell and I let my eyes scan his body. *A horseman? How old was he?*

It was difficult to tell, as the stranger possessed the same ageless demeanor of my father, though skewing a bit younger in comparison.

Seeing me, the man smiled, and I allowed myself another hurried examination of his body.

No deformities, no horrific amalgamation of horse and man. The reaper shrugged out of a tan trench coat revealing dark brown pants, a suit jacket, and a crisp white shirt underneath. He wore a silk scarf draped over his shoulders with a matching pocket square. If this man *was* a reaper (and what else could he be, having magically appeared in my house?) he could pass for a human on his way to a formal party.

Albeit, a stunningly beautiful example of a human.

"Hello, I'm Hexley," the man said.

"He's no one."

I whipped around, surprised to see a brunette girl crossing the marble floor in our rotunda. She had that same un-pinnable age and wore a silky silver dress, not too unlike my own. As the girl moved, I was unable to settle my gaze upon one feature, bouncing from high, dewy cheekbones and sculpted brows down to pouting pink lips, before settling upon her uncommon amber eyes.

I realized I was gawking.

"Although he tells the many ladies he beguiles to call him *Hexylicious*," the girl cooed in that same polished tone Hexley used.

Pulse racing and with no small amount of disbelief, I looked back and forth between the two horsemen. *These are horsemen, right?* I wondered. Both reapers looked so utterly human. Which made sense, I supposed, since Death appeared mortal too.

"I'm Embrette," the girl introduced herself, "and it's lovely to finally meet you. Why, you're absolutely *divine,*" she gushed, encircling me like I was an item she'd long wanted to purchase. "I always knew you would be something special for Eligius to have raised you. But then—and don't tell him—I *may* have skirted the rules and peeked at you once or twice, from afar."

"Peeked at *me?*" I echoed, blinking.

"You're as legendary to us as I think we are to you," Embrette said, pointing a perfectly manicured finger at me. "Taken under Death's wing? The only human Eligius has welcomed into his life in, well, ever? You've been forbidden from us too." Embrette gave a careless shrug. "You know… Eligius didn't want us to corrupt you with our wicked ways and all."

So that was all this was? Eligius saw his reapers as too wild, and he didn't want them to be a bad influence on me?

But then, why did he so suddenly change his mind and insist on today?

"Your house is lovely," Embrette said, sighing. "You know, I've never truly explored all the rooms."

On the surface, both horsemen's accents sounded American, and yet there was a curious articulation I couldn't put my finger on. It was like those who'd studied English later in life… Although that wasn't quite right as there wasn't the strain of any other accent struggling underneath. I couldn't say the reapers sounded like upper-class Englishmen, yet there was a slight poshness to the enunciation of their speech. It rang as aristocratic, but from an aristocracy unknown to the world.

Perhaps that's what they were, these non-monsters who seemed more high-born than hideous. I licked my lips, astounded and still struggling with a sense of disbelief. I'd had not a single glimpse my whole life, and now *two* reapers were suddenly standing in front of me.

"Embrette—" I began, but she cut me off.

"You can call me Em or Brett if you like," she said, giving me a friendly, almost conspiratorial smile. "Everyone does."

"Everyone calls you Brat, you're mistaken," Hexley mumbled to the floor.

Embrette examined her fingernails, mock-bored. "No one calls me Brat."

Hexley chuckled. "To your face."

Embrette ceased the fake-fingernail study. Unamused, she chided, "Watch your tongue."

In a roguish, seductive voice, Hexley asked, "Would you like to watch it for me?"

"You're… female?" I breathed, interrupting their banter.

"I should hope so," she said airily. "Rather sexist of you."

"It's just, I always pictured the horsemen as, you know," I mumbled, blushing, "men."

Embrette laughed and it was a beguiling sound from her lips. "And Death wasn't some indication that things aren't always as the stories say? Tell me, which form of your father's will we be dining with tonight? A classic, tall and bony as a skeleton? Or a hulking specimen with a barrel of a torso and muscles bulging at the seams? Slim and female perhaps? That one looks better in silver than I do so maybe I should change."

"I… *wait.* Can you change your appearance too?" I asked, unclear as to whether she meant her dress or her body. I had so many questions that I felt like I wanted to sit the two reapers down and barrage them for hours. Having waited for this moment for years, only to have it unfold so suddenly and casually, made me wonder if I'd struck my head and was dreaming the whole thing. *And where in the world was Eligius? What could he be doing that was more important than this?*

Em sighed. "Alas, we are stuck as we always were." She flicked her hands dismissively over her body, as if being stuck that way was anything other than being dealt the luckiest hand possible.

"It's not true," Hexley interjected, crossing the room to join us so that I now stood between the two bickering horsemen. He carried himself like a king as he moved, graceful and sure.

"What? That we're not stuck as we are? Or that you don't leave a body count of beguiled women in your wake?" Embrette smiled and it had a feral, cat-like warning. "Or are both of these things really the same?"

Hexley grinned on one side of his mouth and winked at me. "I confess to enchanting my fair share of the fair sex—" he began.

"I see nothing fair about the number," Embrette countered. "When you're through there's nothing left to share."

Hexley's grin widened. "Is that a request? I'd be happy to share with you." He held out his hand. "Come, my dear, we shall away this very moment in mutual amorous conquest."

Embrette leveled her gaze at Hexley. "That's not what I meant."

Pointedly ignoring her, Hexley said to me, "I have never in my life heard the word *Hexylicious* out of anyone's mouth—but hers.

And I'll admit it's odd, but I've also never in my life met a man who minds whatever a woman wants to cry out when she's in the throes of that much passion—"

Before Hexley could finish, a creature flew into the room and headed straight for him, whizzing past my head. The flying blur resembled an amber, iridescent butterfly, with a small, deadly-looking stinger. Its body seemed vaguely humanoid, albeit miniature, making the creature appear like a cross between a butterfly and a faerie.

"Ouch!" Hexley exclaimed, slapping his hand over his bicep. "Your bitch bug bit me."

I guessed it had little fangs too. Embrette only shrugged, smug.

"Do you have familiars?" I asked, surprised and delighted. So much about the horsemen had been kept from me and suddenly, a lot of information was coming at once, making me both want to speed up and need to slow down. "Helpers in reaping, like Eligius?"

"Of course," Em replied, waving her hand. "If Death himself can't even collect his share of souls without assistance, however could we manage?"

"What are yours called?" I asked, gawking at the fascinating creature flitting through the air to its mistress.

Embrette lifted her hand and the insect landed gently on one finger, gossamer wings flapping softly.

"Bitch bugs," Hexley said, rubbing his arm.

"I call them butterfae," Embrette replied, cooing to her striking familiar. The name made sense, and I nodded.

Spinning to face Hexley, I asked, "And what do you have?"

"Ronemin," Hexley said with a grin, and a different creature tore into the room. It leapt onto Embrette's arm, knocking her butterfae onto the marble floor and pinning it helplessly.

This new magical familiar looked as if a large, cat-like predator had been given strange wings. I squinted, searching my mind for an appropriate mythical comparison. The creature was partially reminiscent of a manticore, and yet wholly different. Blinking, I realized its wings were made of *fur,* not feathers.

Are all familiars winged? I wondered. And, more urgently, *had I stepped into some kind of enteral animosity between Hexley and Embrette?*

The female reaper could barely contain her fury as she ordered, "Unless you want your ronemin swarmed with *all* of my butterfae, you will command him to release her this instant."

Hexley gave a mocking bow but he relented, alleviating the pressure on the struggling butterfae and allowing it to escape. I braced for their continued arguing, but Embrette's eyes shifted to something behind me and I turned to see a third horseman enter the room.

I guess knocking at the front door isn't customary for reapers.

Another ageless boy-man stood in the doorway, long, pale limbs an echo of the doorframe itself. Light blonde hair fell past his ears, and sunken green eyes stared out above pronounced cheekbones. Two swords were sheathed onto either side of his waist. I had to blink and shake my head, marveling at the appearance of a third non-monster, right here in the manor and after all these years.

The blonde newcomer worked his gaze from my toes to my head, and I shifted nervously. He said nothing, and though only a few seconds passed, the silence grew awkward. No one moved except for Hexley's ronemin, who stretched lazily, and Embrette's butterfae, who folded its wings onto its back.

"Avalia, this is Sevastian," Embrette offered with exaggerated politeness. "Sevastian, may I present… Death's daughter?" I thought the slight elevation in her tone was to lighten the mood, which had inexpiably darkened at the new reaper's appearance.

Sevastian's reply was a slow blink. He continued to stare at me, though not at all with curiosity or friendliness. If I had to guess, I'd have said he seemed dismissive or bored or… angry? Had I done something wrong?

The newest reaper wore similar attire to Hexley, though a shade less formal, and three shades less pressed. His gray pants and shirt were the same cut, but he wore no jacket, no scarf, no pocket square, and the wrinkles made it look as if he'd slept the night in his clothing. Or the past several nights. Plus, he'd left his blades strapped to his waist while Hexley and Embrette had glamoured whatever they used to reap.

Finally, the newest horseman nodded. I supposed that was the only greeting I was getting because he spun on his heel and, without a word, walked out onto the adjoining terrace. When Sevastian left, I was surprised to find a weight had lifted from my chest. It was as if a hopelessness filled the air around him that had, thankfully, departed when he took his leave.

"Don't take it personally," Embrette said, sighing. "He's like that with everyone."

"We can't all charm the ladies," Hexley said, taking my hand and gallantly kissing it. Embrette shot him a displeased look and he quickly straightened. "Shall we join Sevastian and get to know one another?" he asked. "We've been as curious about you as I imagine you have been about us. As Em said, in all the millennia of reaping, Eligius has never taken an interest in a human before you."

"Shouldn't we wait for Noric?" Em asked, cocking her head as if listening.

"You know he's a workaholic," Hexley dismissed with a wave of his hand.

"Mmm," she agreed with a shrug, "a reaper's work is never done."

My mind spun as it tried to process everything that had just occurred and I held up my hands, needing everyone to give me a minute. "You're the horsemen?" I marveled, half to myself. "Father's reapers?"

"In the flesh," Embrette replied.

"Do you… have another form?" I asked, astonished, as I once again pictured transformations into actual horses.

"You're quite literal, aren't you?" Embrette remarked, arching a brow. "No, we can't shift as Eligius can. Not unless you count our skeletal images when lightning strikes, same as Death, and we have no control over that. This is all we've got. Disappointed?" Em tucked her chin as she looked up and batted her lashes. The coy move struck me as having long been practiced, but that didn't diminish its effect. "Where do you keep the champagne?" she asked, changing the subject.

"Um… in the cellar."

"I'll go fetch it," she said.

"Allow me," Hexley offered with a friendly smile, taking the stairs with a skip in his step. His familiar—the fur-winged manticore he called a ronemin—disappeared into the air.

"Take your time. Or don't come back at all," Embrette called over her shoulder as she laced her arm through mine. "Although, we would be bothered to have to fetch the champagne ourselves," she added thoughtfully.

"Come. Let us talk as the best friends I'm sure we're going to be," Em declared boldly as we walked. "You don't know how long I've been waiting for an estrogen injection into this group. You do like champagne, don't you?"

"I… yes?" I didn't mean it to come out as a question, but I was more than a little overwhelmed. I'd had champagne plenty of times—Eligius said we were citizens of the world, and the regional statutes on the drinking age didn't apply. In fact, he'd always encouraged my developing a *responsible attitude* toward adult beverages under his supervision, rather than abusing alcohol at a wild party some night.

Eligius missed the fact that I'd need to have friends in order to be invited to a party at which I'd get drunk in the first place.

Although… did I suddenly have a friend? And, was she trying to get me drunk, first thing?

I bit my lip, suppressing a chuckle.

Not that this beguiling creature next to me seemed likely to slip into anything as inelegant as inebriation, unless Hexley could provoke her into such a state. I didn't know what their deal was, and I'd have to possess psychic abilities to figure out Sevastian's problem.

Also, who was Noric, the mysterious fourth and final reaper?

I shook my head, bewildered. Finally having met father's horsemen, I had more questions than ever.

Arm-in-arm, Embrette and I made our way to the terrace overlooking the grounds at the back of the house. A chill hit us as soon as we stepped out, and I scurried to turn on the heat lamps and fire pits. Immune to the cold, Embrette draped her body over the chaise lounge as if she were sunning herself. At dusk. In a gown.

Hearing our entrance, Sevastian made no move to break his study of the rolling lawn below. The terrace granted a view to the darkening forest beyond our gardens. Come summer the landscape would turn lush and leafy, but now the trees were bare, with only few bearing a hint of spring buds.

"Won't you join us, Sevy, baby?" Embrette cooed.

Grudgingly, the tall, blonde horseman shuffled over to the table but did not sit or speak, as taciturn as he was handsome. I thought I'd overcome those pesky feelings of inadequacy from my youth, but seeing three preternaturally perfect specimens brought a new and unwelcome challenge. I sat upright in my chair, leaning on years of rigorous ballet lessons. Grace was what I relied upon, what I retreated into, when all else failed me.

Hexley returned and distributed glasses of champagne. Sevastian took his and turned again, studying the grounds. Clouds had rolled in, obscuring the view, but in the distance, I glimpsed Olga's hunched back as she gathered the first few wild dandelions. I was sure our elderly housekeeper would bring Sanderson the bounty if she remembered, and Sanderson, our chef, would prepare them for a salad later. Olga's mind had weakened with her advanced age, and she needed a lot of reminders. The advantage was that, unlike Sanderson, father didn't have to magically obscure her memories every so often. Human knowledge of immortals was strictly forbidden.

I, however, had been a lucky exception the gods granted Eligius.

"Sevastian?" I called, curious. He reluctantly turned from his study. "Can I ask what your familiar is?"

Wordlessly, the blonde reaper conjured his helper and I *gawked*. The creature was the rough approximation of an adolescent dragon crossed with a sea serpent. It looked like a beast right out of legend, its scaled body the same green as Sevastian's eyes. His familiar was entirely fitting, because Sevastian reminded me of a Viking warrior or Nordic prince.

"Oh my gosh," I breathed. The creature was larger than any of the others I'd seen thus far, undulating as it levitated and lazily flapping its large wings every so often to maintain air. A storm was rolling in, and it looked particularly menacing against the darkening sky.

"They are my drasyg." Sevastian bit out the words. His voice was soft but proud, dangerous.

"Yes, yes," Hexley interrupted, waving a hand to conjure the reaper blades he'd previously glamoured. Hexley's weapons were slightly smaller than Sevastian's and curved to resemble a scimitar.

"Sevastian has the largest weapon and the biggest familiar," Hexley grumbled, slicing his blades through the air with skill and showmanship. "It doesn't correlate to anything, you know."

I burst out laughing. "I wasn't going to—that's not what I was thinking." Turning to Embrette, I asked, "Can I see yours too?"

Embrette un-glamored her lethal weapon—a unique, hand-held blade. Curving before straightening, it reminded me of her butterfae's stinger, smaller than the others but just as deadly. I knew from Eligius that a reaper's weapon was utilized in the same manner as their Time Strider. Neither were necessary, as they could reap with their hands and whisk at will, but both were employed for pleasure or convenience.

For the next half hour, I pelted Hexley and Embrette with all kinds of questions about their powers and their lives, but sometimes it was difficult to get a word in because they had so many questions about mine. I couldn't understand their curiosity—my life was dull compared to theirs.

There was a break in conversation and Hexley paused. He cocked his head as if listening, then announced, "Noric's still tied up. Eligius will be here in a moment and asked us to head inside."

"Workaholic," Embrette groaned, rolling her eyes. "I hope he doesn't arrive with blood on his clothes."

"You can all talk to one another… telepathically," I said, awed. "Just like Death."

"Mm-hm," Embrette agreed, nodding. "But when it comes to mortals it only works in one direction." She wagged her finger and chided, "You can't talk back."

I let out a breathy laugh and we all rose for dinner, my heart as light as my steps. I'd half-forgotten about the mystery of why Eligius kept his reapers from me and why he'd suddenly changed his mind.

Until the ominous, storm-charged air lifted the hair on my arms, and the rising wind blew onto the back of my neck, as if it tried to whisper secret warnings into my ear.

But I was no reaper, and whatever the world wanted to say, I couldn't hear it.

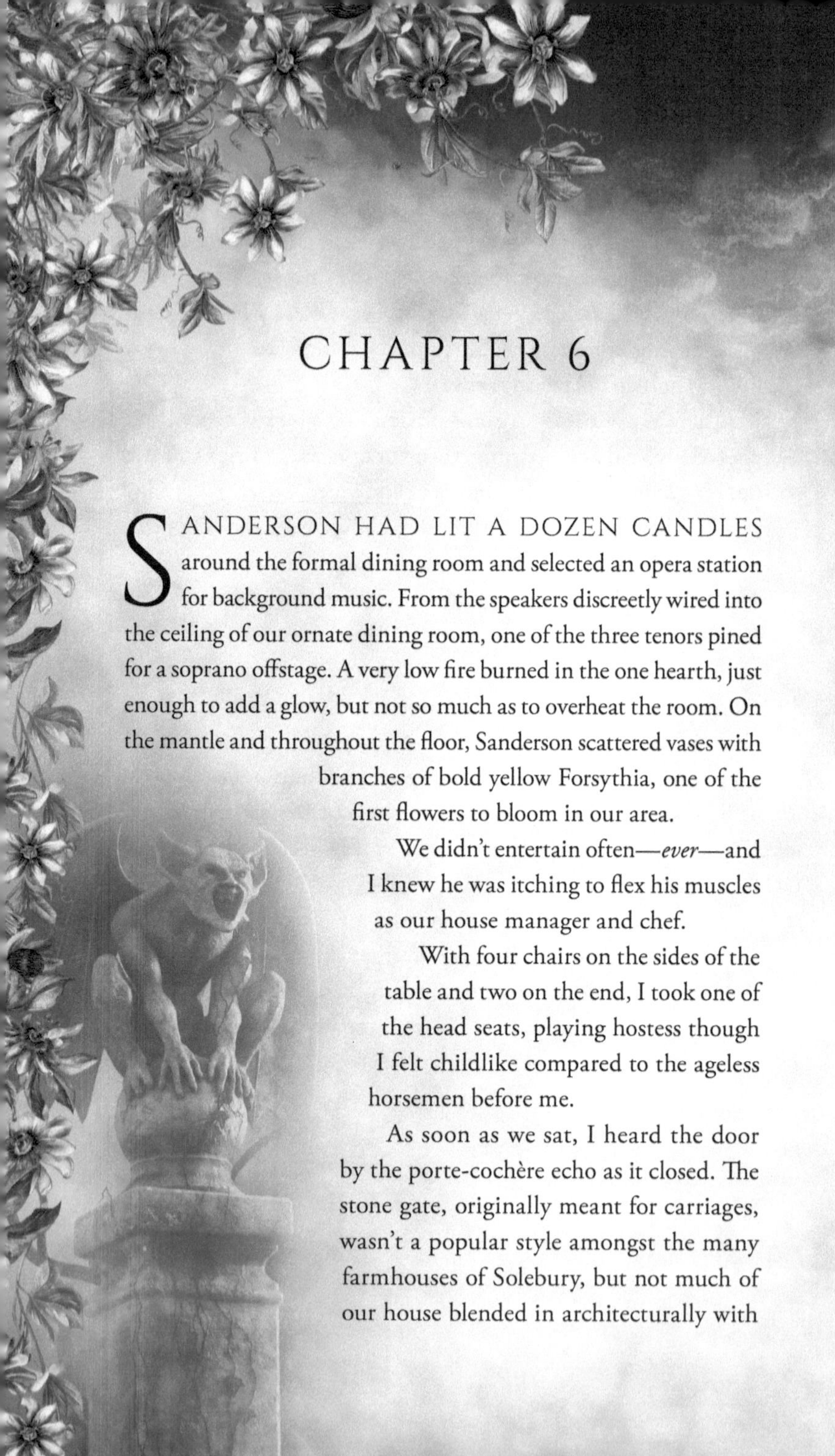

CHAPTER 6

SANDERSON HAD LIT A DOZEN CANDLES around the formal dining room and selected an opera station for background music. From the speakers discreetly wired into the ceiling of our ornate dining room, one of the three tenors pined for a soprano offstage. A very low fire burned in the one hearth, just enough to add a glow, but not so much as to overheat the room. On the mantle and throughout the floor, Sanderson scattered vases with branches of bold yellow Forsythia, one of the first flowers to bloom in our area.

We didn't entertain often—*ever*—and I knew he was itching to flex his muscles as our house manager and chef.

With four chairs on the sides of the table and two on the end, I took one of the head seats, playing hostess though I felt childlike compared to the ageless horsemen before me.

As soon as we sat, I heard the door by the porte-cochère echo as it closed. The stone gate, originally meant for carriages, wasn't a popular style amongst the many farmhouses of Solebury, but not much of our house blended in architecturally with this region. Or any region, really, since Eligius constructed it by combining pieces of his favorite styles from all over the world.

We turned our heads in unison, listening to the nearing footfalls of what I assumed to be my father or the mysterious fourth horsemen, Noric, entering Grimsmere the mortal way.

Eligius appeared in the dining room and I was immediately taken aback. My father usually kept to the body I knew best—bony, pale, and with straight black hair falling almost to his shoulders. Whatever business he'd been on left him harried today, because he hadn't shifted from yet another form, this one his most intimidating. Death's body was bullish, his facial features menacing, his gait forceful.

Very rarely, souls didn't ascend or turn spectre… sometimes they went elsewhere. Had Eligius used a more frightening form for such a transition?

"What kept you?" I quickly asked.

"There's been a mudslide in southern India of unprecedented magnitude," Eligius replied, taking a seat at the head of the table and making me wonder if the antique chair could bear his weight.

I frowned. It took more time to ferry the dead when their bodies were buried beneath layers of earth. But wasn't as if Death had more or less power in any form, so it didn't seem this overly-muscled body wasn't necessary.

"Noric is still working on the last few dozen," Eligius said. His voice was unusually deep and rough, but he looked at me with the same black irises. I always knew my father by his eyes. "We can start without him."

Sanderson poured a Burgundy wine and set before us a dandelion salad. It made me smile to know that Olga had enough of her mind today. We all ate except for Sevastian, who pushed the salad aside as if it was poisonous. The huffy gesture seemed rude, but I told myself that maybe he just wanted to wait for his friend before starting.

My wineglass was pressed to my lips when I heard a noise outside the dining room.

In a teasing voice Embrette announced, "Ah, the high horseman has finally arrived."

When the fourth and final reaper sauntered into the manor and into my life, I knew I gave a little gasp, though I didn't know if anyone heard.

I couldn't see his face at first, because at that moment lightning struck, and with the door still open somewhere, it was close enough that the magic illuminated Noric's skeletal form. I supposed everyone else in the room appeared in their true reaper body as well, but my gaze was riveted by the towering horsemen in the doorway.

It only lasted for a flash. The lightning died and a man of cruel beauty appeared, borne of the storm like a dark and deadly inversion of the fair Aphrodite, birthed from seafoam upon her shell.

Noric was tall enough that if he'd entered the older wing of the house, he would have needed to duck. His hair was brushed back in a neat manner, and with only the low glow of the candlelight, I couldn't tell if it was light or dark brown. However, I couldn't possibly mistake his uncommonly gray eyes. Though human they were large and keen, reminding me of the reaper's skeletal form he'd just displayed. Noric's black pants and black shirt fit his trim waist like his clothing had been expertly tailored somewhere in Milan, and for all I knew, it had. He was as muscled as any dancer, though nothing in his stern countenance made me believe he enjoyed dancing. Certainly not ballet.

Yvette would have taken one look at Noric, leaned back appreciatively, and christened him *a tall drink of water.*

I'd taken one look and felt a surprising and unfamiliar desire to be physically close to him. To get inside that beautiful head and to know all *his* desires. Or really anything at all. How he took his coffee or if he liked the color red or any mundane, everyday detail about this man—this reaper—who was anything but ordinary.

Of course, there was the immediate and obvious issue of Noric's *extraordinary* nature. As an immortal, he'd probably known countesses and queens, starlets and seducers, and any number of renowned beauties throughout all of history.

That was considerable competition for an orphan. Were it not for Eligius, there'd be nothing interesting about me at all, and even my adoption was nothing special but rather a stroke of luck. Perhaps my diligent training counted for something, but I'd given up pursuing ballet professionally.

"Avalia," my father said formally, "I'd like to introduce Noric, my high reaper."

"It's lovely to meet you," I replied in an unusually breathy voice that I hoped no one noticed.

Noric nodded politely and looked back toward my father. He didn't even *speak;* he just nodded in my direction, sat, and began talking to my father about the mudslide.

I recoiled a bit, as if I'd been struck. The stunning reaper had technically done nothing wrong, but the physical reaction I had upon seeing him cried out to be met in kind or at least met with... *something.* But like Sevastian, Noric was utterly unenthused about meeting me.

No, this was worse.

Noric had been *indifferent* as he'd nodded, and that stung more than Sevastian's open contempt. With the blonde reaper, I could reason that whatever caused that chip on his shoulder, I had nothing to do with it. But when it came to Noric, I had simply failed to capture his attention in any meaningful way.

I'd lit up when he'd entered the room, but now I dimmed a bit, slouching in my chair. Stealing glances left and right, I worried that someone had noticed my immediate attraction and Noric's instant dismissal.

It stung.

For the first time in a long time, I'd *wanted* someone's attention.

And I'd been abruptly rejected.

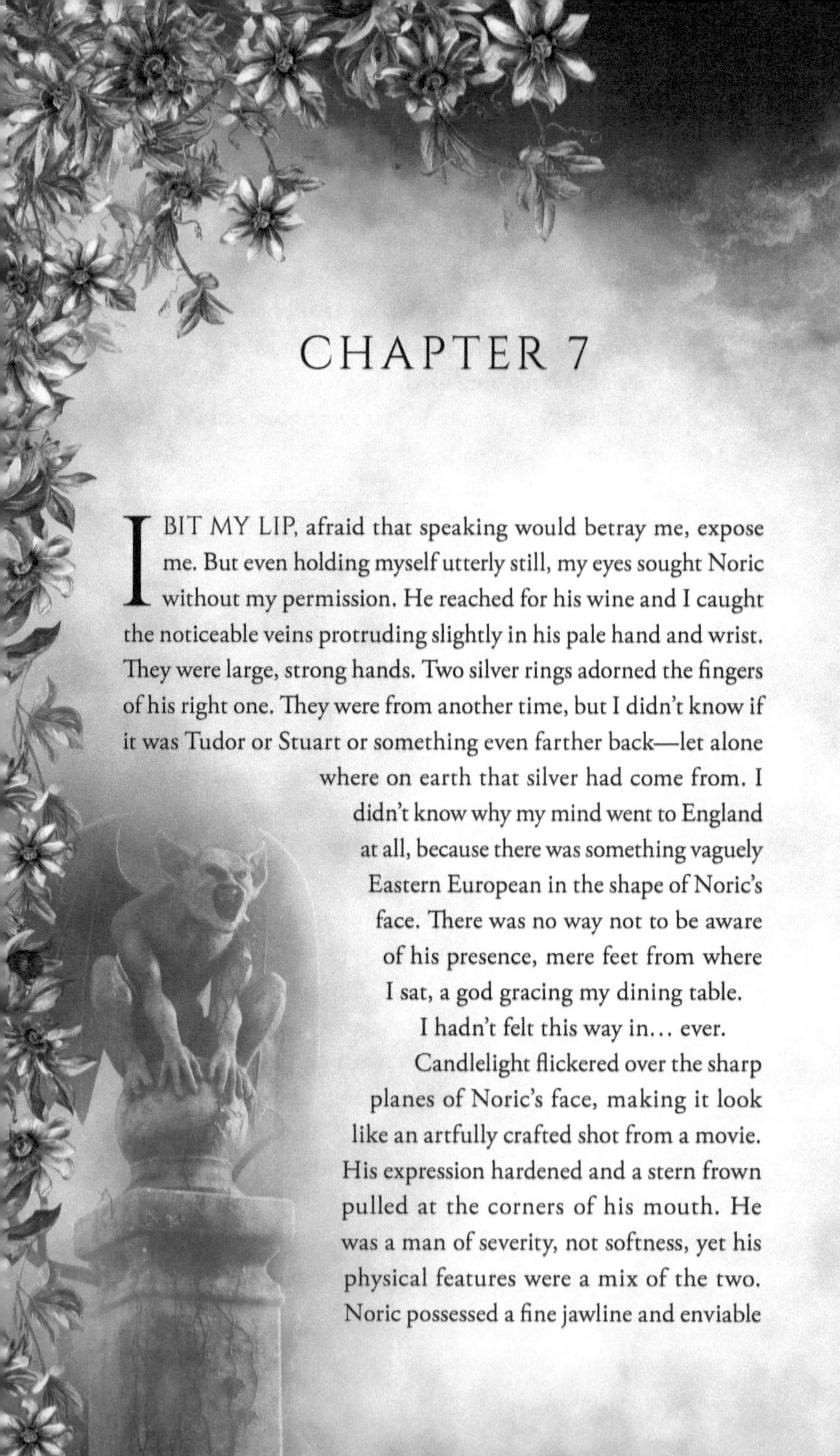

CHAPTER 7

I BIT MY LIP, afraid that speaking would betray me, expose me. But even holding myself utterly still, my eyes sought Noric without my permission. He reached for his wine and I caught the noticeable veins protruding slightly in his pale hand and wrist. They were large, strong hands. Two silver rings adorned the fingers of his right one. They were from another time, but I didn't know if it was Tudor or Stuart or something even farther back—let alone where on earth that silver had come from. I didn't know why my mind went to England at all, because there was something vaguely Eastern European in the shape of Noric's face. There was no way not to be aware of his presence, mere feet from where I sat, a god gracing my dining table.

I hadn't felt this way in… ever.

Candlelight flickered over the sharp planes of Noric's face, making it look like an artfully crafted shot from a movie. His expression hardened and a stern frown pulled at the corners of his mouth. He was a man of severity, not softness, yet his physical features were a mix of the two. Noric possessed a fine jawline and enviable cheekbones, but his eyes were large and wide and his lips had a boyish fullness.

For a moment I worried that frown had something to do with me, but then my father spoke and I realized they discussed work.

Only seconds had passed since he'd entered the manor, and I knew my life would be forever bifurcated into the moment before and after I first saw him. I certainly didn't believe in love at first sight, but desire was another matter. And who could blame me?

Noric's haunting, aristocratic bone structure might as well have been taken from some book about vampire princes lording over ancient castles in faraway lands. Strong brows framed eyes of stone gray. Whenever something caught his fancy, they glinted with a hint of silver, like the flash of gunmetal. Noric blew into the manor like the wind carried him fresh from a dangerous, daunting, mountain peak.

Before I could think of anything to say, Eligius looked over and asked, "So have you given any more thought to college next year? I can pull the necessary strings for late enrollment."

Everyone turned toward me, and my mouth fell, stunned by the unexpected topic. *Is that what this meeting was really about?* I wondered, narrowing my eyes at Eligius in his unusually intimidating body. Was this an ambush? Had he wanted to gather the reapers as an audience to pressure me somehow?

"Avalia is an accomplished dancer," Eligius announced to the table, both gracious host and doting parent. "But she doesn't wish to pursue ballet professionally. And yet she hasn't chosen another career path. It is something we discuss often."

"The discussions have been getting more frequent and more… public," I mumbled, not hiding my displeasure as I took a sip of wine.

Eligius grinned on one side of his mouth. Whatever he was about, I knew there was no way to outmaneuver Death. My father was like a powerful river; it was best to give yourself up and go along with it, because fighting the current was pointless and only led to your doom.

The only time I'd ever won with Eligius was when I was four and he'd taken me from that Slovenian cabin... and tried to leave me somewhere else.

"College presents complications," I noted for the hundredth time. Why were we talking about this today, now? Sanderson arrived with dinner, saving me for the moment. I glanced down at what looked like pan-seared duck in a cherry demi-glaze.

"A private tutor, then?" Eligius suggested, as he had in the past. He cut his duck as he asked, "What is your secondary interest, if not ballet?"

I stifled a groan, but out of the ether, a wild idea popped into my head. And it wasn't even a lie.

"History," I announced. "But even tutors have drawbacks. What if I want time off to accompany you on an interesting reaping? What if there are questions about our life that I cannot answer? There'd have to be some mind-tampering to make it work."

With the mention of a tutor and Noric sitting *right there,* I had the idea that maybe... possibly... he'd offer to teach me, or that Eligius would ask him. Who knew more about the history of the world than a reaper who'd lived through it?

"That is the first time you've expressed an interest and I'm holding you to it straight away." Eligius leaned back, surprised but pleased. His hulking body made the chair creak in protest. "I know just the perfect tutor for such a subject."

My hopeful heart picked up speed with his declaration.

"I'll have Archibald put together an introductory curriculum and you can begin tomorrow."

"No," I protested too quickly, gripping the table and trying not to steal a glance at Noric, who'd cocked a confused brow in my direction. I flushed as the other reapers had turned to me, equally curious at my tone. "I mean, yes, I want to learn but," I shifted in my seat. "Do you really think he's best suited for the job? I mean, he only knows as far back as his own time."

"Archibald has had hundreds of years to study," Eligius pointed out. He furrowed his brow in an expression I knew well, even if he wore another face at the moment.

"Right," I breathed, stomach sinking. I was an utter fool, caught by my own trap.

"Good, it's settled then," Death said, taking a long sip of wine. The glass looked like a child's toy in his overly-large hand.

Great. *Fantastic.* Spring was just around the corner and then I'd be spending my summer stuck in the old schoolhouse with Archie.

Before any further discussion began, my father paused, and his eyes took on a faraway look I knew well.

"There's been an update in the Book." He announced it to the table, but it may have been for my benefit because all the reapers had keyed into the information now. "An explosion in Houston… more names are appearing, but it looks like a dozen will be dead within the hour."

"I'll take care of it," Noric declared.

I nearly fell out of my chair as a living, moving gargoyle appeared in the dining room. I had been so preoccupied by Noric's beauty that I'd forgotten all about his familiars. Never, however, would I have imagined *this.*

Head bowed, the stone gargoyle knelt before Noric like the reaper was his king. The act wasn't much different than any other familiar's deference, but it was odd to watch this large, vaguely human creature prostrate itself before the horseman.

Noric wordlessly communicated something, and his familiar disappeared.

"I've got it under control," Noric said matter-of-factly. He flashed a handsome grin, easy and in direct opposition to the stern expression he'd been wearing. But it wasn't aimed at me.

"Thanks," Embrette said, lifting her glass in a toast and taking a sip. "I really didn't feel like changing and the butterfae are having so much fun playing outside."

"And what do you call them?" I asked Noric, finally plucking up the courage to speak to him. "Your gargoyle creatures."

Noric turned the full weight of his gray stare on me and the look alone made me want to squirm. His beautiful brow knit, as if perturbed.

"Gargoyles."

Oh. Right.

"Oh," I stammered, looking down at my plate. "Right. Of course."

My entire face flamed with embarrassment. *Genius, Ava,* I chided, pushing my duck across the plate and leaving a trail of dark sauce. *But then, how was I to know when every other reaper had a different name for their familiars?*

My mood shifted to anger as I suddenly wanted to bring up that point, but the conversation had moved on and interjecting it now would have only made me look childish.

When there was a break, I desperately wanted to recover and asked, "Can any of your familiars satisfy the deathlust or must you reap your own as well?"

Eligius had had to serve the Reclamation of Souls book, but he also regularly needed to reap mortals of his own choosing. Any human would satisfy his craving and all were fair game—as long as the person wasn't a static, marked to remain in the mortal world until such time as the gods chose. When I was younger, I pictured Death hunting like a dark wolf stalking its prey in the forest. But when I grew up, I realized most of his victims would be in cities, towns, and other crowded places.

I was hoping to hear Noric speak, but it was Hexley who responded. "It's a powerful force inside us as well," he said, putting down his fork to give me his full attention. "Usually, deathlust is easy to satisfy with a reaping here and there, but there's the rare occasion when it's as if the gods turn up a dial on the desire." He shook his head. "The duration and intensity varies. It can be deep and prolonged or sharp and fast."

I nodded; it was the same with Eligius. He tried not to add to the pain of the world by reaping children, but so many were listed in the Reclamation of Souls book anyway that it made little difference overall.

"We crave a culling the way a human hungers for food or a vampire thirsts for blood," Sevastian said, lazily circling the rim of his wineglass with one finger. He spoke as if vampires were real, and I was surprised to hear him speak at all. "We won't die, can't die. But we grow ravenousness for the reaping in a way we're powerless to withstand."

Sevastian bit out the words and it made me wonder if he'd tried and failed to deny the urge in the past. Was that why he was so withdrawn? Did he resent his job?

"And, in turn, the humans are equally powerless to withstand our blades," the blonde reaper added with a wild—almost excited— gleam in his green eyes. One side of his mouth rose into a maniacal grin, as if ready to reap at that moment and to take pleasure in it.

I frowned, reconsidering his reluctance.

"And does time spent with a mortal increase the desire to reap that particular human?"

I asked the burning question trying to sound casual.

"We're the same," Embrette said, sighing softly. "It's not as if we'll go berserker with the craving, but it does get harder to fight as time goes on." Grinning she added, "But don't worry, we're talking about years, not *days*."

I knew from Eligius that it wasn't something sharp and sudden, but more like a dark, cursed cloud that hung over any mortal-im- mortal relationship.

Familiarity breeds contempt, went the human saying. For reapers, it would be, *familiarity breeds craving.*

The conversation continued and I'd barely eaten, too distracted by Noric's magnetic presence. Only half-looking, I cut a piece of duck and swallowed without paying too much attention. In my carelessness, it did not go down into my stomach, as it should.

I knew that, without my name appearing in the Book, I wasn't going to die. And yet I couldn't stop panicking. Not being able to breathe tended to do that to a person, and the spate of recent choking deaths was fresh in my mind. Instead of excusing myself or drinking water, I shot to my feet and *thrashed*. My flailing prompted Hexley, who was nearest, to rush behind me and perform the Heimlich Maneuver. As bad luck would have it, when Hexley successfully dislodged the chewed bit of duck from my throat I was at an angle. It flew across the table—

—And of all the spaces it could have gone, it landed on Noric's plate.

Right in the middle of his pristine platter, my gray and brown lump of half-eaten duck meat sat like a declaration of all my mortal inadequacies.

I supposed it could have been worse. I could have hit his face.

Noric stared down, trying to conceal his disgust and obviously debating how best to kindly push aside his meal.

I wanted to die. There were plenty of reaper blades at the table, and I briefly debated throwing myself onto one.

And yet, I was not so easily defeated. *Oh no,* I was Avalia Thrailkill, my father's daughter, raised with propriety and sixteen governesses teaching me how to behave. I knew that the best way to navigate an uncomfortable situation was to proceed as if it hadn't even occurred at all; to remove the spotlight from the unfortunate victim or transgressor. I would simply employ that magnanimous tactic for myself.

"My apologies," I said, managing what I hoped was a charming smile. Surely, the disturbance had reached Sanderson's ears, and he'd check to see what was wrong. He'd hastily remove Noric's platter and all would return to normal.

Needing to leave this part of the night behind me as quickly as possible, I fell back into my chair with less grace and care than was required for the gown I was wearing.

The gown I'd been warned against wearing.

Because of the questionable construction.

The sound of a seam tearing in the back of my dress was like a rip that could be heard around the world. It might as well have been the very fabric of the earth itself tearing. In the quiet dining room, the sound of a ripped seam rang out like a shot of gunfire.

Air caressed my backside, telling me exactly where I'd torn my dress. Mortification overwhelmed me to the point I felt dizzy, violent waves drowning me in a sea of shame. One mistake I could manage, two broke my resolve.

Everyone stared at me with their heaps of mounting pity, wanting to be helpful and unsure how. Less than five seconds had passed since I'd stopped choking, but the memory of what happened in this tiny slice of time would be scorched into my brain forever. Never had my cheeks flamed so hot; I imagined even the second-hand embarrassment for everyone at the table was difficult to bear. Yvette was right, the gown's quality was poor and I paid the price for my vanity, but not even her defenses would have helped me now. I might have been plastered in pearls or dripped with diamonds and it would not have been enough to protect me from myself.

Do. Not. Cry.

The only course of action was to leave, but a dignified exit wasn't possible. I released a half-hysterical laugh into the stunned silence, which only made things worse.

If I turned to exit the room, they'd all see my exposed backside.

I stood slowly, horrified as hot tears welled.

"I've had a bit of an emergency… with my dress…" Awkwardly, I shuffled away from my chair. "Excuse me, please."

"Do you need help?" Em asked with genuine concern. Hexley and my father both tried to rise and remove their jackets, but I waved them all off.

Still facing the table, I stepped backwards at an excruciatingly slow, ridiculous pace. I couldn't spread my legs too much for fear of further ripping the gown, and I couldn't turn and show my rear.

There wasn't enough money in the world that could have paid me to meet Noric's eyes. Not only had my face flushed as red as my dress, but my neck and arms flamed too. I shuffled out of the room in what had to go down in history as one of the most painfully awkward events ever. It was my own, personalized horror. I didn't bat an eye at the most grotesque images of death and decay. Noxious, oozing wounds of pus, stumpy limbs torn from bodies, crushed skulls… none of it frightened me. But this dinner would haunt my nightmares.

Once I made it out, I turned and sprinted up the stairs. Safe inside my bedroom, I didn't cry at least. Maybe that would come later. I felt like I was in a state of shock as I changed into the first dress I found. It was loose, knee-length, and gray with black trim.

But I couldn't make myself leave, so I sat on the bed, debating. As much as I didn't want to move, I knew that if I didn't face everyone quickly, I'd only make it worse by delaying it.

What in the world did the reapers think of me now? What a horrible first impression.

At least it's an opportunity to show your bravery.

By the time I'd dragged myself downstairs, I was half-relieved to find the dining room empty and the table half-cleared. Not ready to face any of Eligius's questions—or worse, plans for my history lessons—I grabbed a long, warm coat from the hall closet and slipped out the side door. Brisk, April air blasted my face and I wrapped the jacket tighter around my body.

I planned on heading to the old graveyard, as it was the place I always strolled when I needed to think. Grimsmere was built upon the aptly named *Devil's Acres,* a plot of land early settlers had chosen to construct a small community, including a one-room schoolhouse and a place of worship. Sadly, the little church had been destroyed ages ago, and nothing but a few stones remained to mark the building. But the graves persisted, and they always gave me a peaceful, homey feeling.

Before I made it around the side of the manor, however, I heard voices. Slowing my steps, I peered over the bushes and saw Noric and Embrette lingering under the porte-cochère. I didn't think they saw or heard me—moody gas lamps flickered above their heads, but it was dark where I stood by the bushes, and they weren't paying attention.

"She wishes she were one of us?" Noric scoffed. "She wants eternity and she's bored in a few short years?"

A chill ran up my spine as I realized they were talking about me. Earlier on the terrace, when we were getting to know one another, I'd told Embrette and about my mortal life and how I envied hers. I might have used the word *bored.*

"That's not fair," Embrette argued on my behalf. "Think of what her life must be like. It's almost cursed. Ava is more than human—at least, she knows more than mortals—but less than an immortal. Fitting in nowhere and unable to connect with anyone on a deeper level. You of all creatures should understand that. You said so yourself."

"She's directionless and lacks ambition and that has nothing to do with being a mortal or not. Imagine immortality when she has no goals now."

I clutched my stomach, which felt as if it were suddenly filled with heavy rocks, and hot tears stung my eyes. I wanted to jump out and argue that Noric didn't know what he was talking about. There *were* things I wanted but I couldn't do them for reasons he didn't understand. Even if I joined the ballet world, changed my life and hid my past… well, it was really none of his business anyway.

"You know the malaise is rising—" Embrette said.

"Don't use that as an excuse," Noric cut her off. "She's spoiled and lazy."

My cheeks burned at his cruel accusations and I realized I'd been wrong. This was *worse* than his previous indifference. It was a step down to a deeper level, one of dislike.

I didn't know how to recover and maybe I didn't want to.

Quietly, I fisted my hands. It was rude of him to make judgements like this about me anyway. Who did he think he was? And what had I ever done to him—besides accidentally ruining his dinner and that wasn't something you could vehemently dislike someone for. Was it? And how *dare* he? I wasn't lazy, I practiced *at least* four hours a day—and often double that, for five or six days a week. Just because I didn't perform for strangers didn't make me any less dedicated to dance. The constant aches in my muscles and the irreversible wear on my feet were testaments to my commitment.

He was the spoiled one, if anything. Flitting around the world on a whim—no stress, no fear.

How did I ever find him attractive in the first place?

Noric had hardly spoken at the table, which was impolite at best and ignorant at worst. Now that I thought about it, he was freakishly tall, more like a monster. And his eyes were too big for his face—bug eyes, really. And, and… without gel, his hair was that floppy sort, I could just tell.

What girl anywhere wanted a boy with floppy hair?

I retreated silently back into the warmth of the house. I didn't care about Noric one way or the other, which meant that I didn't care what else he had to say.

My stomach quieted. No waves, no rocks, no lepidoptera. The butterfly larva within shriveled and petrified before the creatures even had a chance to emerge into a state of limerence.

CHAPTER 8

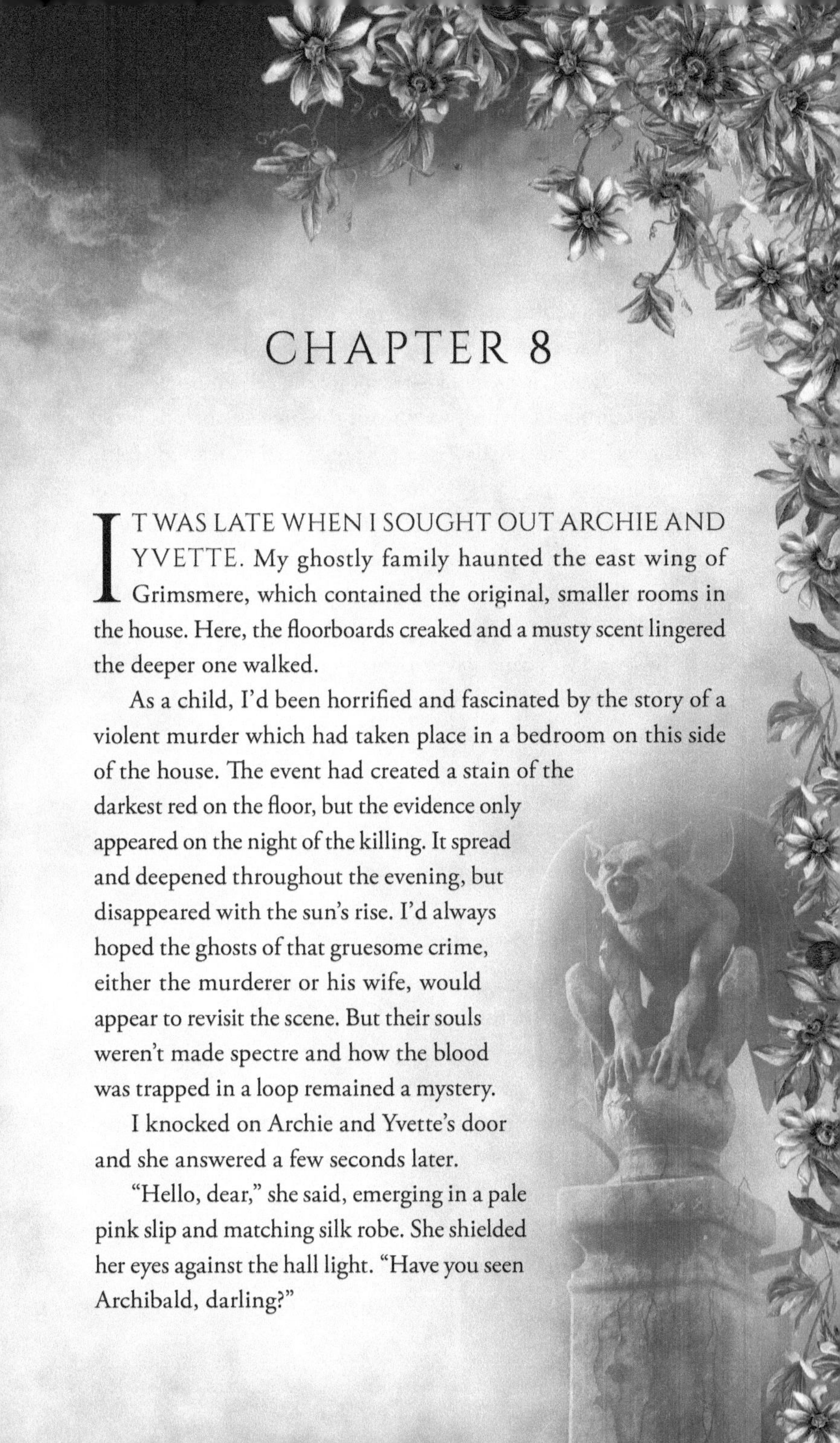

I T WAS LATE WHEN I SOUGHT OUT ARCHIE AND YVETTE. My ghostly family haunted the east wing of Grimsmere, which contained the original, smaller rooms in the house. Here, the floorboards creaked and a musty scent lingered the deeper one walked.

As a child, I'd been horrified and fascinated by the story of a violent murder which had taken place in a bedroom on this side of the house. The event had created a stain of the darkest red on the floor, but the evidence only appeared on the night of the killing. It spread and deepened throughout the evening, but disappeared with the sun's rise. I'd always hoped the ghosts of that gruesome crime, either the murderer or his wife, would appear to revisit the scene. But their souls weren't made spectre and how the blood was trapped in a loop remained a mystery.

I knocked on Archie and Yvette's door and she answered a few seconds later.

"Hello, dear," she said, emerging in a pale pink slip and matching silk robe. She shielded her eyes against the hall light. "Have you seen Archibald, darling?"

I shook my head. "That's what I came to ask you."

"He must be on a winning streak. Oh, he'll be half-seas over in no time." She gave a small laugh. "He's going to slip up and give a guest quite the scare."

"He'll be sleeping at the inn, I take it?" I asked.

"Mm," Yvette agreed, fussing with her bob and her hair ribbon. "Likely. But what is it you need to tell him? I can deliver the message."

"It's nothing," I sighed, waving off the suggestion.

Eligius had already declared my continued education would start tomorrow, and I was hoping to somehow talk Archie out of it. Not that I didn't enjoy his company and I truly did have an interest in history. But what was the urgency? Twenty wasn't too old to not have a career path; plenty of forty-year-olds still didn't know what they wanted to do with their lives. Besides, it wasn't as if the world was conducive to growth right now anyway. Who planned for the future when everything was so unstable?

"Thanks anyway," I said. "Goodnight."

THE NEXT MORNING, I stalked to the little schoolhouse beneath a cold, gray sky, skirting father's Grim Gardens and reminding myself of two things. One, Embrette had sent a note saying that the horsemen were swamped with work but wanted to meet again at the end of the week, a prospect which thrilled me more than anything else. And two, my routine would return to normal after class, when I headed to my dance studio.

I only had to survive a few hours.

Like a prisoner, I sat at my old desk in the one-room schoolhouse, just as Eligius had instructed the night before. Over the years I'd been educated here by the parade of tutors he'd employed.

I sank my head into my hand, bored. That torture had ended almost three years ago, and I resented returning to it.

It's better than college, I reminded myself. *Just a few hours and you're free to dance the rest of the afternoon.*

Archie was late. I opened my laptop and checked the time.

Why wait? Why not leave if he doesn't show in a minute or two? Or maybe right now? Impatient, I snapped the laptop shut and scooted to the edge of my seat.

But at that moment, a reaper whisked into the room, scaring the living daylights out of me and causing me to nearly knock over the scalding cup of Earl Gray I'd perched on the corner of the desk.

Noric.

My stomach dropped to the floor.

He was dressed similar to the night before, though the cut of his dark suit was more casual now. He had the nerve to sneer when *I'd* been the one startled into nearly getting third degree burns.

"Your father has asked me to take Archibald's place, for the time being." Noric spoke sternly and with no attempt to conceal his irritation. "He's overslept, and upon further consideration Eligius has determined that Archie is unlikely to be a reliable tutor going forward. I will instruct you in history from now until summer break, at which time you are free to focus on… whatever it is you do with your time."

Instruct me? Was he serious? I'd wanted nothing more during our dinner last night, but after, I wanted nothing less. And he made it clear the feeling was mutual.

"Noric—"

He held up one arrogant hand. "I would ask that you address me more formally in this setting."

My mouth fell and I scoffed. Eligius insisting we utilize the old schoolhouse was about as much tradition as I could take.

"Such as?"

"You can call me Mr. Thrailkill." Noric offered it as if being magnanimous, as if it were a privilege.

Wincing I replied, "That's kind of weird for me. You forget that I'm a Thrailkill too, and Mr. Thrailkill is my father."

"Right," he muttered, lips twitching with something like resentment. "I suppose your father would have shared our name when he adopted you."

I narrowed my eyes. *You know, you were hot until you opened your mouth.* The thought made my skin warm and itch.

"I should hope so." I drummed my fingers on the desk, making it clear *I* was resentful for any doubt.

"Right. Well, call me Professor, then," he ordered, half-sitting on the larger desk and folding his arms.

I smirked and reminded, "But you're not, are you? Do you even have a legitimate degree? Or any employment at an institution for higher learning?"

Noric leveled his large, steely eyes at me and I swear they seared my flesh. I tried not to wilt under the angry heat as he stepped forward. He was way too tall and toned for me to take him seriously as a professor; he looked completely out of place in the little schoolhouse.

"Then you can call me *sir*," he said, taking two steps toward my desk.

I fought the urge to cough as I flushed. Noric's arms were still folded as he towered above me. I didn't even think he meant to intimidate me, it just came naturally.

"Professor's fine," I squeaked. Cursing myself, I cleared my throat and said, "Professor will do."

At Noric's smug satisfaction, a fire rose within me. *What was his problem anyway?*

"Although I'd like to go on record as saying *teacher* would be more apt," I couldn't help but push, "and you know what they say. Those who can't do, teach."

"You wound me," Noric said evenly as he sorted through papers.

"Only a wound?" I mused. "Well, I can't expect to do more, given that a reaper can't die."

"Keep trying," he replied, tossing the papers on the desk and dwarfing the small chair as he took a seat. "Maybe you'll be the one to find a way to kill me."

I blinked, remembering what Embrette had alluded to outside the manor—some sort of dissatisfaction Noric possessed. Curious, I asked, "Do you have a death wish?"

Noric folded his arms behind his head with the natural arrogance of someone who'd had centuries to embody the trait. "No, I rather like immortality. For the most part," he added as an afterthought.

"Then why goad me like that?"

"It is not my intention for a statement to cause you to feel the need to engage in any way at all, outside of broadening your historical knowledge," he replied, matter-of-factly. "I've been instructed to instruct you. That is my purpose here today, and once it's complete I'll depart."

I blinked. *What a jerk.* As if I wanted to be here any more than he did.

Noric rubbed his chin, "Do you have a particular interest in any place and time, or should we start with a basic, introductory curriculum?"

Folding my hands on the desk, I smirked and asked, "Why don't you start as far back as you can remember and we'll go from there?"

I suspected that particular weakness might be a sore spot for a man like Noric. My father's earliest memories were hazy, as if the gods intentionally obscured them, so Noric's couldn't be much better. Eligius described his origins as similar to the fuzzy memories of a mortal childhood.

I was rewarded with Noric's dark stare and an evasion of the question.

"We'll start with Mesopotamia," he declared, turning to the old-fashioned chalkboard and writing the word as if I were an idiot who needed the visual reminder.

And thus, my compulsory education began.

I couldn't escape *Professor Noric* for one second. Without a classroom filled with other students, all the focus was on me, which made daydreaming impossible. The few times my mind wandered, Noric would inevitably catch it and quiz me on whatever he'd just said. Even without an audience, the way he rode me so closely and so contemptuously called me out on any misstep nearly made tears well.

Which only made me hate him more.

"Avalia." It was the first time Noric said my name and his voice snapped it like a whip. "Were you paying attention? What did I just say?"

God, what was his problem?

I was sure he'd wanted to call me *Miss Thrailkill* but didn't want to use the name he shared.

"I don't know." Instead of letting tears pool, this time I fought back. Noric's choice of exceedingly boring topics seemed intentional to torment me. "Perhaps you should be a more engaging teacher."

"The most skilled teacher in the world couldn't help a student determined not to learn," he retorted.

"Then why don't you just leave?" I shot to my feet. "I have no desire to learn from you and you clearly have no desire to teach me."

You clearly hate me.

"Sit down, Ava." Noric barked the order.

I huffed, debated my options, then sat.

"I have already told you. Your father has asked me to step in for Archibald. I will do as he asks, and you will do as I say." Noric arched a brow. "Unless you want to take it up with him?"

I fumed but said nothing. We stared at one another in battle of wills until finally, I looked away. Not because of Noric, but because he had Eligius backing him.

I could practically feel the reaper's smugness radiate as he continued the history lesson. Those two hours made for a painful first day, and the plan was to increase my time in the classroom as we established a rhythm. When the lecture was over, Noric simply whisked away, as if I wasn't worth so much as a goodbye.

"What the—" I started, when I found myself suddenly alone. "Ugh!"

What was Noric's problem?

Beyond irritated, I left the little schoolhouse and steered clear of the manor. I didn't want anyone to find themselves collateral damage of my bad mood, and I felt a scream building. Quickly, I discarded my laptop and jumped onto Orsha's back, flying to the New Mexico desert. I hated that dusty landscape, with its prickly shrubs and unbearable temperature, but that loathing suited me right now. I didn't want to be soothed by the beauty of sweeping mountains or lush forests.

Within seconds I landed on the arid, cracked earth of my destination. I slid off Orsha's back, stomped into the empty desert, and screamed at the top of my lungs, again and again. I let that thirsty land drink my screams as if they were water. My hands shook and I clutched my shirt to help still them. Noric made me so *mad*.

To my right, an alarming rattle sent chills up my spine and ripped me from my indulgent release. I scurried back to the safety of Orsha and exhaled once I'd slung into her saddle. But it only made me angrier because I couldn't even vent the way I wanted to.

Too mortal, too delicate. Even a little snakebite could end me.

It occurred to me that I wasn't only mad at Noric, I was furious about the unfairness of it all. But I sure as heck wasn't ready to examine that feeling too closely now, especially as a breeze kicked up. The hot wind blew at my face like the opening of an oven's door and sand pelted my cheeks.

With a final grunt, I flew Orsha back to Solebury, feeling like I'd turned the wheel of a release valve just a little. Enough to face Noric again tomorrow, at least.

After leaving the pasture, I headed straight for the barn we'd converted into my dance studio. But as I warmed up on the barre, I was distracted. Not only did I not truly understand why Eligius had changed his mind about the horsemen, I wondered why Sevastian was so moody and withdrawn, and what the situation was between Hexley and Embrette. Clearly, they'd had some kind of relationship in the past.

But most of all, I wondered why Noric was so hateful.

And I hated that I wondered even more.

CHAPTER 9

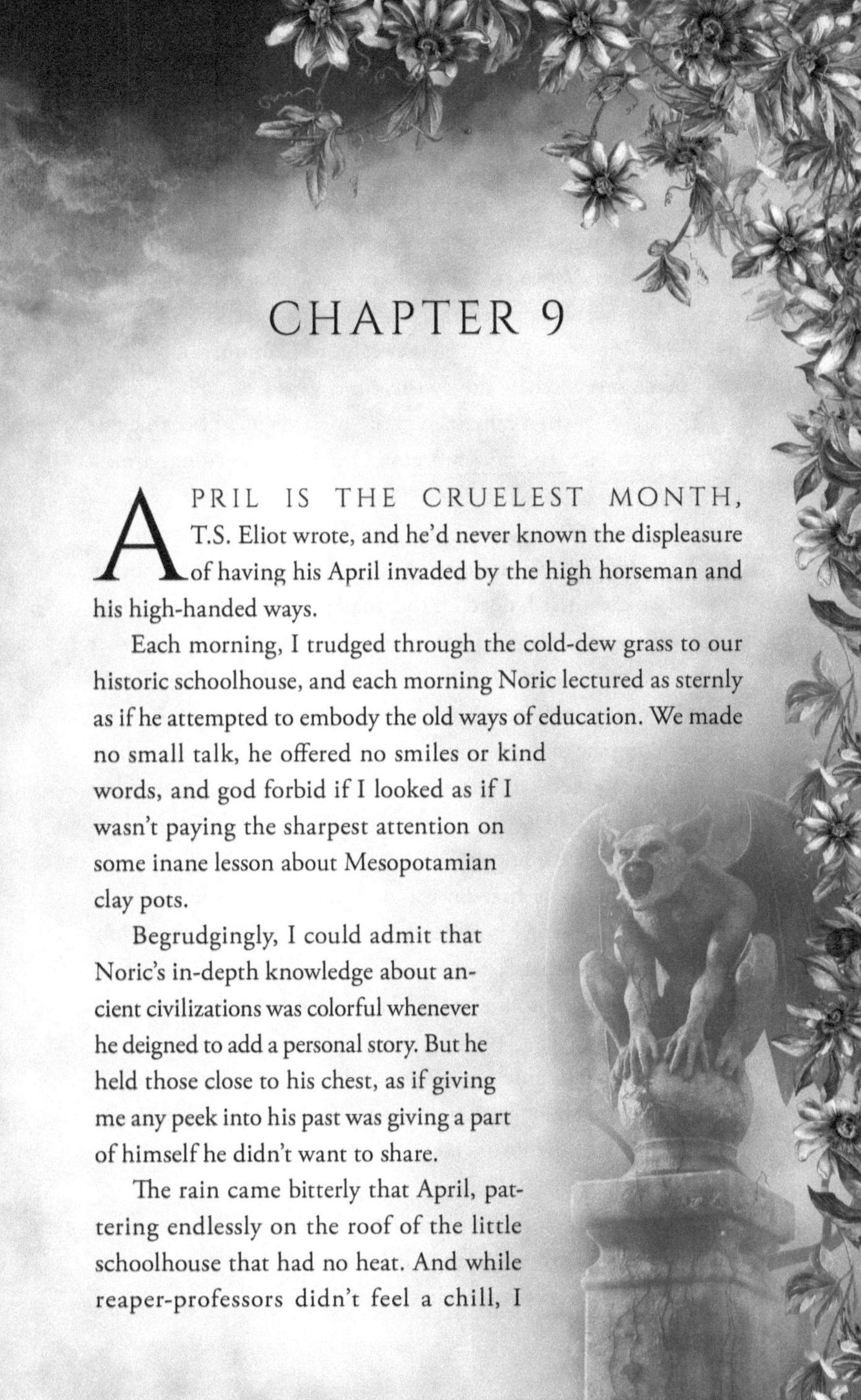

APRIL IS THE CRUELEST MONTH, T.S. Eliot wrote, and he'd never known the displeasure of having his April invaded by the high horseman and his high-handed ways.

Each morning, I trudged through the cold-dew grass to our historic schoolhouse, and each morning Noric lectured as sternly as if he attempted to embody the old ways of education. We made no small talk, he offered no smiles or kind words, and god forbid if I looked as if I wasn't paying the sharpest attention on some inane lesson about Mesopotamian clay pots.

Begrudgingly, I could admit that Noric's in-depth knowledge about ancient civilizations was colorful whenever he deigned to add a personal story. But he held those close to his chest, as if giving me any peek into his past was giving a part of himself he didn't want to share.

The rain came bitterly that April, pattering endlessly on the roof of the little schoolhouse that had no heat. And while reaper-professors didn't feel a chill, I certainly did. Noric never offered to move locations, and I wouldn't give him the satisfaction of denying my request.

Let alone allowing him the gratification of seeing me shiver.

My mornings of extra sweaters and large cups of steaming tea under *Professor Noric's* stern gaze were at least balanced by a phenomenal source of happiness that month—getting to know Eligius's remaining reapers, usually when they came to Grimsmere for dinner.

I made sure to chew slowly this time.

Though Sevastian remained chilly towards me, I became fast friends with Hexley and Embrette. One balmy evening, after a delicious meal of prosecco-braised rabbit, Em and I took a walk in the old graveyard together. She let her butterfae loose, twinkling about the half-sunken tombstones and through the eager spring grass. Two creatures landed on the small graves marking the infamous *Hessian and the Harlot* from our revolutionary days. Higher in the sky, father's veishkas flew, darting so fast they might have passed for birds or bats if a human spotted them.

Thinking she might be likeliest to shed some light on my father's half-truths, I asked, "Embrette, I understand why Eligius didn't want me to meet all of you sooner… sort of… but what made him suddenly change his mind?"

Everything about that day was odd. Eligius's nervous attitude, the one-eighty spin on his reaper rule, the rushing of my education.

Okay, maybe that last one had been a growing point of contention, but getting to know his horsemen was an abrupt change of heart.

"Ah, you can blame me for that," she said, waving me off. "I used to nag him about getting to know you and he probably caught me peeking, so," she shrugged, "it all wore him down."

I chewed on that. *Maybe.*

"So why does Noric hate me so much?" I asked, after another meal in which he avoided acknowledging my existence. "And don't say he doesn't. He resents having to teach me."

"Well, you know he's a workaholic," Em said. "And teaching you is not just a few hours out of his morning, he has to prepare lessons the day before too."

I hadn't thought about that and was about to give Noric some grace when Embrette added, "So he's spending his time doing all this while it's obvious you'd rather be spending your time doing something else."

Half-rolling my eyes, I said, "But that's mainly because *he* clearly doesn't want to be there! So why would I? And I know he thinks I'm a directionless, spoiled mortal," I said, hoping she wouldn't ask *how* I knew.

To my relief, Em only laughed. "He might have misjudged you, and Noric *hates* admitting when he's wrong. So he's only going to dig in his heels."

"Fantastic," I breathed.

ANOTHER MORNING IN the classroom came to a tense conclusion, and I felt particularly itchy to begin the day's practice. Each April, I danced *The Rite of Spring*. Perhaps I'd always been drawn to ballet because no art more closely resembled life, as so many shows ended in death.

Denying Noric the opportunity to whisk out of the room first, I shot to my feet and collected my laptop. I thought he'd be gone by the time I looked up—he was always in some kind of race to beat me—but this time he hadn't moved.

To my surprise, the overbearing reaper only blinked and remarked, "You're tall," as if noticing for the first time.

I raised my eyebrows and said airily, "Disappointed you can't look down on me as much as you do everyone else?"

"Oh, I don't need others to be short for me to look down on them," he replied, though his boyish smile cut any real bite from the offhand statement.

That must have been the reason for my lapse in judgement when I offered a more personal reply—his disarming grin, which contradicted so stunningly with his cruel cheekbones and the severity of his reaper's jawline. It hindered my sense of reason.

Or maybe it was pride.

"I'm a dancer and I'm pushing the limits of what's desirable," I said softly. "It's not always easy to find a partner at this height."

"You're not desirable?" Noric asked the question bluntly. It sounded like disbelief, but I couldn't really believe there was a compliment in it somewhere.

Unsure how to reply and not trusting him or this conversation, I only shrugged.

"But you're not pursuing a professional path any longer," he noted, narrowing his judgmental eyes. With a reaper's sense of entitlement to the world, he demanded, "Why not?"

"It's none of your business," I snapped. "But contrary to what you might believe, I don't just sit around and bedrot. I dance almost every day. I dance until my feet bleed and my human heart nearly bursts." I could tell my passion surprised Noric, who'd dismissed me as directionless. "You wouldn't understand what it's like to love something like that, to *need* it."

"I understand perf—"

Before he could finish, I spun and stalked to the door.

Two gargoyles appeared from the air, blocking my path and making me jump.

"Class is dismissed when I say it is."

His edict was forceful; the high horseman didn't like not being in control.

In response, I fisted my hands and gritted my teeth. It wasn't as if I could power my way past stone monsters. Not physically.

But an idea struck and I relaxed my fingers. Throwing a look over my shoulder, I challenged, "Would you *like* to hang around longer to teach me? Are you trying to spend more time here with me?"

Noric opened his mouth and scoffed. Then he snapped it shut, scowling as he realized I'd backed him into a lose-lose corner. One wave of his hand and the gargoyles disappeared.

A childish sense of victory raced through me as I exited the little schoolhouse.

Especially because, I swore I heard a frustrated reaper growl at my back.

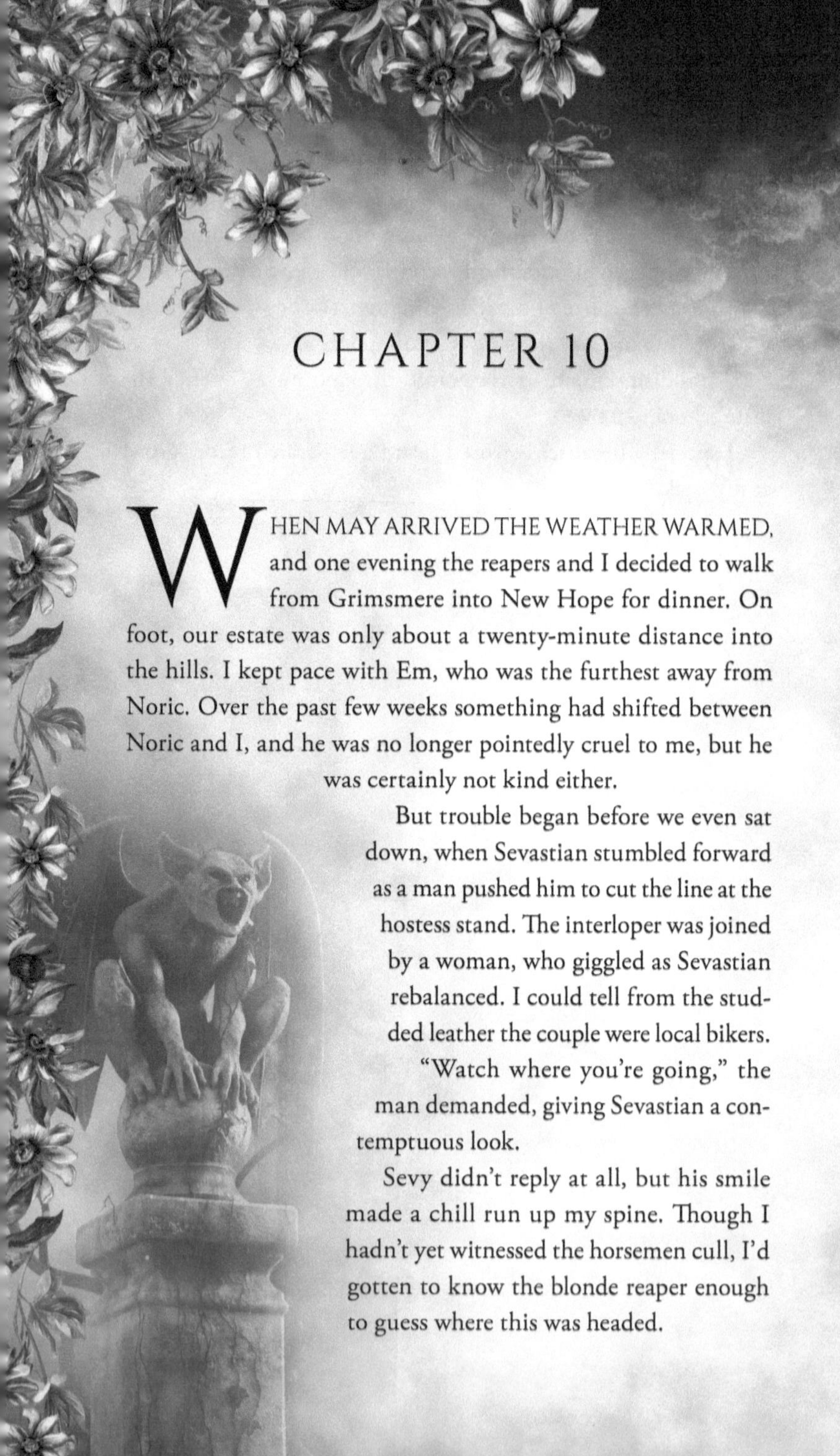

CHAPTER 10

HEN MAY ARRIVED THE WEATHER WARMED, and one evening the reapers and I decided to walk from Grimsmere into New Hope for dinner. On foot, our estate was only about a twenty-minute distance into the hills. I kept pace with Em, who was the furthest away from Noric. Over the past few weeks something had shifted between Noric and I, and he was no longer pointedly cruel to me, but he was certainly not kind either.

But trouble began before we even sat down, when Sevastian stumbled forward as a man pushed him to cut the line at the hostess stand. The interloper was joined by a woman, who giggled as Sevastian rebalanced. I could tell from the studded leather the couple were local bikers.

"Watch where you're going," the man demanded, giving Sevastian a contemptuous look.

Sevy didn't reply at all, but his smile made a chill run up my spine. Though I hadn't yet witnessed the horsemen cull, I'd gotten to know the blonde reaper enough to guess where this was headed.

"The owners are friends of Eligius's," I said, eyeing Sevastian warily as we were seated. "Don't reap where we eat, okay?"

Sevastian licked his teeth.

"Can you at least save death-dealing until after dessert?"

He grinned and promised, "I'll be on my best behavior until then."

"That's actually not saying much," Noric pointed out, leaning back in his chair.

Embrette shot him a look, "You're one to talk."

Noric ran his hands through his hair, smug, and I watched him carefully. I was sure Sevastian would always choose violence, but Noric could go either way.

"I said we're not ready!" the motorcyclist's voice carried across the restaurant as he scolded the server who'd come to check on him.

His waitress scurried away, lip trembling as she fought to hold back tears, but when she passed our table, Noric's strong hand shot out and clamped around her wrist. I gasped, looking around nervously and wondering what he was doing. He stared into her eyes so deeply, I thought he might be communicating telepathically.

"See?" Noric whispered. "It never happened."

Oh...

"You checked on the table and the couple was well-behaved, boring even," Sevastian added.

"You don't want to return," Hexley said to the waitress.

"You want to take a long break," Embrette suggested, smiling with encouragement. Her eyes flicked to the side. "That big, bearded man over there? Your coworker? Ask him to cover your shift for now."

"I can't... my boss..." the server protested, as if in a trance.

Em jumped to her feet. "I'll take care of him too."

Once she'd departed with the server, I leaned forward and whispered, "You used your reaper powers on her? Do you have the same ones as Death?"

Hexley folded his hands on the table and explained, "Four of Eligius's mind powers are divided amongst the four of us. Embrette can *compel,* motivating any mortal to do as she desires, and I can *dissuade,* deterring a human from whatever they'd set their mind to."

He pointed discreetly at Noric and Sevastian. "Noric has the ability to *obscure*—to wipe a person's memory, and Sevastian can *ingrain*—implanting a new, false memory within a mortal."

I knew how each power worked from Eligius, but I hadn't considered how they'd manifest separately in the reapers.

I would have given my soul for just one of those powers, any *one.*

As Embrette returned to the table, the biker knocked his drink over and began an expletive-laden tirade as he shouted for someone to clean it up, causing the entire restaurant to turn in their direction. I winced in sympathy for the staff and wondered if they'd kick him out. Instead, several employees hurried to soothe the man. I didn't know him, but I got the feeling he might be someone with local influence, and with so many businesses struggling lately, they didn't want to bring trouble.

"You know, I haven't culled all day either," Noric said in a low, dangerous voice. His gray eyes flashed silver as he stroked his chin thoughtfully. "Shall we make a home visit later?"

Sevastian's grin was maniacal. His hand had disappeared beneath the table and I guessed he gripped his sword. "Maybe something a bit more dramatic?"

"Oh, Sevy," Embrette tsked, rolling her eyes. "Thousands of years and you're still determined to put the *psycho* in *psychopomp.*"

I clutched my glass tightly, pulse racing. "Can you let them enjoy their last meal so that we can enjoy ours?" I pleaded, not wanting any drama to befall the owner, who was very kind. From the few chats we'd had, I knew he'd emigrated from Sicily when he was just a boy and had worked his way up in the world to achieve his dream of owning his own restaurant. "Sevastian, *please.* Not here."

To my surprise, Noric's sharp gray eyes flicked between me and Sevastian. He gave Sevy a stern look and the blonde reaper sank into his chair, sullen.

Did Noric say something, mentally?

"Mm," he mused aloud, stroking his chin and leaning in toward Sevastian. "You know, those blind turns can be deadly on a night like this, especially on a bike."

Sevastian perked up, green eyes shining.

Hexley growled, drawing everyone's attention. "I've got work in an hour and I want to try these dishes Ava's been raving about." He let his menu drop onto the table. "Can we order already?"

I wasn't sure if he'd said it to be a peacemaker or because Hexley loved to eat. Probably both.

After dinner, Embrette and I walked back to Grimsmere the mortal way, Hexley whisked to St. Petersburg for scheduled reapings, and Noric and Sevastian followed the couple into the moonless night. River Road was treacherous in the dark, and the couple's imminent motorcycle accident would be one of many over the years.

I wondered if Sevastian would knock their bike off course or if Noric would simply appear in the middle of the road, causing a deadly swerve. It was a worse way to go than through a quick culling from Sevastian's sword after dinner.

I still pondered it as I went to bed that night.

Noric didn't seem to take sadistic pleasure in reaping the way Sevastian did, but why else would he have suggested it?

THE NEXT AFTERNOON was a Saturday, and thankfully, Noric was busy working. The other reapers and I sat on the terrace of Grimsmere, similar to the day I'd met them. In a rare move,

Sevastian let his drasyg fly and the sight of those creatures over our dark estate was mesmerizing. He seemed to be in a particularly good mood after having taken his vengeance on the couple the night before. Em's butterfae, on the other hand, chose to frolic in the Grim Gardens below.

"We all have our talents we agreed to pursue long ago," she told me. "Your father enjoys gardening, Noric is passionate about music, and Sevastian chose painting."

Music? My ears perked at the word. Did he enjoy playing classically?

I bit my tongue, too proud to ask.

"And I chose singing and fashion design," Hexley announced loudly, having been pointedly left out by Embrette. She grinned at having riled him and when his eyes darkened, she grinned wider.

"Two talents? Overachiever," I remarked, impressed.

Hexley snorted. "I had to make up for Em who didn't choose one at all."

"I chose seduction, but you don't consider it an art. Plus, I helped Noric decorate his castle, so that counts for something. If you like a good view," Embrette said, sweeping her hand to the treetops, "then you should see Noric's house. I've got a flat in Tokyo right now. Gorgeous, but not much of a view."

"Where do you live?" I asked Hexley.

"Coincidentally, on the same street as Em," he answered, but he wasn't looking at me, he was staring intensely at Embrette in a way that made me feel I'd interrupted something. "And I've got a view too."

In the heated silence, a blush skirted my cheeks. Did he… live across from her?

"Where do you live?" I asked Sevastian, wanting to escape the tension.

"North," he answered. "And I don't share my view."

Embrette sighed dramatically. "No one wants to see your shack,

Sevy baby." Changing course, she smiled prettily and suggested, "Let's go to Noric's. Ava should know where he lives in case of emergencies."

"Emergencies?" I asked, a chill creeping up my spine. "What kind of emergency could there be?"

Hexley threw his arm around me. "She just wants an excuse to raid Noric's rare collection of scotch. Let's go."

My stomach lurched suddenly, similar to the feeling when one drops down a rollercoaster hill. Seeing Noric's home was too invasive, too intimate.

"I don't need to—"

"Too late!" Em announced, clapping her hands. "I already told him we're coming."

I frowned at the speed of their telepathy and debated refusing. But I reluctantly kept quiet and followed the reapers to our pasture. Though they could just as easily whisk, the horsemen seemed to enjoy flying as much as I did—and I had no other choice. Their pleasure in employing Striders was similar to the way humans enjoyed walking, biking, or riding regular horses when they could more easily drive and save time.

When Hexley was a bit further away and busy with his Strider, Atheon, I leaned toward Embrette and whispered, "Em. Can I ask you something?"

"Mm-hm," she agreed absent-mindedly.

"Well, I was wondering, have you and..." I stumbled, sighed, and tried again. "Well, it just seems like maybe... have you and Hexley dated, in the past?"

Embrette's mouth dropped into horrified disbelief. "Absolutely not!"

I chewed my lip and quickly averted my eyes, hoping I hadn't offended her.

"I don't know where you heard that," Em snapped, taking the reins. She shook her head angrily. "Never, not since our last divorce."

Then she stormed off into the air, and I bit my lip harder as I tried not to laugh in her wake.

I knew it.

Following her lead, the four of us left the sunny afternoon in Solebury and flew toward the night in Romania.

I SUCKED IN an awed breath as we arrived and tightened my shrug against the cold once I dismounted.

Billions of stars shone down on the Carpathians like twinkling jewels the gods had spilled from their cups. Around us, mountain peaks rose and rolled, cresting and falling like waves soft and sharp in every direction. And straight ahead, a sickle moon slashed the cloudless sky over Noric's estate.

My blood sang with the first dark notes of a haunting melody as I laid eyes upon his house—part castle, part chateau.

Of course he lived here. I'd been eerily accurate when imagining it.

Every turret had been adorned with stone angels, demons, and plenty of gargoyles. I wasn't sure which were made of actual stone and which were his familiars, other than his two favorites looming like menacing sentinels on the roof high above the front door.

As if the scene wasn't dramatic enough, several howls pierced the air and my stomach tightened at their nearness.

"It's just the local wolves," Noric said condescendingly, appearing from thin air and making my heart thump. He wore full reaper regalia, and I couldn't help but wonder if he intentionally stalled the sheathing of his lethal daggers to scare me. As he walked toward us, he tucked his blades into a hidden holster strapped across his chest and beneath his jacket. I'd grown up with father's scythe so I wasn't frightened by magical weapons, but I'd never considered anyone could look dangerously alluring wielding them.

Not that Noric does, I thought, scowling.

"They're a part of my home now," he said, walking toward me and standing too close. He was obviously trying to intimidate me with his towering height, but his nearness had the benefit of sharing his bubble of warmth, so I was forced to stay. "I've tamed them."

"Yes, yes, Noric has a way of taming wild creatures," Embrette agreed, rolling her eyes. "He's very *intimidating.*"

Smoothing my hair, I asked, "Isn't that really just a nice way of saying *threatening?*"

"We are the apex predators of this world," Sevastian pointed out. "It is our nature to threaten, and to make good on that threat."

Noric laughed, smug. He cupped his hands to his mouth and made a howl-like sound. Then, turning to the reapers, he said, "If only the three of you listened as well as they do."

"You may be the high horsemen but you're *actually* high if you think I'll heed you like a dog," Sevy returned.

Half a dozen wolves appeared on the mountainside. I tried to hide my gulp as they wove around us, but any predator was just another reminder of my mortality. They were larger than I expected, and while one let me cautiously pet it, another playfully bit the wraparound tie on my shirt and pulled until it ripped.

Noric took his time in chastising the wolf. It quickly backed off, but I *swore* Noric hid a grin. I scowled at both my torn shirt and the tall reaper. Had he delayed intervening to let me squirm, or was it his way of telling me I wasn't welcome here? The whole thing felt weird, like being in my teacher's house, which was technically accurate.

But I forgot about that once I stepped inside his stunning castle.

Grimsmere was glorious, but it was also a bit chaotic, with each room a different study in time and place and a reflection of my father's infinite life. Noric's home was dramatic but more cohesive.

Embrette sighed happily as she watched my reaction. As if she could read my mind, she said, "It's kind of like what whimsigoth would look like if the style matured."

Design wasn't my forte, but as Noric gave us a tour, I grasped the intention. The mountaintop chateau was gothic, but there were fanciful and otherworldly elements throughout, like the Gustavian clock and the four-story library of Prussian blue, with a celestial painting across its domed ceiling. The elegant music room, filled with every instrument known to man, took my breath away. Noric filled his house with plenty of antiques and artifacts, too. I was insatiably curious about a horned skull in a prominent glass case, wondering if it was some sort of Viking headdress. But I was too stubborn to ask.

Nothing could have prepared me for Noric's bed, however.

It was like a poster bed, but instead of wooden pillars, two tall, thin gargoyles perched upon the lower corners. I didn't know if they were his familiars or actual stone, because the wings were folded and their eyes closed. At the top of the bed, one enormous gargoyle rose several feet in the air. It too had his eyes closed, as if sleeping, but the creature's spread wings made up the terrifying headboard, poised as if ready to attack.

There wasn't a single girl in the world whose fantasies wouldn't be haunted by such a bed.

Except for me. Knowing Noric was an insufferable jerk, the last thing I ever wanted was to find myself in that big, pretentious bed, at the mercy of that big, pretentious man.

Seriously, who crafted something like that?

I wondered if Noric wanted me to squirm from this too, but I couldn't tell because he kept his back to me the entire time.

Still, I swore arrogance radiated from him like a tangible energy filling up his suggestive bedroom.

"Shall we have a drink downstairs?" Embrette proposed, proving Hexley at least partially correct.

Everyone filed out of Noric's bedroom and back toward the celestial library.

How many girls over the centuries had writhed on that bed anyway? I wondered, as I followed the reapers to a built-in bar of burled walnut. *Hundreds, probably. Did he ravish them, then obscure their minds?*

It was a terrible thing to consider, as I sipped some rare, expensive liquor that made heat spread throughout my body. I wasn't even sure what was worse—remembering a ravishment or having your memory wiped to forget you'd been overpowered.

Not that Noric even needed to coax a woman, let alone did he seem likely to do anything as terrible as force himself on someone. Girls probably threw themselves at his boots before jumping onto that gothic bed. They probably presented themselves like animals, like one of those wolves outside. I could just imagine them preening on all fours, tossing a coy look over their shoulders and waiting for him to come up behind them.

I clasped the glass of scotch tighter.

They probably clutched the plush bedding in anticipation of his large hands all over their bodies, pulling their hips and running through their hair...

Except for me, of course, I remembered, realizing Noric was staring darkly at me as he sipped his own drink. I quickly looked away and tossed back a casual swig of the stinging, brown liquor. *I would sooner throw myself onto his blade before I fell into his bed.*

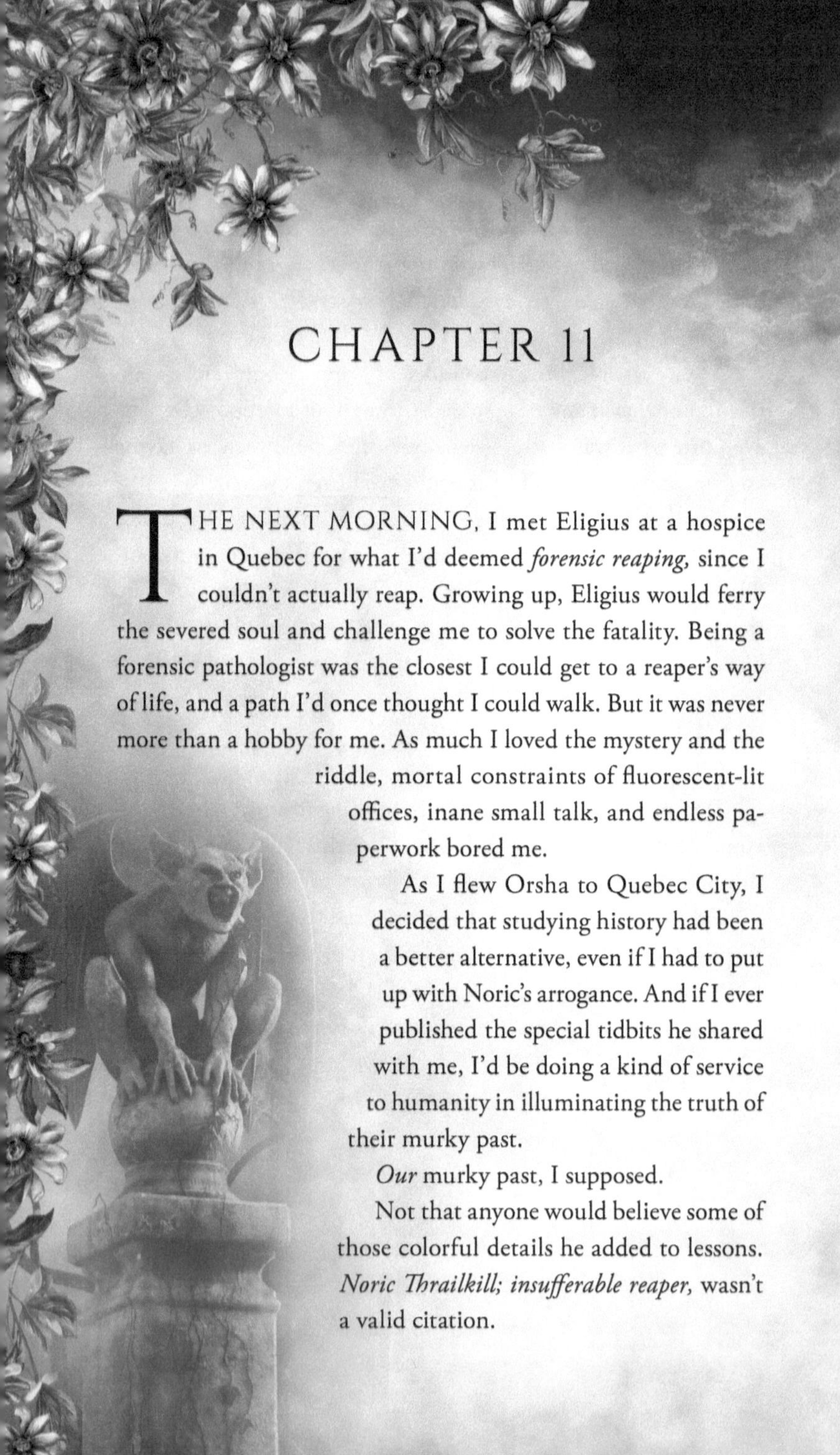

CHAPTER 11

THE NEXT MORNING, I met Eligius at a hospice in Quebec for what I'd deemed *forensic reaping,* since I couldn't actually reap. Growing up, Eligius would ferry the severed soul and challenge me to solve the fatality. Being a forensic pathologist was the closest I could get to a reaper's way of life, and a path I'd once thought I could walk. But it was never more than a hobby for me. As much I loved the mystery and the riddle, mortal constraints of fluorescent-lit offices, inane small talk, and endless paperwork bored me.

As I flew Orsha to Quebec City, I decided that studying history had been a better alternative, even if I had to put up with Noric's arrogance. And if I ever published the special tidbits he shared with me, I'd be doing a kind of service to humanity in illuminating the truth of their murky past.

Our murky past, I supposed.

Not that anyone would believe some of those colorful details he added to lessons. *Noric Thrailkill; insufferable reaper,* wasn't a valid citation.

Perhaps, I pondered, *I could weave those facts into fiction, writing historical stories with hints of the truth sprinkled throughout.*

I considered the idea as I landed outside a brown and gray building, choosing a sparse patch of grass to leave Orsha on this chilly Canadian morning. A moment later, Eligius appeared in the parking lot to escort me inside. My father was in an elderly, feminine form today—dark hair graying at the crown and wrinkles splaying out like short rays around the eyes—and I knew the dying mortal was about to receive a more personal reaping. Since humans tended to picture Death as masculine and no more than middle-aged, the change piqued their interest, as well as calmed them. Sharing invisibility, Eligius escorted me inside the building and to the fourth floor. We entered a small room with a frail, old woman occupying a single bed.

I stood in a corner while Eligius relinquished invisibility, approaching the bed quietly. The woman, seemingly half-asleep, immediately snapped to attention. Her eyes widened and she stared at Eligius for several long seconds.

"I'm dying, aren't I?" the bedridden women croaked, surprising me. Her voice was raspy, like her breathing, but her mind was sharp. Eligius wore the most classic-looking of Death's reaper's robes, however, so I supposed it would be hard to mistake the role.

Death nodded.

"But my family isn't here," the woman moaned, looking around in panic.

"I want you to know that it won't be long before you see them again," Eligius said, taking her hand and clasping it.

"Heaven?" The woman asked. "Am I going there? Will they be there too?"

"I don't want you to fear," Death answered. "In a moment, you will be in the Above, and they will join you when it is their time."

The woman's pale blue eyes were clouded, and they began to redden as she teared. I thought she might ask "Why now?" or "Can I speak with my loved ones one last time?"

But she scrunched up her face and whimpered, clearly in pain and struggling to breathe through it. When she re-opened her eyes, she said simply, "Thank you for telling me. I'm ready now."

It didn't matter if she was ready or not, her time was mandated by the Reclamation of Souls book and not even Death could change that. But the declaration gave her a sense of power Eligius was happy to permit.

"There will be a bit of pain first. But once you're through it, you'll be happy on the other side."

"Oh!" Just as Eligius finished speaking, the woman curled into herself, weeping and shaking. Death watched sympathetically and after a few seconds, Eligius leaned forward. With a quick wave of the hand, Death severed the woman's soul and channeled it to Elysia.

It was done. Ascending to the Above was one of the biggest things to happen in a person's life, and it took but a moment.

No monitors beeped or blared as the room held no hospital equipment. The woman laid on the bed as peacefully as if she were sleeping, and I wondered how long it would take the staff to notice she was not.

"Cause of death?" Eligius quizzed, as he'd done thousands of other times throughout my childhood.

I glanced up, noticing his voice had deepened. Death had taken on the fatherly form I knew best, slim and pale with sleek dark hair, likely because it was the one most familiar to me.

"Old age," I replied, shrugging.

"That is not an official designation," Eligius scolded. He knew that I knew that.

But did it really matter? If it wasn't cancer or pneumonia, it was some other affliction of the elderly. One of them was inevitable.

"Organ failure," I whispered. "Her heart gave out."

Eligius nodded.

It was only a guess; I hadn't applied any science here. But I'd seen it enough to know the odds.

I didn't know why, but I didn't feel like reaping today any longer. Eligius and I hadn't worked together in a while, and I had been looking forward to it.

But I suddenly needed to dance.

"I need to go," I said abruptly. "I didn't practice yesterday and I feel… behind. I'll reap with you next weekend."

Startled, Eligius stared at me with concern, blinking his black eyes once but letting me leave. I slipped out of the building the mortal way, disappearing when I found Orsha in the grass where I'd left her. As soon as I arrived at Grimsmere, I ran upstairs for a shower and washed the hospice off me, though I'd only been inside for a few minutes. Then I dressed for practice in a white leotard with a white skirt to practice *The Rite of Spring*. Making my way to the barn under a low, gloomy sky, I rounded Eligius's Grim Gardens at the back of the house.

Some flora in those flowerbeds were so deadly, my father didn't even want me walking near them. Others were simply gothic in the dreamiest sense. That a mere petal could poison me was an irritating reminder of my mortality. Sometimes, when Death wasn't looking, I skirted those gardens or even challenged myself to a run-through.

The transparent petals of skeleton flowers were my favorite, but they wouldn't bloom until mid-summer. The toxic corpse flower would open to a bright red blossom then too. But now, for spring, the dainty white Hemlocks dotted the edges of the garden, and the pretty-but-deadly bells of the foxgloves were just beginning to bud. Those deceptive, pastel blooms shot up at the garden's center, piercing the air like a snare straight from a dark fairytale.

Staring at the Grim Gardens with the sky threatening rain, I admitted what spooked me. Even knowing what I did. *Because* I knew what I did.

I didn't want to end as a withered woman in a wrinkled bed, with dance but a memory, a pleasure caged only in my mind as I was caged in a body that couldn't express it. I wanted what they had. Father and his reapers.

With fisted hands I hurried to the barn, turned on my sound system, and keyed up the set list. I'd only laced on my pointe shoes when a voice cut the air.

"So this is your dance studio?" Noric remarked, sauntering around as if he owned it, yet sneering as if dust assaulted his nose. "A barn."

Narrowing my eyes at him and in *no* mood for his condescension, I demanded, "Why are you here?"

"Your father asked me to check on you. Said you seemed upset after this morning's reaping."

"Everyone's upset," I pointed out, waving my hand and shooting to my feet so that he wouldn't tower above me any more than necessary. "That's how the world is now. It's everywhere."

Noric paused, and, funny enough, so did I. I'd only said it to deflect, but now that I'd spoken, I realized how true it was.

"What's it like to you?" Noric asked, curiously. He stepped closer. "How do you feel it?"

Closing my eyes, I inhaled and exhaled slowly. "It's a hopelessness. Like no one is excited for the future any longer."

"Mm, yes," he agreed, nodding thoughtfully. "Hope is missing."

"Yes," I said quietly. "That's how I feel, at times. It's a creeping despair inside me."

"No, it's not," Noric declared, searching my face.

"Excuse me?"

"You feel it coming from elsewhere, from everywhere. But it's not coming from within you, is it?"

"I—I don't know what you mean."

I knew we were discussing the general state of the world, but I felt like I was missing something. The pressure grew and the sky beyond the barn door darkened—it would rain any minute.

"If you were truly hopeless, you'd give up. Why do you train so hard every day? For an audience that will never see you perform? Something keeps you going." Noric cocked his head, studying me. "You're sensitive to it coming from others, from the very air even. But it's not innate to you."

I gave a low laugh. He made me sound plucky when he'd once dismissed me as directionless. Was it a compliment? I couldn't tell if we were on friendlier terms now and wasn't sure I even wanted to be. After all, he hadn't apologized for his rude behavior.

"You know, I can simply turn on the news to see it's worsening everywhere and I'm just more insulated because of this," I pointed out, waving my hand around to indicate the estate. "Father's money. I'm lucky. But ultimately, it doesn't matter because it's all around me and I live in this world. I'm affected by it too."

Noric studied me, brow knit. Then he shrugged abruptly. "It will pass regardless. It always does."

He was curt, telling me this discussion was over. I was confused but didn't want to admit it and risk Noric rejecting any explanation. Instead, I changed the subject. I'd seen his music room and now he'd seen my dance studio, so why not?

"I noticed a lot of instruments in your house last week." I hoped I sounded casual and not overly interested. "Which do you play?"

"All of them," he replied without hesitation. Noric's response was so earnest, and to my surprise I didn't detect any bragging from it. "Including several that no longer exist."

I'd *meant* to reply with sarcasm, but I could only breathe an awed, *"Oh.* Which is your favorite?"

"I enjoy the piano," he said cautiously, rocking back on his heels. "There's only so many keys because anything beyond the standard number is past the range of most mortals' ability to distinguish frequencies. But reapers can hear those notes, and I have my own, custom-built version. I compose on it for the horsemen only," Noric explained, and I listened, stunned that he was revealing so much. Other than lecturing, this was the most I'd ever heard him talk—although it was a bit of lecture in itself. Had I just hit the correct mark to get him to open up, or was he trying to distract me because Eligius had ordered him to make sure I was okay?

Both?

"Oh. I wish I could hear as you do."

I frowned at myself. *Did that sound awkward?*

Did I care?

Noric's attractiveness was confusing me again. He wore fitted, all-black reaper attire and it flattered his muscles too well.

"Lately I've been considering a piece inspired by butterflies," he said, tilting his head. There was a strange look in his eyes, but I didn't know what it meant. "The ethereal notes of their wings."

"Oh! I love moths and butterflies," I whispered, surprised. "Although I haven't studied them in-depth or anything. Birds, too. I mean, I love anything that can fly, really."

I quickly folded my lips between my teeth to shut myself up. I'd been wistful; too vulnerable by offering up personal information. Or I sounded like an impassioned misfit of some kind.

Although, so had he.

Not that powerful, towering reapers cared what they sounded like to mere mortals.

"The piano is not my favorite though," Noric said, running a hand through his soft brown hair. "My preferred instrument is the violin, or those in that family." He tilted his head, considering me. "Do you play?"

I lifted a hand to the barre. "No. My body is my instrument."

A beat and then Noric asked, "Where did you train?"

"I tried the usual schools for a time, but it always grew too complicated, so Eligius found willing instructors, privately. Several of my Russian teachers were discrete enough that he hardly needed to obscure their minds, and he still works with them from time to time to coordinate... things for me." I ended vaguely, not wanting to get too deeply into the specifics about the rotating male partners we sourced for my practice.

Another beat and then Noric commanded, "Dance for me."

I blinked, suddenly realizing that as I'd rambled, his eyes had darkened, focused.

"Excuse me?" I nearly choked out my laugh. "I don't think so."

"You don't dance professionally. Why not? It's not your feet. It's not your form," Noric declared, gaze freely wandering my body. Wearing only a white leotard, I felt very exposed to those sharp gray eyes set within his haughty, aristocratic face.

"Technique?" He threw out the last word with a teasing arch of the brow, challenging me to prove him wrong. "Dance for me," he said again. But this time, curiosity softened the roughness in his order.

It was still an order.

"No thanks." I spun away from him.

"Dance for me," Noric called at my back, his words reaching out as if to grip and turn me around. *"Please."*

He didn't plead the word—*oh no.* It slipped through his teeth, like a mouse through a cat's claws. Noric gritted his *please* out with resentment, and that intrigued me more than if he'd begged softly. It had cost him to use that word, and I liked making the stoic reaper spend emotional coin.

At that moment, the sky broke and the first patter of rain hit the earth. Noric had left the door wide open and the fresh smell of a spring shower spread into the studio, energizing me.

With a breath, I turned around and took position.

"Play Brahms. *Die Mainacht,*" I requested, and Noric walked over to my laptop to play the selection, then sat back on one of the metal chairs. The first notes of the piano streamed through the speakers overhead. And then… I glided on the back of the wind like a sylph, my body composed of air. I lost myself in the movement as if I were under a spell; the studio fell away and I saw nothing but the dance. When the music stopped, it was as if I'd been released from the magic hold, and I opened my eyes to find myself back in the barn with Noric.

But the faraway look on his face told me he'd been there with me in that magic other world the whole time, and he was still partially there.

How very odd. In order to get there, he needed to watch me, and I needed to lose him.

Instead of racing, my heart seemed to hold off on beating as I waited for Noric's assessment.

"You gave that up," he breathed, mystified, and I grinned at the praise in his voice. But suddenly, he sneered and declared, "Then there can only be one reason. Your heart. There was a boy."

His voice dripped with so much disdain it was as if he'd drowned me in it and I had to swim to the surface just to reply. When I did, I met his scorn with haughtiness and drawled, *"Wrong."*

Noric's gray eyes narrowed with annoyance, and I remembered how Embrette said he didn't like being wrong. But I liked besting him. I wanted payback for the night we met, for the way he looked down on me without even knowing me.

No thunder rolled, but the rain grew heavy. Outside the barn, it pounded the earth, and that wild energy spread into the studio, charging my body, my words.

"Then why did you quit?" he demanded. "Explain."

I laughed, dismissing the reaper so used to having others follow his curt commands. I had a vision of leaving him alone in the studio and I took two steps, but he blocked me.

Only this time it wasn't his gargoyles, it was *him*.

Noric whisked himself into my path so quickly that I bumped into him and gasped. This close, I was forced to tilt my head back to take in his height and my skin tingled at his proximity.

"We're not in the classroom," I reminded, trying to keep my voice steady… trying not to let my gaze linger on those sinister lips. "You don't have power over me here, *sir.*"

Why had I said that?

It got a reaction out of Noric—his eyes flashed.

I wanted more of that, of making the stoic reaper respond. Oh, I was playing with fire, and I liked it. He'd been so dismissive of me when we'd met, now every reaction like this was a tiny victory.

"Would you *like* me to stay? Would you *like* to spend more time here with me?" I challenged him, just as I'd done a few weeks before when he'd blocked me.

To both our astonishments, Noric frowned as he replied, "I don't know." Then he shook off his confusion, shrugged one arrogant shoulder, and added casually, "You're not the most insufferable human I've ever met."

"You're the most insufferable reaper I've ever met," I quickly returned. "And that's saying something, since I've met Sevastian."

Noric scowled, but I pushed past him. Exiting the barn, I held my head high as the rain pelted my body.

My power move cost me my pointe shoes, soiled as I stalked through the mud, so I wasn't truly sure I'd won this round. Not to mention, I was quickly looking like a drowned rat. But I could *feel* Noric staring at my back as I crossed the wet lawn. With the rain soaking my white leotard and diaphanous skirt in mere seconds, I wondered if the game hadn't slightly shifted again.

I wondered if that's why his gaze lingered. It felt heavy, like a pull.

I wondered if that's why… I almost turned around and returned.

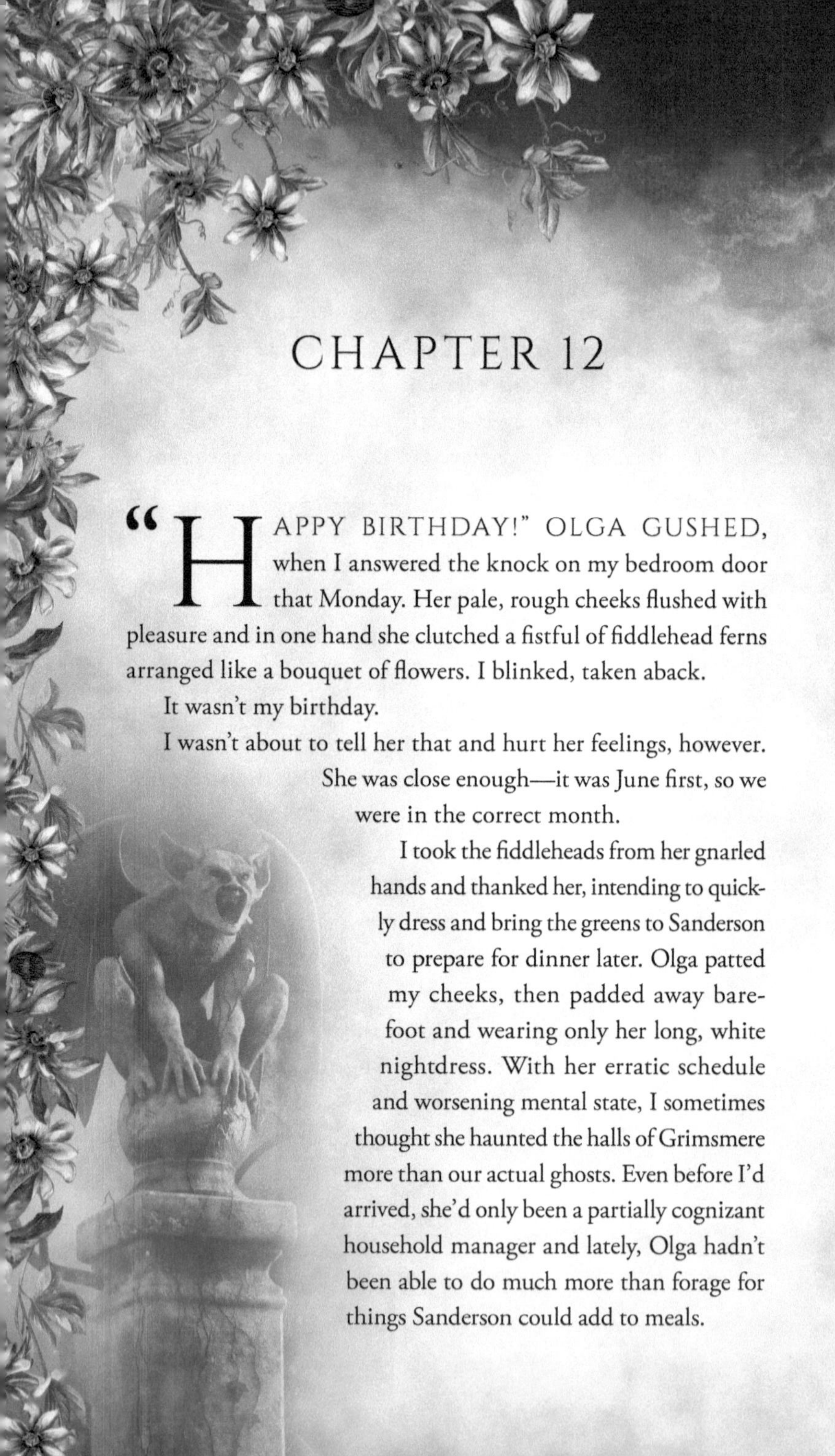

CHAPTER 12

"HAPPY BIRTHDAY!" OLGA GUSHED, when I answered the knock on my bedroom door that Monday. Her pale, rough cheeks flushed with pleasure and in one hand she clutched a fistful of fiddlehead ferns arranged like a bouquet of flowers. I blinked, taken aback.

It wasn't my birthday.

I wasn't about to tell her that and hurt her feelings, however. She was close enough—it was June first, so we were in the correct month.

I took the fiddleheads from her gnarled hands and thanked her, intending to quickly dress and bring the greens to Sanderson to prepare for dinner later. Olga patted my cheeks, then padded away barefoot and wearing only her long, white nightdress. With her erratic schedule and worsening mental state, I sometimes thought she haunted the halls of Grimsmere more than our actual ghosts. Even before I'd arrived, she'd only been a partially cognizant household manager and lately, Olga hadn't been able to do much more than forage for things Sanderson could add to meals.

We had to be careful as she was just as likely to choose poisonous mushrooms as edible ones.

But Eligius had a penchant for taking care of lost and broken people, so Olga had a permanent place here. The elderly woman was the very opposite of Sanderson, who had his full mental capacities but didn't *want* to remember many things... the shame, the addiction. He'd *asked* to forget, which made it easy for father to adhere to the overlord's rules, and obscure Sanderson's mind whenever he saw too much of the truth.

After quickly delivering the fiddleheads to our chef, I crossed into the foyer and my heart stopped when I crashed into Noric. He simply appeared in the middle of the floor.

What the—

"What are you doing here?" I blurted, stepping back. Being flustered angered me—it wasn't *my* fault he'd whisked into my personal space. I wasn't due in the classroom for several minutes.

"I was just making sure you were attending class today," he answered stiffly. Noric's eyes darted to my skirt. It was gray and pleated, a schoolgirl's skirt. Maybe shorter than usual, as I'd decided to wear shorter skirts because of the warmer weather. Even if yesterday's rain had carried a lingering chill. Gooseflesh rose on my skin from our drafty house, coincidentally in time with Noric's roving gaze.

"I—why wouldn't I?"

"How should I know what goes through your mortal head?" he countered defensively. "Maybe someone texted and you made other plans."

Texted? The word sounded wrong coming from his lips. *Was Noric...* I narrowed my eyes... *nervous I wouldn't show? Because his pride would be wounded or because....* Did he mean some*one* or some *guy?*

"I'll be there in a minute?" It came out like a question. Whatever was happening, it made both of us awkward. Again. *Had I wounded him by calling him insufferable?*

Noric nodded, then disappeared. He'd whisked to the little schoolhouse, I presumed. To wait.

Noric never waited. He always made me wait for *his* arrival.

As I stared stupidly at the empty air, Archibald and Yvette floated into the room.

"Well, isn't he a tall drink of water," Yvette mused, apparently having watched from the parlor. "No wonder he's rendered you senseless."

I meant to scoff in protest but it came out squeaky. Yvette knew me too well, having raised me like her own daughter. While I stammered trying to form actual words, she turned to Archie.

"Of course, I could never be with a beardless man," she added, stroking Archibald's perfectly, supernaturally groomed facial hair. "A boy like that wouldn't know what to do with me."

"No, he wouldn't," Archibald reminded with a dark and dangerous grin. He grabbed Yvette by the waist and she giggled.

"Going to class now!" I announced, bolting out the door with a wave. I knew Yvette only soothed Archie's jealousy, but calling Noric a boy was wildly inaccurate. And I was sure the immortal reaper with eons of experience knew what to do with most women.

Except for me, of course, I remembered. Although I couldn't remember exactly *why* I was an exception. I didn't even know what to do with myself in that situation, if I were honest.

As I walked across the lawn, an unwanted image of that pretentious, gothic bed flashed in my mind. This time with me in it.

I gasped, not having realized I bit my lip hard enough to hurt.

Noric was waiting at his large desk when I entered the historic schoolhouse.

Waiting.

He always wore mortal clothing to teach, but the formidable reaper sitting at the head of the classroom never looked quite right. His sculpted arms didn't fit the professor image. I'd never had much of a thing for arms before now, and I was used to feeling the strength in dansuers who possessed plenty of power to lift their female partners.

They couldn't reap with a flick of the finger, however.

I often found my eyes freely roving Noric's body whenever he turned to write on the chalkboard, like now. But this time, with his back turned and without that penetrating gaze on me, it made talking easier.

So I did.

"It wasn't a boy that made me stop dancing professionally," I confessed. It wasn't Noric's business, but for some reason I wanted him to know the truth. "It couldn't be because I haven't even been with anyone that way... ever."

The chalk in Noric's fingers snapped—he must have applied too much pressure against the blackboard.

"Oh," he replied, turning around and putting his hands in his pockets.

I didn't know what to make of it. I broke out in a light sweat as silence filled the room. What wild demon had possessed me to offer such a confession?

"I shouldn't have—"

"No, it's," Noric began as he stroked his chin, "it's that I haven't been with anyone... in some time now."

"Oh."

I looked down and smoothed my skirt. *What was some time to Noric? Weeks? Years?*

"It's not that I don't want to—I do," Noric quickly insisted, chuckling and coming around to the other side of his desk. "But it's pointless as I can only bring someone pain or death. I can have one-night stands and short flings, sure. I've had more of those than any human in history."

Something hot and unpleasant flared inside me. *Of course you have.*

"But if affection grows and the longer I stay..."

"The more you'll want to reap them," I finished softly. I knew the cruel system the gods created to ensure that bonds of love didn't develop between reapers and mortals.

"I can't even share the truth with a human woman, only lies. It is the only thing that makes me think about my immortality. I'm rarely bored," Noric said, flashing an impish grin. "The world is my playground and it constantly changes, entertaining all of us horsemen. But…" he trailed off, running a hand through his hair.

But you want more than a string of meaningless flings, I thought, butterflies in my stomach taking wing.

Noric coughed and cleared his throat, reminding me that we were student-professor in this environment and the discussion was inappropriate.

"So why *did* you stop dancing?" he asked.

I took a deep breath. "When I can't say how I feel because there are no words in any language, when they all fail me… I can dance it instead."

"That's exactly how I feel about composing and playing music," Noric quickly replied, gray eyes dancing as he searched my face.

I nodded, a warmth spreading through me at our mutual understanding. "But it morphed into something darker."

Averting my gaze, I whispered, "My face doesn't suit modern beauty standards—don't argue with me," I quickly scolded before he could try to disagree… or not. "It turned even my best feature, my eyes, into a negative. The boys at school said I stole them. *'Give them back, witch,* they'd taunt. *'Give them back to the beauty you took them from. Did you leave her blind? Or did you at least give her your own eyes in return?'"*

I repressed a shiver; the childhood memory still made shame trickle up my spine.

"But when I danced, I felt like the goddess of beauty herself moved through me, channeled from the Above and offered as a benediction to anyone who watched."

I pursed my lips before continuing. I'd never confessed this to anyone.

"For many of the girls in my class it only made them hate me more. And the more they hated, the harder I danced… until I realized there was no pleasing them. Others, though…" I shook my head. "I quit because I started to only feel worthy when I danced. Like it was my currency in the world and I couldn't earn my place unless I spent it." I shrugged and concluded, "So between that and the complications of my life here, I just gave up trying to fit in."

"The taunts of children," Noric dismissed, sneering with those cocky lips. But when it was directed this way, I kind of liked it. "I've seen you dance. Surely if you continued you could have the world at your feet."

"Maybe I've moved past all that, but what about all this," I said. "I'd have to keep this world separate and secret from that one, have to keep one foot in each."

"Is it really that you're afraid of worlds colliding?" Noric asked, keen gray eyes staring right through me, "Or is it that you're scared to truly plant a foot in the human world?"

I gulped and shifted in my chair, taking time to smooth my skirt again. "It's more like hope," I whispered, looking up with only my eyes. "I hope my feet, my entire body… I don't know." Silence fell once more. What was there to say? That I wished I could be something else? Toying with my hair, I muttered, "It's fine. I know how the universe works. You can just—start the lesson."

With reluctance, Noric retrieved his chalk. But before he began, he stared at it and mumbled something I could barely hear about hopelessness or helplessness. His sharp gaze pinned me and he asked in his blunt reaper way, "With so many ballets ending in death, do you feel dancing them gives you control over an inevitability you can't master in life?"

My heart stuttered. "I—I don't know."

Noric's assessment made me feel exposed, bared to his view in a way more personal than if my body had been displayed.

"Maybe," I admitted, stunned that I'd come close, but hadn't considered the aspect of control before. "Maybe that's one part of it."

It certainly wasn't the only reason I loved dancing, but it might be a significant one.

Weighty seconds passed as Noric held my eyes and my mind ran wild, trying to guess what he was thinking. Finally, he turned around to begin and I let my fingers relax, barely realizing I'd been clutching the edge of the desk.

Luckily, we'd moved onto more interesting topics, like Mesopotamian agriculture and leisure and ancient gods. I suspected Noric kept the early lectures intentionally dry, focusing on things like pottery and arithmetic to torture me or maybe even to make me quit.

But now… did he *want* me to stay?

CHAPTER 13

T**HE NEXT SATURDAY I WAS IN THE BARN** dancing *La Sylphide,* and when I stopped mid-scene to adjust my shoe, I swore I felt something move in the air. Hair rose on my neck and I froze, scanning the barn while the haunting, hopeful melody played on.

Though clearly alone, I felt like I was being watched.

No. My heart skipped a beat. *Clearly, no* mortal *was in the room with me. But that didn't mean…*

Suddenly, the barn door creaked open and Embrette walked through the human way.

"Hey," she called out over the music. "We've got a reaping in the Philippines, all hands on deck. Tsunami. We're heading to Nede after, do you want to come?"

"Oh," I said sadly. "That sounds bad."

"Actually, it's a smaller one that's been scheduled for a while, but it's hitting a popular beach hotel and water reapings are tricky."

"What's Nede?" I asked.

"That's what Sevy christened the isle," she said, rolling her eyes. "It's just Eden, backwards. Though it might as well be forwards—it's a paradise and it's ours."

Hexley appeared next to Embrette and explained, "We maintain a glamour around the island. But for such a large territory and from a distance, our magic's not infallible and sailors do find it from time to time. But even if they stumble upon it once, they're never lucky enough to reach it twice, and no one believes their reports when they return. *If* they return."

Noric and Sevastian popped into the room, and suddenly I was very interested in joining them. Each horsemen wore the simplest of black clothing—no draping, hoods, or cloaks, only fitted pants and shirts.

"Let me just get cleaned up," I said, hurrying out of the barn and back to the manor.

A few minutes later, I flew Orsha over a stretch of powdery sand and sparkling water on a near cloudless day in the Philippines. An earthquake had already struck offshore but no sirens blared. Either there weren't any or there hadn't been enough time. A few dozen mortals were going to lose their lives in the next few minutes. Though there was nothing I could do to defy the Book—nothing even an immortal could do—my heart ached for the unknowing tourists and locals below. I'd only had sixteen years to adjust to the true nature of the world, after all, unlike reapers who'd had millennia. But the alternative, leaving a soul writhing in psychic pain, only to have the overlords pull it through when they got around to it, wasn't any better. Not to mention, I knew from Eligius that a reaper could be punished with a similar unbearable agony for the defiance.

A moment later, a racing sea wall tumbled forth.

Though I'd seen more than my share of death and disasters, the wave thundering to shore was horrifying, as were the screams. Mercilessly, it crashed into the main hotel and surrounding buildings.

From the safety of the sky, I watched as the reapers did their duty, delivering death, severing souls, and ferrying them back to Elysia.

It was difficult work when it came to waves and water, because the horsemen had to be close to the dying. As I watched, I could easily see why Noric had been declared the high reaper. No one moved as quickly and precisely as he did, diving and whisking from one body to the next. I searched for him whenever he disappeared beneath the sea and couldn't tear my eyes away whenever he re-surfaced, hair slicked and body dripping. There was a terrifying beauty to his work that riveted me.

When the worst of the waves subsided, all four reapers were drenched as they flew up to meet me. Noric shook out his soaked hair and declared, "Our familiars will take care of the rest of today's cullings."

Sevastian stripped off his shirt and tossed it into the sea. "Come on," he said. "Let's dry off in Nede. Treat ourselves for the hard work."

We left the devastation behind and flew our Striders somewhere in the middle of the ocean. Nothing but blue waves spanned in every direction, until finally, a small island appeared amidst the cerulean sea. It immediately made me think of Bora Bora, because this one also possessed a lagoon and was as close to paradise as I thought possible. Our Striders landed and their long horns, leather wings, and deep scarlet eyes looked wildly out of place in the sun-soaked paradise.

So did the reapers. I couldn't help but think we were all snakes in a garden here, a glamoured island that was wild and raw and pure.

"You keep this from humans," I breathed.

Sevastian snorted. "They'd only ruin it."

Noric laughed his agreement, and I thought instead that maybe reapers were the only creatures who belonged here.

Hexley threw his arm around my shoulders. "Consider us her eternal caretakers."

"And we take good care of what matters to us," Embrette said, side-eyeing me.

There was something weighty and enigmatic about her tone, just like when she'd spoken of needing to know where Noric lived, in case of emergencies.

I frowned. *Was I in some kind of danger Eligius hadn't told me about?* No, that couldn't be. My name wasn't in the Book, and what care could I possibly require?

We found a spot on the sand facing the lagoon, and I self-consciously stripped to the bikini I'd worn, while the rest of the reapers simply stripped down to their underwear.

Thank god I was far away from Noric because when I saw him, I laughed and couldn't stop. I didn't know how to react, other than with hysteria, because his body was ridiculous. Of course he looked like *that.* Like raw masculinity laid bare. Bodies like that weren't meant for teaching or playing violin. They were made to reap and ravish.

That stupid gargoyle bed popped into my mind again and I felt my face heat. A very wet, dripping, Noric turned and started walking in our direction.

"Ugh," Embrette groaned. "Does Eligius ever burst into your brain with orders? I told him we're taking a break today and our familiars will handle all our work."

"Eligius doesn't speak to me telepathically very often," I said, training my gaze on her to avoid the wet god of death coming closer. "It's not as if I can mentally reply. Like the overlords sending wispingers to you, it's a one-way conversation for me and that feels… invasive."

"Good to know," Noric said. I felt him staring but I refused to look at him. I *couldn't,* as my whole body already ran too hot. I wanted to tell him that with another person and under different circumstances, telepathy wouldn't feel like a violation at all…

it would be a welcomed intimacy. But how could I say that and especially when he was slick and half-naked next to me?

Perhaps Noric misunderstood my stiffness because he quickly left and my heart sank.

"Hexley," Embrette cooed. "I have a craving."

"No," he grumbled, flopping back in the sand and closing his eyes. "Tell Frederick to get it for you."

Who's Frederick? I wondered.

"But *Hexley,*" she protested, reaching over and running her fingers down his smooth torso to an area just beyond what was socially acceptable for others to witness. Hexley peeked one eye open. "Pistachio is an aphrodisiac."

"No," he repeated, closing both eyes again.

"What do you want?" I asked her.

Without opening his eyes, Hexley answered, "She wants gelato from this little shop in Florence."

"What time is it in Florence?" I wondered aloud.

"They're in tomorrow," Noric answered.

"We're in yesterday." Sevastian remarked, off-handedly.

"Whatever. They're open. And it's not like you couldn't grab a container even if they weren't." Embrette pouted, then smiled. "Remember Sainte-Maxime? That little hotel with a balcony right up against the sea? I've been wanting to return someday."

Hexley's eyes popped open. A slow, sly grin spread over his face. "When you say return do you mean—"

"Repeat," Embrette said, looking up through her lashes. "Return and repeat."

Hexley shot to his feet. "I'll make a run."

"Mm, thank you. Gelato is my favorite." She sighed happily. "And the malaise feels a million miles away when I'm here."

I snapped to attention, sitting up straighter, and asked, "Okay, what *is* this malaise?"

"Oh, you know," Hexley replied, waving his hand. "It's just what we call that disillusioned feeling in the world right now. When you've lived as long as we have, you go through up and down times."

"I see," I said slowly, although I wasn't really sure I did. Perhaps the horsemen were more sensitive to what everyone was feeling the last few years—that dark cloud over the world that pressed like a weight on all of us. Economic downturn, plummeting birthrates, another world war nipping at our heels...

"Anyone else want gelato?" Hexley quickly asked. We all gave him our orders, and he whisked away to Florence.

"Hey, did you see that gray yacht?" Sevastian asked Noric, lightly slapping Noric's leg. The blonde reaper tied his hair into a short ponytail at his neck. "I have a different craving. Want to nip over there?"

"I'd say you have a preference for reaping the rich and the rude," I mused, looking at Sevastian, "but I'm not sure you discriminate at all when death-dealing. You crave, you cull. No questions asked."

"We *are* the terrestrial chaos variable," he declared with a lazy, wolfish grin.

I furrowed my brow. "Well, that's a very scientific way to put it."

Noric grinned, tossing a fruit he'd plucked from a tree between his hands. "Think of us as being introduced into the environment as an apex predator to keep it all in balance."

"A predator whose prey isn't even aware of your existence. Not really."

"There's plenty of work to keep us busy on the daily," Em pointed out. "And it's not like we'll die if we don't," She knocked her sunglasses down from her head and over her amber eyes. She didn't need them, she simply liked the look. "But we reap as the mood takes us."

I pursed my lips against making a comment about being a *mood reaper,* but in my own head I thought it was a dark and disturbing thought. From Eligius, I knew that reapers couldn't over-cull either, similar to when a human filled up on food. But they had to randomly reap as a part of their existence.

Hexley returned with the gelato and when we finished, Sevy and Noric momentarily disappeared. When they reappeared, I involuntarily shuddered. It all happened so fast. Growing up, Eligius had explained but tried to keep that side of his role from me. I couldn't help but think about whoever was in that yacht, blissfully unaware they'd been chosen one second and dead the next.

If I weren't Eligius's daughter, would Noric have randomly selected me someday?

Noric must have caught something in my eyes—fear? Because he'd been walking toward me but abruptly stopped. He clenched his jaw and his mouth formed a tight line. I couldn't make out the emotion on his face before he turned away. *Frustration? Shame?* I looked down at the sand, confused and a little guilty. I hoped that I hadn't made him feel bad for something he couldn't help, something he'd been designed to do. And it wasn't all bad, of course, since he'd channeled the soul to Elysia.

"Your birthday is coming up," Hexley announced, coming over to sit with me in the sand. I gave a small smile, amazed that he knew. "Shall we surprise you?"

Embrette clapped happily and answered for me. "Oh yes. Leave everything to us!"

The reapers shared a conspiratorial look, communicating silently, and a warm feeling spread throughout my body. It gave light and heat, like a cozy fire lit from within.

The realization that came was so stunningly simple, yet so deep, I stilled as I considered it.

All my life, I was never really bored.

I was *lonely.*

I had Eligius and Yvette and Archibald, sure. But as parental figures they were never going to be friends. No wonder I'd pursued endless diversions without finding fulfillment. It wasn't *things* I'd wanted to do, it was *people* I'd wanted to do them with.

Well, reapers, specifically.

I'd been lonely.

How stunningly simple.

I gave myself a little grace for not seeing the obvious some amateur therapist would have called out in two sessions. Because I'd always thought it impossible to connect with anyone socially, I'd banished the idea from my mind before it even had a chance to fully form.

But now, four horsemen welcomed me into their fold and for the first time in my life… I had friends.

I glanced at Noric, but he'd turned to face the lagoon.

And what was he, to me?

Nothing, I reminded myself.

Except perhaps the one who might reap me someday, when the time came.

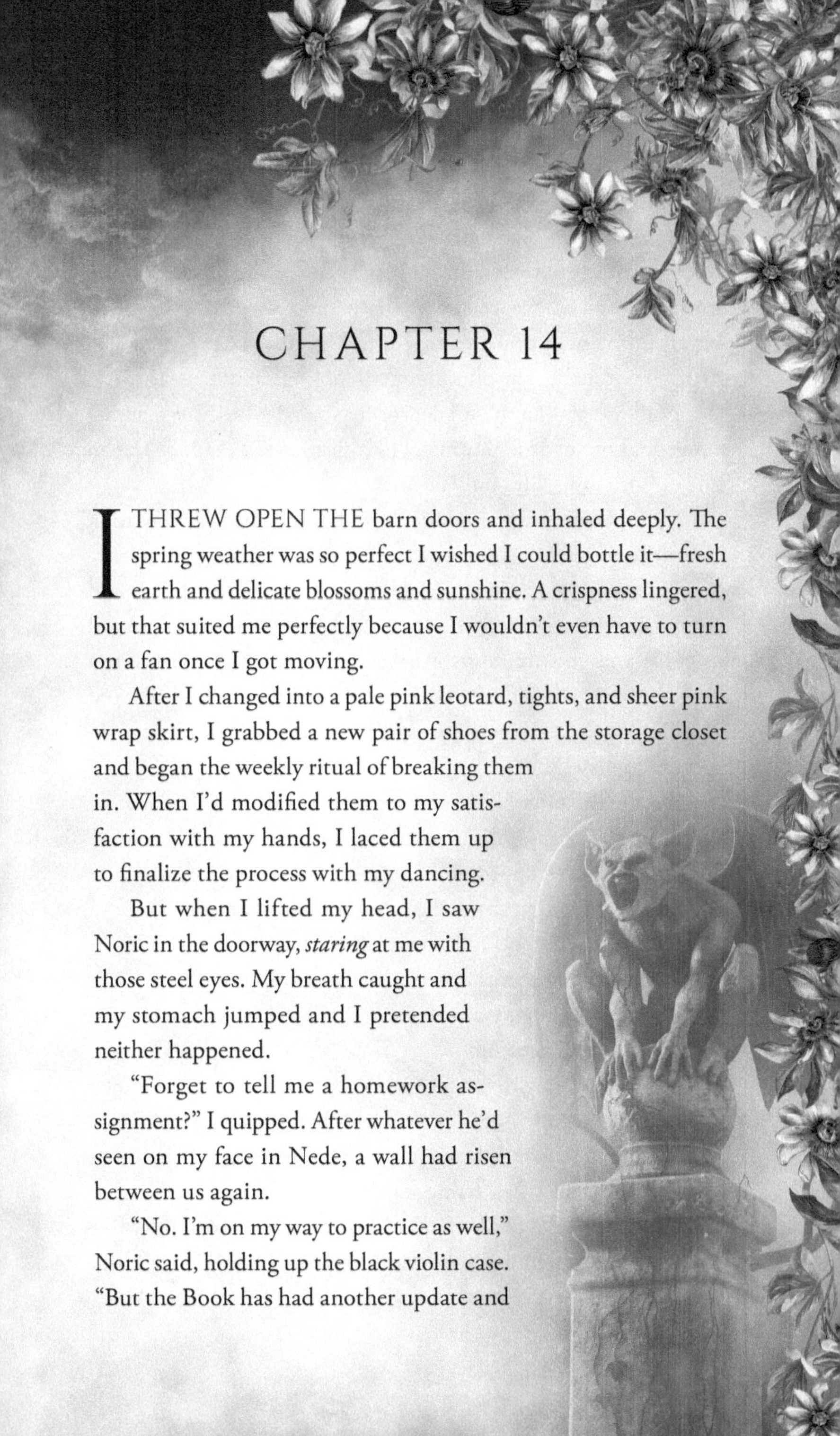

CHAPTER 14

I THREW OPEN THE barn doors and inhaled deeply. The spring weather was so perfect I wished I could bottle it—fresh earth and delicate blossoms and sunshine. A crispness lingered, but that suited me perfectly because I wouldn't even have to turn on a fan once I got moving.

After I changed into a pale pink leotard, tights, and sheer pink wrap skirt, I grabbed a new pair of shoes from the storage closet and began the weekly ritual of breaking them in. When I'd modified them to my satisfaction with my hands, I laced them up to finalize the process with my dancing.

But when I lifted my head, I saw Noric in the doorway, *staring* at me with those steel eyes. My breath caught and my stomach jumped and I pretended neither happened.

"Forget to tell me a homework assignment?" I quipped. After whatever he'd seen on my face in Nede, a wall had risen between us again.

"No. I'm on my way to practice as well," Noric said, holding up the black violin case. "But the Book has had another update and

I've got a calamitous reaping in Beijing tomorrow. I'll be late for class."

So many unusual updates lately. I supposed such chaos matched what we all felt in the world.

Noric walked deeper into the barn and a tingle of excitement began in my belly. He'd changed into his all-black reaper's garments, contrasting the pink confection of standard ballet attire.

"Will you play for me as I danced for you?" I asked. The question came out hot, loaded. Gunmetal like his eyes and ready to fire on one or both of us. "It's only fair."

Noric debated, then nodded and opened his case. He took position and I held my breath.

A moment later, Noric moved his bow across the strings and the music swept me away to a state of immediate frisson. I gasped as chills and goosebumps spread over my skin and warmth ran down my spine. It felt illicit, like he penetrated me with his notes. *Piloerection music,* I knew it was called, a skin orgasm from transcendent music.

Oh my. If I took Noric to that other world with dancing, he did the same for me with his playing.

Abruptly, he stopped and I struggled to speak. I realized he waited patiently to hear my thoughts as I had for him.

"You're gifted… beyond the reach of mortals."

Noric laughed as if that was a hilarious thing to say.

"What?" I demanded, defensive again. Were we hot or cold today? I couldn't keep up.

"I wasn't playing to my fullest. Over the centuries, I've grown to a point where my music can reap for me, whether I want it to or not." He ran a hand through his light brown hair. "There was a woman long ago. Her name was Frou Troffea and we had a… relationship." A sad smile touched his lips. "She was a little like you. Uninterested in the conventions and customs of mortals, and she loved to dance."

Frou Troffea. The name sounded familiar but I couldn't recall why.

"I played and, as the ecstasy seized her, it seized me too. I'd acquired a new talent but I hadn't yet learned to control it. I coaxed music from my instrument and she danced and soon the townsfolk joined in, but they couldn't stop." Noric paused, squinting as if he could see into the past. "No one could stop."

"Wait," I protested, holding up a hand. A fuzzy memory from some governess or other came to light. "The Dancing Plague that happened a long time ago? That was you?"

He gave a tight nod and I sucked in an astounded breath. *Dear God.* History lessons were much more illuminating when Noric offered a personal memory. I desperately wanted him to continue sharing these stories of his life. His words were like a much-needed breeze, blowing the clouds aside to reveal the light of the moon, and I basked in the haunting glow of his past.

"Strasbourg, 1518. Even when I managed to stop, they danced on, convinced that if they continued, they'd hear the heavenly music again."

I tried to recall everything I'd learned about the event, but no one ever knew for sure what had happened.

"Did she…" I probed gently.

Noric nodded again. "That was how I was able to stop in the first place. We were both caught in the ecstasy but only one of us could die. I don't know what would have happened if Frou Troffea hadn't saved us all with her death. Before she crumpled to the ground… that look in her eyes told me she knew. When she fell, I dropped my bow. Her death stopped me from enchanting more, but it was too late for those already dancing. They continued spinning until they all fell."

Centuries ago, and the guilt still etched onto Noric's face when he talked about it. The reaper capacity for pain caused a bolt of fear to tear through my heart, because if something ever developed between us, it would condemn Noric to everlasting agony. I would die and find peace in the Above, while he would suffer eternally.

"It reminds me of *La Valse*," I murmured, referencing the ballet about a girl seduced by Death himself, succumbing further until she danced herself to her own doom. Of course it had been a favorite of mine as a child. "Perhaps you've inspired tales like that."

"Perhaps." His eyes took on a faraway look again and he said, "There isn't a single true artist who hasn't engaged in some misdeed, some shame, in pursuit of their art. It is our manifestation of the divine and we sin in its name as guiltily as any crusader slaughtering with determination in a battle they've deemed holy."

Oh, I knew that feeling too.

"I understand, though I haven't reaped anyone," I whispered. "I was raised as Death's daughter and I've been as starved for dance partners as a vampire child with a fresh appetite. But instead of bringing humans for me to drink, Eligius… he brings me partners to dance with. Since I was young, through bribes or obliging, he finds talented danseurs for me… for the night or for a week's worth of evenings if I chose. They are dissuaded from asking questions and he obscures their memories once we're done, one man after the next."

Noric gave me his rapt attention as I told him what I'd never told anyone before. I'd been practicing solo lately, but eventually, I would need partners again.

"What am I to them?" I asked, rhetorically. "I suppose they see a mystery, a twirling ballerina in an old barn beside a windswept manor, a magical girl who calls them to dance, then sends them away with the sun's rise. It's the plot of a ballet in itself. Sometimes I wonder if I haunt their dreams, every now and again, should a memory peek through."

Amusement played on Noric's lips. "Perhaps you'll inspire a production someday."

"Perhaps." I smiled, distracted by his face when he allowed it to soften.

"What a pair we make," he said, running a hand through his hair and bringing me back to the moment. "You do not *want* to dance for others and I *cannot* play for them. Not in the way I want to." Noric's long fingers stroked his violin with the adoration of a lover, and I was jealous of the wood. "Masters are able to play so beautifully they will make you weep. I am able to play so divinely my music can ferry the listener down the River Styx."

Noric wasn't boastful when he claimed it; he was melancholic.

"Reaping with music," I mused. From our conversation I decided that we were hot now, not cold. "I don't believe you. Show me. Holding the secrets of the universe in my head," I countered, "I might not be subject to the same mortal limitations."

Noric cocked his head as he considered me. "You are different, it's true."

"Play," I insisted, boldly spinning a circle around him. "And if I'm wrong and you're right, you can always stop and jar me out of it. You said so yourself, you now know how."

"I said I know how to stop now. Not that I can snap someone out of it once I've begun."

I crossed my arms and tapped my slippered foot impatiently. "Then start out slowly and offer me more incrementally. We'll see how I can handle what you can give, bit by bit."

I chewed my lip because my words came out more suggestive than I'd intended. But Noric didn't budge.

"Trust me," I looked at him pleadingly. "Trust yourself."

Trust us, I wanted to say.

Which sounded ridiculous, but it was what I felt in my bones, my blood.

I wondered if Noric felt it too, because he slowly retrieved his violin once more. Noric tucked the instrument beneath his chin and positioned his bow, silver rings glinting on his fingers. The intensity in his eyes and the messy, casual way his hair flopped down to obscure his gaze created a haunting image that made my heart pound.

"Slowly," he agreed in a cautious tone.

But as soon as he struck the first notes, I gasped. There *was* something different in his playing, right down to his posture, his stance. The way his bow flew over the strings was nothing less than a spell evoking the divine. He was beyond a virtuoso. I didn't even know what level to call it. Godlike? I wasn't moving, wasn't breathing.

Noric's dark gaze lifted from his violin. *Dance* his eyes commanded me. And in that one look I lost my worries. Because it didn't matter how sublimely he played, I knew that Noric, the man, the reaper, had the power to call me back to him.

I moved, somehow both running from the grip of the music and chasing it at the same time. Noric was right, the sound was too much for my mortal body to contain. But through my dance I was able to channel and release it. I'd never heard such a composition before. Noric spoke the words of creation to me through his notes, and I replied back with the entirety of my being, using my own instrument of choice, my body. I gave myself over to the notes and let them lead me, transcending my physical form and floating as I danced steps I scarcely knew.

Whirling, spinning, faster and faster.

I realized I'd leapt into a saut de chat when the floor disappeared beneath my feet. But, carried upon Noric's notes, the name was woefully insufficient to describe what I'd done. *Spin. Spin faster!* It was killing me, perhaps, but murder had never been more melodious. Had I an audience, would they weep to see the final performance of Avalia?

My head fell back and my chest thrust forward as if both were yanked in opposite directions. It was like an invisible, steel cord tugged me toward... something gleaming. My arms curved gracefully behind me as I submitted to the ecstasy. *Oh, how that glow beckoned.* My heart never wanted anything more...

...Except... one thing. *Didn't it?* I couldn't recall. Gray spheres flashed before my eyes, but the golden glow expanded, encompassing them. And weren't they one and the same, anyway? The owner of those dancing, silver spheres was somehow linked to the illumination before me. My body jerked back and forward again, and I wasn't sure I could take full credit for the illustrious move. Was I commanding the motions of my body or was something else dancing its will upon me?

It didn't matter when the result was heavenly to behold.

Yes, my body screamed, contorting with dreadful loveliness as I bent backwards a third time, yielding to whatever it was that wanted me, that craved me as much as I craved it in return. I offered myself to its will. My pirouette seemed unnaturally fast and still I spun faster, breaking only to leap, each time hoping I'd leap into the Elysian chasm that beckoned me.

Take me, I begged, throwing my arms wide. *Take me now. Now!*

The abrupt vacancy of divine music assaulted my ears so terribly I thought they'd bleed at the onslaught of mortal white noise. All at once the world was horrid and harsh and my soul yearned to return to the harmony.

I collapsed on the floor, limp as a puppet whose strings had been cut. At the same time, I heard a voice shout, "Stop!"

I slapped my hands over my ears and cried out. This silence was not life, it was death. The divine music I'd heard—that was the truth of being.

"Avalia," Noric yelled, or it sounded like shouting to my ears, still longing for the melody of that other place. Gray eyes were the first thing to come into focus, and I was aware that my head was in Noric's lap.

Perhaps he'd been saying my name for a while. Skeletal white and wide-eyed, Noric's face was the picture of abject horror as he stared down at me. Understanding dawned gradually as the world returned, piece by piece. I'd been succumbing to the spell he'd warned me about. Maybe I'd held out longer than most, but in the end it was taking me just the same.

No—not the same. Noric's voice had called me back.

Suddenly my body was yanked upwards and into a crushing embrace. Noric clung to me as if I'd disappear if he slackened his grip.

"Too tight," I gasped.

He loosened his powerful arms and lifted my face in his capable hands. My heart skipped several beats; being in his lap felt like where I belonged. This close, I could smell the reaper on him, that scent of centuries of knowledge, of unimaginable adventure.

I'd dance to the edge of death every day if it meant Noric would take me in his arms like this.

"Are you okay?"

His demand was harsh. My answering grin was perhaps maniacal.

"I want to do it again."

Between ragged breaths, Noric laughed. His grip on me loosened and he pulled away, suddenly aware of how inappropriate we were. My body screamed so badly to return to his hold, the ache was painful. But I said nothing.

"I think not, Ava," Noric said, shaking his head. "Your father just might find a way to kill me if anything ever happened to you."

CHAPTER 15

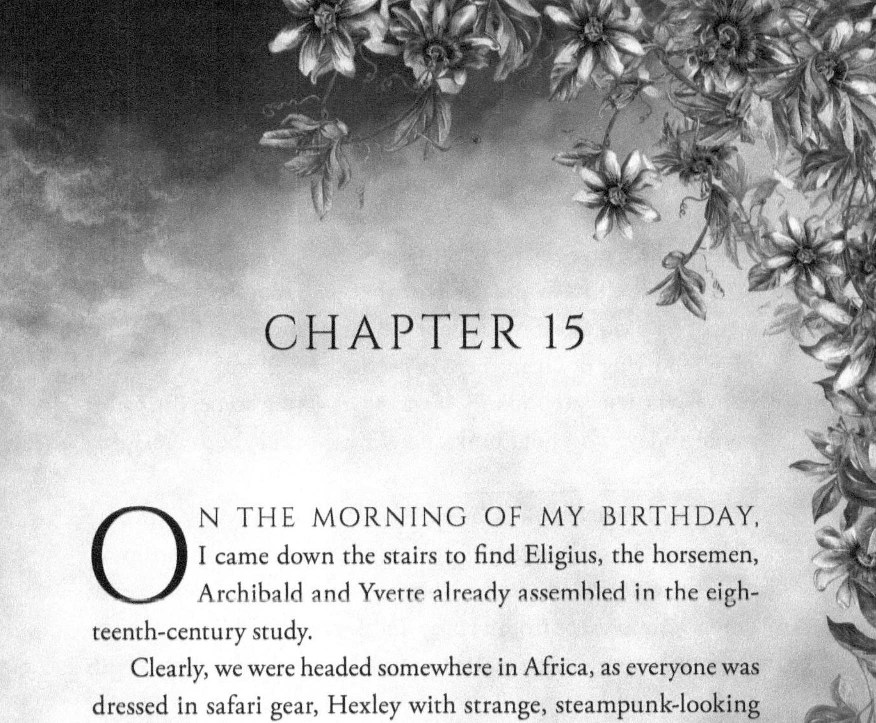

ON THE MORNING OF MY BIRTHDAY, I came down the stairs to find Eligius, the horsemen, Archibald and Yvette already assembled in the eighteenth-century study.

Clearly, we were headed somewhere in Africa, as everyone was dressed in safari gear, Hexley with strange, steampunk-looking goggles resting on a hat resembling a pith helmet.

"Where are we going?"

"Where *aren't* we going?" Hexley replied.

Embrette's amber eyes twinkled. "There's four hemispheres and four of us," she announced, braiding back her shiny brown hair as she spoke. "So we divided up the world into quadrants, each of us planning for one of them."

A thrill ran through me. I loved this day already and it hadn't even begun.

"But first, open your presents," Hexley urged. He threw himself onto the couch, one leg over the arm, and grinned as excitedly as if it was his own birthday.

My first gift, from Yvette, was a vintage Christian Dior slip of the palest pink and as soft as rose petals against my skin. Next was Archibald's present, a book on Benjamin Franklin which I was sure he'd quiz me on within days.

I could tell from the package that Sevastian had gifted me artwork, but I gasped when I opened the wrapping to find a stunning rendering of Grimsmere in all her dark glory and with my barn in the background too. It was a late spring scene, fitting for my birthday, with bold pink and electric purple buds emerging on the trees.

"This is masterful," I breathed. Sevastian only gave me one tight nod. An oil painting of this skill belonged in a museum.

I knew I wanted to save Noric's gift for last, so I next moved onto a joint present from Hexley and Embrette. Pulling back the thick wrapping paper revealed a small ebony chest, studded with rubies. When I opened it, however, I gasped as the crescendo of Rachmaninoff's haunting *Isle of the Dead* played on what I now realized was a music box. The scene inside was a work of art, depicting a dark and mysterious island of towering rock walls surrounding thick pine trees. Like many music boxes, this one held a twirling dancer, but she was not alone. A girl, and what was obviously a reaper, spun together at the stone gates of the moody isle.

"My god, this is incredible," I said. I was so hypnotized by the mysterious scene and eerie music that I could scarcely breathe. I knew I would play this nightly, staring into the isle and wanting to transport myself there. And from the dancers, I wondered if Hexley and Embrette thought something was going on between Noric and I.

Next, I opened my father's red velvet box to find a chunky necklace of garnets and lapis lazuli. It was gorgeous on its own, but it immediately became one of my most prized possessions when he told me it once belonged to Anna Pavlova, the famous prima ballerina.

When it came time for Noric's gift, however, he said he wanted to give it to me in the barn, before leaving. So I hastily dressed for safari and packed what Embrette instructed I bring. Then I hurried to meet Noric while everyone else made last-minute preparations back in the house.

He was standing in the middle of the barn with his violin at his chin, and as soon as I entered, he made it sing. It was the type of music where the melody wrapped itself around my heart and tugged. From our speakers Noric was accompanied by a full orchestra he must have recorded earlier. He only played for a few minutes, and I was left dying to hear more.

After I'd finished clapping, he said quietly, "It's for you. This is just a part of a ballet I composed for you."

Oh.

Oh, it was *perfect.*

"I love what I've heard so far," I breathed. "Did you choreograph it too?"

"I have some vague ideas, but I don't dance ballet." He gave me a look like the idea was crazy. "You'll have to do that part."

"What is it about?" I asked.

"You two finished?" Embrette's voice called from the doorway, and I let out a frustrated sigh when Noric began putting away his violin.

"I'll tell you later," he said.

"Sevastian's craving," Em declared, sauntering inside with the other reapers.

"Gonna reap some poachers I've been eyeing," Sevy announced, sliding across the floor with his arms wide in a showy move. Turning, he licked his lips with exaggeration.

"Ah. So every now and again you do some good," I remarked.

"He's got a soft spot for animals," Embrette corrected. "Humans, not as much."

"I'll try not to take that personally," I mumbled.

Sevastian shrugged. "You can try."

Noric rolled his eyes at his brother, pulled him down into a headlock, and mussed his hair.

"Let's go," he commanded, dragging Sevy out of the barn without releasing him.

IT. WAS. MAGICAL.

Pure wonder.

Once we landed, we rode our Striders like regular horses, racing and laughing and getting close to the wildlife without alerting them to our presence. Every vista was a work of heavenly art. The land possessed its own music that sang to my blood, making me want to dance through the zebras and to run alongside the giraffes.

Noric and Sevastian showed off, competing as they hooted and balanced on their Striders' backs, part acrobat, part ancient warrior. I knew they enjoyed riding or flying when they needed to slow down and think, but also for the pure fun of it.

When Noric and I neared a lake, a group of flamingos took wing in unison. When I pointed at the flock, he said, "It's called a *flamboyance.*" Noric winked and turned his Strider, Orphnaeus. "Come on."

We took to the sky and followed the flamboyance through the air, our dark and menacing Striders a haunting juxtaposition against the bright pink and orange birds. I'd reaped in Africa before, but I'd never taken the time to explore; never had friends to explore *with.*

After sharing a bush lunch of meat and banana stew, Sevy announced, "My turn. We're headed to Scandinavia."

"Sevastian gets the region where he lives? That doesn't seem fair," I pointed out.

Noric shrugged. "We cast lots and promised to keep to the outcome."

The five of us mounted our Time Striders, headed north, and within seconds we arrived at a hot spring. The scent of sulfur assailed my nose and chilly air bit my skin as I left Orsha's warmth. Steam rose from the pools and people splashed about in small groups or soaked alone in a meditative state.

"We've got sort of a hot and cold theme going," Embrette explained.

I choked on my laugh and tried not to look at Noric.

Well, that's fitting.

We showered first and it felt luxurious simply washing the dust and grime from my body. Then I put on the bikini Embrette had instructed me to pack and we met the men, who'd already found their way into the steaming waters.

I grinned as three faces covered in white-gray clay turned to us in unison. It was hard to get used to reapers in casual environments like this, despite my experiences. The world was just their playground, and humans, well…

We were just their playthings.

After we soaked for a bit, Embrette and I took our time cleaning up in the spa's spacious dressing rooms. She brought makeup we shared, and I put on the one dress I'd packed.

It was nighttime when we left Scandinavia, but still light when we landed in Buenos Aires. It was Noric's turn, and he'd chosen an Argentinian steakhouse. I'd worked up an appetite after the hot spring and was happy to simply eat good food, but when a band struck up the unmistakable music of a tango, I realized Noric's real surprise.

He cocked his head at the dance floor while those large, gray eyes twinkled.

"You don't dance," I reminded.

"I don't dance ballet," he corrected. "I never said I don't dance."

Noric pulled me to him and we moved with the crowd to the sensual beat. He was good, of course, and my heart pounded so forcefully being spun in his arms that *I* was the one who struggled to keep up.

Within the boisterous restaurant, I could still feel the so-called *malaise* affecting the world, but it was as if it was being kept at bay here, temporarily denied. It had been the same in the bush and the hot spring. There was no escaping that feeling, any more than one could escape gravity. But in places like this, it was as if it encroached but hadn't yet conquered.

Noric spun me and I put it from my mind, determined to enjoy my birthday even if the state of the world tainted events like this.

Breathless and flushed, I returned to the table after several songs, and Embrette fell into the seat next to me. She'd been dancing tightly with Hexley, and Sevastian had offered his hand to a girl who looked ready to swoon at being chosen by the sexy stranger.

"I've lived long enough to know one thing is true," Em said, pulling lipstick out of her purse and touching up her makeup. She leaned into my ear and advised, "You can tell what a man or woman is like in bed by how he or she dances."

I flushed a deeper scarlet and was relieved for the distraction when Hexley moved our party along by announcing, "My turn."

Departing the restaurant and returning to our Striders, I considered the next surprise. We'd certainly run hot again, so we had to be headed somewhere to cool off. The Canadian Rockies? A lake in Vermont?

Having imagined something deep in nature, I was dumbfounded when I followed the horsemen to an indoor water park. The place was massive, with towering, twisting slides, a wave pool, waterfalls, and a lazy river. It was also entirely empty, so I assumed they'd either rented it out or obliged and dissuaded our way to privacy. Music was already blasting, a full bar had been laid out upon a table, and a cake was set beside it with the candles already burning.

It was unexpected and silly and perfect. It was perfectly Hexley.

"Happy twenty-first birthday! Make a wish," Embrette prompted.

As I blew out the candles, I tried not to make eye contact with Noric, fearing he could see it all over my face.

Hexley whooped loudly. "Now let the partying begin," he shouted to the empty park as he shoved a cocktail into my hand.

It didn't take long for all of us to find our child-like sense of wonder again, aided by the copious amounts of alcohol. We ran beneath the tropical foliage from one water ride to the next, laughing and spilling our drinks. When I found myself at the top of the longest slide, I hesitated. I wasn't afraid, but I'd consumed a lot of liquor and wondered if it was wise to throw myself into a tube built to toss me about in partial darkness.

"You can ride with me."

Noric's voice rasped in my ear from behind, making me shiver. He held up an innertube meant for double riders.

"Wet, dark things can be scary for mortal girls, I know."

Even in my drunken state, I knew that had a double meaning. Loosened by the liquor, I bit out, "Why do you tease me?"

Noric's eyes danced and one side of his lips pulled into a half-smile. Being the recipient of that impish grin was like being graced by a god. I wanted it all for myself; wanted to coax it, to preen beneath its glory.

"For the pleasure in seeing your frustration."

My heart jumped.

For the pleasure in seeing your frustration.

There was more to the statement, I was sure of it. And yet, Noric laid down his tube and positioned himself on it, moving on as if it meant nothing. I tried to calm myself as I slid into the front part of the tube and between Noric's long, strong legs.

Our laughter echoed off the long, twisting slide as we barreled down toward the end. When we exited the pool, Noric helped me up the steps, which seemed excessive. Was I drunk and unstable? Because when we next waded into the lazy river, he gripped my arm and chuckled.

"You can ride with me," he said again, as he laid on the innertube. This time it was a large one but made for single riders, or at least nothing more than a parent and a child.

My heart stopped and I stared, frozen and dumbfounded. Did he want me to just… climb on top of him? Like, against his bare chest? Was he drunk too?

Noric crooked a finger at me, bidding me to come.

Right. Okay. Just…

I climbed onto the innertube and on top of Noric's body as gracefully as I could manage. Every part of my skin that met his was set aflame while the lazy river gently-but-swiftly pushed us along.

I couldn't help but think that without the alcohol, I would be having a panic attack. Hexley, Embrette, and Sevastian bobbed along elsewhere—I could hear their drunken cries, splashes, and laughter echoing through the empty water park.

"Tell me the story of your ballet?" I prompted, wanting to distract myself as we floated.

As I floated along *on top of Noric's wet body.*

"It's the tale of two faerie-like creatures," he answered from behind me. "Part human, part Lepidoptera. I was inspired by the Zebra Longwing Butterfly emerging from her chrysalis. The males surround her cocoon and sometimes even break into it to get to her. It's called pupal rape, but that's just because mortal men named it," he dismissed. "In reality, the female puts out her scent to attract the mates, as she doesn't want to waste time finding a partner with such a short lifespan."

I listened attentively as we floated past potted palm trees and a bucket of water that was timed to tip over and splash every few minutes.

"In this production, the male lead is nearby as she's emerging, but he is not of the same species. She is a creature of the day and he is a night moth. He scents her, fights off her other suiters, and whisks her away."

I let my feet trail through the lazy river, imagining the choreography and intrigued by the story, which felt perfectly crafted for the ballet world.

"The male was lucky that it had been twilight when she emerged, as the pair can only meet in the mists before daybreak or in the gloaming prior to nightfall. If he were to face the sun, he'd burn to a fiery end, and if she were to exposed to night's moon completely, she would shiver and freeze to death. The couple meets by the river, falling in love in the blue-gray predawn and in the afterglow of many sunsets."

I held my breath as I waited for Noric to finish, knowing what happened next wasn't going to be good. A story always needed its obstacles, and ballet was often tragic.

"One day, there's a rare eclipse in their world. It's an event that has never been seen before. To make matters worse, the male had been inside drinking, celebrating the fact that he'd decided to propose to his love. So when the moon blots out the sun, he becomes disoriented. He stumbles in the darkness to find her. Morning mists always follow the starry night; the sun always rises slowly after the darkness. But not now. When he's in an open field with no cover, the male is caught as the sun reveals her hidden position behind the moon, and he burns to his death."

My stomach knotted, finding more meaning in the story than Noric probably intended.

"When her love fails to show up at their meeting place, the female seeks him out and finds his charred corpse in the grass," Noric said. "She dances around him until the sun sets—that's the solo you'll love. The prima ballerina twirls until the moon rises and claims her life as well. Shivering, she curls into her lover's body and freezes in his lifeless arms."

Ah, tragedy then. I exhaled slowly. *Literally* star-crossed lovers, since the very firmament conspired to keep them apart.

"It's beautiful," I whispered, as the water pushed us along. It wasn't a lie, I just felt a prickle up my spine from the tragic ending. Involuntarily, I yawned. What time was it? How much had I drunk? Noric's tale had been like a bedtime story. "Tragic, but beautiful."

It was a dream, floating with Noric beneath the lush, tropical foliage. The rocking river soothed me until…

I fell asleep, aided by the liquor and the long day. I was only aware of the fact when I awoke just before dawn and *still in Noric's arms.*

After a moment of sheer terror, I sat up with a jolt, nearly knocking us both into the river. Outside the large walls of foggy windows, the sky was gray, light. I must have been out for hours.

"You let me sleep here?" I squeaked. The artificial smell of chlorinated water hit my nose. In the silence, the *whirr* of amusement machinery sounded. I cocked my head, listening, but didn't hear the other reapers. We were alone.

"I didn't want to wake you," Noric said, watching me intently. "You looked like you needed sleep. Hexley and Embrette brought Orsha back to Grimsmere."

His hands held my waist. Was it to keep me from falling into the river?

"You've been floating here all night?" I whispered, disbelieving. "You could have whisked me home. To my bed."

"You're all wet," he pointed out. "I didn't want to disturb you."

"Oh. I'm sorry."

"I'm not."

Noric's voice was deep, rich. Goosebumps rose on my flesh. With just two words, he'd said so much. *Hot, we'd grown very hot again.* I licked my dry lips and he watched me with those keen gray eyes. I swallowed thickly, aware of my post-drunken state. Hair askew, breath stale, legs stubbly with hair, and badly needing to use the bathroom.

Looking down at the bright blue innertube, I mumbled, "Can you whisk me home now?"

Noric reached up and moved a strand of hair from my face, not answering. "Did you have a good birthday?"

The best, I wanted to say. *And this is my favorite part and I don't want it to end but I can't stay on top of you in this state.*

"Yes," I whispered. "Thank you."

A few seconds passed before he said, "Okay. Are you ready?"

When I nodded, he sat up and wrapped his arms around me. The next second, we were in my bedroom and my already-queasy stomach lurched at the transition. Morning sun peeked out between the trees and through my window.

"I'll leave you alone to get more rest," Noric said. "I'll see you for class on Monday."

He stood close, unmoving, but I didn't know why. He was *so* hard to read. A tingle spread throughout my body as I wondered if he might do anything as wild as kiss me goodbye. But he couldn't. Not *now.* Not when I hadn't brushed my teeth and my face was streaked with makeup and my bladder was near exploding.

Noric leaned back slightly.

Was I giving off signs of disinterest? Was I misreading the signs he was putting out?

I had no answer, because the next second, he was gone.

He was always gone, just like that. Leaving me wanting.

I flopped on my bed, still wet, and replayed every second of the morning, over and over.

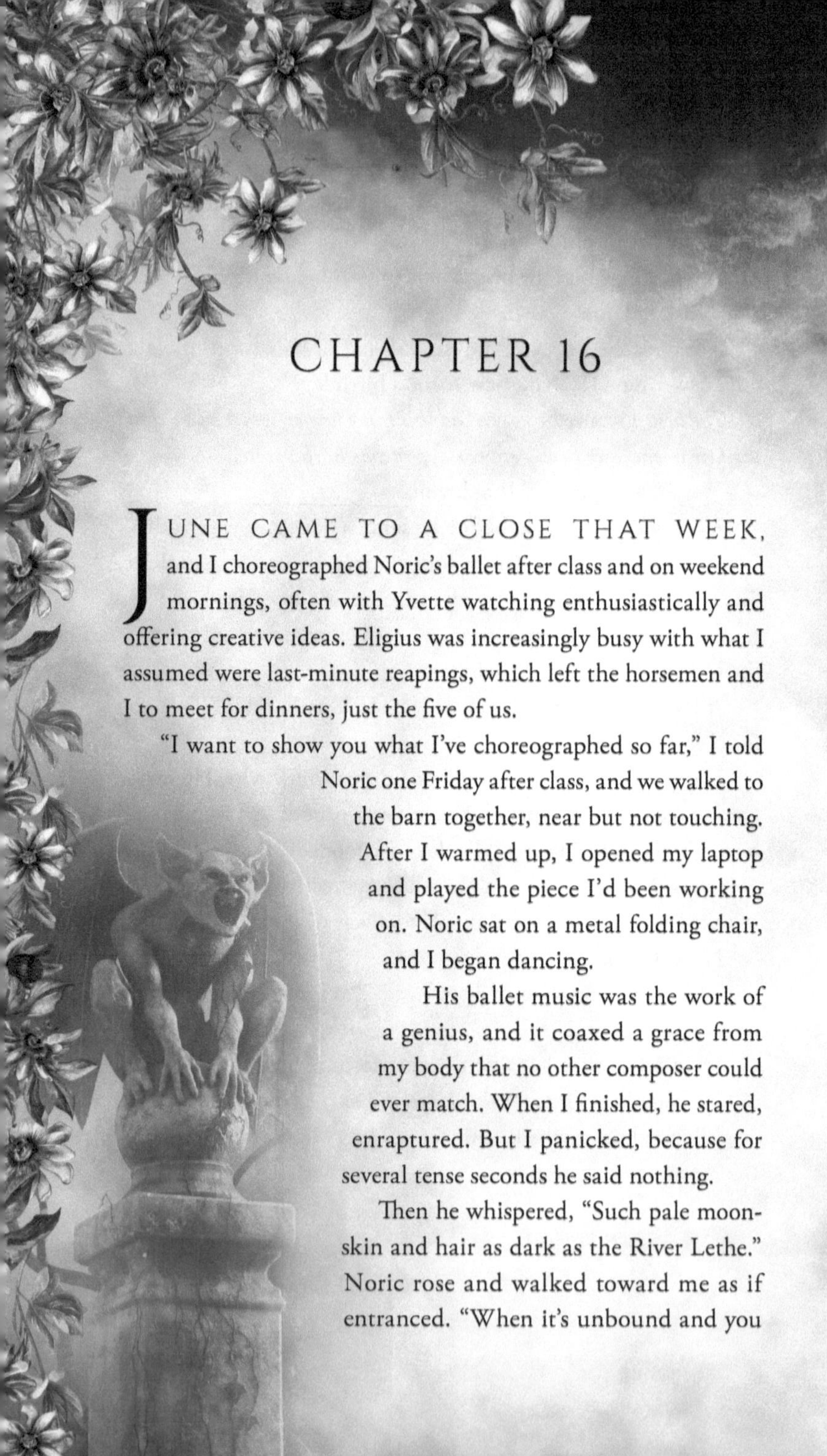

CHAPTER 16

J UNE CAME TO A CLOSE THAT WEEK, and I choreographed Noric's ballet after class and on weekend mornings, often with Yvette watching enthusiastically and offering creative ideas. Eligius was increasingly busy with what I assumed were last-minute reapings, which left the horsemen and I to meet for dinners, just the five of us.

"I want to show you what I've choreographed so far," I told Noric one Friday after class, and we walked to the barn together, near but not touching.

After I warmed up, I opened my laptop and played the piece I'd been working on. Noric sat on a metal folding chair, and I began dancing.

His ballet music was the work of a genius, and it coaxed a grace from my body that no other composer could ever match. When I finished, he stared, enraptured. But I panicked, because for several tense seconds he said nothing.

Then he whispered, "Such pale moon-skin and hair as dark as the River Lethe." Noric rose and walked toward me as if entranced. "When it's unbound and you dance, it's like night's orb shimmering on those black, flowing waters. In Ancient Greek mythology they say that mortals are made to drink from the river to forget before… before returning to the earth." Noric swallowed. His eyes roved my body. I'd never heard him speak like this before and it set my heart to hammering. Something *was* happening between us, I wasn't crazy.

"When I see you dance it's like I've drunk more than my fill from those mythic waters and forgotten everything of this world… including my place in it."

I forgot to breathe and when I remembered, the sound of it was the only thing in the room.

Noric was close enough to kiss me. This time, I was ready.

"Your eyes are like the rarest Tanzanite," he said softly. "Those children weren't jealous enough; humans can't see the spectrum of colors that reapers can."

I felt lightheaded. My father had once said something about reapers and the cones in their retinas. He told me that my eyes were really a violet-blue hue—but the compliment had an entirely different effect coming from Noric's beautiful mouth.

He gently clasped my chin, holding it in place, and my knees nearly buckled. It was finally happening.

Kiss me. I want you to. Silently asking, I parted my lips.

Noric's grip suddenly tightened on my chin, almost enough to hurt.

Abruptly, he tore his hand away and stepped back.

What? No.

I fisted my own hands to keep from reaching out and grabbing him. Pulling him back. Had I misread everything? Was he simply studying my irises for curiosity's sake?

"I like how you've interpreted the music," he said, matter-of-fact-ly. His eyes were still clouded, gray clouds threatening rain. Or was something else ready to burst forth? Was it hunger? For me or for culling?

"I have a busy weekend reaping, though. I'll see you for class on Monday."

What? Now I wasn't going to see him all weekend?

Before I could think of anything to say, Noric gave me a curt nod, then whisked away. Just like that, I was alone in the barn wishing I *had* grabbed him. I fought back a scream. He was always doing that—whisking away beyond my reach.

With Noric's absence, I spied myself in the mirror behind where he'd been standing. My cheeks were flushed, lips pinked, and my body shimmered with a light sheen of sweat. I hadn't put my hair into a ballerina bun, so it was the first time I'd danced for Noric with it unbound, falling dark and wild down my back.

I looked breathless, as if I basked in the afterglow of pleasure. That was what dancing to Noric's music, while he'd watched, had done to me.

Was that why he'd disappeared so quickly?

Later that evening, before I went to sleep, I threw my balcony doors wide. *Forget birthday candles,* I thought, determinedly scanning the sky. The moon was low and heavy, pregnant with magic ready to burst, and fireflies twinkled in the air, like wispingers to carry it forth.

Only a few seconds passed when I spied a shooting star. My heart leapt at the streaking beauty, but I didn't wish on it. It was not a star at all, I knew, just a hunk of rock careening in space. I wouldn't wish on cosmic debris or even the unreliable moon.

Instead, I located the brightest star I could, wanting something more permanent and powerful. I didn't know the star's name, but there weren't many options here, given the light pollution. I wished on that twinkling mystery, whispering my plea to the night air… hoping the wind would carry it up to the one I'd chosen, and that it would shine upon my desire, in return.

SPRINGING FROM MY bed, I dove through my dresser and tossed aside leotards until I found the red and orange one.

Firebird. I felt like dancing *Firebird* today.

Hastily, I dressed, then headed for the barn. I closed the door and turned on the air conditioning at full blast before warming up. Then I danced for hours, pushing my limits to the point of recklessness.

Everything that aids life has the power to claim it, I thought. Fire. Earth. Water. Air. Through absence or abundance. Elements were the ultimate duality, with survival laying in the narrow channel in between. Around the corner and ever lurking on the sidelines—just one step too far to either side and death snapped its jaws upon the unlucky mortal.

That duality was how I felt about Noric. I'd burn if I got too close, and I'd explode if I stayed away. I needed a third solution, and that didn't exist.

Because it was all pointless in the end, I thought angrily. Everything would end, I would die, love didn't last.

I danced *Firebird* and then moved on to my own choreography for the ballet Noric created—all the parts that I could dance solo. I danced until I collapsed in total exhaustion.

Yet I wasn't spent. Not the way I wanted to be.

After a quick glance at the closed barn door, I stripped my sweaty leotard from my body and laid back on the parquet. Spreading my legs, I moved my hands to where I ached. I'd never done anything like this in the studio before. Desperately, I stroked, giving my pent-up energy the release it truly yearned for.

I wondered if Noric *had* been spying on me that day I'd felt a presence in the barn. If so, how often did he invisibly whisk inside and watch me dance?

Would it excite him to watch me now? Would those gray eyes widen in shock and lock in on my rocking hips? Perhaps he'd be unable to resist touching himself too.

Or would he be too much of a gentleman to watch me now?

I thrilled at the idea that he might not be and peaked hard and loud imagining it.

THAT WEEK IT was exceedingly difficult to concentrate when Noric lectured. I'd blush furiously when he inevitably caught me daydreaming, because my thoughts were always scandalous. His desk was *right there*. Noric moved around it as he spoke, standing in front or half-sitting on the edge. I'd squeeze my legs together as I imagined him bending me over it and lifting my skirt.

I wore short skirts all the time now. I pretended not to know what I was doing when I crossed my legs, and Noric pretended not to notice.

Neither of us was very good at it.

I could tell by his white-knuckled grip on the chalk, like he might break it again. Or the strain in his shoulders, like he held himself back. Or the darkening of his eyes, like his entitled reaper nature might take control of his body and compel him to claim mine too. In those moments, the tension between us crackled like a storm. But each time I thought those clouds of lust had filled to bursting… each time when it seemed like satisfaction would rain down and wash over us… Noric would abruptly step away and resume lecturing from nearer his desk.

It continued like this until nearly the Fourth of July, which meant the summer break I'd negotiated was fast approaching.

I no longer wanted it.

Thursday was to be our last day of class before the holiday, and the evening prior I found my father reading in the red room. I smiled, wondering how many evenings I had seen him like this, hearthside and buried in a book. It didn't matter if the summer was sweltering, he loved his fires.

A creak pierced the air as I curled into the old, wooden armchair across from Eligius in his usual form, tall and slender. The fire crackled as a log broke and I inhaled deeply the scent of soot, smoke, and flame.

"Narcissist," I teased, noticing the book he held showed a hooded figure embossed onto the cover. "Do you never tire of reading books about yourself?"

My father looked at me, considering. Then he closed the worn volume and placed it gently in his lap. "I never used to. Couldn't stand the misinterpretations."

I laughed. He picked up his glass of scotch from the side table and stared into the amber liquid.

"Then one day, I broke my rule. I don't even know why. It's funny, the way we look for meaning in an event that precipitates a change of that magnitude," he reflected.

I cocked my head, unsure where this was going.

"I remember everything about that day. I browsed the seemingly endless rows in that old, used bookstore downtown, you know the one. Chopin's *Fantaisie-Impromptu* played on those dusty speakers atop the shelves. They had two cats back then, each considering me from a perch upon a stool. Just before me, a gentleman in a tan hat and a plaid jacket rejected the tome in his hand. Put it back on the shelf and walked away. And for no particular reason whatsoever, I picked it up. On the back, I read a story of myself. And I was... curious. I paid the lady behind the counter and returned home to read a... version of myself," he repeated as he looked at me. "With an adopted daughter."

My heart thumped and I sat up straighter. Eligius had only spoken vaguely of the events leading to my adoption before. Why was he telling me this now? Like meeting his horsemen, the decision reversal bewildered me.

"I was reading the book when I found you and in the back of my mind, I saw an opportunity… for another version of myself, my life. Another version of your life."

Mouth parted and eyes wide, I listened to the fire crackle as his words sunk in. A full minute passed before I found my way to speak.

"I've never understood. Of all the orphans throughout all of time, why me? Are you saying… if you weren't reading that book, at that moment, you wouldn't have chosen me?" My voice cracked at the end.

Eligius inhaled and exhaled slowly. "I didn't just choose you, Avalia. You chose me too. Don't you remember? I think you do. The Miller farm, the Hovarth estate, the Dunns with the little house at the end of the road."

Death held himself very still as he waited for me to answer.

He thought I'd forgotten? Oh, I remembered, I simply didn't want to any more than I'd wanted to stay at those places. It made me so angry, and not because I felt like my father wanted to abandon me, but because he thought himself unworthy of raising me. It was too risky to turn the gods' gaze to me, he'd said. Three times he'd tried to house me where he thought I'd be safer and three times he'd failed. Once because I'd raged and wailed and clung to his cloak. The second time because I quickly ran away to find him. Eligius had plucked me from the dusty road I'd been storming down, directionless but determined to reunite with him. The third time I'd taken a kitchen knife, screamed, and cut my palm. I still bore the horizontal scar today, one that I tried not to look at. Only four years old and dripping blood, I'd threatened to keep cutting until I could see my *skeleton papa* again.

By the time he'd returned, the Dunns were more frightened of that bloody, knife-wielding child than they were of the grand reaper himself.

But I knew in my heart he wanted me too, because Eligius could have obscured my mind as he had worked his magic on the Dunns. Instead, he sighed deeply—not with resignation, but with love. Eligius carried me to Grimsmere and we never spoke of it again and it had all worked out because he was granted an exception to raise me.

"I remember," I whispered.

Eligius released a soft sigh and sipped his scotch. He paused overlong before speaking again.

"I cannot promise you that if I had I found you on another day I would have made the same decision," Eligius confessed softly, placing the glass back on the side table. "I cannot promise you that a part of me still doesn't wish you had a normal life." His dark eyes held mine. "But I can promise that you are now and will always be the most important thing in the world to me, Ava, and that there is nothing I wouldn't do for you."

I nodded, gently at first and then more assuredly. "I know," I said. And I truly did. How our small family came to be, how we wound up here together, did not matter. What we built from there mattered.

My childhood wasn't perfect—I missed out on friendships, sure. But that probably would have happened anywhere, and what I gained in return was priceless. After all, it wasn't as if Eligius hadn't tried, but my stints in local schools and even foreign ballet classes never took. And though Eligius kept away at times to curb the urge to reap me, he never missed a birthday, a holiday, or anything important in my life. If he was busy at work some night when I was younger, I never felt neglected. Archibald and Yvette were always there to tuck me in with a ghostly bedtime story, or to patiently applaud as I practiced in the barn, day after day.

My life might not have pleased every girl, but it perfectly suited *me*.

"So, we have a book about Death and his daughter to thank for our family," I pondered aloud. "Life imitates art."

"Death imitates art," he quipped, leaning forward.

In sync, we both released the same breathy laugh.

Like father, like daughter.

I said goodnight, and as I climbed the stairs for bed, the idea struck me. *I'd* made this life happen. If Eligius had his way, I'd have been raised in a tedious, mortal family. It was only my insistence that got me what I wanted, my pushing for it.

Maybe I couldn't reach out and *pull* Noric, but maybe that's what he needed instead.

A little push.

CHAPTER 17

I T WAS THE LAST DAY OF CLASS BEFORE THE HOLIDAY, but I didn't come to learn today, not about history. I wanted to learn the truth of Noric's heart. Or at least, to find out if he'd secretly watched me dance in the barn.

I was going to do the boldest thing I'd ever done in my life.

I sat at my desk, as usual. I'd worn a cute skirt, as usual. Red, pleated, flirty.

But underneath…

When Noric moved in front of his desk, I moved my lukewarm cup of Darjeeling to the empty desk next to me and took a deep breath, readying myself.

Then I parted my legs, revealing the absence of underwear and displaying my bareness beneath the waist.

Don't blush, don't you dare blush, I scolded myself. *This is to make him squirm, not you.*

But with Noric standing so close and all his towering, formidable height looming over me, my blood ran hot anyway—and I had no control over where it rushed. His eyes blew wide and he couldn't hide that any more than he could conceal their darkening. Or the desire slackening his jaw. I wanted to shout for joy because if lust were a picture, it would be his face in that moment.

"For the pleasure of seeing your frustration." I threw his own words from the water park back at him, swollen with pride and with my own desire.

Noric moved too fast for me to see him shake off his catatonic state, but the next thing I knew I was pushed against the wall and Noric had pressed himself tight to my back.

Yes.

He used one hand to pin my wrists high upon the brick and the other to fist my hair at the nape of my neck, securing my head and bending it slightly to the left. My neck tingled where Noric's cool breath caressed it, and I shivered at his nearness and the idea that he might kiss me there.

Best of all, I could feel the delicious length of him on my lower back, hot and hard as a victory torch.

"You'd use against me what I told you in confidence?" he demanded, and my stomach sank at how angrily he'd hurled the unwelcome words.

"What? No," I quickly swore. Why had this taken a wrong turn? "I'm giving you what you desire, I'm… trying to. Someone you can be with whom you don't have to lie to."

"You are lying to yourself," he said, scoffing.

What did that mean?

"Which is preferable, Ava?" Noric asked. His voice was so cold, goosebumps rose along my skin. "That you're lying to yourself about how I might desire you? Or that you're lying to yourself about how there's any hope of happiness to be found here, given your short life? One or both of us comes out wounded either way. Which would you choose?"

"Neither," I insisted through clenched teeth, "I want a path forward where neither of us comes out hurting."

"Utter childishness," Noric said with a laugh, and I flushed in embarrassment. His words made me feel reckless with my attempt at seduction, so clumsy and unartful. How could I compare to the princesses and the courtesans, the starlets and the warriors and who knew what other kinds of women throughout history who'd thrown themselves at Noric just as I had?

And yet.

Noric hadn't let me go and I could feel his erection pressed into my back.

"What am I to you, Ava? A version of your father you can kiss?"

What the… He had to be joking.

Noric was nothing like my father. How could he think that? For a man who hated being wrong, he certainly had enough familiarity with the concept to get used to it.

I remembered why I started this game in the first place—not just to arouse Noric but to find out if he'd aroused himself, watching me.

I laid all my cards on the table, hoping to force his hand as well.

"And what am I to *you?* Entertainment? Are you secretly watching me while I dance?" I demanded, jutting my chin. "What is it you do there in my barn, Noric? Do you look away before I change?" I turned my head so that my cheek was pressed to his shoulder, which was as much movement as his grip on my hair would allow. "Do you ever do anything while you're watching… or whisk home to do it?"

"And what would you know about any of that?" he asked, voice cruel. "Never having experienced it yourself."

My flush deepened, but I refused to be embarrassed. What was the point? Noric already knew about my lack of partners and I could *feel* the hard truth of his desire. So he was lying about that, he had to be.

"You haven't answered the question," I noted.

Noric's hand tightened on my waist and I instinctively arched. It wasn't meant to tease. My body reacted innately to Noric's grip, similar to when a human strokes a cat's back and it curves into the caress. The feel of Noric, so delicious and firm behind me, caused my hips, of their own volition, to seek *more*.

And oh—I was rewarded by the dangerous, rumbling moan he tried to stifle. It was pained and cut short, but I was thrilled to cause it. Even better, a second later his hips snapped against my back and his hand gripped the bare flesh of my thigh. My skin burned, my blood heated—I was on fire. If Noric wanted to do *anything* in that moment, right there in the old schoolhouse, I wouldn't refuse him.

Touch me, kiss me, move your hands along…

With a groan, Noric abruptly released me and stepped back. I couldn't stop the pitiful whimper before it left my lips. My heart sank.

"Class is over for today," he declared in a low voice. "Over for the summer."

What? Not again.

He was gone so fast that I was still pressed against the wall, alone, positioned there by only my own leaning. I bit my lip, holding back both a scream and tears. I'd made an offer and been rejected. I'd laid out all my cards out on the table and Noric had risen from his chair, walked away, and left the game.

Idiot. Fool.

I straightened my skirt, stalked out of the little schoolhouse, and did what I always did.

I headed straight for the barn to dance away the pain.

This time, I was sure Noric wouldn't be hiding and watching, and I was glad for it. I couldn't bear to face him right now.

And had no idea what I'd do after the holiday either.

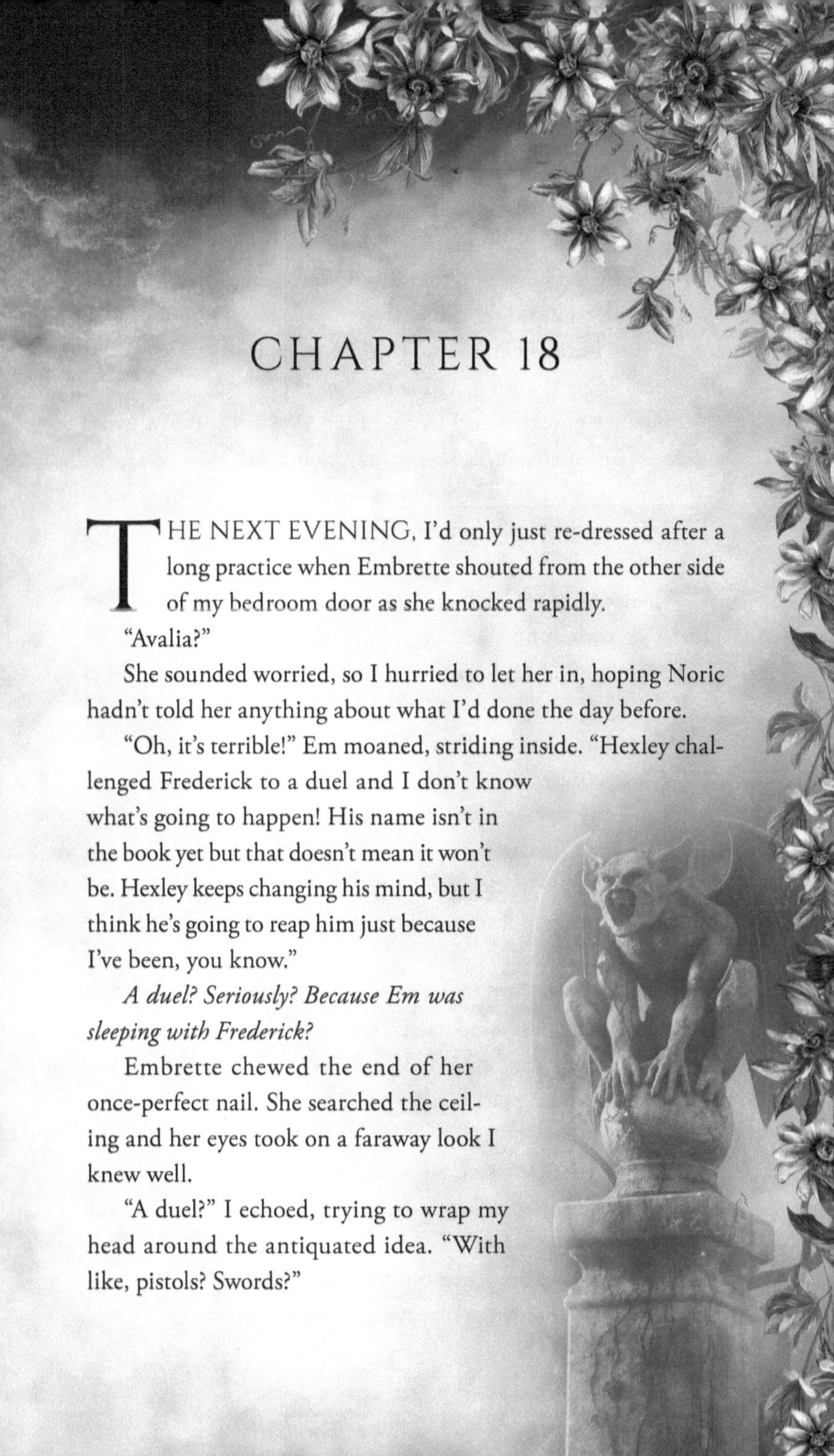

CHAPTER 18

THE NEXT EVENING, I'd only just re-dressed after a long practice when Embrette shouted from the other side of my bedroom door as she knocked rapidly.

"Avalia?"

She sounded worried, so I hurried to let her in, hoping Noric hadn't told her anything about what I'd done the day before.

"Oh, it's terrible!" Em moaned, striding inside. "Hexley challenged Frederick to a duel and I don't know what's going to happen! His name isn't in the book yet but that doesn't mean it won't be. Hexley keeps changing his mind, but I think he's going to reap him just because I've been, you know."

A duel? Seriously? Because Em was sleeping with Frederick?

Embrette chewed the end of her once-perfect nail. She searched the ceiling and her eyes took on a faraway look I knew well.

"A duel?" I echoed, trying to wrap my head around the antiquated idea. "With like, pistols? Swords?"

Embrette froze, mouth parted. For several seconds she didn't move, then she sprang into action.

"What?" I asked, trying to pull her back from the door.

"Yes, exactly! I can stop this duel. Or at least, render it useless. I have to go!" she said, breaking free.

"Wait!" I called before she whisked away. I was getting tired of reapers doing that to me. "Let me come!"

Embrette quickly considered. "Take Orsha. I'll ride a spare. In case of an emergency a Strider may be helpful."

Then she bolted down the stairs and I stumbled behind her.

"Tell me what's happening," I begged, as I slung onto Orsha's back.

"There's no time!" Embrette declared, taking the reins. "But Hexley's a stickler for tradition."

She took off and I hurried not to lose her in the misty in-between as we headed toward Hexley and Frederick. Seconds later, we emerged into a forest I couldn't readily identify.

"Telum eligere," Embrette shouted breathlessly as she leapt from her Time Strider with supernatural grace and control. Before us, Hexley and Frederick faced one another with coiled muscles, poised to attack. Frederick had curly blonde hair, a square jaw, and a thick, linebacker look about him… but a human would never be a match for a horseman.

"Telum eligere!" Embrette repeated with force, storming up to the two men who immediately stopped and turned toward us. Hexley folded his arms, annoyed, and Frederick stared with open-mouthed confusion as he tried to comprehend Embrette's sudden appearance out of thin air.

"Em?" Frederick asked, blinking.

She pushed herself between the two men and declared, "I claim the right to choose arms."

Hexley's frown deepened but he said nothing.

"Embrette?" Frederick repeated, rubbing his eyes.

"The duel is over *me*." Embrette said, pointing to herself as she spun to face the men. She was so terrifyingly beautiful that, as odd as this scene was, it wasn't entirely unexpected to see lovers dueling over her. "It is an ancient and lesser-known rule that a lady has the right to select the weaponry if she be the subject of the duel." Em flashed a devious smile as she turned to me. "Some say it was to grant favor to the preferred suitor."

Nervously, I darted my gaze between the two men. How did this help? Embrette favored Hexley, I presumed, but choosing a weapon in which he'd be more skilled didn't solve the problem of keeping Frederick alive. A mortal couldn't kill a reaper—even with the reaper's own blade. I knew their lethal daggers could *wound* them, but a horseman would quickly heal. Is that what Em intended?

"What—what's going on?" Frederick sputtered, finally catching up. I could see from his handsome face why Em had taken a liking to him. "How did you get here?"

"Do you accept?" Embrette asked Hexley, ignoring her befuddled human suitor.

Hexley studied Em with his fingers pressed thoughtfully to his lips. After a moment, he nodded reluctantly.

Frederick's frustrated cry cut the air. "Can someone tell me what in the *world* is going on?"

"Darling," Em said gently, laying a hand on his pretty cheek. "When I heard of your duel I came as fast as I could. Since I cannot convince either of you to cease this ridiculous conflict, I am evoking the right to choose the weapon."

"I never heard of that before," Frederick protested, scowling. He was in over his head and he knew it, probably wondering how he'd wound up in a tradition as outdated as dueling in the first place. Stubborn male pride was the only thing keeping him in this situation, but such folly was an adhesive more powerful than any cement mortals would ever invent.

Embrette batted her lashes, once. "Do you agree?"

"I…" Frederick spoke slowly, unable to find a way to break free with his ego intact, "… guess."

Embrette twirled. "No matter the weapon I select, you both agree to fight using only what I choose?"

The men nodded.

"To the death," Hexley bit out.

Em relaxed her shoulders, but I still couldn't see how this would help. Pistols, swords… even if she chose a rock for the men to bludgeon each other, the result was the same.

"Get on with it, then," Hexley commanded, lifting his chin. "Weapon?"

Em tapped her lips thoughtfully, making a show of it. "Sinister manus."

My ears pricked at the word *"sinister"* and panic wove through my gut. That sounded bad, very bad. Why hadn't I paid more attention to Latin, as my father had wanted?

"Particularly, the palm," Embrette added, examining her nails.

"What are you saying?" Frederick asked, clearly as confused as I was.

Gritting his teeth, Hexley announced, "She's saying she wants us to slap each other to death." He cocked his head and said dryly, "With our left hand."

"And just to be fair, I will tie your right hand behind your back," Em announced.

She tore two strips from the bottom of her shirt, perhaps intentionally revealing her waist. Then she wrapped each duelist's wrist in the cloth and tied it through a belt loop at his back. They were putty in Embrette's hands, and each man's unwillingness to back down made the other dig in his heels.

But I still didn't understand how any of this saved Frederick's life.

At Embrette's signal, they began.

Hexley shouted a war cry that echoed through the forest and he ran full-speed to Embrette's lover. Eyes blazing, Frederick charged in return, and the men clashed in the middle of the clearing. While their left hands exchanged a flurry of slaps, each tried tripping the other to the ground. Hexley wasn't using his full reaper strength, either because he wanted the thrill or the honor of beating Frederick man-to-man. But I winced because that only made it worse. I'd never seen anyone have the life slapped out of them, but I guessed it would escalate to something as prolonged and brutal as being beaten to death.

"No kicking!" Em admonished from the sidelines. If I wasn't mistaken, she giggled under her breath.

Smack, slap, grunt.

The men thrust their chests at one another in an animal-like fashion, trying to knock the other off his feet with the strength of their pectorals alone.

Whack, smack.

As they attacked, I definitely heard another snicker from Embrette.

Finally, the duelists fell to the ground and tumbled, bodies thrusting and twisting in ridiculous contortions. Each struggled to roll on top of the other with only one hand. It was both horrific and absurd. Nearly as many steps behind as Frederick, I finally caught up to what was happening. Or, more importantly, what *wasn't* going to happen. I released a breathy laugh through my nose, but when Embrette's eyes sparkled with encouragement, I intentionally giggled louder.

Hexley gained the advantage, pinning Frederick with his legs and straddling the man's body beneath him. He unleashed a fury against the man's cheek—*slap, slap, slap.* Embrette and I chuckled louder, covering our mouths and doubling over as our laughter carried through the clearing.

I was sure Frederick would have a ringing in his ears later, but it would take many blows to kill him with Hexley's unsteady left hand. In the meantime, the ancient reaper looked ridiculous, and he knew it.

Noric and Sevastian appeared in the clearing and my heart leapt. Embrette didn't look up, but I assumed she'd called them to have more of an audience. Hexley noticed and scowled.

"Argh!" he roared, grabbing Frederick's left shoulder with his left hand and shaking him. Then he threw Frederick back onto the dirt as he stood.

"There is no honor in this!" Hexley cried, circling the ground with the pent-up frustration of a caged animal.

"No," Embrette agreed, not looking up as she examined her fingernails. "You look ridiculous."

"You want me to relent? Fine! Have it your way." He tore his arm free from the binding. "I will not continue to debase myself in this manner. Declare me the loser if you want." His shoulders squared in defiance of his defeat. "You think it will change anything for me, Em?" Hexley asked in a husky voice. "It will not."

Hexley's confession was bold, but I wasn't sure if it meant he wouldn't stop loving her or that he wouldn't stop fighting for her. Probably both.

I glanced at Frederick, bruised but hopeful on the ground. A slow smile spread across his face and for a moment I wondered if I was mistaken about Embrette's affections. Had she done this to save Frederick because she loved him?

"You have both shown great courage here today," Em said. She spoke like a mythical princess both praising and scolding two errant knights. "But you have also shown pigheadedness, foolishness, and pride." She stared hard at each man. "Historically, a duel is between two parties, and only one may win.

Embrette lifted her chin and announced, "However, today's battle of honor was actually the lesser-known *truel*, a three-way duel of opponents, and the true weapon was not our hands but our wits. And gentleman," she said, sauntering to the middle of the clearing and smiling prettily, "I therefore declare myself the winner. As such, I will bestow mercy upon you both. None will die today."

Frederick's face couldn't settle upon an expression, anger warring with disbelief as he noticed Noric and Sevastian for the first time.

"Where'd you two come from?" he asked, blinking.

Embrette, however, ignored him. She and Hexley stared deeply at one another across the clearing, and it was like watching something illicit. I wondered if they spoke mind-to-mind or if they didn't need to, because their eyes were saying a lot. Hexley was sweaty, sexy, and had been ready to fight a mortal to the death *in a mortal manner*, just to show Embrette how much he loved her.

I understood the hungry look in her eyes.

But to my shock, Hexley whisked out of the woods and Embrette stared at the space he'd once inhabited.

"What in the world is going on?" Frederick shouted.

"Come, darling, let's get you home," Em said, suddenly remembering he was there. "Ava, can you bring the Striders back to the stables?" she asked, and I nodded. Some of the pent-up adrenaline dissipated from my veins but some remained, because Noric stood so near it was electrifying, magnetizing.

"Noric, Sevastian. Would you mind following us to obscure and ingrain?" Em asked. "I think this has… ran its course."

Embrette whisked Frederick away so quickly I didn't hear him scream, though I imagined he did from the shock of it.

"We're back at this part," Sevastian mused, shaking his head. "I give it two weeks until they're together again."

"I give it one," Noric said, folding his arms and smirking. "Care to make a wager? Five spelunking and five mountaineering cullings for the loser. Reaper has to do it, no familiars."

"Ugh, those people are the worst," Sevy groaned, but he struck out his hand. "Fine."

From the corner of my eye, I saw the two horsemen shake on it, but I refused to give Noric the satisfaction of my attention. In fact, inspired by what had just occurred, an idea formed in my mind of doing the very *opposite* of giving him any attention.

I spun away and, without a word, mounted Orsha and flew off with the spare Strider beside us.

I needed a man—any man would do. If Noric *was* attracted to me in any way, it would make him jealous. And if he was hesitant to touch me because of my inexperience, I'd be rectifying the problem by experiencing *everything* I could.

And in the worst-case scenario where neither of these things were true… well, at least I was moving on with my life.

I returned to Solebury to find night had fallen and fireworks now exploded over the river. I'd completely forgotten that it was the Fourth of July, but I took their colorful bursts and celebratory booming as an encouraging sign. As I paused in the air to watch the show, I vowed that tomorrow night I was going to find a man and take him to bed.

Er, let him *take me to* his *bed?*

Whatever. I was going to do everything a person could do in any bed, gargoyle-styled or not.

PART II

To Claim
a Mortal

CHAPTER 19

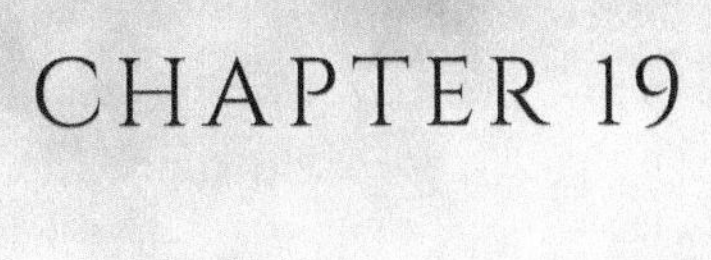

GOING OUT FOR THE NIGHT WITH A PLAN to have sex didn't excite me as much as I thought it would, but I told myself it was because I hadn't yet selected a man. Closing my eyes, I tried picturing someone ridiculously good-looking to motivate myself, but when Noric's sculpted, aristocratic face filled my mind, I snapped my eyes open and quickly resolved not to do it again. Instead, I focused on my own appearance in the mirror. I'd chosen a lacey red underwire bra and a matching red thong, hoping it would manifest passion.

Passion? I squirmed at my own reflection. No, no. This wasn't for pleasure, this was for purpose. A man or two under my belt and Noric would have no qualms about my experience.

How much time is sufficient to qualify as experience? I wondered, slipping on a loose, short black dress. *Five minutes? Ten?* I supposed it was over when the man was done. Unless I was able to finish as well, and I wasn't counting on it.

A few minutes later, Orsha and I circled Philadelphia from above. Despite considering myself fairly worldly, the imposing buildings intimidated me a little for this particular task. What if I choose somewhere fancy, misread the rules somehow, and walked out unsuccessful? Surveying the low, crammed buildings ringing the city, I thought it better to pick somewhere amongst those neighborhoods.

Leaning down to Orsha's ear, I whispered, "Take me to a bar on the outskirts of the city. Somewhere locals go. A dive bar."

Closing my eyes, I allowed Orsha to select my destination and when I felt her gentle landing, I opened my eyes to find a street lined with bars and various rowhomes. It seemed safe enough, but Orsha neighed when I dismounted, as if she knew what I was doing and didn't approve.

"I'll be okay," I whispered in her ear while patting her dark mane. "Just stay close."

It warmed my heart that her red eyes followed me as I ducked into the nearest establishment without even noting the name.

There was only one bar inside, but it was crammed with bottles of all sizes. Several dart boards covered one of the walls and a smattering of neon beer signs hung from the other. To the right, a pool table with pieces of baize torn or missing around the edges. About a dozen men sat the wooden bar stools or faux-leather booths, and five women chatted with the various male patrons.

The air smelled like stale beer, which definitely wasn't an aphrodisiac to me but I thought it might be to the men. What did I know about normal humans, really? I was familiar with their grief and pain at the end. *But this?* The beginnings mystified me. First meetings and dates and intimacy. Those things I had only ever seen or read about, which was just another reason I didn't fit in. Everything commonplace to me was rare to mortals, and vice versa.

A drink, I commanded myself, shoes squeaking on the sticky floor as I walked. *You're too in your head right now.*

Sidling up to the bar, I took a seat on a free stool and jumped a little when a man immediately claimed the one beside me.

"Can I buy you a drink?" he asked.

I blinked. Was that a pick-up line? Was he interested? Could it be that easy?

Before responding, I considered him. He wasn't especially fit, but he was tall. Not as tall as Noric, though. I studied his face and decided he was conventionally attractive. Not as attractive as Noric, of course.

He'd do, I guessed. The man had warm brown eyes, wavy hair, and I gave him bonus points for confidence.

I smiled, but it faltered. What did customers here commonly drink? I grimaced at the idea of sipping beer, and the few, half-empty wine bottles looked rarely touched and likely skunked.

"Um, a rum and coke?" My order came out like a question.

The man ordered the drink for me and a beer for himself from a bartender who looked both bored and equally annoyed at being disturbed.

"I'm Evan," the man said.

"Aurora," I responded with my practiced lie, having chosen the name for the ballet and as a kind of test. I was curious to see if anyone at least knew it was from the tale of Sleeping Beauty.

"Aurora," Evan said, leaning closer. "That's a pretty name for a pretty girl."

"Thanks."

Evan and I made small talk for a few minutes, and I couldn't say he was the most interesting person I'd ever met, but he was enthusiastic enough. His frequent touching of my upper thigh told me so.

Except... I didn't really like it.

In fact, the more the both of us drank, the higher his hand moved, as if he needed to grab or stroke my leg to convey a point whenever he spoke. Shifting uncomfortably on the stool, I scolded myself. Wasn't the goal of the evening for us to do a lot more than touching?

A quick scan around the bar told me Evan was my best option. To be fair, he was good-looking. As handsome as I could expect for the task. His full hair looked soft, if I were to run my fingers through it, and his brown eyes shone with eagerness.

"Am I boring you?" Evan asked.

"What?" I straightened, slightly embarrassed, and dropped the straw I'd been twirling. "No."

"I can back off if you're not interested. I've got a buddy coming to meet me soon. Blonde, if you're into blondes."

My face heated but I laughed. "No, I'm not particularly into blondes."

Noric's hair looks a dark blonde though, when the sunlight hits it just right.

I frowned, annoyed that thoughts of him were spoiling my evening and thwarting my goal.

Evan leaned in as he picked up a lock of my black hair. "Me neither," he said, wagging his eyebrows theatrically.

Ugh, ick. Something about the move turned me off.

"Would you like another drink then?" he asked.

I nodded my acceptance, but it was too late. A kernel of doubt had been planted and quickly sprouted. It wasn't just Noric, it was *me.* I wasn't… in the mood. Didn't feel any arousal. Didn't want to be touched.

As we waited for our order from the bored bartender, I grew surer by the second that I didn't want to proceed. But I reasoned that it couldn't hurt to have a drink and forget the reaper who didn't want me. At least, not enough to do anything about it.

It would be a celebratory cocktail too. Maybe I hadn't succeeded in making it to bed with someone, but I'd taken a step in the right direction by putting myself out there. I deserved a reward for that. I'd have one more rum and coke, return home, and try again tomorrow. Maybe it would be better to try a different city… heck, maybe a different country? It would be like a vacation, and that always loosened people up, right?

Yes, I decided, sipping my cocktail. *Tomorrow night I'll go to*

New Zealand. High up in Queenstown. I'll find a masculine, out-doorsy type. The kind of adrenaline-junkie who travels for thrilling adventures. We'll return to a cabin somewhere with a view of the mountains and make love while the snow falls.

Yes, that will suit for a first time.

Glass shattered and a man shouted as a fight erupted by the pool table to our right. I looked down at my drink, not remembering when I'd finished most of it.

"Oh, shit," Evan cursed, as the fight quickly spread to nearby patrons who'd begun throwing fists. He grabbed my hand. "Come on, I know another way out."

Another way? The front door was clear of any fighting, but I let Evan pull me around the bar and to a back exit. We slid into a dark alley, which set my heart racing with alarm, but Evan continued yanking me along as he strode quickly.

"They're gonna call the cops," he exclaimed over his shoulder. "I can't get caught in a brawl and have another incident on my record."

Incident? Record?

I tried to ponder the meaning and his words and it must have taken me a while, because when I refocused, I didn't know where we were. The street with the bar had been lower-income perhaps, but everything was tidy. Clean sidewalks, functioning streetlights, and petite, happy gardens. The area where I now stood was dark, abandoned, and non-residential. Crumbling buildings surround-ed us, the streetlights were very far away, and not a single other person was in sight. In the distance I heard cars whiz down a busy road, and I could see a deserted business district ahead, but the immediate area was empty.

I felt… funny. It must have been a very strong rum and coke. Or did I have two? Three? My head was thick, heavy, and wading through memories to recall specific information was too much work. What I most wanted to do was sleep. I'd try another bar in Queenstown, tomorrow, after a nice nap. If I found my way to Orsha, I could sleep on her back right now and no one would even see me doze.

Where had I left her? Where was I now?

I seemed to be teleporting, whisking to destinations as if carried by a Strider or a reaper, but Evan was neither. So why was my memory so patchy?

To my immediate left was a neglected brick building. To my right was a bit of sparse grass and crumbling pavement. Asphalt sprawled behind and ahead and everywhere underfoot. The hair on my neck rose.

This was a bad place.

Or a bad dream.

The thought came suddenly, surely, but slippery too. It felt as hard to hold onto as my vision because the scene jumped, like they do in dreams, and next I was in a small bedroom. Before me was a stained, twin mattress on the floor with the sheets askew, and the poster of a band I did not know on the wall. The open window provided some air, but it was still sweltering in the tiny space.

Why was I here? And where was my dress?

Evan faced me, mouth slack, hands on his belt…

…*unbuckling* his belt…

A noise like large, flapping wings whooshed past my ear and I gasped, because it didn't come from the half-open window and it wasn't some kind of gigantic bird or even a Time Strider.

It was *Noric.*

What in the world was going on?

He flew past me, reaper's cloak beating the air at the same time his fist smashed into Evan's face.

My scream filled the room. Hexley, Embrette, and Sevastian appeared beside and behind me and the next instant, Hexley's arms locked around my waist, restraining me. Why did he want to stop me from stopping Noric? And why weren't they?

Embrette moved to block my vision of Noric pummeling Evan, but she couldn't block Evan's screams or stop my own.

"Avalia, can you hear me?" she asked. "Do you understand what I'm saying?"

"Stop him, help me!" I cried. But Noric *had* stopped beating Evan, and somehow I'd missed it. Why was everything so patchy and jumbled? He tied Evan's hands behind his back. Absolutely nothing made sense. Maybe I was dreaming. I certainly didn't feel myself.

"Stop him!" I cried again. "What is going on?"

Embrette seized my shoulders. With her mesmerizing amber eyes, she looked dangerously beautiful in her reaper's robes. "Ava, you've been drugged. This man put something in your drink and he was going to… attack you."

"You broke my nose, you asshole!" Evan shouted, struggling against the ropes Noric had used.

Evan couldn't have drugged me. Could he? And if he had, why would Noric waste time tying him up when he could simply reap him?

I was really confused, it was all too much to consider, and maybe it wasn't even happening anyway.

My eyelids fluttered. Hexley could support me if I fell asleep in his arms right now.

So tempting.

I must have blacked out for a second because the next thing I knew, my cheeks were in Noric's hands and his impossibly gorgeous face was inches from my own, examining it as he turned my head from side to side. My entire body tingled and I wore my black dress again, which I swore had been gone a few seconds before.

"Noric," I breathed his name, unable to believe he was standing before me somehow, in a strange bedroom. I wanted to touch him, to smell him—but I was still restrained by Hexley and the only thing filling my nose was the garbage below the window carried in by the breeze. Noric's eyes locked on mine and I ached for him to say something I could hold onto, to give me some shred of hope that those stoney eyes weren't sheer walls of rock he'd built between us.

He did not.

"Take her home," Noric ordered, looking up harshly. "Sevy, Em, stay with me and finish the job."

Sevastian nodded and pushed back his shoulders, like a beast ready to pounce…

On Evan, who screamed and thrashed on the floor…

Why would he do that?

What job?

"Hexley…" Noric began.

"I know what to do," Hexley replied from behind me. His voice was clear and confident.

Why was anyone doing anything at all and how were they here?

I wanted to scream these questions but instead, I slumped in Hexley's arms, losing the battle to stay awake.

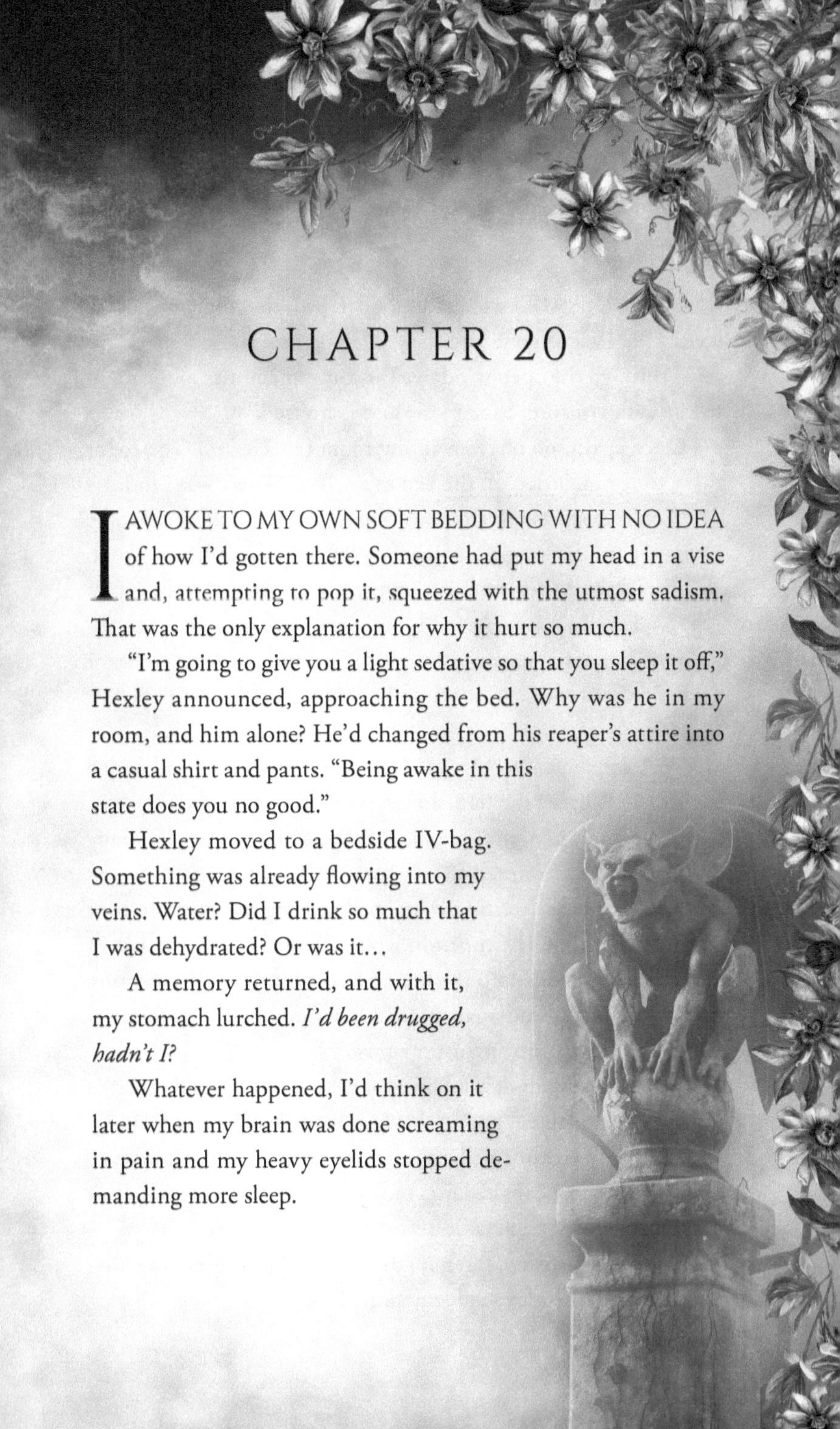

CHAPTER 20

I AWOKE TO MY OWN SOFT BEDDING WITH NO IDEA of how I'd gotten there. Someone had put my head in a vise and, attempting to pop it, squeezed with the utmost sadism. That was the only explanation for why it hurt so much.

"I'm going to give you a light sedative so that you sleep it off," Hexley announced, approaching the bed. Why was he in my room, and him alone? He'd changed from his reaper's attire into a casual shirt and pants. "Being awake in this state does you no good."

Hexley moved to a bedside IV-bag. Something was already flowing into my veins. Water? Did I drink so much that I was dehydrated? Or was it…

A memory returned, and with it, my stomach lurched. *I'd been drugged, hadn't I?*

Whatever happened, I'd think on it later when my brain was done screaming in pain and my heavy eyelids stopped demanding more sleep.

THE NEXT TIME I woke, I shot up in bed, clutching my downy cover. The IV was gone and the golden light of late afternoon filtered through the open window. This time, memories of the night before came rushing back to me and I shivered.

Once again, no one was in my room but Hexley. One of his furry ronemin curled on the bed at my feet. Where was Noric?

"You've been asleep since last night," Hexley told me, gently. "Would you like water? It's there on your nightstand, along with some crackers if your stomach is upset. How are you feeling?"

"I—I'm okay. I mean I will be," I insisted, ignoring the provisions. "What happened last night? What did Noric do to Evan? I don't understand… if he wanted to hurt him why didn't he just reap him?"

"Release his soul to Elysia?" Hexley shook his head and folded his arms. "Where's the punishment in that?"

On second thought, I grabbed the glass of water to soothe my cottony mouth. I wanted to brush my teeth but needed answers first, and my head had finally stopped hurting too much to hear them. As I stirred, the ronemin woke. Though it was the size of a large dog, it padded up the bed in its cat-like way. The creature nudged its furry head against me a few times before tucking its wings and curling up against my torso.

"Noric… saw you. He followed you out of the bar and called to us," Hexley explained, pacing slowly as he spoke. "You were clearly drugged, but we confirmed it through the friend, too. When Evan texted his friend, he invited him to… join in." Hexley snarled, then continued, "And spelled out his heinous intentions."

"I see," I whispered, though I didn't. Had Noric been watching me all night? The idea made my heart flutter.

"What happened to the friend?" I asked, petting Hexley's ronemin, who released a melodic purr as I stroked.

"We didn't have time for the same special brand of justice," Hexley announced. His nostrils flared with a slight snarl. "While he'd declined to participate, he didn't stop his friend either, so we reaped him. Well, we scared the hell out of him first and made it hurt."

I blinked at Hexley's rare use of strong language.

"What happened to Evan?" I asked, nibbling a cracker. I wasn't at all hungry, but Hexley was right. My stomach needed settling.

He took a deep breath. "Noric tortured him through the night, physically and mentally. He and Sevastian obscured and ingrained memories, Emrette compelled future actions, and I returned briefly to dissuade him from going near women again. It wasn't clean—we scrambled his brain. The memories of last night weren't wholly stripped from his mind but instead, obscured in a manner to skim the conscious surface. Noric allowed parts to occasionally burst forth, but even those flashes will be darkened, distorted."

I listened attentively, waiting to feel horrified, but I did not. Not at all.

"We drove home one lesson throughout Evan's torture—something horrific will follow, as it did before, if he *ever* goes near a woman again. Or any person, for that matter, if the intent is sexual," Hexley said. "You could call it a psychological castration, but it goes beyond that, because Evan will spend the rest of his life haunted by a torment he can't quite recall. He'll awaken from nightmares screaming, but he'll never be able to remember what they were about. He'll fear any intimacy with women, but he'll never be able to understand why. Most importantly though, he will never harm anyone again."

I sucked in a deep breath, considering. Was I sorry for Evan? No, I was not. Not in the least. They'd served a fitting punishment; gave him the scarring he'd planned to give me.

As I waited for him to continue, Hexley took a seat on the cushioned window-ledge, the one facing the other side of the room from the Juliette balcony.

"Noric made sure Evan is driven mad and miserable for the rest of his life. If you think that's extreme, well," Hexley shrugged. "He picked the wrong woman to assault."

I hadn't moved throughout Hexley's recounting of the night and I needed to use the bathroom. My skin was sticky, grimy, and I could only imagine how my makeup must have smeared down my cheeks. I still wore the lingerie set I now planned on burning, along with my dress, and the sheets needed changing. I hopped out of bed and excused myself. Hexley watched me with his hawk-like gaze, as if he was afraid for me.

I paused, realizing he worried I'd hurt myself.

"I'm okay," I insisted, giving him a weak, but genuine, smile. "Thanks to all of you. I just need to clean myself up."

I took my time in a steaming shower and threw on a fresh shirt and a loose pair of shorts when I finished. Hexley waited outside my bedroom while I dressed, but when he returned, he insisted I rest again.

"Thank you," I said, noticing he'd changed the sheets while I was in the bathroom. I had no idea how he'd found clean bedding on his own; he must have spoken with Sanderson.

I hoped he hadn't told Eligius of the incident. Though he'd gifted me my own Time Strider, my father constantly fretted over where I traveled alone, and I worried this would only prove his fears right.

"Why did Noric tell you to take care of me?" I asked curiously, tucking myself beneath the covers and drawing my knees up to my chest. The cuddly ronemin immediately hopped into bed and curled up beside me again. They were much better companions for snuggling than Noric's gargoyles, or any of the reaper's familiars. "I hope I don't offend you—you're good at this. But I would have thought he'd ask Embrette. Girl to girl and all," I said, averting my eyes. "You know."

Hexley returned to the window ledge, gazing out onto the Grim Gardens, and I wondered if my question had been rude. My heart sank, hoping that was not the case. I was just curious as to why he was immediately asked, especially when his powers of dissuasion were critical the night before.

Hexley remained quiet so long I didn't think he'd answer, but finally he said, "I took care of Embrette once, when she experienced something bad."

Bad? How could anything bad happen to a horseman? Gooseflesh rose upon my skin as my mind raced. It couldn't be an assault of any kind. Embrette was more powerful than any mortal, so no human man could hurt her. At least, not physically.

"What happened?" I whispered.

He turned to me, shaking his head. "It's not my story to share." He rose from the window seat. "But it was a long enough healing process that I became adept at playing nurse." He picked up a cracker from my nightstand. With a wink, he added, "When she finally improved and asked me to *wear* a nurse costume, however, I absolutely refused."

I barked a laugh. "No, you didn't."

"Bah!" he cried, waving his hand as he struggled to swallow the cracker and speak at the same time. "Alright, I didn't. You know how she can be when she wants something."

"And I know how you can be when you want to make her happy."

Hexley's long lashes grazed his cheeks as he gazed down, smiling.

"It's not easy, you know. Immortal love. It takes effort to make forever work."

"I can only imagine but…" I swallowed, then whispered, "it's better than the love between a mortal and an immortal, which has no hope at all of achieving forever, of being anything other than fleeting."

Hexley didn't embarrass me by saying anything specific about Noric, and for that I was grateful. Instead, he rolled up his sleeves and announced, "I'm going to put the kettle on. Green tea okay?"

I didn't particularly like green tea, but I nodded. The way Hexley always sought to make everyone around him happy and comfortable made me want to make *him* happy and comfortable.

He returned a few minutes later holding out two cups of tea, and at the same moment Embrette appeared in my doorway. She wore a beige mortal dress that looked anything but plain on her, and not at all as if she'd just come from a night of torturing someone.

Leaning over the porcelain mugs Hexley carried she scoffed, "Ugh, that smells like catnip and wouldn't fortify a butterfea. Get her a strong cup of Darjeeling."

"It's fine, really," I insisted.

Embrette bestowed an apology kiss on Hexley's cheek for speaking so roughly, then held his gaze for several seconds. That was all it took for me to know—I could practically *see* the sparks flying between them as Hexley grinned and she giggled softly.

Abruptly, as if knowing she'd been caught, she brushed past him and sat on my bed. I wanted to inquire about what had happened to her, but now wasn't the time.

"How are you feeling?" she asked with concern.

"I'm fine, really. Thanks to all of you." Trying my best to sound casual, I asked, "Where, um, is Noric?" I tucked my hair behind my ear. "I'm just wondering if he's okay."

Embrette didn't try to hide her knowing smile.

"He said he'll be busy for a few days," she answered. "Said he had things to take care of back at his house."

I considered what that might mean. Embrette didn't say that he actually was busy or had things to take care of, just that he'd *said* that.

"Oh, okay." I tucked my chin as I gave a one-shouldered shrug. "Of course. I'm sure he's got things to catch up on after all that."

For the rest of the evening, Hexley and Embrette needlessly fussed over me and even Sevastian stopped by to see how I was doing. Impatiently, I watched the clock and when it turned eight, I told Hexley and Em that I needed more sleep.

A lie.

All I could think about was Noric. He'd been watching me… but he hadn't stopped me from going into the bar, looking like I had every intention of finding someone for the night. Did I want him to have stopped me? Did he want to, but had stopped himself?

He cared enough to follow me and to dole out the harshest of punishments.

So what did that mean?

After the horsemen said goodnight, I sat in bed for another few minutes, debating on speaking to him. *Confronting him.* What if there was a reasonable, non-romantic explanation for everything?

Groaning, I let my head fall into my hands.

At the very least, I could thank Noric for saving me. And if I was bold enough, once I got him talking, I could persist.

Because something *was* going on between us; I felt it in my bones, my blood.

My confidence grew with my resolve, and I slid out of bed. I changed into a simple black skirt, a light gray tank top, and a soft gray shrug that wrapped around my waist and tied in a bow.

Hot, heavy air blasted me as soon as I slipped out the side door and headed for the pasture.

A storm was coming.

I looked to the east, picturing the Carpathian Mountains.

Maybe I was bringing it with me.

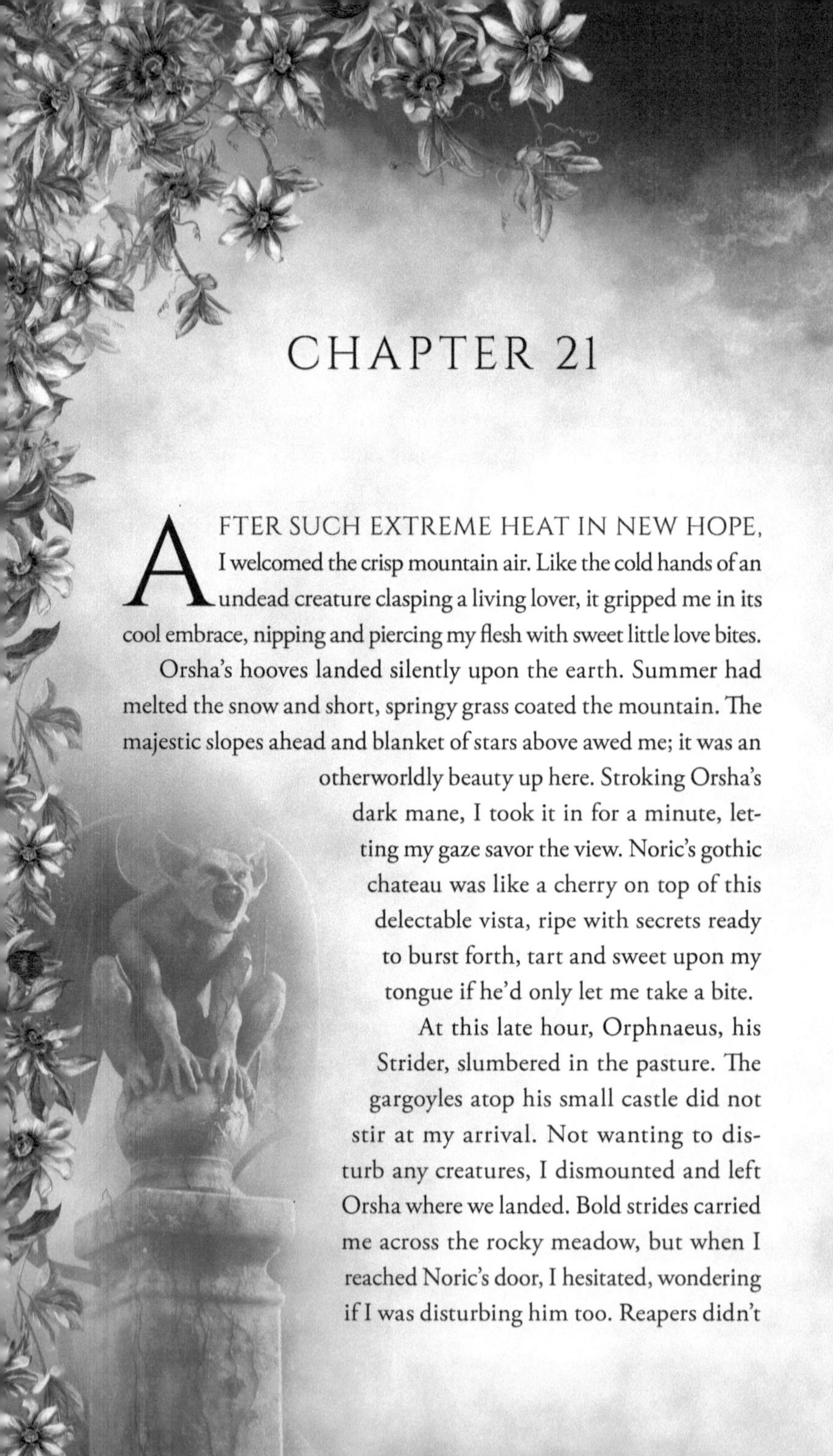

CHAPTER 21

AFTER SUCH EXTREME HEAT IN NEW HOPE, I welcomed the crisp mountain air. Like the cold hands of an undead creature clasping a living lover, it gripped me in its cool embrace, nipping and piercing my flesh with sweet little love bites. Orsha's hooves landed silently upon the earth. Summer had melted the snow and short, springy grass coated the mountain. The majestic slopes ahead and blanket of stars above awed me; it was an otherworldly beauty up here. Stroking Orsha's dark mane, I took it in for a minute, letting my gaze savor the view. Noric's gothic chateau was like a cherry on top of this delectable vista, ripe with secrets ready to burst forth, tart and sweet upon my tongue if he'd only let me take a bite.

At this late hour, Orphnaeus, his Strider, slumbered in the pasture. The gargoyles atop his small castle did not stir at my arrival. Not wanting to disturb any creatures, I dismounted and left Orsha where we landed. Bold strides carried me across the rocky meadow, but when I reached Noric's door, I hesitated, wondering if I was disturbing him too. Reapers didn't have to sleep, but they could if they chose. Maybe he'd wanted to rest after taking such brutal revenge?

Leave a note? I wondered. It seemed an almost antiquated thing to do but Noric had lived through centuries of letter-writing. *Yes, a note if he's not home or if he's sleeping,* I decided.

It had to mean something that he'd avenged me so ruthlessly. My heart insisted it.

I chewed my lip, shifting my weight back and forth as I debated. A thank-you note wasn't tearing down walls, it was simply good manners. Politeness and all.

I pushed the door, grimacing at its creaking hinges. The staccato beat shot through the echo-y hall like the composition from *The Door and the Sigh*, complete with an ominous, heavy woosh of wind channeling through. It was an especially creepy ballet, and the way it fit the moment unnerved me. As I slipped into the entry, Carpathian moonlight spilled onto the tiled floor, spreading further the more I shouldered my way inside. Stepping sideways, I moved out of the light and toward the small Queen Anne table I hoped contained some paper.

I never made it.

A force slammed me into the wall so hard my head banged against the stone and stars spun in my vision. I let out a cry of pain and terror tore through my chest as I focused on Noric's shadowed face, twisted with fury. He'd bent his muscled forearm and pushed it forcefully against my throat, pinning me. His other hand gripped the reaper's dagger, poised to slice my cheek with its gleaming, lethal edge.

Once again, I was pressed to a wall by Noric, but this time was entirely different.

This time he meant to kill me.

I tried to speak—to protest or beg for my life, but no sound came from the desert in my throat and he was crushing my windpipe anyway. My knees had weakened to the point I suspected only his punishing forearm held me up. I didn't know this terrifying Noric before me, mad with rage and bent on reaping. The only other time I'd seen him like this it was directed at Evan.

As a pitiful and woefully common final act in this world, I could only gasp and sputter. My beginning may have been unique, but my end was just like everyone else's.

Noric's already large eyes blew even wider, and he released his grip on the dagger as abruptly as if it burst into flames and scorched his flesh. The weapon clattered onto the tile and echoed throughout his petite castle. His face was contorted in a mixture of bewilderment and anger. Roughly, Noric gripped my shoulders and shook me, as if to shake out the truth of who I was.

It dawned on me that he'd whisked into the room—ready to reap first and ask questions later. He must have believed me to be some rogue intruder who'd mysteriously snuck into his manor…

…A home he never locked because what would be the point? Who would he possibly bar the doors against?

"Noric?" I whispered, voice breaking as I reached forward.

He shoved me backwards at the same time he leapt away from me, and he wasn't gentle about it. Noric stared at his hands as if he witnessed gut-twisting horror there. Those uncommonly long fingers curled slightly, loose and limp… as harmless as he could make them while still attached to his body.

He snapped his gaze back to me and roared, "I was less than a second away from reaping you!"

The dagger was back in his hand so fast I didn't even see him grab it, and Noric pinned me against the wall once more. He made an L-shape with his thumb and forefinger, cupping and lifting my chin to expose my neck. The rage vibrating from his entire body was enough to make me tremble, to make tears well in my eyes.

"Do you see this?" he demanded, indicating the lethal dagger he'd raised back to my bare throat. "One prick and you'd be gone from this earth forever. Is that what you want? Do you want me to reap you?"

"No!" I protested. I struggled to move but didn't get far, both because of Noric's harsh grip and the threat of the blade. My heart slammed a rapid beat against my chest and I fought to hold back the hot tears. He'd never been violent like this in the past. Arrogant, cruel, and insufferable, yes. But never threatening or vicious. Not toward me.

"It looks to me as if you have a death wish, sneaking into my house like this. Either that or you're an utter fool."

"I—I came to thank you," I said stupidly. My stomach churned with an unfamiliar mixture of embarrassment and fear. "For saving me from harm, not to seek it."

Noric's laugh chilled me, rose the hair on my neck. I couldn't guess what he was going to do next. His unpredictability had always frustrated me but for the first time, it frightened me. I'd been around Death my entire life, but my father's power never scared me. He never used it that way, intentionally or not. Since I was four years old, I'd been sheltered from that power, protected from the threat. But Noric didn't shepherd or shield me; he made no attempt at all to conceal how dangerous a reaper truly was.

And yet… despite my terror and like the foolish girl he'd just proclaimed me to be, I dropped my gaze to his mouth. Sensuous. Sinful. My legs screamed at me to run, my lips begged me to stay, and the more intimate parts of my body tingled with newly-awakened desires.

He'd hunched to pin me. Despite my being tall, Noric was taller by several inches, and the way his back and shoulders rounded gave him the appearance of a predatory beast. An image flashed in my mind—him prowling his mountaintop manor like a dark hunter as he awaited prey to wander into the trap he'd constructed.

I didn't let the fact that no one else could actually *see* the castle deter me from the fantasy.

Fantasy? I swallowed thickly and Noric watched my throat dip. Why deny it? The idea called to me. Power radiated from every pore in his body, wrapping me in a spell of desire until it dripped from me.

There was nothing beastly about Noric's aristocratic face though, dreamt into existence and carved by the gods. More blood rushed to my swollen lips, wanting him to kiss them, *aching* to feel the press of his mouth against mine.

A muscle in Noric's cheek feathered.

I heard my own sharp intake of breath.

Was he going to…

He lowered his dagger and stepped back.

No, no, not again.

His brow knit in displeasure and a frown of disgust pulled his lips in the *wrong* direction.

A chill swept over me and it wasn't coming from the open door. Whatever was happening, I liked this even less, feared it even more. Noric spat his order.

"Get out."

Two simple words, but he'd hurled the demand with such loathing I absorbed it like a physical blow. Tears pricked my eyes because he was probably right to be angry. I'd been wildly stupid to break into his house, to appear without knocking just like horsemen did. I wasn't one of them. He could've reaped me.

"Noric, I'm sorry, I—"

"Ava, get out of here, now!"

Noric roared the command with his reaper voice—the one that sounded rough and supernatural, like the scraping of gigantic, ancient stones. He'd never before directed that kind of anger towards me and I hated that it made me want to cry. Noric's words were like shards of ice slicing my heart and crystalizing along the bones of my spine. The prick of his dagger would have hurt less; I wouldn't have felt anything at all as my life slipped from me in an instant. But this… pain trailed in the wake of blooming ice, until my whole body trembled terribly and wouldn't stop.

I fled.

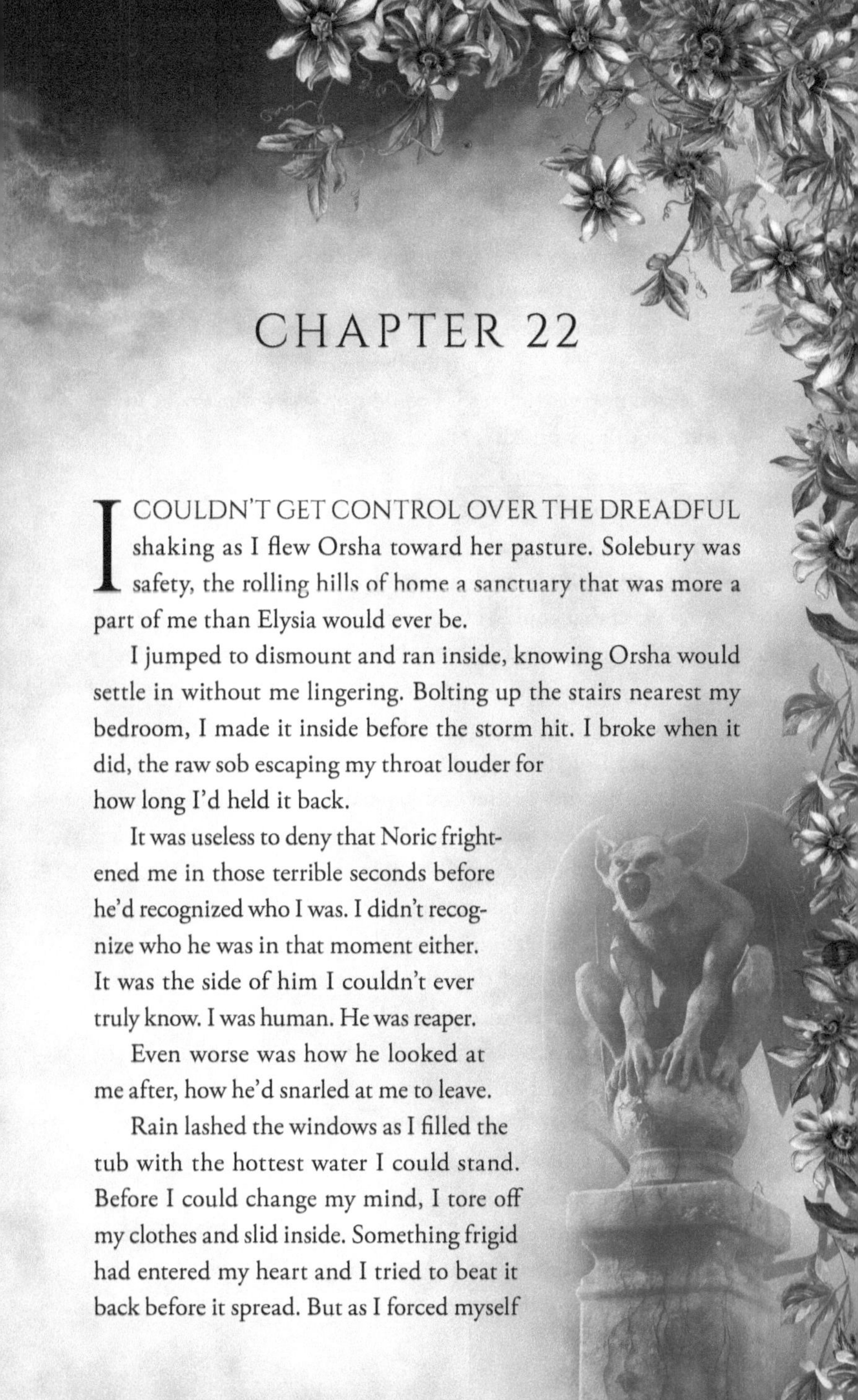

CHAPTER 22

I COULDN'T GET CONTROL OVER THE DREADFUL shaking as I flew Orsha toward her pasture. Solebury was safety, the rolling hills of home a sanctuary that was more a part of me than Elysia would ever be.

I jumped to dismount and ran inside, knowing Orsha would settle in without me lingering. Bolting up the stairs nearest my bedroom, I made it inside before the storm hit. I broke when it did, the raw sob escaping my throat louder for how long I'd held it back.

It was useless to deny that Noric frightened me in those terrible seconds before he'd recognized who I was. I didn't recognize who he was in that moment either. It was the side of him I couldn't ever truly know. I was human. He was reaper.

Even worse was how he looked at me after, how he'd snarled at me to leave.

Rain lashed the windows as I filled the tub with the hottest water I could stand. Before I could change my mind, I tore off my clothes and slid inside. Something frigid had entered my heart and I tried to beat it back before it spread. But as I forced myself beneath the scorching water, all that happened was that my skin turned an angry shade of scarlet. Steam rose from my reddened flesh, dissipating into the air. Inside I felt so cold it hurt, and no heat could penetrate to the depths I required.

Get out. Ava, get out of here, now.

Noric's wrath played on a loop in my head. Clawing at my skull, it was as if I tried to physically remove the memory. Failing, I squeezed my eyes tight as if I could stop seeing the image in my mind. Nothing worked.

Get out of here, now!

How to make it stop? Maybe I'd wait for the rain to cease, then I'd go to the barn and spin and leap until I exhausted myself beyond any ability to *think* any longer.

Yes. Pain that couldn't be contained demanded to be danced.

By the time the water cooled, I welcomed it, having finally reversed my temperature—perhaps too much. My heart raced and I realized I might have given myself the first stirrings of heat stroke.

Jumping from the bath so quickly that I sloshed water onto the floor, I raced to my dresser and yanked a thin white slip over my head. I couldn't bear to wear anything more, but exposing my naked self to the world beyond my room didn't feel right either. Throwing open the doors on the Juliette Balcony, I arched backwards, letting the chilly night air wash over me. The storm had rolled eastward and rain no longer beat the earth, but a pleasant breeze caressed my skin and I could hear the rumble of thunder not far off.

Something dark and fast rushed in the distance. I blinked hard, wondering if a combination of my heartache and the scorching bath had caused me to see mirages in the night sky.

The mirage flew in my direction, and I jumped back on instinct, breath catching. As the image neared my heart thumped faster, because with each passing second a clearer outline formed.

A horned, winged horse. A man astride its back. A reaper's cloak, snapping wildly in the wind behind him.

Noric.

I blinked again, but he remained.

Noric is riding his Time Strider to my window. Right now.

I couldn't move, hardly daring to hope. Had he come to… *why?*

He must have jumped distance at some point to span the world between us, but he flew the last leg of his journey the slower way, right through the storm. *Needing time to think?* His hair, darkened by the rain, was slicked to his head, and Orphnaeus's leathered wings dripped. Noric rode his Strider through the rain with the effortless control of being born to it, which may have been the case. Everything about him spoke of power and danger and I found it only half as frightening as I did intoxicating.

He flew to me like a fairytale, but instead of a prince on a shining white Pegasus, it was a reaper on an inky black Strider. Of course that was how it would be for me, Daughter of Death. Was there ever a time I'd thought otherwise? This dark fairytale gripped my soul in a way the light version never did, even as a child. It felt like home to me more than any angel, golden king, or dashing hero could ever hope to.

When he reached my window, Noric struck out his strong hand, wordlessly offering, and I put my own in his. He pulled me against the railing and then hands were upon my waist, lifting me backwards onto his Strider so that I faced him. My heart pounded in my ears and every part of my body tingled. I didn't turn and he didn't want me to either; I straddled Noric's lap, my legs resting over his powerful thighs.

He picked up the reins, caging me with his arms, but said nothing. Not *I'm sorry* or *are you okay* or any explanation of why he'd come. What was he thinking as he stared at me with those cryptic gray eyes? More than ever, they seemed like a stone labyrinth that I had no chance of solving.

I wasn't sure if I spied desire on his face, but I knew it was plain on mine. Bare. Desperate. I was certain Noric, with his thousands of years of experience, could know from a dozen little tells whether or not a woman wanted him. Was there ever one who *didn't?*

I held onto his shoulders and Noric took off into the sky. Orphnaeus's leathered wings beat the air and Noric's cloak danced in the wind behind us. I didn't know what we were doing, I only knew I never wanted to dismount.

We headed toward the storm but only skirted the edges of it. Light rain pelted us, cool droplets coating my skin and slicking my negligée to my flesh. Did he know I was overheated? Or did he want to show me something in the rain?

The storm raged harder, violent enough that lightning flashed, illuminating Noric's skeletal form. I couldn't help but gasp as I blinked away the rain. The sockets of his eyes were as large and black as any skull, but they were not empty or lifeless to me. I saw the man in that darkness and that dark man saw me. Noric's fleshy, human face reappeared immediately after the lightning stopped, but it was only seconds before another strike flared.

I want you. *Whatever the form.*

I tried to convey the message with every fiber of my being.

Raw hunger grew in Noric's eyes as they darkened, intensified.

No more hiding, no more fighting. Fighting it or each other. Please.

He glanced downward, taking in all of me. Noric's gaze lingered on my wet lips and the tips of my breasts, mesmerized by what my now-sheer slip revealed. I arched into his stare, asking, offering. My hands fell to his waist, longing to pull him closer but not daring. My breathing grew ragged as that hungry, haunting stare lowered to the flat of my stomach and the dip in my hips. I wasn't sure how much Noric could see between my legs, but he clenched his jaw as he stared. It wasn't long, however, before that searing gaze trailed a line back up my body and to my face once more. My heart thumped against my ribcage.

If he did this, if he kissed me, it sealed both our fates. Such a kiss would condemn.

I want you, *I will only ever want* you.

A pleading whimper escaped my swollen lips. Engorged with blood, they ached for Noric's own cool mouth to soothe them. It felt like a madness ravaged me and only the touch of his skin to mine could heal it. Several streaks of lightning splayed across the dark sky and Noric's face flickered between beautiful human and other-worldly skeletal. Back and forth the man and the monster alternated so rapidly they merged to create something new entirely. It was like a thaumatrope—that old-fashioned child's toy where two different pictures on either side of a small piece of paper are quickly spun upon a string, so that the eye cannot tell one from the other and a new image is created. I'd often seen it designed to give the illusion of a bird stuck in a cage... or flying free.

The change in Noric's face happened so fast that I did not actually know which was presenting when his mouth crashed into mine, claiming it for himself.

Yes.

Thunder boomed like my heart as his tongue swept inside with a dominance I was sure only a reaper could possess. The moan I'd been yearning to release tore through my throat and into his mouth where he swallowed it, swallowed all of me that I ached to pour into him—my overheated body, my human heart, my lonely soul.

Take all of me. I'm yours, I've always been yours.

Nothing had ever felt like dancing before, *nothing*. Not even flying.

Until now.

Noric locked one of his hands into the hair at the nape of my neck and pressed the other to the small of my back, keeping me to him even as our lips broke apart. The lightning ceased, for the moment, allowing Noric's face to remain human. Raindrops coated his sensual mouth and I had the erotic thought that his lips might look similar, wet with an even more intimate act.

As if I could be more breathless. Sometime during our kiss I'd fisted his shirt and slid further into Noric's powerful lap. I wanted him so badly I was sure my body shouted it with signs noticeable to all, reaper or human.

Noric's finger traced my lips and he eyed them greedily. He dipped his thumb inside and I sucked on instinct. It made Noric close his eyes and groan softly.

Did the gesture remind him of something else? Was he also imagining the other, more intimate act it evoked?

My cheeks had truly reddened now but were at least cooled by the flight. Noric loosened his hand but kept it splayed on the back of my head and neck. His other moved to hold my waist.

"I can't stay away from you, Ava," he declared, impassioned. "The gods know I've tried. With each day passing it's as if another golden string of your being has woven itself into the fabric of my soul. It has fused; there's no separation possible and I don't want one. I only want to bind you more to me until you are wholly and completely mine, as I am yours."

A strangled cry of joy escaped my throat and tears welled.

"I am sorry. I wasn't angry with you, I was angry at myself," he rasped. A new intensity gripped Noric's face as he tightened his hold on me. "Furious. I couldn't live with myself if I lost you, I'd go mad. I think I started to."

"And yet I lose you, *again and again*," I cried. Boldly, I pushed aside Noric's overshirt, found the holster strapped to his chest, and withdrew his lethal dagger. Noric stiffened but allowed it, watching me cautiously as I brought the blade to his neck.

"I tell you that I am yours and your response is to hold my own dagger to my throat?" Noric chuckled with disbelief and his gray eyes twinkled. "You know it can't kill me."

"I know, but it can wound you," I reminded, pressing it more firmly to his pale flesh. Orphnaeus soared through the clouds in no general direction, simply maintaining air. "You always whisk away, leaving me wanting. How do I know you won't do it again? And you hated me before we even met. Why?"

Noric's lips twitched. The breeze blew through his hair, mussing it sexily. "That night at your manor was the first time we'd met, but it wasn't the first time I'd seen you."

I narrowed my eyes.

"When you received Orsha, you struck out on your own more. I was bid to keep an eye on you from time to time. Usually at times highly inconvenient for me."

"As in following me?" I asked, frowning. *Oh, my father had a lot to answer for.*

"Yes," Noric admitted. "You didn't travel solo often, or too far, but it was always spontaneous. I only trailed you at a distance," he quickly insisted. "Your father didn't want me to get too close, not unless you were in trouble. He didn't want to draw unwanted attention from the overlords."

"Oh."

"Try to understand from my point of view," Noric said, an edge of pleading in his voice. "I was often in the middle of something—reaping or practicing or even showering—and I'd be ripped from my task at your father's whims to keep an eye on you, but never too near. It was boring, as I couldn't even hear your conversations and I resented—"

"Babysitting me," I finished for him, looking away into the heavy, clouded sky. I may have pouted.

Noric took my chin in his fingers. I resisted and he persisted, turning my head to face him whether I liked it or not. "Don't hide from me, Ava. Don't ever hide from me."

I nudged his blade closer and whispered, "That's rich coming from you. Tell me, were you ever hiding in my barn, watching me while I danced?"

Noric only grinned his guilt. I pressed the blade into his flesh.

"And were you there that day when I laid back and touched myself? If so, did you stay and watch or leave?"

Noric made a hissing sound as he sucked a breath through gritted teeth, and I knew. It was like he tried not to lie and tried not to show that he'd liked it.

"You ask too much of me. I'm a reaper, not a saint."

Just when I was about to give his flesh a little prick, he quickly said, "I *had* almost forced myself to leave, I swear it. But then you moaned my name."

I gasped and was sure I'd turned the color of my Firebird costume that day. To be fair, I had fantasized about him watching but I didn't at all remember calling his name.

Seeing my mortification, Noric laid both hands on my cheeks and swore again, "I am yours, Ava. As fully and completely as you are mine, if you'll allow it."

Listening to his words and looking into his earnest gray eyes, I forgot how to breathe.

"Lay your claim on me, I'm begging you, as I have laid my claim on you. I love you."

My heart threatened to burst at his bewitching declaration, from another time and place.

"What is a vow of love when sworn with a dagger at your throat?" I whispered, teasing just a little. After all, he'd secretly *watched* me. Followed me, spied on me.

Noric cocked a brow and slowly reached up. He laid his hand over mine and took the dagger in his own. Then he spun the weapon around and carefully brought his blade to my neck. My eyes blew wide but I remained *very* still. One prick of that magical steel and I'd die, but I trusted Noric knew what he was doing.

"I love you, Ava," he repeated. "Do you believe me now, with my blade at *your* throat? I will never hurt you, reap you, or leave you wanting again. Do you feel anything for me?" And then I supposed he wanted to tease me too because he said, "I mean, other than the lust that made you writhe on the floor repeating my name, and the desire that urged you to show your delights to me beneath the desk?" His eyes gleamed with pride and his smile was completely smug. "Not that I didn't thoroughly enjoy both."

My mouth fell and I wanted to deck him, but I couldn't move until he dropped the dagger.

By the time he'd lowered it, however, I could only breathe, "*Yes*. My heart knew I loved you from the first moment I saw you, I only needed my head to catch up. I am sure of us, Noric, I… have thought I loved before, when I was younger, but it wasn't like this. I know, without any doubt."

As I struggled to explain, the image came to me.

"Love is like dreaming," I said. "You almost never know when you're dreaming, you think it's real. But true love… True love is like being awake. You can't prove it to anyone, you just know it's real."

"Is that so?" Noric asked, sounding both wistful and melancholic. There was something odd in his voice, and for a second I worried that he didn't feel the same. But then he stroked my cheek and said, "Yes, that's a beautiful way to put it and exactly how I feel. I love you Ava, and it is more powerful than anything I can fight."

"Don't," I pled, clutching him tighter.

Noric pulled me into another deep kiss and his hard muscles set parts of my body tingling. Minutes ago, I'd wanted to hide in the barn and dance my pain to *Giselle*. Now I needed to spin and leap like an awakening Aurora.

We descended back to my balcony. It was sensible—I would catch my death if I continued to fly in the cold wearing only a soaked slip. Part of me still feared Noric would disappear again and I couldn't truly blame him for trying to stay away from me. This was reckless, foolish—a sentencing to his eternal agony.

"Noric," I began, hating myself for saying the words but knowing I'd hate myself more if I didn't. I'd just told him *not* to fight us. "By doing this… like you said, we'll both come out wounded in the end, but you more so. I—I don't want to hurt you. Unless we broke apart someday, I can't—I won't—one day I'll die—"

Noric put his finger to my lips. "Let me decide how much pain I can handle, and what is worth it. And you are."

Noric cocked an arrogant brow at me, not releasing his finger until I nodded.

"Did you ever… like watching me? Back when Eligius made you?" I asked, realizing there was no good answer. If he enjoyed it too much he would sound creepy, and if he didn't like looking at me at all, I'd be kind of insulted. Noric's face told me he knew this.

"Of course I thought you were beautiful, but I also thought you were a spoiled mortal brat. And I was wrong," Noric revealed, matter-of-factly. "It wasn't until later that I fell in love with who you are." He stroked my cheek with the back of his knuckles and my heart melted at the look in his eyes. "So in love, Avalia."

I swallowed again, wanting to be mad at Noric and Eligius for the secret, stealthy observance, but all I could think about was the way I ached for Noric to kiss me right now —

— which he did. Leaning close to take my mouth in his. He gently grabbed my waist and I wanted to imprint the memory of this moment on my brain forever. I was putty in Noric's hands and feared he could end any disagreement with a kiss.

When we pulled apart, Noric mused, "I need to talk to Eligius. He's like a father to me."

"That's… weird," I pointed out, wrinkling my nose. "That would make us step-siblings."

Noric pondered for a moment. "Not really. It's more like if your father had a secret, second family on the side. One that you'd never met."

I winced. "You just made it worse."

Noric laughed, "Well, without any of us actually being related, of course." He thought a moment, then said, "In another sense, Eligius is my boss."

I grinned and ran a finger down his hard chest, "Does this mean you're dating the boss's daughter?"

Noric's gaze darted to my transparent slip, courtesy of the rain. "When you say it like that, there's something hot about it."

He kissed me again and too soon, Noric lifted me off Orphaneus and into my room.

"Sleep," he ordered, reaching over to stroke my cheek again. "I'll return tomorrow."

"It is tomorrow," I breathed. By now, dawn couldn't be far off in New Hope and it was midday in Romania.

"Later today," he corrected, flashing that dashing grin that weakened my knees.

When I didn't move, Noric raised his eyebrows, admonishing, and cocked his chin toward the bed. Sighing, I moved—he was right after all—but I wasn't about to sleep in a soaked garment. Facing away from Noric, I lifted the slip over my head and gently tossed it aside, revealing my bare backside to his gaze.

I threw a coy look over my shoulder and said, "Until later today."

Even in the moonlight I could make out the whites of Noric's knuckles, stretched to breaking as he fisted the reins. I laughed and his muscles relaxed, but his heated gaze remained glued below my waist. Giddiness that I could drive Noric to a state of any kind of desire went straight to my head.

His fiery expression might have sworn, *I'm going to devour you once you're rested.* But all Noric actually gritted out was, "Tomorrow."

And then he took off into the sky.

CHAPTER 23

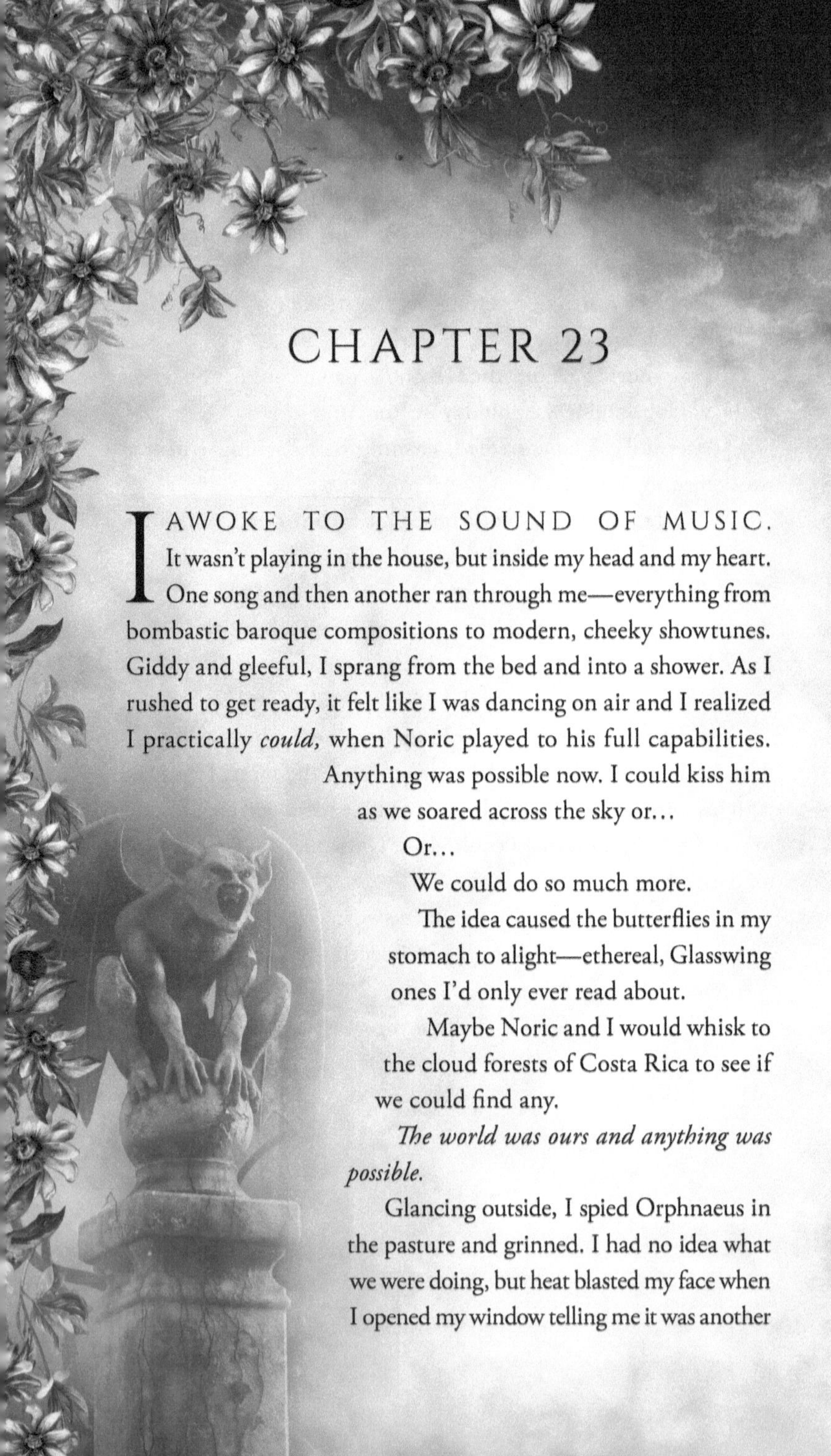

I AWOKE TO THE SOUND OF MUSIC. It wasn't playing in the house, but inside my head and my heart. One song and then another ran through me—everything from bombastic baroque compositions to modern, cheeky showtunes. Giddy and gleeful, I sprang from the bed and into a shower. As I rushed to get ready, it felt like I was dancing on air and I realized I practically *could,* when Noric played to his full capabilities.

Anything was possible now. I could kiss him as we soared across the sky or…

Or…

We could do so much more.

The idea caused the butterflies in my stomach to alight—ethereal, Glasswing ones I'd only ever read about.

Maybe Noric and I would whisk to the cloud forests of Costa Rica to see if we could find any.

The world was ours and anything was possible.

Glancing outside, I spied Orphnaeus in the pasture and grinned. I had no idea what we were doing, but heat blasted my face when I opened my window telling me it was another scorching July day. I put on a simple white tank top and a white skirt that looked more ballet than tennis and raced out of my room.

No one was around when I fled down the steps and spied Noric in the hall. He was wearing a black shirt with the sleeves rolled up to reveal his toned forearms, and a pair of black pants that shaped his long legs perfectly. I gave a little jump and at the same time, Noric easily lifted me. I wrapped myself around his waist and he kissed me.

The feel of him was delicious. It was all I ever wanted.

"We should talk about the future," he said when we broke apart. His nose drew a line up my cheekbone and he planted kisses in its wake, making me shiver. "If we're going to do this… and make no mistake, I want to do this… but we should talk about how."

We rode our Striders north of New Hope, where the crowds thinned and the path wasn't as established. Chunks of debris floated quickly downriver. Last night's storm had felled many branches and the current was swift today. The way the heavy rains stirred the muck and churned the soil pleased my nose and created a competing scent on the air—green and loamy with hints of sharp, pungent mud. It made me think of freshly-dug graves, of cemeteries with their grassy smell blanketing the rot of corpses below.

"Let me talk to Eligius first," Noric stipulated, and I agreed. He was so tall he sometimes had to duck beneath branches as we rode, and I thought even that small move was adorable.

"We'll tell the horsemen together?" I asked, and he agreed.

We rode northward for another hour, stopping to kiss every few minutes. When we finished, Noric and I flew directly back to Grimsmere where the reapers were waiting, as Noric had already called them telepathically.

Hexley and Embrette just laughed and declared, "It's about time."

Sevastian, of course, did not jump for joy. But he held his tongue as he stared at me accusingly, and at Noric with open pity.

I wished I could say that it didn't make me feel guilty—like I was the darker of us two, like a demonic temptress condemning Noric to eternal torment. I had to remind myself that he was fully in control of his own choices, his own heart.

In the evening, I waited in my bedroom and Noric disappeared to have a long talk with Eligius, who was busy working another last-minute update in the Book. This one was particularly sad because it hadn't originally been planned, and many died when the plane crashed. Not only that, but Eligius lingered to cull those who lost their lives later, sustaining injuries when the accident hit a heavily-populated area.

With so many disasters in the world, was it any wonder that people everywhere felt the way they did?

"What did he say?" I asked Noric as soon as he whisked back to Grimsmere. He seemed distracted and I supposed it was due to the unusual increase in culling updates.

"Eligius is… withholding any judgements on us until he sees how it plays out."

I clucked my tongue and remarked, "You mean, if we last?"

Noric flashed a wry grin, and with our tasks complete and seeing me on my bed, his eyes darkened. He quickly crossed over, gently guided me onto my back, and held himself on top of me. We'd waited all day for this moment and when he reached beneath my skirt, I knew what he intended.

It was what we planned, but the moment was all wrong. Maybe it was the plane crash or Sevastian's look or my father's strange reply.

"Wait," I protested, grabbing Noric's hand to stop his exploration. He stilled, raising one eyebrow in question.

"You made me wait," I told him with a teasing smile. "Now you must wait."

"Oh?" His voice strained to hide his disappointment. "Is this punishment?" He shifted his hips, trying to conceal his discomfort. "How long would you like to wait?"

I gave a breathy laugh. "Not punishment and just until Hallow's Eve," I announced, coming to the decision as I said it.

A muscle in his cheek twitched, indicating he'd clenched his jaw as he tried to feign patience. "You want to wait until Halloween to have sex?" he asked.

Did I?

I did.

"Mm-hm. I've waited this long, might as well choose a special night," I told him.

Now I shifted uncomfortably because it was only partially true, and not the primary reason. Putting it off a bit quelled my anxiety. The truth was, waiting so long had built the event up in my mind, and knowing it was *Noric* on top of all that... *oh god.*

Halloween was a special day, because the veil really did thin between the human world, the spectral one, and Elysia. If I was going to have my first time on any day of the year, that's the one I wanted.

But mostly, I needed time because I was nervous as hell.

As he pulled himself off me, Noric released a low grunt, almost a growl.

He took a few seconds to get himself under control, but his eyes were still dark with desire when they flicked back to me and he declared, "Until Hallow's Eve, as my lady commands." Scanning my room, he mused, "To be fair, we probably should find a better location than your bedroom. That gives me plenty of time to set up something worthy."

I thrilled at the idea but wasn't sure it didn't make me even more anxious.

IT WAS THE happiest summer I'd ever had, and it was only July. Maybe the world was falling apart but I was falling in love.

With the river warming, sometimes the horsemen and I headed northward, away from the crowds near town. We'd *borrow* a small boat and anchor ourselves for the day, jumping off the stern and swimming until I was breathless. For dinner we'd alternate whims, just as apt to try a dish from Hexley's favorite market in Peru as we were to grab a bottle and enjoy the views from a vineyard in Sonoma that Sevastian liked.

The world was truly ours.

Sometimes I slept alone in Solebury, and Noric used the time to catch up on work. Other times we stayed up late talking in his gargoyle bed, which inevitably led to a discussion on babies.

"I don't want children," I assured Noric. I'd been laying beneath him but now sat up in bed as I spoke. "And I find it infantilizing for you or anyone else to say that I'm young and that I'll change my mind. I know my mind, and I certainly know my heart. Even with another human, I still wouldn't have a child."

My shoulders rounded but I fought the urge to curl entirely in on myself.

"I hope with your passion for music you can understand," I whispered. "I will dance until my body betrays me. Slowly and heart-breakingly, every year a little more diminished than the one before. That is what it means to be a mortal ballerina. Immortality could never rob me of something I will never want, it could only grant me the priceless treasure of being able to dance eternally."

I sighed in relief when Noric said, "Ava, I believe you. I just wouldn't forgive myself if I didn't mention it."

"There is so much more to life than that. If I were immortal…" My sigh turned into a moan and I cupped Noric's cheek. "In you, I see a partner who cannot die, one who can dance with me forever."

He grinned and half-rolled his eyes as he reminded, "I don't dance ballet."

"With eternity, I could teach you."

And a few days later, we all did dance together, though it was at Yvette's request and with old-time music for the Foxtrot and Charleston. Hexley and Embrette laughed and spun with her butterfae flitting about. The sounds even drew Olga from one of her wanderings and into the ballroom. She twirled alone in her white nightgown, lost in that world inside her head. With Eligius busy at work and Sevastian not wanting to join us, Sanderson eventually stepped in and partnered with her for a few songs.

"The moves had to be simple because back then, everyone danced," Archibald explained, taking a break to light up a ghostly cigar, "so the popular steps became those most easily followed."

Yvette giggled, covering her mouth. "Back then, the popular dances were the ones that allowed couples to press close together without being seen as scandalous and ruining their reputations." She swished her hips and the fringe on her ghostly skirt moved along with it. "The steps hardly mattered when your heart was racing from such delicious proximity to a man."

Archie's brown eyes flared with jealousy as he stubbed out the cigar he'd just lit. He pulled Yvette to him, lifting and twirling her in the air while she threw back her head and laughed.

"If they weren't all dead already," Archie vowed, "I'd kill every man who touched you in your corporeal state."

I had to admit that Yvette had a point. Without the distraction of complicated steps, my mind was free to linger on the little things.

Noric's reaper scent and how it beckoned, like a cave of mysteries begging to be explored. That sardonic curve of his lips, as if he was ready to break into a taunting grin at any moment. The strength in his muscles, which made me yearn to feel their power on my body, be it to lift me up or pin me down.

I bit my lip and very quickly, Noric's eyes darkened and lingered on my mouth. The intensity of his gaze flared the heat in my belly, and I marveled at our connection, at how the simplest movements in one of us spurred desire in the other.

October started to feel very long away.

AUGUST CAME IN hot and hard that year. Now that I'd thought about it, it wasn't just the Book that seemed unstable, the world's weather was unusual too, with temperatures breaking records in several regions.

One scorching August evening, Noric and I rode our Striders to dinner in Monaco, and we were shown to a table on a curved terrace overlooking Port Hercule. When we sat, however, I was taken aback by the menu.

"Wow, how fancy," I remarked. "They don't even list the prices. Rather presumptuous of them."

An amused smile tugged at Noric's lips. "You're a lady, clearly on a date."

I let the menu drop back to the table with an unladylike *smack*. "So what?"

"I'm assumed to pay at a restaurant like this," he informed me. His gray eyes twinkled and he took my hand in a genteel kiss. "It would be vulgar to share the cost with you."

My cheeks flushed as I struggled with too many feelings at once. *I* was the one who always knew more than everyone else—at least when it came to matters of life and death—but since meeting Noric my world had upended, in the largest and the smallest of ways.

Out of my depth, I thought. No mortal man could knock me off axis because we didn't inhabit the same worlds—not when it came to what really mattered. But Noric existed in a realm separate and above my own, and that imbalance always made me feel a little off-kilter.

"It must be odd for you," I remarked, once we'd ordered and were alone again—once *he'd* ordered for us both, as was expected here. "Watching the world grow and change. Visiting these last vestiges of a time gone by."

"It's no different than your passage of time really," Noric replied. "Mine's just longer."

Infinitely longer, I thought, heart sinking.

I was human. He was reaper. I could no more understand the workings of his mind or his magic than a bird could comprehend the mortal brain.

It was pointless to try.

And yet I could no more tear myself from Noric than I could escape the earth's gravitational pull. So where did that leave me?

I bit my lip to keep tears from welling and tried to appreciate such a perfect evening. The people around us were so elegantly dressed. The yachts and sailboats dotting the water made a picturesque tableau. And with twilight approaching, a cool breeze stirred the air, carrying the fresh, clean scent of the sea to our table.

Not to mention, in the distance and glamoured from everyone's view but mine, two of Noric's gargoyles dipped and soared over the bay in playful flight.

But I was as ephemeral as the moment. Compared to Noric's life, mine was that of a leaf, and I'd soon wither on the branch. One day he'd watch me fall to the ground, turn brittle, and scatter into dust.

A bottle of Chateunuf-de-Pape arrived and as Noric sampled it, his eyes bore into me. I knew he was going to make me tell him what I'd been pondering as soon as we were alone.

The best I could ever hope for was to be the helpless human trailing his steps. Even if he wanted to treat me as his equal, he couldn't risk it. I'd be a protected pet, the mortal who could easily fall into danger and he'd come running to my rescue, saving me.

The image of a thaumatrope struck me again, with its oft-depicted bird, caged or flying free. Two contradictory images and yet I felt both in my soul, simultaneously. With Noric I was utterly spellbound, unable to think of a world beyond him, as chained as his prisoner. Yet it was only with him that I was truly able to be myself, to soar, to love, to live the life I desired.

Once we were alone, Noric waited for me to speak.

"Thousands of women throughout history, perhaps hundreds of thousands," I whispered, "must have badly desired you."

Noric's gaze was weighty, penetrating. "But this is the first time I've badly desired someone in return."

"Why?" I tried, and failed, to keep the disbelief from my voice. I forced a smile and sipped my wine; a transparent attempt at looking casual.

"I could list a thousand little reasons, from the way—*just now*—your mouth shaped that one word you uttered, to the counterclockwise direction in which you stir your tea."

I blinked. Did I do that?

"I could tell you better reasons. That I love you for what I see in your heart—your passion, your spirit, even your dedication to dance. And all that would contribute to the way I feel. But it's as you once said. True love is like knowing when you're awake. You can't explain your assuredness any more than you can explain that you're aware you're not dreaming. You just *know* what's real. I know you as I know myself. I am as sure of you as I am sure of me." Noric shook his head ruefully. "I believed in love but never believed it would happen for me. I think I was so married to that belief that when I found it," Noric flashed a grin, "it was difficult for me to admit that I was wrong."

And I barely believed in it at all.

I let my eyelids flutter shut as I smiled.

It was enough—*no,* it was more than I could ask for. And the best we could make of our impossible situation.

I would have to be satisfied. I would have to focus on the present.

There, at that elegant table above the picture-perfect harbor, I vowed not to waste the time Noric and I had by being preoccupied with my eventual death.

After all, with every reaper protecting me, I had a better shot than most at a long life.

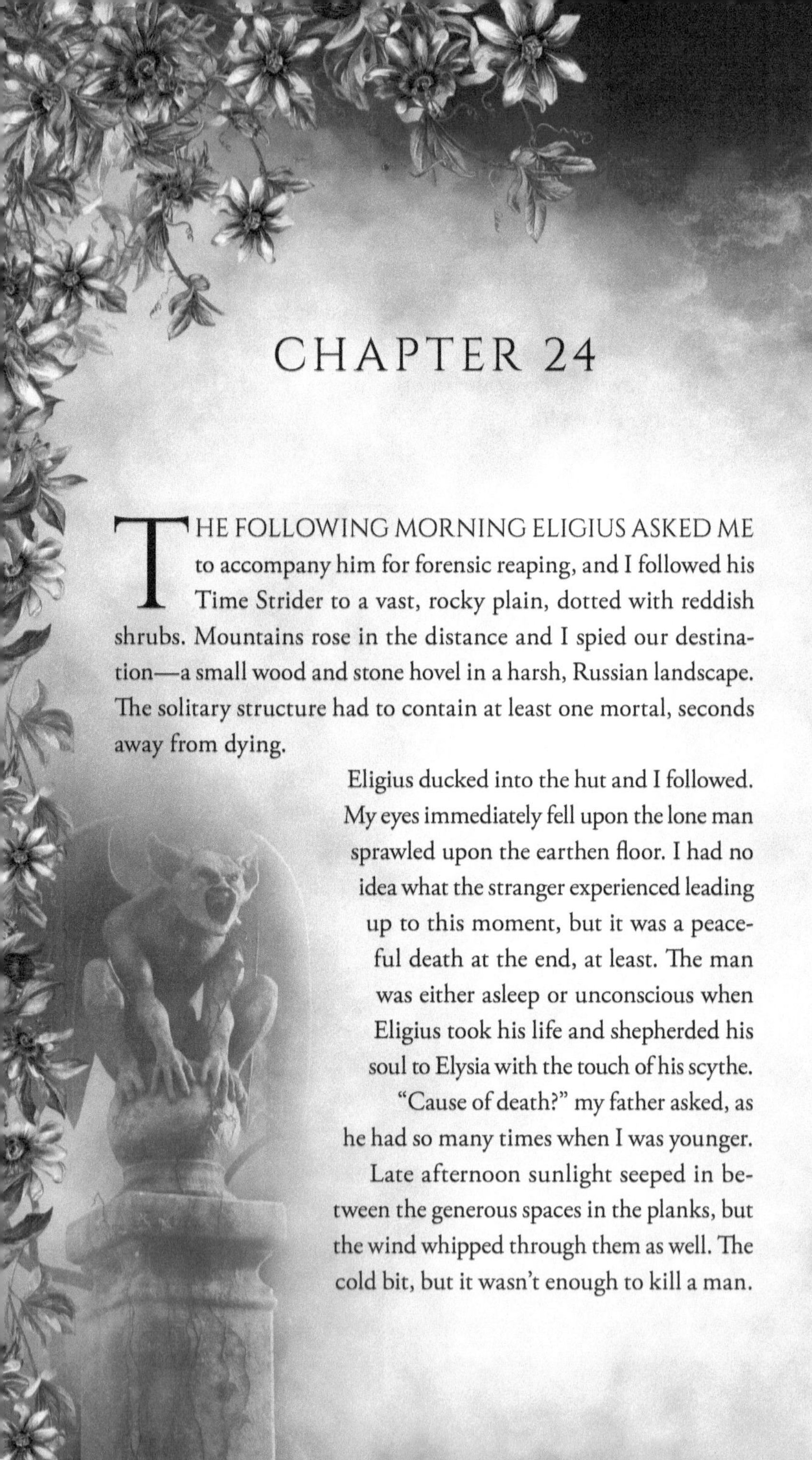

CHAPTER 24

T HE FOLLOWING MORNING ELIGIUS ASKED ME to accompany him for forensic reaping, and I followed his Time Strider to a vast, rocky plain, dotted with reddish shrubs. Mountains rose in the distance and I spied our destination—a small wood and stone hovel in a harsh, Russian landscape. The solitary structure had to contain at least one mortal, seconds away from dying.

Eligius ducked into the hut and I followed. My eyes immediately fell upon the lone man sprawled upon the earthen floor. I had no idea what the stranger experienced leading up to this moment, but it was a peaceful death at the end, at least. The man was either asleep or unconscious when Eligius took his life and shepherded his soul to Elysia with the touch of his scythe.

"Cause of death?" my father asked, as he had so many times when I was younger. Late afternoon sunlight seeped in between the generous spaces in the planks, but the wind whipped through them as well. The cold bit, but it wasn't enough to kill a man.

Slipping on a pair of disposable gloves, I examined the body. His unkempt hair and beard were long and stringy. Dirt crusted the man's face and loose, crooked teeth poked out of his slackened mouth. No blood, no severe wounds. He was thin but not emaciated, and some fish bones littered the corner, although they looked old.

"Heart attack?" It was a weak guess and I'd only said it because I was thinking of our last reaping.

"Think about his lifestyle," Eligius prodded. "What kind of man is this?"

We were more miles from civilization than he could walk in a day. I turned around the hovel, looking for clues. Some flies had found easy entrance, lured by the stench. A short stack of books lay on the dirt floor beside him, along with a filthy pile of bedding, some candles, and a canteen. We had passed a nearby river on our ride, so he hadn't died of dehydration. Unless…

"The water? Was it tainted with a bacteria of some kind?"

Eligius shook his head. "But you're getting closer."

I pursed my lips. The recluse didn't value personal hygiene, so perhaps an infection came from the food.

"Botulism?" I tried. "He didn't properly cook his meat? Or some other type of food poisoning?"

My father shook his head again but a smile curved his thin lips. "Very close though."

What was like food poisoning but not that exactly?

I examined the body again but couldn't find any tell-tale clues. "It wasn't something he ate that killed him?" I asked.

"The opposite." Death said.

I frowned.

"He didn't eat… something…" I pushed aside his collar with my gloved fingertips. No marks on his neck. No signs of choking. "But he didn't starve," I mused aloud.

I sat on the dirt floor beside the corpse, fingers clasped. Several minutes passed and more flies buzzed by my head.

"I need a hint," I admitted.

"Argh," my father growled, and it was so unusual coming from his mouth that I burst out laughing.

Was he killed by pirates? But we were thousands of miles from the ocean and the tent bore no signs of a struggle. Was there such a thing as tundra pirates? No, they would be more like highwaymen, I supposed. I hadn't seen any large bodies of nearby water on our descent, save a distant river. He couldn't have drowned because he lay in his hovel, not the riverbed. Dry, not wet. Unless...

"Secondary drowning?" I guessed.

My father shook his head and replied, "You're getting colder. Remember the food."

"Okay, so it had something to do with something he ate. Or rather, didn't eat. And pirates."

What did pirates not eat and die?

I smacked my forehead. But no... not in modern times and not here, inland. It couldn't be.

"Scurvy?" I asked tentatively, almost embarrassed.

"Aye," Eligius replied sagely, and I laughed again.

"How does that happen here, on land?" I asked in disbelief.

"Insufficient nutrition happens everywhere."

"Huh," I said, looking down at the corpse and swatting the air with my hand. The flies were really getting to be a problem. "I'll be sure to finish all of my carrots tonight."

"Is this all it would have taken to get you to eat them yourself when you were younger, instead of sneaking off to feed them to the Time Striders? I would have brought you to a scurvy victim long ago, had I known."

"Oh joy, another box to check in your scared straight method of parenting." I rolled my eyes and laughed, remembering how I used to hide the bland, hard sticks in my pocket as a child. After dinner I'd sneak to the pasture and give them to Time Striders, believing I'd fooled Eligius.

Of course I hadn't.

I always tried coaxing one of Striders to bring me to the Rotunda, where the Reclamation of Souls Book was kept.

Of course Eligius had dissuaded them all not to do so.

"Come," my father said. "Let's leave this hovel and have a talk."

His voice was weighty, making the hair on my neck stand on end. Something was happening, and this forensic reaping was just a prelude. Whatever it was, I knew it had to do with Noric, because Eligius and I hadn't discussed our relationship yet.

We exited the dead man's hut and Eligius took a seat on a small boulder. I was close enough that the bubble of his power reached me and the cool wind disappeared in his warmth.

"Lee Lee," Death began, folding his hands. "The world is not everything I've represented it to be… you were not the exception I represented you to be." His gaze swept the land as if he searched for something, but we were alone on this eerie plain. "At least, not to the gods, though you were to me."

My heart pumped faster. It felt like I'd secretly, subconsciously waited for something like this, but now that it was here I wasn't sure I was ready.

"I'm going to tell you everything and then we can decide what to do from there."

I could only nod.

"The horsemen and I ferry souls to Elysia, that much is true," Eligius said. "But it is not permanent. They return."

That… wasn't what I expected. I paused a beat, then asked, "Like reincarnation?"

"Yes, precisely," Eligius said. "Except for those few slated for Elimination, usually because the soul is too rotted to repair—history's most monstrous men and the like. They are not sent to a hell or any other realm as I've allowed you to believe, the soul itself is destroyed, annihilated. But those cases are rare."

The wheels in my mind spun and I inhaled deeply. "Okay," I breathed on my exhale. *Okay. Reincarnation is real.* I could handle that. "So reincarnation exists. I can see why the gods wanted to keep that secret."

"It's more systematic than you are imagining," Eligius cautioned, one bony hand raised. "The Rotunda isn't just where souls pass through on their way back, it's where they return to leap again. We can only access an aspect of the structure, however. It's as if the true passage up and down exists in another dimension, layered behind this one."

"Leap?" I echoed softly. "Does this mean I can see the Rotunda now?"

"No, that is a step far too far." Eligius's dark eyes gave a sharp warning. "And yes, that's what we call it. Leaping back to earth. It's more intentional than falling. Unless, for whatever reason, the unwilling soul is thrown by the gods. Either way, this world was designed with intention. Those who leap return to live again, to play again. Noric would say it's like a game, except it's all quite real."

Suddenly, I felt hot and claustrophobic, even though we sat on the open tundra. A light sweat broke out on my body and I wanted to leap out of my own skin.

"What are you saying?" I tried to slow my breathing. "Oh my god, are we in a simulation? Am I asleep somewhere dreaming this? Feeding an alien race with my body's energy, like in the movies?"

"No, as I said, you are real, as is the world around you. But it's… moldable. And the overlords do quite a bit of molding," Eligius explained. "Elysia exists, but souls are free to leave and return to Earth. Each time a soul chooses to leap, their memory is wiped. Think of it as drinking from the River Lethe. A mortal may have recalled a bit of the truth when they created that tale, long ago."

I gasped, remembering something Noric had said.

Hair as dark as the River Lethe… When I see you dance it's like I've drunk more than my fill from those mythic waters and forgotten everything of this world… including my place in it.

He'd been using what I thought was a myth to speak the truth.

"Sometimes there is a delayed effect, and that is why children are more prone to see ghosts or remember past lives," my father explained. With a wry grin he said, "Sevastian christened it *BAD*, short for Biologically Aware Disorder, and it stuck, because the overlords don't like it. Occasionally, it persists in glimpses throughout adulthood, and those BAD specimens may become artists who hide messages in plain sight. Sometimes they're unaware it's forbidden and sometimes they want to see how much they can get away with. But if the overlords grow annoyed, it leads to reaping and resetting. Ghosts are not just supernatural, Ava," Eligius explained. "They are beings that have had the right set of conditions to let them slip through the cracks. They are literally ghosts in the machine, beyond the reach of a reaper's blade and somewhat of a blind spot to the gods. Until they're caught and collected in a systematic sweep."

Mouth slack and eyes glazed, I knew I looked dumbstruck. Trying to let this new information settle so that I could file it away and accept more, I quietly studied the mountains in the distance. Come autumn, they'd be snow-capped, but now the jagged peaks were gray and barren. I wondered if any tribes had populated this land long ago, and if they ever retreated to those mountains for cover. Because here on the plain, there was nowhere to hide. Here, everything was laid bare, vulnerable and exposed.

"If memories break through," I asked slowly, thinking of the sharp mountain peaks, "is Déjà vu real?"

Eligius nodded. "A true memory coming though from a light case of BAD."

"The Mandela effect? Is it real?"

Eligius nodded again. "Mass reprogramming, blanket enchantments."

"So my mind is susceptible?" I cried angrily, bringing my hands to my head as if I could protect my memories. The idea that I'd ever lose them, lose my life or myself, was unbearable. "Is everyone's? Can our lives be rewritten?"

"As far as I can tell, it's only utilized for insignificant updates. If there's a malfunction, they're more likely to recall a soul to Elysia."

"I don't understand. If it's not a simulation, if I'm real—if this is all real," I exclaimed, waving my hand around me, "how can anyone alter it? And which is it? Reprogramming or sorcery?"

"Think of it as the power of the gods, if you like. The same way I block a person's memory, the gods cast enchantments to bring something into being or to erase it."

"So is it science or magic?" I pressed, increasingly lost.

"Neither. Both. They are one and the same, and something else entirely. Think of either you prefer, if you cannot fuse them together," Eligius advised. "Although I have often wondered if creating a false separation between science and magic, galvanizing and polarizing the followers of each, is the deepest illusion ever created."

For a moment I just stared, wide-eyed. Then I collapsed my face into my hands. "I need a minute."

After a few seconds of studying the ground, I grabbed a stone from the rocky land, sprang to my feet, and threw it as far and hard as I could. I picked up three more, tossed them, and shouted into the air. I didn't know what I intended to accomplish, I just needed to direct my energy somewhere.

Thoughts flew at me in rapid fire.

Reincarnation was *real*.

This was all some sort of game but it was also *real*.

My father had kept the greatest of secrets to protect me.

Glancing at Eligius, my heart warmed, because I could have been an orphan somewhere, raised by anyone. Whatever was true about this realm, I was incredibly lucky, because I faced this world with someone who loved me. More than one person, now.

I re-sat, intending to ask questions. But Eligius, who'd been watching me patiently, spoke first.

"There's more," he intoned. "Brace yourself. You might as well know it all now."

I bit back a mad laugh. *What more could there possibly be?*

"Many creatures of myth have truly populated this world throughout the ages. Most aberrations that you can think of did in fact exist at one time." Eligius rubbed his chin, distracted. "The ikavorn are different from the others, however. The gods permit their continued existence, and their creation is a mystery to me. Humans would call them vampires."

"Vampires?" I breathed, disbelieving.

"Not exactly as they're portrayed in the media but a similar concept."

Eligius announced the news gently, but it turned my world on its axis anyway.

"We can reap them—in fact, our craving to cull an aberration is difficult to resist. But we are forbidden to interact. Eons ago, a wispinger reported their existence to me. Perhaps they were intentionally created or perhaps they have some leverage over the gods, I do not know. I know only what I observed from one I've… encountered… more than the others." My father rubbed his forehead. "I violated the edict to track down the ikavorn known to me, and to learn what I could from his kind."

A kernel of hope grew in my heart. Vampires didn't die. *Maybe I could…*

"They have ichor in their blood, the ever-essence that grants them immortality and makes them difficult to kill," my father explained. "But not only is it rare to possess the ichor, most humans do not survive the transformation process. Still, I thought maybe," Eligius looked at me sadly. "I violated the decree to speak to Vasilios, a very old vampire, and I requested that he scent you but… the required ever-essence does not run through your blood."

In the span of a heartbeat my hopes rose like a wave, only to be smashed upon the rocks. Still, I was insatiably curious.

"What are they like, the ikavorn?" I asked.

"I only know what I've observed from afar," Eligius answered, rubbing his chin. "We may crave the culling of a mortal we grow close to, but it is a prolonged process. An ikavorn is more like an animal. If a mortal appeals to them, they want to drink, and if they want to drink, they want to drain."

"Are there werewolves too?" I asked, feeling ridiculous, but nothing seemed out of the realm of possibility now.

"That glitch has been eradicated. There have been no known werewolves since the seventeenth century." Eligius thought it over a moment, then shrugged. "Which doesn't mean the bug won't resurface."

My mouth dropped. "You're kidding me. Right?"

"No, it's all real. Zombies have arisen when systems malfunction. Mermaids." Eligius made a noise in the back of his throat. "Bigfoot. There are even whispers of witches, which I have not personally confirmed but, where there's smoke, there's fire. Some spellcraft must be real for the rumors to persist."

At my look of shock, my father said, "Is it so hard to accept that unicorns existed in the thickest parts of the forest, or that sirens swam in the depths, when you ride a Time Strider every day, and commune with ghosts?"

"I guess not," I said slowly, "but that's different. It's—"

"Familiar to you. And those creatures are not. But believe me, I've reaped them. When these special cases crop up, it is not like normal animals, which are handled outside of our care. In these instances, we are inevitably sent to eradicate them. Despite the powerful craving, there is no grief like culling a species the overlords declare an aberration, wiping them from existence. Sevastian wept the day we killed the last unicorn."

"But why?" I pled. "What makes a horse permissible but not a unicorn?"

Death shrugged. "You have a power that I do not. One day, you will return to Elysia. Perhaps you can ask the gods if you meet them. Though I wish there was a way you would remain here forever."

Return? An idea popped into my mind and I froze, though my heart thumped harder. *Reincarnation is real.*

Now I understood.

That was why I feel so drawn to Noric, and he to me. We must have met many times before and fallen in love each time! He'd been keeping it a secret from me because he wanted to protect me. *Of course.* It all made sense.

"I need to talk to Noric," I announced, springing to my feet. I hugged my father and said, "Thank you. We'll talk more later, but right now I need to see him."

"Lee Lee," my father called out as I sprinted to Orsha. "Wait, please. There's more."

"I need to talk to Noric," I yelled, swinging onto Orsha's back. "I'll be home tonight and we can finish, I promise!"

"Ava," my father cried, but I was already in the air.

It wasn't that I didn't care about vampires and unicorns and everything mythical and wonderful. But the idea that I'd been with Noric in my past lives temporarily obscured all that magic.

I now understood why I loved him the first time I saw him. I'd known Noric before; we'd fallen in love countless times in our past. I was an old soul, and our connection had formed over eons.

And now that I knew the truth, he was free to tell me *our* truth.

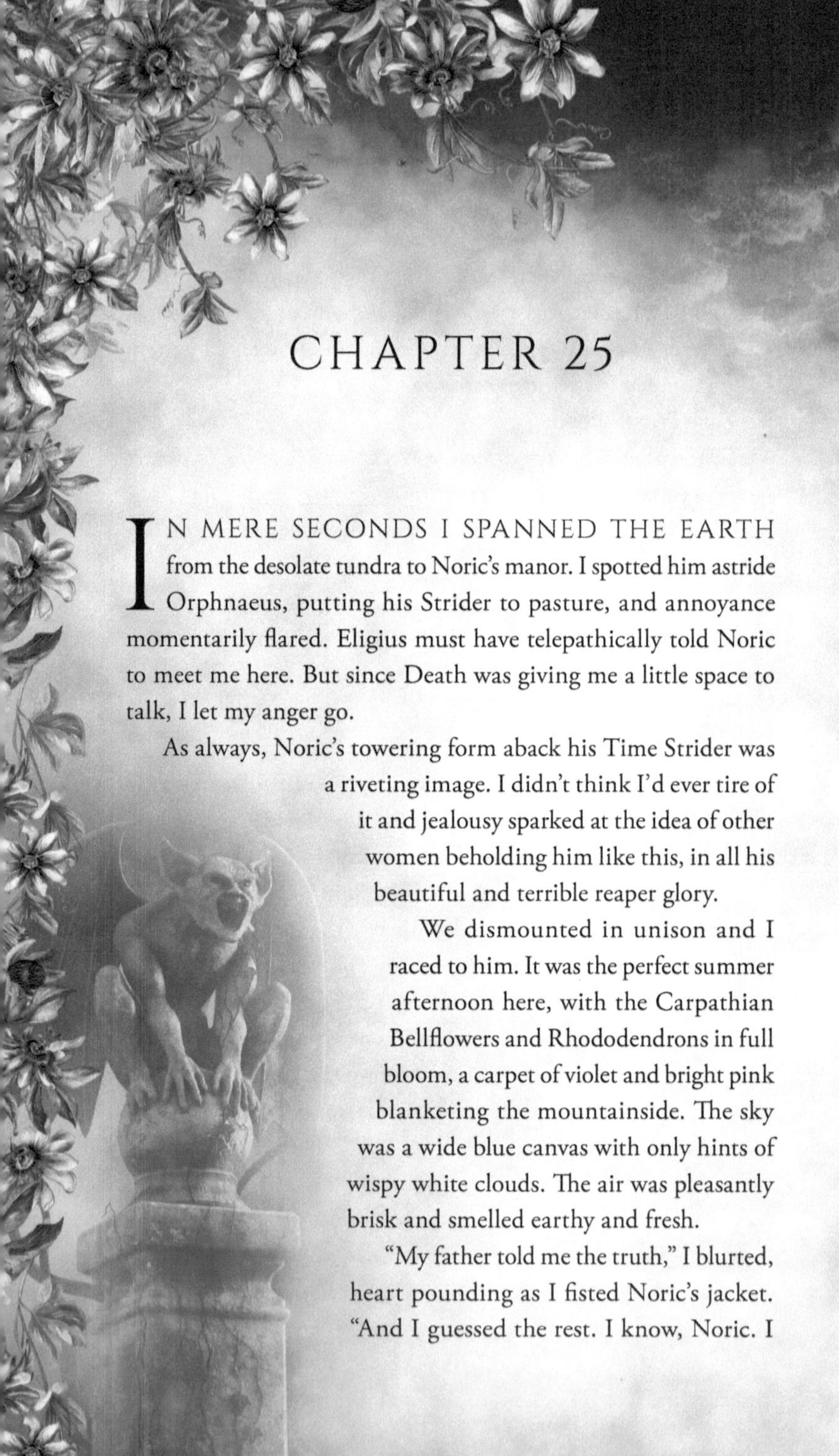

CHAPTER 25

I N MERE SECONDS I SPANNED THE EARTH from the desolate tundra to Noric's manor. I spotted him astride Orphnaeus, putting his Strider to pasture, and annoyance momentarily flared. Eligius must have telepathically told Noric to meet me here. But since Death was giving me a little space to talk, I let my anger go.

As always, Noric's towering form aback his Time Strider was a riveting image. I didn't think I'd ever tire of it and jealousy sparked at the idea of other women beholding him like this, in all his beautiful and terrible reaper glory.

We dismounted in unison and I raced to him. It was the perfect summer afternoon here, with the Carpathian Bellflowers and Rhododendrons in full bloom, a carpet of violet and bright pink blanketing the mountainside. The sky was a wide blue canvas with only hints of wispy white clouds. The air was pleasantly brisk and smelled earthy and fresh.

"My father told me the truth," I blurted, heart pounding as I fisted Noric's jacket. "And I guessed the rest. I know, Noric. I know why I love you so much, why I feel as though I've known you before. Because I *have,* haven't I? We've met in my other lifetimes."

Noric seemed to pale, if that was even possible. He took a moment to reply.

"I knew your father was going to tell you everything, but I never dreamed you'd come to that conclusion." His face fell and his eyes softened. "No, Ava. We've never met before," he declared.

Defeat hit me like the strike of a sword and my entire body shrank protectively in on itself. Noric took my hand and the sympathy in his gaze only embarrassed me, made me feel foolish for hoping. "You're a new leaper, maybe even a new soul," Noric said softly. "I can feel it on you."

I paused, then laughed. Madly.

Oh, our gap was *worse* than me being younger in this physical reality alone. My soul was young too. Angry and ashamed, heat prickled my flesh. It itched, like a skin I needed to shed, like a shell I had to discard to grow into something new, something older. Something ancient, like Noric. Learning that reincarnation was real and that my soul could be so much older gave me hope of leveling the playing field between Noric and I in another way.

Instead, it only served to make the imbalance greater.

"So the gap between us widens," I spat with disbelief, stepping back and scowling. "When I think about how much more time you've *existed* than I have…"

"It's not like that," Noric said. "Stop assigning time more meaning than it deserves."

"It's not just the concept of time," I argued, fisting my hands. "It's my experiences, my growth and knowledge. Who I am as a person. *Being* a person in the first place. You see me above all other mortals, on a level to be your partner, but don't you understand that you are still on a level above what I can ever achieve? I could live to be a hundred and we still won't be equals. You can't pull me above the mortal level, it's not in your power."

Tears stung my eyes and I wasn't sure what we were talking about any longer. I'd gone from discussing the difference in our age to the difference in our experience to the difference in our lifespan to the difference in our power, but all of it was connected and extremely frustrating.

"I wanted… I don't know. The way I fell for you to have more meaning," I breathed, circling back. "For us to have a history, to have met and loved a hundred times before."

"Why is it a disappointment, Ava," Noric asked gently, turning my chin so that I looked at him again. "That this is not the middle of our story, but the beginning?"

I opened my mouth, then closed it. *Why, indeed?* We had to start somewhere, didn't we?

Noric cocked his head at me and asked cautiously, "Ava, did your father explain it all to you?"

I searched his face. What did he mean?

Noric was quiet a moment.

"Are you speaking with my father now? Stop doing that."

I tensed as Eligius appeared, whisking onto the grassy mountainside.

"May I please speak with my daughter for a moment?" he asked Noric.

Noric nodded and stepped away, a move which brought a chill up my spine. I wasn't ready to hear more and what else could there be?

Once Noric ambled a bit further down the mountain, Eligius confessed, "Ava, I haven't been honest with you in more ways than one. I couldn't. I don't think you remember," he said, taking my hand in his and turning it over to show the scar on my palm. "The Dunns."

I stared at him blankly.

"Avalia, you're not an exception, you're a secret. When I first left you with those families, I thought you were young enough to forget me. I wanted to raise you, please believe me. But I didn't want to risk your life by breaking the overlords' rules."

I stared at my father, confused.

"I was afraid for you, so after the Dunns I obscured your memory. But it was too late, it didn't fully take. Every time you looked at your palm, you'd remember me. It's not so unheard of for mortals, when there's a physical reminder like that."

Eligius gently ran his thumb over my scar and my lip quivered as flashes of memories returned.

"I was afraid you'd cut yourself again and again to bring me back to you. So I took you to Grimsmere, which is what I truly wanted in my heart. I tried to raise you with the least exposure possible—nothing beyond what you'd already seen or was absolutely necessary. The less you knew, the less likely it was for the overlords to take you from this world. That is why I kept the horsemen away."

Tears ran down my cheeks by the time Eligius finished—not for myself, but for him. I knew how much my father loved me and could only imagine how hard it was to have to make these choices.

Suddenly, I knew where this discussion was going and my stomach sank.

"Something happened the day you changed your mind," I stated, wiping my tears with the back of my hand as I worked it out. "The gods threatened my life, didn't they?"

Death nodded. "Possibly. I received a wispinger that day. The gods might have always known, waiting and watching. Or they might not have paid attention until recently. We immortals have all had human companions in the past, here and there, skirting the rules in our own little way. It's always a bit of a risk," Eligius explained.

"Whatever the case, I received a wispinger that day telling me two words," Eligius rasped. "*We know.*"

The shiver that ran through me was fierce.

"It was like a taunt, another game the gods play," Death said. "I'd once asked Vasilios to scent you for the ichor. That day, I violated the rules and contacted him again. He agreed to meet just before our dinner the night the horsemen came, which is why I was late. There have been whispers of forbidden information their kind possesses and I was hoping Vasilios would have something to help, but those rumors turned out to be false. The overlords are as capricious and fickle as the gods of myth. I am afraid they'll take you from me, and also…" his voice took on a weighty tone. "…that they might take *me* from *you.*"

I scrutinized my father and a new, creeping fear crawled over my skin.

"Something is wrong with the world, Ava. Even humans can feel it, this growing malaise. And it's both similar and different from those in the past, because this time, it's difficult to pinpoint a source. I don't know if the realm is failing. I've felt this before and it righted, but it's different each time. It's not a circle, exactly…"

Eligius knit his brow as he tried to explain. "Have you ever heard the saying that history doesn't repeat, but it rhymes? It's as if time goes 'round a spiral and we travel through a similar region, but never exactly the same spot. It's more like we're moving along a coil; perhaps it is that of the golden ratio, the Fibonacci Sequence, as it presents in the overlord's time. Or another pattern that is naturally common to them, but unknown to us." Eligius shook his head. "We're in a troubled period but it won't last. Something always causes a reset, a push forward."

"Like… what?" I asked.

"It can be anything. A great flood. A great war. The culling of a great mortal. These things can trigger a new era. We're not always privy to the solution, but we can feel when a cycle begins and ends."

"And this malaise is an indicator that it's happening again?"

Death nodded. "That, and the spontaneous, catastrophic cullings." He considered me and said, "These things usually take time to unfold, and it could be a long way off. It might not even happen in your lifetime."

My stomach flipped. As reassuring as it was to know the world might not face a reset anytime soon, being reminded of my short and finite lifespan as the reason I wouldn't live to see it wasn't a cheerful thought either.

"However, once I received the wispinger, I wondered if a reset was coming sooner and that this time," Eligius looked at me and laid a meaningful hand on his slim chest, "a sacrifice might be required to sustain the system."

"You?" I asked, horrified.

"Me," he confirmed. "I thought between this widespread… ennui," he said, waving a hand, "and how I'd defied the gods by raising you, that they might demand my life as payment and punishment. That a reset involving my death in the form of Elimination would be forthcoming."

The idea of my father no longer existing made my heart ache as painfully as if someone fisted and squeezed it. "But they haven't done anything," I pointed out. "And I still don't understand why you were in a hurry for me to meet the horsemen."

"Yet," Eligius clarified. "There is a looming threat, and I don't know whose life is in the balance, if anyone's. But if I were to be taken away, I wanted my reapers to take care of you. Noric and I were discussing it telepathically when he arrived at dinner, the night I introduced the horsemen."

For a moment I froze, then snorted a laugh. *Noric babysitting me again.* I cast a glance at where he stood, waiting patiently on the mountain slope. No wonder he'd been both distracted and so grumpy when he met me.

"I'd have to be blind not to notice your blossoming attraction, but I did not expect you and Noric would fall in love," Eligius said. "You've always shunned the idea, and he hadn't been keen to—"

"Spy on me for you," I said, crossing my arms. "I know."

Eligius almost looked sheepish. Almost.

"We've realized it's pointless to try to keep the knowledge from you any longer."

"Because I'm going to die for what I've already learned anyway?" I asked, gripping my neck on instinct.

"Because the two of you cannot truly love if there are lies between you."

Oh.

Seeing my blushes my father said, "I'm going to step aside and let Noric take over for the next part."

Eligius quickly disappeared. I had no idea where he'd gone but figured he waited nearby, while Noric walked back up the mountain.

Licking my lips, I looked up and asked, "Did you force my father to tell me?"

Noric smiled on one side of his mouth. "We've been arguing about it. Not necessarily on opposite sides, just considering the pros and cons."

"I would have liked a say in this debate," I remarked tightly.

"I know," Noric replied in a deep, resigned voice. "Ava, I can give you almost anything in this world, including the whole truth of it. But the decision on whether or not to tell you wasn't something I could share, at least not initially."

I blinked. *Initially?*

"If you'd rather not know what Eligius told you, some or all of it, I can obscure your memory. It's safer that way. Should your name ever appear in the Book, there is nothing I can do at that point to reverse it."

"No," I protested, taking a step back and covering my head like it helped. Now that I knew the truth, the idea of having lies in our relationship was unbearable. A wall would exist between us, one where only he would be aware of its existence. "No, swear you will never tamper with my mind."

Noric raised his hands in a surrender motion. "I will not ever. Unless you want me to now."

"No, I want to *know*," I cried. It didn't matter the risk, I wanted to know everything, foolish girl that I was. Noric had been right when he'd said it. I was like some careless explorer opening an ancient, cursed tomb, simply because she had to see what was inside. No—I was like Pandora herself, and I couldn't close the box any more than she could.

Correction… I *wouldn't*. And anyway, hope had escaped and that was a good thing. Right?

"What do *you* want?" I asked, tentatively.

"I want you," Noric declared, impassioned. "And I've been terrified that you'll choose to forget and terrified that you won't. I've hated myself for not making the decision for you and hated myself when I tried to."

I scowled, hating the idea of losing control over my own mind.

Noric licked his lips, considering. "Given that the gods have already sent that wispinger though, I don't think knowing any more or less makes too much of a difference now."

A shiver ran through me.

"Can I talk to my father again?" I asked.

Instantly, Death appeared, and Noric strolled down the mountain once more, giving us privacy though I hadn't requested it.

"I told Noric that I want to know everything," I said, just to be sure we were all firm on my decision. "So what's the plan now?"

"I admit, I do not have a good one," Eligius replied, rubbing his cheek and scanning the mountains like they might have a solution. "I've tried seeking out aberrations, but Vasilios is the oldest ikavorn I know, and he cannot help. It's been months since I received the wispinger, and nothing has happened yet—but such a timespan is mere minutes to the gods. This game of theirs may be designed solely to make me worry for nothing. There is no telling, when it comes to the overlords and their whims."

"So we wait and hope? How very mortal."

How much time did I have left? Or father? *Or any of us, if some kind of reset was coming?*

I glanced nervously at Noric, who looked hauntingly beautiful perched on the slope and framed by the setting sun. I bounced on my feet a little, which caused Eligius to laugh.

"Go to him. Nothing is likely to be resolved today, at any rate."

I kissed my father lightly on his cold, pale cheek, and raced to my reaper. Before he could ask questions, I laid a finger on his lips.

"That's more than enough talking for now, I absolutely *cannot* process any more information. Not only do I need to digest all this, I need some actual food. Can we go inside and eat?"

Noric pulled me into his embrace. "I've got a better idea."

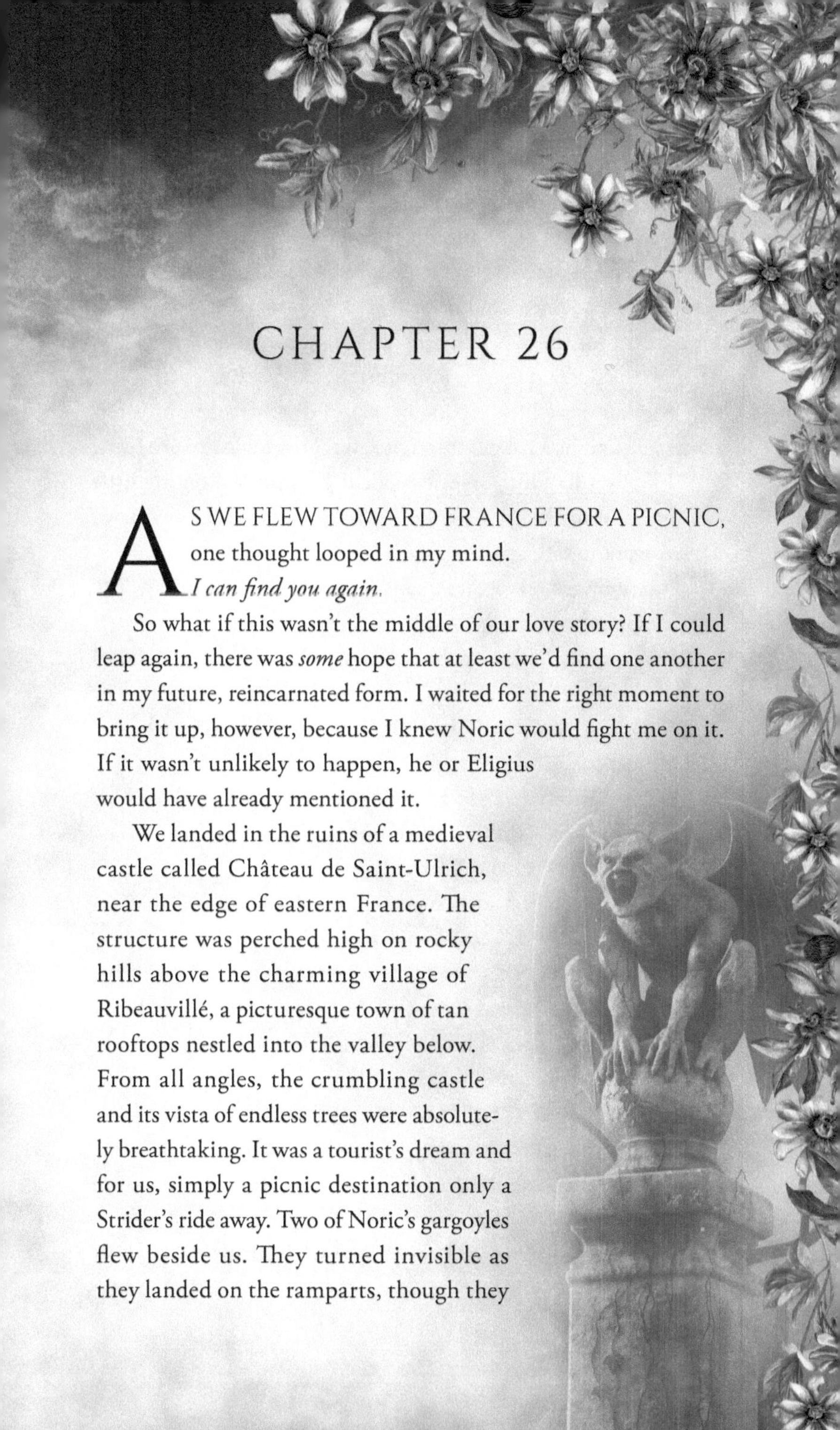

CHAPTER 26

AS WE FLEW TOWARD FRANCE FOR A PICNIC, one thought looped in my mind. *I can find you again.*

So what if this wasn't the middle of our love story? If I could leap again, there was *some* hope that at least we'd find one another in my future, reincarnated form. I waited for the right moment to bring it up, however, because I knew Noric would fight me on it. If it wasn't unlikely to happen, he or Eligius would have already mentioned it.

We landed in the ruins of a medieval castle called Château de Saint-Ulrich, near the edge of eastern France. The structure was perched high on rocky hills above the charming village of Ribeauvillé, a picturesque town of tan rooftops nestled into the valley below. From all angles, the crumbling castle and its vista of endless trees were absolutely breathtaking. It was a tourist's dream and for us, simply a picnic destination only a Strider's ride away. Two of Noric's gargoyles flew beside us. They turned invisible as they landed on the ramparts, though they wouldn't have looked entirely out of place if they remained seen. The air, much warmer than the Carpathians, motivated me to remove my shrug, revealing a lacey white bralette underneath.

"I bet you know stories of the lords, ladies, servants and stablemasters who once lived here," I said, leaning back. Some light remained, but the sun had already set, keeping visitors at bay. Though the sky said *dinner,* my stomach said *lunch.* Moments like this were always a little jarring because I'd only woken up a few hours ago and had passed through several time zones since then.

"I knew a handful," Noric replied, gaze pinned on my little bra-top. I bat my lashes. "But I don't want to talk about that now. I don't want to talk at all."

As he climbed on top of me, I playfully pushed him away. "My mortal appetite demands food first."

We took a seat on one of the castle's rough, old walls, and shared a meal of tête de moine, a baguette, and thick slices of some type of dried meat. Noric had picked it all up from the village below, including a crisp white Sancerre to wash it down with.

As dusk kissed the castle, I couldn't help but ask wistfully, "Were there dragons too? Did they exist, once upon a time?"

Noric's face lit up and I gasped.

"That must have been something," I said, wide-eyed. "What were they like? I wish I could have seen it."

"No, you don't. They were far more dangerous than even the stories make out," he said seriously. "Although, if you were able to hatch a baby, there was a fifty-fifty shot it would bond to you. In that case, yes, you could ride it. But the odds that another dragon might burn you off its back were even worse."

"I'll bet you rode a dragon," I remarked, envious.

His grin was diabolical. "Of course. Sevastian and I used to race them."

"Were you made to cull the dragons?" I asked, sadly. "Like the unicorns?"

"No," Noric replied, smile quickly fading. "Whether they were unsanctioned or experimental, I don't know, but they died out on their own. The last…" he trailed off. "The last one roared and roared for a mate he never found. You could hear it for miles, shaking the very earth."

"Oh god," I put down my bread, unable to stomach it. "That's one of the saddest things I've ever heard."

"You've reaped mortals alongside your father for years, seeing all kinds of grief and horror, but *that's* one of the saddest things?" he asked, eyebrow quirked.

"Well, you have to admit there's something particularly awful about being the last of your kind and not knowing it, of never having the possibility to find a partner."

A shadow passed over Noric's face and I realized that both his and Sevastian's fates weren't too dissimilar. Not for the first time, I wondered if Eligius wanted a partner or if he didn't have the desire at all. It was an awkward conversation to have, his being my father.

"Now that you know the truth of the world, how do you feel about it?" Noric asked.

"I don't know," I admitted, taking a swig of wine. "Other than wishing I'd been alive to see the mermaids and the unicorns—and wanting to steer clear of these vampire creatures, since I have no hope of being one," I added ruefully. "I'm going to need a lot more time to process it."

"I've had eons, and I still don't know the *why* of it," Noric confessed, looking to the rolling green hills that stretched for miles and running a hand through his hair. I'd once thought it floppy and now I found it terribly sexy, especially when it fell carelessly over his forehead, obscuring his eyebrows, or when he slicked it back. "Your father sees reason, patterns. But sometimes I wonder if it's all a game, a kind of distraction in the Above. A dream within a dream," he mused, reaching over to stroke my cheek. His words jarred the memory of what we'd said the night we first kissed—about true love and waking up. Had he wanted to tell me then?

"Maybe that's why there's repeat leapers," Noric theorized, "something like adrenaline junkies or gaming addicts, falling over and over."

Noric's words jogged yet another memory, this time of lyrics I'd once heard.

"Do you know the old song *Free Falling?*" I asked tentatively. "By Tom Petty?"

He grinned and to my relief he said, "Oh, he at least had *some* recollection. I'm surprised those taunting lyrics didn't get him reaped right away, but perhaps the gods liked his music too much."

I tried recalling the words to the song but could only remember a bit of the chorus.

"A famous musician," I mused, cutting up more bread and cheese. "What are the odds?"

"Actually, pretty good," Noric replied. "Most people who try to tell the truth are artists."

"Or madmen," I said, shrugging.

"Or both."

"So artist or madwoman?" I wondered aloud. "What does that make me?"

Noric grabbed my hips and pulled me to him. "Mine."

We were so close I could smell the wild reaper on him. When my laughter died, I asked, "So if we're reincarnated, don't you think there's a chance we could meet again?"

Noric's eyes fluttered shut. "I *knew* you were going to ask that."

"Of course I am!"

"Ava, I don't know the souls I reap or who they were in the past. I can only feel when someone has leapt often, or not, which is pretty meaningless. Even if you jumped again, you'd be setting us up for disappointment. You will not remember, you will not find me. Humans retaining even a hint of memory is rarer than those turning spectre. And there are billions of people in this world. I cannot magically look into the eyes of each and recognize you. But if you insist on trying…" He gritted his teeth. "Ava, it would be like when someone loses a loved one and they don't know what happens. The *not knowing* drives them to madness. There is peace in accepting the truth, even if it is a terrible one. I'd rather know *you're* at peace in the Above, than jumping to what could likely be a life of suffering down here, with no chance of us finding one another."

I sighed and bit my tongue. Noric understood how it worked better than I did, and I wouldn't put him through an eternity of false hope that would drive him insane. But I knew the topic wasn't over for me, because I still wanted to find some kind of miracle through it.

"Okay," I whispered, laying my hand on his.

A full moon shone by the time we finished our meal. Noric tidied up and I bolted into the depths of the ruins. I hid for Noric to come and find me, wondering if hundreds of years prior medieval men and women played similar games in this very same spot. Tipsy from Sancerre, I giggled so much I practically gave away my position, but I hid again, telling Noric that he'd earn a kiss each time he caught me. I was blissfully happy as we loved like this—beneath a blanket of stars, hiding and running and chasing and kissing. Once, Noric brought the bottle of wine with him and when he caught me, he poured it onto my shoulders while I squealed and laughed as he licked it off.

Eventually, giddy on love and Sancerre and French moonlight, I climbed the steps of the box-shaped tower and stood on the wall. Searching for me, I spied Noric's head of light brown hair darting below.

"Catch me!" I called to him.

He immediately froze and looked up, muscles tensed. I could tell he was going to whisk and prevent me from jumping, so I held up my hands.

"Don't!" I warned. "Catch me, my love, and I'll let you kiss me wherever you want."

Noric immediately took a catching position and I threw my head back as I laughed to the sky. Spreading my arms wide, a thrill raced through me. I trusted Noric completely, but the idea of giving myself to the air was a rush.

With a pounding heart I tipped forward, swan diving to my reaper.

Did leapers feel a similar exhilaration when they jumped? I wondered. *Is that why some souls repeated the game again and again?*

Before I hit the ground Noric easily caught me in his arms.

"My hero," I proclaimed, smiling.

"Oh, I don't think a hero would claim his reward where I plan to."

My breath quickened and I amended, "My dark hero."

Noric laid me down on one of the grassy patches inside the ruins. He bent low and gave me a *frustratingly* single kiss—just one, right on the part of my body that was throbbing for more.

"Until Hallow's Eve," he said, lifting himself up.

I swallowed thickly.

"Until Hallow's Eve," I agreed.

We flew over the Alps and back to Noric's castle, swooping and swan diving as we raced until my sides hurt from laughing. Craving a culling, Noric reaped two mortals in Zurich on our return, and I imagined it must have been a relief for him not to hide his true nature from someone. I neither gawked nor recoiled at his work, having had time to adjust to it. A reaper was a part of the world's ecosystem to me, the same as a bear, a wolf, a lion. I had grown up understanding part of the cycle—how reaping returned a soul to the Above—and it helped even more now that I knew one could leap again.

THROUGHOUT THE REMAINDER of summer, the horsemen and I explored the world together. Not even the richest billionaire on earth could travel as we did, or enter the exclusive clubs we slipped into, or have any food craving satisfied in such a short time. It was magical.

When September came to Solebury, the warm weather lingered, and people carried themselves differently now, as if the carefree days of summer were over and they had to quickly get down to the serious business of fall. Yet some, sensing the imminent closure of those sweet days, of hot beaches and sunny barbeques, whipped themselves into a final frenzy to squeeze every last citrusy drop from the season. Noric and I people-watched couples and families as they shared one last lemon ice cream by the river, or lazed on skiff boats below, one foot dipped into the waters. The air carried a bittersweet anticipation of autumn, an almost palpable charge, with the faint hint of fall whispering on breezes down the Sourland Mountains.

I loved autumn the same way I loved twilight, for the splendor of its enchanted, in-between nature. Transitionary, fleeting, ephemeral. The riot of colors that would soon burst onto the trees and over the hillsides were like nature's terminal lucidity—a phenomenon in which a dying mortal re-gained clarity and renewed energy in their final moments before the very end.

Noric and I were on a random walk, halfway across the bridge connecting the river towns, when the moment struck me as perfect for no specific reason.

I closed my eyes and tried to capture it, to sear it into my memory. I felt the sun's warm rays on my cheeks and the cool river breeze on my forehead. I heard the crank from the metal bridge as cars slowly rolled alongside us. I inhaled deeply, smelling the valley.

It wasn't just this moment. I knew every moment of that summer—that entire year since I'd met the horsemen—would hold a treasured place in my heart for as long as I lived.

Even if that wasn't a long time, relative to a reaper.

CHAPTER 27

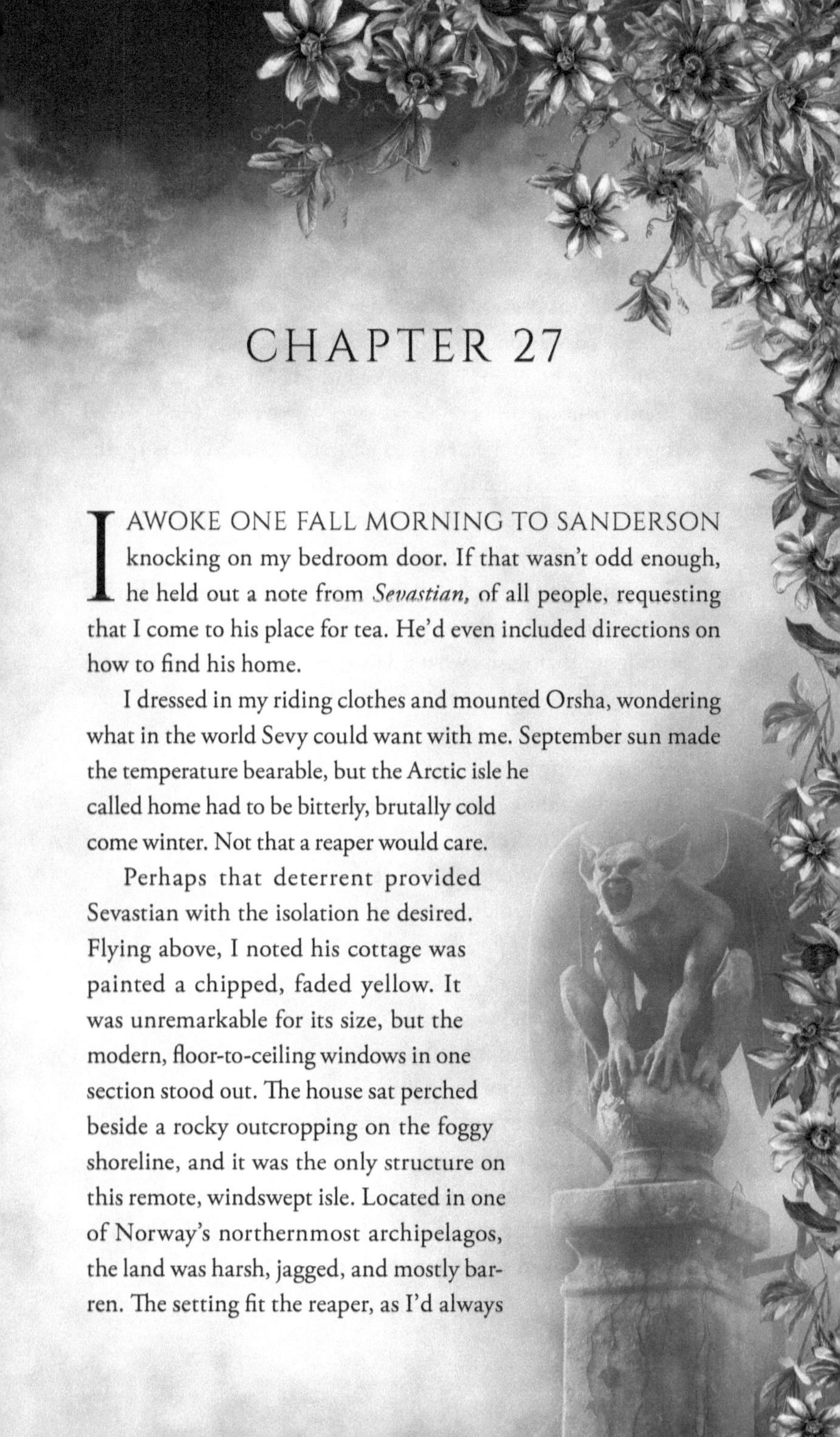

I AWOKE ONE FALL MORNING TO SANDERSON knocking on my bedroom door. If that wasn't odd enough, he held out a note from *Sevastian,* of all people, requesting that I come to his place for tea. He'd even included directions on how to find his home.

I dressed in my riding clothes and mounted Orsha, wondering what in the world Sevy could want with me. September sun made the temperature bearable, but the Arctic isle he called home had to be bitterly, brutally cold come winter. Not that a reaper would care.

Perhaps that deterrent provided Sevastian with the isolation he desired. Flying above, I noted his cottage was painted a chipped, faded yellow. It was unremarkable for its size, but the modern, floor-to-ceiling windows in one section stood out. The house sat perched beside a rocky outcropping on the foggy shoreline, and it was the only structure on this remote, windswept isle. Located in one of Norway's northernmost archipelagos, the land was harsh, jagged, and mostly bar-ren. The setting fit the reaper, as I'd always thought Sevastian looked like a Viking god, or at least a Nordic prince of ancient legend. The very air held secrets in a place like this, and why I'd been summoned was an equal mystery to me.

As I landed, Sevastian held his front door open in a wordless welcome. He was dressed in mortal attire—tan pants and a shirt that I believed was once bright white but had begun to gray. It wasn't slovenly, however. As I walked inside I noted his attire fit the slightly nautical décor of his cottage, where everything seemed weathered and worn, beaten into new shapes and colors by the waves and the wind and the passage of time.

"Your house is enchanting, Sevastian," I remarked, truthfully. "And the solitude must bring you peace."

"I live here for the light," he said, closing the door. "The sun won't set again until summer's end."

The light? That wasn't what I'd imagined. If anything, I'd have thought Sevastian preferred it here for the never-ending dark once winter arrived.

Perhaps seeing some surprise on my face, he ordered, "Follow me. I thought it time I shed some light on… other things."

I trailed behind the fair reaper as he led me into the central room of the small house, which appeared to be a crowded art gallery. Beyond, I could see the modern section with its massive windows, but here, only a few sconces along the walls provided a soft, warm glow.

Craning my neck, I took in the artwork cramming the wall space from the floorboards to the ceiling. Every technique imaginable was utilized—small sketches and pencil illustrations, large watercolors, oil paintings of all sizes and various types of mixed media. The styles ranged from realist, to impressionist, to abstract, to so many others I couldn't name. It was the work of a mad genius, over and over…

…and all depicting the same face in thousands of different ways.

Sevastian looked at me, resigned, and I asked the question he knew I would.

"Who is she?"

The blonde reaper crossed to a charcoal sketch at eye level. He stroked his thumb across the girl's face as if he were caressing the cheekbone of a real-life woman.

"Her name was Zosime, but that's not what you want to know. You want to know what she was to me. And I think you already have the answer."

"You loved her," I whispered. If the obsessive gallery wasn't proof enough, the grief on his face gave it away. Who was this captivating woman? Exceedingly beautiful, she had the look of an ancient princess, and her proud eyes spoke of nobility.

Sevastian's only confirmation was a heavy sigh. "I will tell you, and then maybe you will understand why you are the worst thing to ever happen to Noric."

I flinched. His words stung because there was truth to them, and I didn't know how much.

"Like countless others, Zosime was born a slave on a farm in Ancient Greece," Sevastian began, quickly dispelling my fanciful notions of royalty. "As she grew her beauty became her curse. Her master saw the potential and did not touch her. Instead, he brought Zosime to Athens and sold her. The nobleman who bought her paid a high price. To earn it back, she was made to labor during the day as the rest of the slaves did—scrubbing floors, washing linens, preparing meals. And the nights… he used her or loaned her out for coin or favor. It's a wonder she didn't get pregnant, but her body suffered such trauma she didn't...." Sevastian trailed off, and I wondered if he wanted to say she didn't menstruate.

"Hers was a miserable existence, but she never gave herself up to despair. Whenever Zosime found an opportunity for escape, she'd attempt to take it, even though she was inevitably caught and punished. Like most of her time she was deeply religious, and beneath her barred window she prayed to many gods. Often, she called upon the highest authority to save her, Zeus, her namesake."

Sevastian shuffled over to another image now, this one a framed oil painting in the Renaissance style. Zosime's hair, a golden sunset kissed by a sparkling reddish hue, flowed over her shoulders and down her bare breasts. Her eyes were a remarkable light teal. Her face was softly heart-shaped and her body lithe. Artfully draped silks and the bend of one leg covered her intimate regions, and she sat in a meadow. A dandelion in the different stages of life arced in a semi-circle above her head. First came the full yellow flower evoking the sun, then the white puff of the moon, and finally, a cascade of blowing seeds representing the stars. The painting was slightly reminiscent of the famous *Birth of Venus,* where Aphrodite emerged from the sea upon a clamshell.

"It wasn't Zeus or any other golden, shining god who heard and answered her prayers one night, but a dark master of death. Me."

Ever so lightly, Sevastian's fingertips traced the cascade of Zosime's hair in the meadow painting.

Confirming my thoughts, he said, "She looked like Aphrodite, come to walk the earth, but it was her perseverance that intrigued me, mesmerized me. Her *fire.* It matched mine, in those days. No matter what they did to her, she never stopped looking for a way to escape, even when she had nothing at her disposal but whispered hope."

Sevy's eyes briefly fluttered shut. Drawing away from the art, he fisted his hand, as if he had to force himself.

"Keeping my true nature secret, I saved her as a mortal man. Well, maybe with a bit more skill," Sevastian admitted, amusement curving his lips. "I snuck into her master's house, slayed him and his guards, and carried her away. Together we rode a regular horse, beyond the city and further still. Regardless of my human efforts, Zosime believed me to be the son of a god, and I let her. Better that than her knowing some of the truth and losing her life for it. I wore a mask I never removed, covering all but the lower third of my face. They said a god's true beauty was too much for a mortal to see, so I let that be the reason. We rode past what she called *the edge of the known world* but was just a forest deep within what would become Eastern Europe. I'd built a tower there and I placed her in it, with my drasyg to guard the base. It might have," Sevastian shook his head ruefully, "given rise to the legends about princesses locked away in towers and guarded by dragons, to those who caught glimpses."

"But Zosime wasn't imprisoned," he said. "She could leave any time she desired and, safely flanked by my drasyg—though unbeknownst to her—she often did."

Scanning the crowded gallery, I saw a few pieces depicting the familiars along with Zosime.

"I stayed away most days to curb the urge to cull her, but I returned each evening, always wearing my mask. I didn't want to—" Sevastian cut himself off, gritting his teeth and lowering his eyes.

"I desired her, of course I desired her." He bit out the words with a heated, hungry edge, as if he tried to restrain himself even now. "But I was afraid that after what she'd been through the touch of a man would horrify her. Time passed and we got to know one another the way any couple does—albeit with more lies on my part. I taught her to hunt and to defend herself. She taught me to paint and to…" Sevastian trailed off, catching his breath.

"She wore less and less until one night I arrived and found her sleeping naked in bed, covered only by the hair trailing down her body and falling to the sides of her breasts." Sevastian's eyes glazed, as desirous as if his beautiful Zosime was naked before him in his cottage now. "I didn't want to but…"

He paused so long I thought Sevastian re-imagined parts of their first time in bed together.

Finally, I prompted softly, "But you did."

He clenched his jaw and agreed, "I did."

"From thereafter I came to her each night, not by a mortal horse but through a reaper's whisking, appearing as if by divine magic on her windowsill. Part of me thought that I did it to put up a barrier between us, since one had broken down—to further her belief that I was the son of some god. And another part of me thought I did it for the opposite reason—to share a genuine piece of myself with her. I still don't know which."

Sevastian tucked his pale blonde hair behind his ear and paused again. I didn't interrupt, desperate to hear the rest of his tale.

"Even when I removed my clothing, I never removed the mask. Months passed and I still wore it whenever I took her to bed. Then, one night, at exactly the moment of greatest pleasure when my reflexes were otherwise engaged and I was just a hair too slow to stop her, she tore off my mask."

Sevastian shook his head, yet he smiled at the memory.

"If this story sounds familiar to you it's because over the years, I think word spread through the broken whispers of travelers. I was gone for long periods during which Zosime befriended a few nomads, and it's possible our story inspired myths like Eros and Psyche. Especially because, in the early days, I often hunted in the woods with a bow and arrow, trying to maintain some pretense of humanity."

Especially because, I thought wryly, *your fair beauty makes you look like a Greek God.*

"The night she ripped away my mask, I broke down and told her everything. She didn't believe I was a reaper, so I took her upon Nyctaeus's back as we flew across the sky, killing and escorting souls into Elysia."

A tea kettle whistled, stopping Sevastian in his tale and making me jump. Enraptured, I'd forgotten all about the pretense for my visit. He left the room and returned with two steaming cups of black tea. I took one politely, though neither of us drank.

"Months turned into years. Happy is too weak a word to convey what we felt. I'm afraid none of the modern languages have the right word at all, nor the ancient ones. We existed in a state beyond bliss, tainted only by my worry the overlords would take her from me. But, as you know, time moves differently in the Above. A year to us is but an hour to them. So I hoped perhaps they wouldn't notice."

Sevastian stared at his tea as if debating, then took a long, slow sip. Nervous, I shifted my weight. He'd never been so nice to me, let alone this open before, and as much as I was interested in his past I was a little wary of the softening as well. A blow had to be forthcoming.

"Of course, even if they did not take her soon, there was no happy end possible. Being torn apart was an inevitability and the craving to cull Zosime grew more powerful, intensified by my passion for her. She saw my deathlust and it scared us both, especially whenever it spiked as we were… in bed together." Sevastian winced, then continued, "Unlike you, Zosime wasn't new to the earth, she'd leapt a few times before. I didn't even know who she really was in the Above. Part of me was comforted by the fact that when she returned there, she might find happiness reuniting with her true life, and part of me hated it with every fiber of my being."

Sevastian looked so tired and forlorn as he spoke; his misery compounded through centuries of heartache. I wished there was something I could do, a way to dull his pain. I supposed the only thing possible to help was to leave Noric, so that his friend wouldn't be subjected to the same fate. And that was the only thing in the world I couldn't do.

"Then the awful day came when her name appeared suddenly in the Book, though she was only thirty-two," Sevastian declared, nostrils flaring as he snarled. "It was a clouded death, so I had no information to fight it. Not that I ever could. I was wild with fear and rage in the time leading up to it. On that fateful day I locked Zosime and myself in the tower, brought all my drasyg to guard the base, and removed everything within that might injure her. I smoothed and sanded every splinter of wood and hammered down each nail. I barred the windows and checked every loose stone. I watched her like a hawk for any signs of illness—a sudden heart attack, spontaneous combustion—my mind ran wild with possibilities. But Zosime seemed in perfect health as the minutes ticked down. She was anxious, of course, but that was to be expected, given the proclamation of her imminent death."

Sevastian swallowed thickly. "Nothing and no one could get in to hurt her."

"But," I breathed, when his pause ran overlong, "something did."

Sevastian laughed mirthlessly. "No, I was right. No one could get her. No one *else,* at least."

My eyes rounded with horror, but Sevastian shook his head at the idea.

"I didn't reap her," he rushed to insist, both pained and angry at the idea. "Although my sword did." Sevastian's haunted eyes were unfocused, as if gazing upon the scene. He choked out the words as he spoke, "Zosime kissed me. She told me to come for her, to find her. To demand of the gods that we be united in eternal love. I didn't know what she was talking about. Then she grabbed the blade of my sword and fell instantly dead on the floor."

"Oh, Sevastian," I cried. I had to swallow a lump in my throat to get the next words out and my eyes welled with tears. "I'm so sorry."

But Sevastian laughed darkly, sending chills up my spine. "You think that's the worst of it? If only."

Knitting my brow, I meant to ask, *what do you mean? What happened next?* But one painting caught my attention and I gasped. Amongst the thousands of images depicting the same woman, one artwork alone was of a different girl. Her face was partially obscured by other pictures tacked around it, so I could only make out her eyes and parts of her hair and face. Those eyes reminded me of Zosime, but the face was a bit different. Who was she?

"Why is one girl different from the rest?" I asked.

Noric's sudden appearance beside me made me squeal, then

scowl. The immortal method of whisking into a room wasn't easy to get used to. He was dressed in all-black reaper attire, coming straight from work.

"That's enough for now," Sevastian declared, staring at Noric.

I groaned and cursed Noric's timing, wishing he would have held off for a few more seconds, although I wasn't sure Sevastian would have continued anyway. I did learn much more than I expected, so I was grateful for that.

Noric and Sevastian glared at one another, clearly communicating mind-to-mind. I tried to guess what they were saying from their faces, but I could only tell that it was an argument of some kind.

"Care to share your thoughts with the class?" I asked, folding my arms.

Noric clasped my hand. "School is no longer in session. You've had enough of an education for today."

"Is that so?"

"I am your teacher after all," Noric said, pulling me toward the front door with a temper even shorter than usual. "So yes. If I say class is over, it's over."

Without turning, he gave a brusque wave to Sevastian. He didn't let go of my hand as he led me toward Orsha, who was nosing at the damp earth for something she'd scented. Orphnaeus waited stoically nearby, leathered wings folded. They were hauntingly beautiful here, two dark, magical creatures against the misty gray landscape.

"I'd rather be Sevastian's student for today," I said with annoyance. "If you don't mind."

"I do mind and what's more I forbid it."

I barked a humorless laugh. "Is that how this goes? You make the decisions and the rest of us fall in line? You are not *my* high reaper, remember."

Noric halted and rubbed his forehead.

"No, I just—"

"Let your overbearing reaper nature overrun me?"

"Sorry," he breathed, shoulders relaxing. "Compromise after all these centuries is a bit of a challenge for me. But now is not the time to delve into Sevastian's past."

"Fine, just tell me one thing," I said, relenting. "There was only one painting of a girl who wasn't Zosime. Not exactly, but close. Was she a daughter?"

"No," Noric answered firmly. "Reapers cannot have children. You know this."

"Then who?"

Noric sighed deeply before answering. "She was Zosime. Her true form in Elysia."

I gasped, covering my mouth. *Sevastian saw* her. *So there was a way. If Sevastian and Zosime were reunited in the Above somehow, then there was hope for Noric and I.*

"So Sevastian did it? He was able to find her there—the gods allowed it?" I asked in a rush. "What happened?"

"Contrary to what you believe, I did not forbid Sevastian from telling you," Noric bit out. "We argued, he changed his mind, and now I can't betray my brother and tell you something he's not ready to share."

Convenient. I shot Noric a look of displeasure and crossed my arms again. "You mean you persuaded him and now he's in agreement so you can use that as your excuse."

"It's not my secret to tell."

"But—"

"But it's not something the gods will allow again and it didn't work out anyway. See? This is why I didn't want you prying. Put it from your mind, Ava."

Noric lifted me onto Orsha's back like I was a curious child he handled; one he wanted to distract from something dangerous.

I could admit I *was* a bit distracted by the grace and power of his own body as he slung himself onto Orphnaeus, and especially by his next words.

"Halloween is only six weeks away," he announced. "Do you have any guesses yet as to where we're going?"

Heat coursed through my body but I scolded, "Just because your change in subject is working doesn't mean I don't know that's exactly what you're doing."

Noric grinned like the devil, making me want to push him off his Strider's back, but it also made me want to climb on top of him once I did. We flew back to New Hope at a leisurely pace, and I pelted Noric with guesses of locations all over the world.

But to each he only laughed and shook his head.

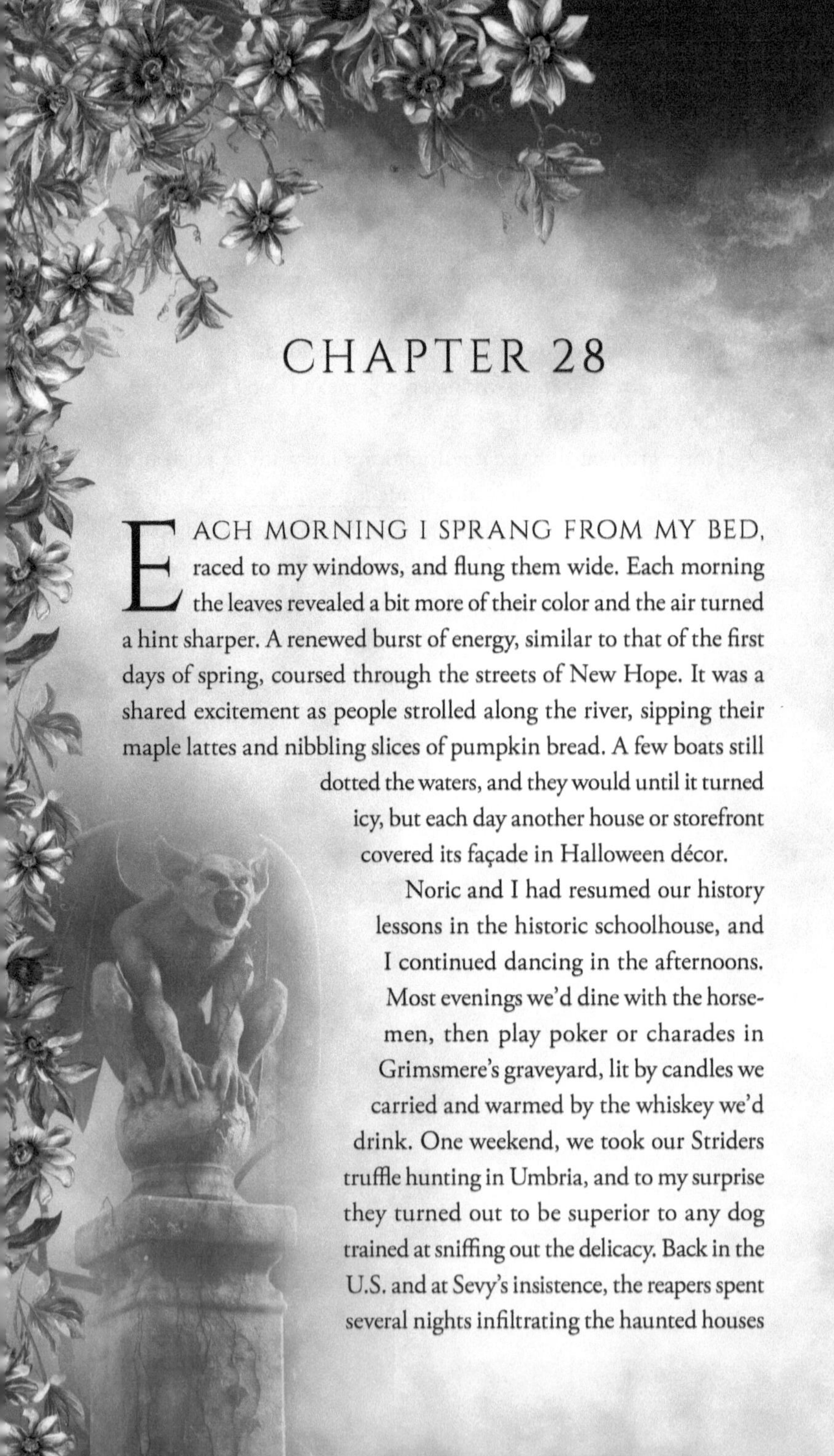

CHAPTER 28

EACH MORNING I SPRANG FROM MY BED, raced to my windows, and flung them wide. Each morning the leaves revealed a bit more of their color and the air turned a hint sharper. A renewed burst of energy, similar to that of the first days of spring, coursed through the streets of New Hope. It was a shared excitement as people strolled along the river, sipping their maple lattes and nibbling slices of pumpkin bread. A few boats still dotted the waters, and they would until it turned icy, but each day another house or storefront covered its façade in Halloween décor.

Noric and I had resumed our history lessons in the historic schoolhouse, and I continued dancing in the afternoons. Most evenings we'd dine with the horsemen, then play poker or charades in Grimsmere's graveyard, lit by candles we carried and warmed by the whiskey we'd drink. One weekend, we took our Striders truffle hunting in Umbria, and to my surprise they turned out to be superior to any dog trained at sniffing out the delicacy. Back in the U.S. and at Sevy's insistence, the reapers spent several nights infiltrating the haunted houses scattered throughout the country. It was all in good fun, he swore, as they used their magic to scare the living daylights out of guests on a level no mortals could ever achieve, applying gory party tricks which had people screaming horrifically and running for the exits.

The world truly was a reaper's playground, and sometimes I laughed so hard I'd fall onto the grass, clutching my stomach and fighting for air.

A week before Halloween, Eligius asked us to reap a lamb for Sanderson to cook for the holiday, and Noric and I whisked to a nearby farm.

"Would you like to choose or should I?" he asked, stalking menacingly through the pasture.

I shivered at the image. What was I to him truly, but a human for the hunting? If I hadn't been Eligius's adopted daughter, I thought again, Noric could have randomly reaped me some day.

And inevitably, when my death came… he would.

I scanned the lamb pen with regret. Though I enjoyed a variety of animal meat, the furry little creatures were so cute, and it was a grisly experience to choose which I would eat.

"You'll leave enough money to compensate the farmer?" I asked, stalling.

Noric nodded.

"That one," I said, pointing at random. "But save one for the one you kill. Bring it to a sanctuary somewhere?"

Noric nodded again, and I watched as he culled the creature quicker and more painlessly than any human could.

The weather was crisp when Hallow's Eve finally arrived, carrying the scent of moss and oak from outside the house, and spiced cider and caramel apples from the kitchen. On the trees beneath my window, vermillion tipped the leaves' edges and spread inward, like parchment lit aflame, scorching the perimeter and burning across the page.

Though I stayed inside to get ready, I knew that New Hope would be a bustle of activity, with people dressed in costumes dipping into shops before jockeying to find a seat at a bar or a restaurant. Halloween soundtracks would play *everywhere* and that thrilling, spooky atmosphere I loved would spread like beacons lit along the Delaware, from one river town to the next.

Inevitably, Archibald and Yvette would spirit off to a party at one of the historic hotels later in the evening, or to Fonthill, but they always joined us for our customary feast beforehand.

Henry, the man who'd built Fonthill Castle, had a suspicion of the ghostly realm before he died. He'd arranged for his estate to be turned into a museum, wanting mortals out of his residence in the evenings, should he turn spectre. It was a gamble that paid off. Now, my ghostly parents frequently joined him for cards down at one of the river inns or back at his manor. Like other artists, Henry even left hints of the truth by setting his motto into fireplace mantles and throughout his castle—*plus ultra*—Latin for *more beyond.*

Olga wouldn't be joining us, however, because she was usually asleep by dinnertime. Sometimes, however, she wandered the house in her ruffled white nightgown, mumbling nonsense before turning in for the night.

Realizing it was now mere hours until I had sex was an electrifying thought. I'd yet to uncover the question of *where* Noric planned to have our first time. The possibilities were as limitless as the world itself, and my heart thumped with anticipation.

Digging into the back of my closet, I found the outfit I'd ordered after a long, nail-biting search online.

The red-and-black bodice wasn't a true corset, but close enough. I squeezed myself into the tight fit and carefully worked each hook-and-eye closure until the garment was practically sealed to my skin. Then I sucked in a deep breath and turned it around until the closures made a line down back and the cups faced forward. The bra section was underwire and padded, giving me a chest where I had none. I pulled on the thong underwear and hooked the black garter belt around my waist, but attaching the garter to the hosiery was a challenge. One strap ran down the front of my thighs and the other down the back, but it was difficult to get it straight without a lot of trial and error, twisting and turning to check the effect. I ruined three stockings by snagging them on my nails before I managed to get it right.

This type of lingerie was more difficult than most of my ballet costumes, and that was saying something.

By the time I'd finished dressing I'd broken out in a light sweat. I plopped onto the bed without care, which only popped one of the godforsaken garter attachments off the stocking and I had to redo that one.

I felt sexy though, minus the pressure on my lungs, the scratching on my skin, and the constant fear of one of the stocking attachments snapping off again. I was thankful that I didn't live in a time when anything like this required daily attire.

But was this Noric's kind of hot? He'd lived forever, so maybe he preferred an entirely different style of lingerie. I frowned. What if he longed for something I hadn't even considered, like girdles or pantaloons or garments even further back? I should have asked him some probing questions, but I'd wanted to surprise him the same way he was going to surprise me with the location.

I put on the black wrap-dress I'd set aside, then I pulled one small section of my hair back with a ruby clip Yvette had given me, leaving the rest long and loose. After finishing my makeup, I walked down our main, grand staircase, and my pulse raced faster with each step. I could already hear the Dark Classical setlist—songs we played each Halloween like *Danse Macabre* and *The Hall of the Mountain King.*

Noric was waiting in the dining room and he stood when I entered, gentlemanly manners forged in a time past. I let out a small gasp at both him and the décor.

My reaper wore all black and had slicked back his hair, which had the dual effect of both making it darker and accentuating the sharp, sinful beauty of his face. He seemed perfectly suited to the dining room's aesthetic, where Sanderson had outdone himself.

A gothic, medieval tablescape had been laid forth with the richest reds and purples. Pomegranates and dark grapes spilled from silver chalices. Black lilies and deep burgundy dahlias rose from onyx vases. Wicked-looking shards of black tourmaline were scattered about the spread. Black candles flickered at random intervals, providing a haunting glow. Antlers—some attached to skulls, some not—pierced the air along both the table and the fireplace mantle. Already plated was an amuse bouche of brie, figs, and scarlet pomegranate seeds. Lastly, a deep wine was ready to be poured into heavy crystal goblets that looked like they came from a storied estate in Bohemia.

It was a feast Hades would set forth to please his Queen of the Underworld.

The horsemen, father, Archibald and Yvette had already arrived, so I took the last open seat next to Noric. His eyes darkened and I preened both at the reward and at my own power. Noric couldn't know exactly what I wore—he wasn't gifted with x-ray vision after all—but his keen gaze caught the ridges from the corset-bra I couldn't completely conceal.

Leaning into my ear, he whispered, "What are you wearing?"

"Where are we going?" I countered.

"I'll tell you if you tell me."

He'd broken down so easily, I grinned.

"I'll show you when you show me," I retorted, power making me patient. "But trust me, you won't be disappointed."

"You could never disappoint me, Ava," Noric whispered, and I shivered for some reason.

I'd spoken with false bravado because I didn't know if Noric cared for the type of lingerie I wore. I didn't know what he'd truly think of my ballet-beaten body, once he'd had it all on display. And I definitely didn't know if I'd be any good at what we were about to do.

I stopped overthinking when the first course arrived, a persimmon and pomegranate salad. The vibrant red and orange dish looked too pretty to eat, like all of Sanderson's recipes, but I dove in and citrus exploded across my tongue.

The main course was the lamb we'd reaped—spiced, pomegranate lamb legs dripped with the scarlet fruit. It was served on a large silver platter, separate from a secondary one containing the roasted, severed head. The creature's eyeballs were still intact, gory and gourmet.

Our chef placed a smaller, personal plate in front of me.

"Heart of lamb, for the girl who is the beating heart of our house."

I smiled for Sanderson's sake, but I felt a pang in my gut. I wanted nothing more than a heart that didn't require a beat to bear my existence.

Wanting to change the direction of my thoughts, I leaned into Noric and whispered, "Am I your lamb for the slaughter tonight?"

"If you'd like to be," he answered, flashing that diabolical grin that made it hard not to jump into his lap. He leaned into my ear, gripped high on my thigh, and whispered, "Would you like to be consumed, Ava? Shall I devour you then?"

I shivered and managed a breathy, "Yes." Beneath the table, I gripped his powerful thigh in return. "I want nothing more. By you and you alone."

"What are you two whispering about over there?" Embrette called across the table, making me start. She swirled her wine and smirked as if she knew *exactly* what we were saying. And whatever she'd guess was probably close enough.

"Yes, tell us, darling," Yvette added. She toyed with her pearls, smirking knowingly.

Heat spread across my face. Being in a roomful of reapers who'd eternally remember everything you'd ever said and done was anxiety-inducing in a way being amongst mortals couldn't compare.

I cleared my throat and dodged the question. Instead I asked Embrette, "Did you reap anyone interesting today?"

She thought about it for a moment. "A surgeon in the middle of surgery."

"Oh," I said sadly.

"Eh, he was a jerk, the patient was fine, and it really gave his staff a chance to step up."

"Oh. Happy ending then. Well, for some."

"Ain't that the way," Hexley offered, raising his glass. "Death is a horror and a happiness, depending on the perspective."

As the table moved onto the more delicate parts of the lamb, I passed on any. Noric sampled some of the brain—less because I think he had a fondness and more to get a rise out of me. When he failed, he upped the ante by reaching for the eyeballs, but Sevastian and Hexley beat him to it. They must have communicated a silent challenge because the boys lunged forward in unison, racing to see who'd grab the prize. I grimaced as Hexley and Sevastian each tossed an eyeball up into the air and caught it in their mouths like showmen. I heard the *squish* as their teeth bore down, popping it.

The gore didn't particularly bother me, but lamb's eyeballs weren't an aphrodisiac and I didn't want to be thinking about them when I was kissing Noric in bed.

Would I be in a solid bed for our first time? I wondered, hoping he hadn't planned something too outrageous.

Dessert arrived and it was a twist on my favorite. Sanderson had whipped up a pomegranate pavlova, tart and lush. Generous spoonfuls of the arils were piled on top of the airy white meringue, and juices ran down the sides in red rivulets, like blood spilling over a cloud and just as impossibly divine to taste.

My heart thumped wildly as we finished. The days had turned into hours and now I was *minutes* away from my first time in bed with Noric—with anyone.

I was half-listening to my father and Hexley converse about some memory from Porto as they drank their after-dinner port, when the air around Archibald rippled. I blinked, unsure if I was seeing things, then quickly noticed a similarly disturbed haze around Yvette. It was as if the ghostly air they occupied expanded around them and *shifted*.

Archie's face froze in shock, eyes locked on Yvette.

Her blood-curdling scream ripped the room in two.

What in the world was happening?

Yvette tried to clutch the table, but her hands passed through as if it didn't exist. Or as if *she* didn't exist. She tried again and again, failing to connect. *What was happening?* Never in all my years of reaping did I see a face with such horror, and it was matched by Archie's. His hands also failed to connect with anything solid in the real world, as if he'd lost his place in it.

Yvette screamed again and it was a sound I'd never forget.

"Remember me!" Archibald shouted, arm outstretched, ringed fingers splayed. "I'll find you! Remember me!"

"Find me! Find me!" Yvette cried, straining and reaching, but unable to make solid contact with Archie. It was as if a wind-like force held them apart, stronger than any earthly gale, and yet, their hair and clothing only rippled softly behind. The sight was perverse. Archibald's dapper coat flapped elegantly and Yvette's dress billowed prettily, as if the most horrendous event possible wasn't occurring, as if the world had a right to carry on and ignore the pain distorting their faces.

"Take care of Avalia!" Yvette screamed. "We love you, Ava."

Take care of me?

Oh god, no. No, no, no.

I didn't want to believe it, but those words were undeniable.

The overlords were scrubbing this sector and my ghostly parents were being collected.

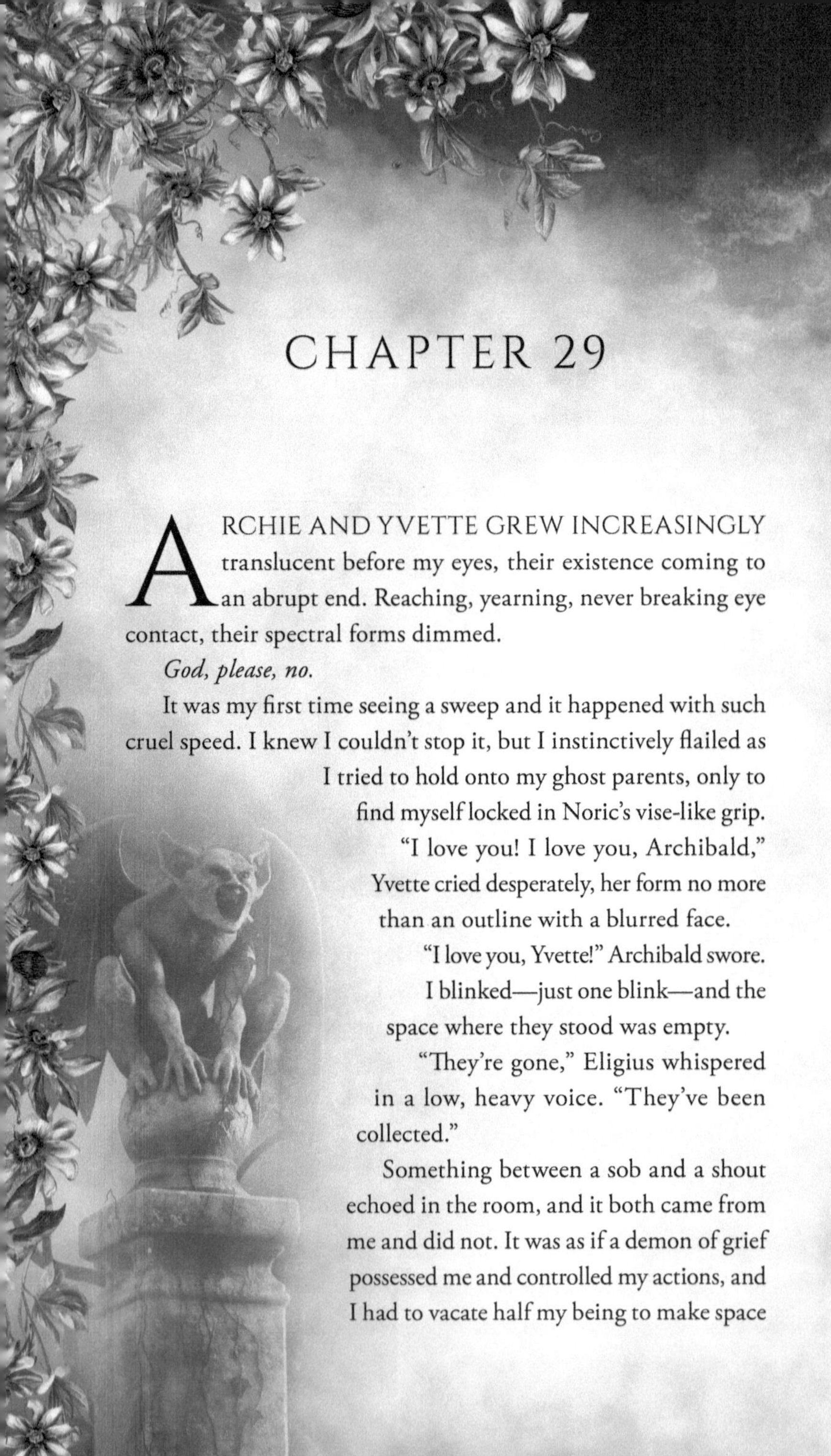

CHAPTER 29

ARCHIE AND YVETTE GREW INCREASINGLY translucent before my eyes, their existence coming to an abrupt end. Reaching, yearning, never breaking eye contact, their spectral forms dimmed.

God, please, no.

It was my first time seeing a sweep and it happened with such cruel speed. I knew I couldn't stop it, but I instinctively flailed as I tried to hold onto my ghost parents, only to find myself locked in Noric's vise-like grip.

"I love you! I love you, Archibald," Yvette cried desperately, her form no more than an outline with a blurred face.

"I love you, Yvette!" Archibald swore.

I blinked—just one blink—and the space where they stood was empty.

"They're gone," Eligius whispered in a low, heavy voice. "They've been collected."

Something between a sob and a shout echoed in the room, and it both came from me and did not. It was as if a demon of grief possessed me and controlled my actions, and I had to vacate half my being to make space for it. I had no power over what tore through my throat. I saw the wood beneath me but didn't remember falling to the floor. Noric's arms held me, but I barely registered them as anything other than restraint when I tried to stand.

They're gone, they're gone, they're gone, my mind repeated the fact but refused to accept it. These weren't human lives to be snuffed in a moment, these were *ghosts.* Here forever, unchanging forever. Here, not gone. Forever. My parents. They couldn't be gone.

Someone was bawling terribly. It couldn't be me, because I didn't cry in front of people, let alone wail with this mucous-laden, scream-cry that put the hysteria of a madman to shame.

I studied my hands as if they could have held Yvette and Archibald to the earth somehow. My hands were useless, I was useless.

Collected. It was done and there was no undoing it. The overlords had claimed my Archibald and Yvette and I would never see them again.

"Get her upstairs," someone said. My father? I felt air beneath me as strong arms swept me up and whisked me into my bedroom. The sudden change made my stomach lurch. All the horsemen stood in a circle around me.

"I can't breathe, I can't breathe," I repeated, tearing at my clothes.

"Leave us," Noric ordered, and the next thing I knew only he and Embrette remained in my room. Skilled hands lifted my limbs and turned me deftly, removing the too-tight lingerie I'd worn and slipping the nearest sleepwear onto my body.

It was the pale pink chemise Yvette had gifted me for my birthday, which only made me wail so hard that I grew too incoherent to explain why I didn't want to wear it.

"Avalia, we're going to give you something to sedate you," Embrette said, making me realize everyone had returned.

Hexley lifted my arm and Noric pierced me with the needle.

It was fast-acting.

I had one coherent thought before I fell asleep.

Archibald and Yvette were a special kind of ghostly light. And they would never again brighten the manor.

THE SKY WEPT violent rain, soaking the earth with grief as it sobbed. Outside my window, trees clung to the last of their leaves, sickly yellows and oranges. Slick, sparse branches held but a few sopping specimens, wind-whipped and dangling precariously. It reminded me of the elderly losing the last strands of hair to reveal the smooth bareness of their skulls underneath.

But trees would regrow their leaves. Elderly humans did not regrow hair. And spectres who'd been collected on a sweep did not return.

My ballet pink room seemed a ridiculously cheerful attempt against the glum outside. I'd existed in this room for days, zombified. I wasn't even scared to know that a real zombie glitch existed somewhere in the world's coding and could happen again at any time. If the undead rose and attacked our manor, I wouldn't fight them. I was already one of them.

Noric would whisk me away to save my life anyway, if that happened. He came with my father, with Hexley and Embrette and even Sevastian. Days turned into weeks as they forced sips of water down my throat and begged me to chew bits of bread. I sat, silent, replaying a lifetime of memories with Achie and Yvette. I was the daughter neither of them had in real life. Did I help bring them joy in their afterlife? *They certainly brought it to each other,* I thought, remembering their decades of lustful side-glances, whispers, and secret smiles.

Their deaths hit me so hard because Archie and Yvette were supposed to be in my life forever. *I* was supposed to die first. Which was backwards for any parent-child relationship, but the way we'd always expected.

I didn't want anyone to talk to me; I knew what they would say. *Be grateful. It's rare for humans to experience a phantom state of being. They lived longer than most, led a richer life than most. Be thankful, Ava. They were lucky, you were lucky, think about the time you had together blah blah blah.*

Without thinking, I threw my balcony doors open to the rain. It wasn't at all like the storm when Noric swept me into the sky for our first kiss. This one was bitter, relentless. A biting wind blasted my face, but it didn't bother me much. I could tell from the forest that it was mid-November, but I hadn't a clue what day exactly. I pressed my body against the railing. The rain soaked me in minutes, and the pale pink slip clung to my wet skin. I stared down at the oaks and maples, helpless to the storm's power. Wind whipped their dark branches and they flailed as if they tried to grip the air, to hold onto anything solid. In a storm this violent, the weaker branches wouldn't make it, and a few trunks might topple as well.

After a time, I slid onto my floor, laid down, and curled into a ball. With the windows open and rain pelting both my body and the hardwood, I fell asleep.

"AVA!" NORIC CRIED, scooping me up into his arms and jarring me awake. "My god, Ava, what were you thinking?" He worked fast, lips tight, while he stripped me out of my wet slip, removed his own long-sleeved shirt, and pulled the soft gray cotton over my head and around my arms. Like a ragdoll, I simply let him dress me, carry me back to the bed, and tuck me under heavy layers of warm goose down.

Noric pressed his hand to my forehead. "Ava, you're burning up! Em, Hexley!" he called in a low, urgent voice, making me think he spoke to them with his mind as well. They whisked into my room a moment later, each in black reaper attire.

"She's got a high fever, at least 103 degrees and likely climbing," Noric announced, voice full of worry.

As he said it, I felt it. A thick, heavy pain in my head and heat throughout my body. Embrette paused, as if mentally checking something. She was. "She's okay, her name's not in the Book," Embrette assured Noric.

Blankets I'd recently hunkered beneath were torn off me, and Noric stripped me of the shirt he'd only just pulled onto my body moments before.

Embrette and Hexley left to give me privacy, while Noric pulled a loose bralette and a pair of underwear onto my body for modesty's sake. The other reapers returned seconds later, carrying medicine and the ice bucket from our bar.

Dizzy, hazy, I swallowed the medicine Noric pressed to my mouth, along with a sip of water. The next thing I knew I was lying on top of my blankets, being rubbed from head to toe with a cold, wet, rag that had the noxious smell of rubbing alcohol.

I found it ironic that Noric pulled me out of the rain only to freeze me with ice water, but I had to admit the cool sensation soothed me. It was as if my skin burned and each pass of the rag helped put out the fire.

I faded back into my haunted dreamland.

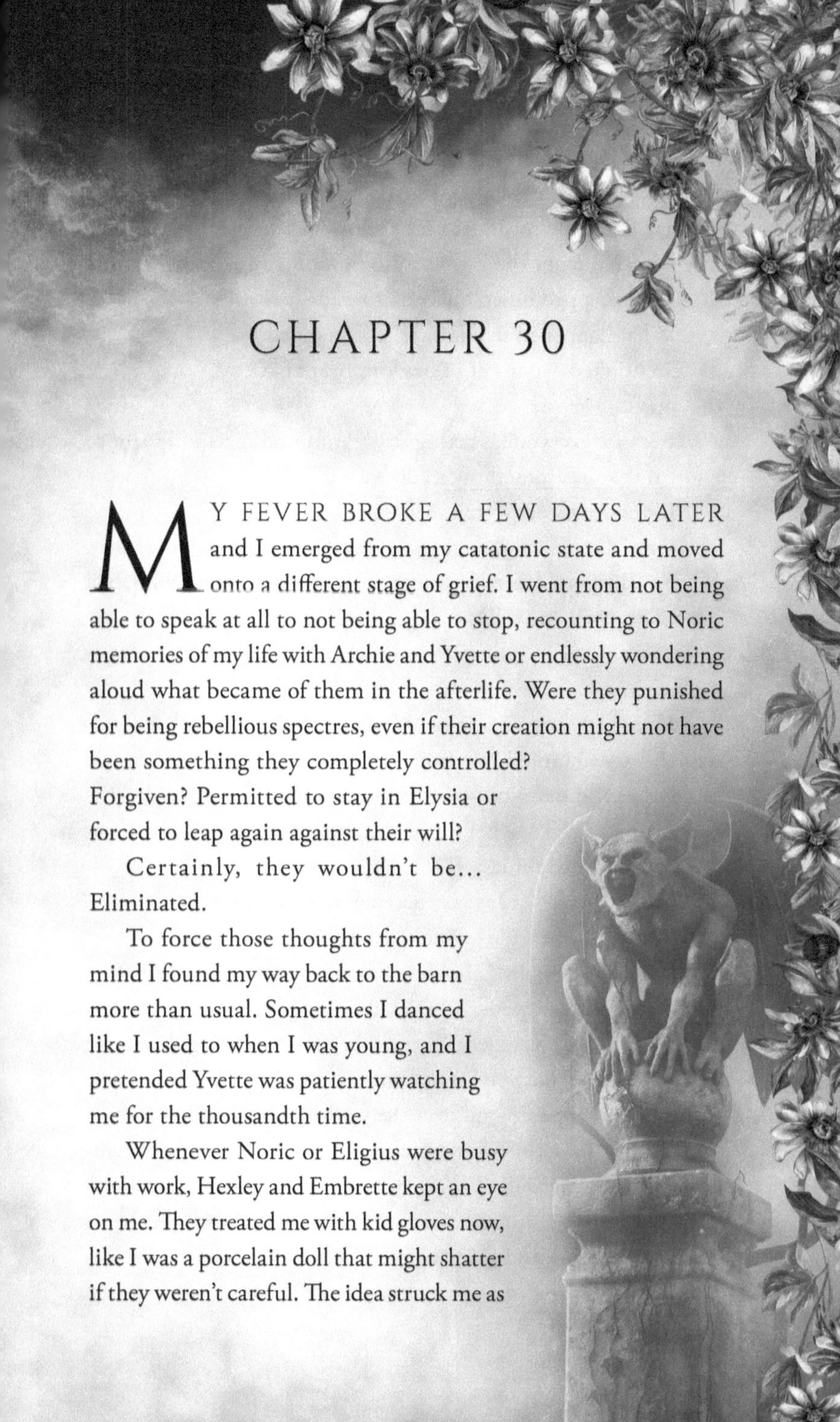

CHAPTER 30

M Y FEVER BROKE A FEW DAYS LATER and I emerged from my catatonic state and moved onto a different stage of grief. I went from not being able to speak at all to not being able to stop, recounting to Noric memories of my life with Archie and Yvette or endlessly wondering aloud what became of them in the afterlife. Were they punished for being rebellious spectres, even if their creation might not have been something they completely controlled? Forgiven? Permitted to stay in Elysia or forced to leap again against their will?

Certainly, they wouldn't be... Eliminated.

To force those thoughts from my mind I found my way back to the barn more than usual. Sometimes I danced like I used to when I was young, and I pretended Yvette was patiently watching me for the thousandth time.

Whenever Noric or Eligius were busy with work, Hexley and Embrette kept an eye on me. They treated me with kid gloves now, like I was a porcelain doll that might shatter if they weren't careful. The idea struck me as ridiculous, considering my countless ballet injuries and the physical limits to which I regularly pushed my body.

One day, dancing under Embrette's watchful eye, I felt entirely disconnected from the music. With a huff, I tore off my pointe shoes and plopped down on a chair beside her.

"What happened to Zosime?" I demanded.

Em blinked—one bat of her long, dark lashes. "What brings that up?"

"Because everyone is acting strange around me and I want to know if that has something to do with it."

"It's not my story to tell," she said.

"Fine," I snapped, then softened my voice. "Then tell me yours. Hexley said he took care of you once before, when something bad happened. Will you tell me about that?"

To my surprise Embrette released an unusual, self-deprecating laugh.

"I tried to reap a static once," she said. Statics were individuals the gods marked safe from random reaping, for one reason or another and pertaining to their grand plans, I supposed. "The overlords stopped me before I could do any damage, and I was severely punished for it."

I froze. Whatever I was expecting, it wasn't that.

"Who did you try to reap?" I asked.

Em laughed again, though it wasn't a happy one. "Hitler."

My mouth dropped. "You're kidding, right?"

"Nope." She shrugged. "You could say I was going through a rebellious phase, but you cannot imagine the despair. Unspeakable things were happening all over the world with no end in sight, I just…" Lost in her memory, Embrette trailed off. Her eyes refocused back on me and she said, "Anyway, I made a plan and didn't even tell Hexley. But the overlords knew somehow, and I was ripped from time and space before I culled the monster. He was eventually Eliminated, did you know that? What was the point of all that agony if he was going to be Eliminated anyway? But the gods play their games and we're bound to their moves, like pieces on a chessboard."

Em paused, then said softly, "I was taken. I don't know where and I don't know what they did to me, not exactly. Tortured me, terrified me. Scrambled my mind so that I could never fully grasp a memory, never heal it. It's not unlike what we did to Evan but far more horrendous."

She pulled her feet up, bent her knees to her chest, and wrapped her arms around them, holding herself. I didn't even think she was aware of it.

"Hexley said I was gone for months. When I came to, I was screaming. I screamed a lot back then. For minutes, hours, sometimes until I was hoarse and fell asleep. Hexley found me immediately and he took me, tended to me... for years."

Years? I chewed my lip, stunned. I'd expected her to say months, at most.

"I spent most of my time in bed, or on a lawn chair outside a cottage he bought, shaking and murmuring to myself. Unbearable memories came to me in nightmares, but I wasn't even sure they were true. I was too weak to reap, though the craving hadn't disappeared. So Hexley brought me humans to cull. Poor things were whisked to my bedside. Sometimes he dissuaded them not to leave, sometimes he physically restrained them, depending on his mood and the mortal. Usually, he needed to shove the blade in my hand and wrap his own around mine, lifting and guiding my arm for the kill. Then he'd whisk the corpse back to wherever he'd found the unlucky mortal."

I imagined the terrified humans, seized from whatever task they'd been doing and whisked to some cottage by what must seem like a demon... then presented to a sickly girl for the slaughter. It was horrible, and I knew Hexley must have felt bad about doing it, but he'd go to any length to take care of Embrette.

"But you healed, eventually," I said, encouragingly. "What happened?"

Embrette let out another breathy laugh, flicking her hair behind her shoulders. "The sixties."

I blinked in surprise. Time was different for a reaper, I knew, but I'd thought when she said *a few years* she'd been healing for two or three and not convalescing for more than a decade.

"I went from relying on Hexley and being terrified of everything, to resenting him and wanting to experience everything that was happening in the world. To be fair, it was a special time in history. The very air hummed with excitement."

Averting her eyes and swallowing, Em said softly, "I struck out against Hexley, the overlords, my position, even myself. My rebellion took the form of endless partying. Men, women, politicians, singers, *bands*. Nothing and no one was off limits. I'd done it before when the mood struck. Rome at its height. Versailles in her grandeur." Embrette smiled beautifully and said, "Fantastic eras for indulgence, Ava. But I went so much harder this time. It's as I told you, seduction became an art form for me."

She fell quiet, lost in a memory before continuing. "Hexley joined me sometimes, pretending to enjoy the scene when I knew his heart wasn't in it. We broke up and got back together more times than I can count. Eventually, the century turned again and I slowed down. The distance between my dalliances grew. But Hexley and I were still on and off again."

She furrowed her pretty brow. "Somehow a competition of sorts grew between us, using the mortals we conquered behind closed doors. Reapers are complicated, Ava. If you think human affections are messy, try adding eternity into the mix."

Embrette's guilty expression told me she thought I didn't understand, but I did. Not necessarily her specific history, but the way love and trauma made a person do things that seemed crazy to someone outside of the situation.

"I was unkind and unfair," she whispered, twisting her deep brown hair into an ever-tighter spiral. "Hexley stayed with me, healed me, and in the end I… I don't know. Misplaced blame or something. Since I couldn't fight the overlords I fought everything and everyone else."

"I'm glad you're together again," I said, laying my hand on hers to still her hair-twisting. "It's obvious to me that Hexley forgives you and that he loves you."

Em winced. "I know, I think… I avoided getting back together with him because I'd have to face what I did. Atone. Even if he doesn't want me to. And to try to forgive myself too." Brightening, she said, "Luckily, I have an endless spool of time in which to do it."

NOVEMBER, APRIL'S CHILLY cousin, was stranger than usual that year. Noric seemed inclined to give me space. He hadn't returned to the sullen arrogance he'd worn when we'd first met, but there was something standoffish about him that reminded me of Sevastian. We didn't speak about what we'd planned to do on Halloween night, and how it was thwarted. He kissed me softly but never let passion consume either of us. And often, I'd find him staring down the hill and toward the river, lost in thought. Every few days I'd abruptly stop dancing, curl up, and cry about Archie and Yvette. I tried not to let Noric see, but it was as if he knew somehow.

"What's wrong?" I asked him one blustery morning in the cemetery. We'd just finished cleaning the leaves from the Hessian and the Harlot's graves. I always liked to keep them tidy, giving them the care in death they never had in life. "I'm getting better every day, but you act as if I'm getting worse."

Noric had been stroking his chin thoughtfully, and he suddenly put his hand down, as if caught.

"Em told me you asked about Zosime," he said, keen gray eyes piercing me. "I talked it over with Sevastian and I've been waiting for the right time to tell you."

"Oh." I swallowed, toying with a stiff, dead leaf and trying not to seem over-interested. "Now is as good a time as any."

Noric nodded and said, "After she reaped herself, Sevastian raged. He screamed in the Rotunda for the gods to kill him. Banged on the doors."

My ears perked. *Doors?* Father never said anything about doors. Noric had just given me more information than I'd ever had before.

"He alternated between slaying entire villages to get their attention and refusing to reap for as long as he could stand it. Eventually, and to our collective shock, it worked. Sevastian was brought to the edges of Elysia. He's the only one of us to have seen what from a distance he describes as a crystal city. But he didn't pay much attention to his surroundings because standing before him was Zosime in her true form. That's the one painting you saw."

I held my breath, fearing the end of this story. It couldn't be good because Zosime and Sevastian weren't together now, but I didn't know how badly it might have turned out.

"Zosime was different, disinterested. With all the memories of her previous lives and her true knowledge restored to her, she no longer loved Sevastian." Noric's voice was heavy, mournful. "Given the opportunity to be together, she declined. She became her true self and that self rejected Sevastian. She remembered another she loved more. They were reunited in the Above."

My heart broke for Sevy. I bit my lip so hard it hurt and squeezed the leaf I'd been holding until it crumpled into pieces.

"Devastated does not begin to cover how he felt. He was broken in a way from which he's never healed."

Is this what Noric most feared?

"I am so deeply sorry for Sevastian." I laid a hand on Noric's and took a deep breath. "But that won't happen to us. I won't reap myself before my time. And when it is my time…" I struggled for words. "We'll cross that bridge when we come to it, but it's not the same. You said it yourself, I don't have any previous lives. When I'm called to Elysia, we'll—we'll think of something."

Noric's nostrils flared and his eyes flashed dangerously. "Ava, you don't understand. The overlords don't listen to our wants—just ask your father. They only allowed their reunion because it suited their voyeuristic sadism. I know it will not be granted again *because* it was granted once. Noric pulled me to him in a one-armed hug and kissed my forehead. "Put it from your mind, Ava."

I knew he would see through my lies, so I whispered, "I'll try."

And though I thought it was the best response, it only made Noric sigh.

The next day, the horsemen gathered at Grimsmere for dinner, and Embrette distributed little white packages to each of us.

"Oh my gosh," I said, feeling the thick sandwich within. "Is this—is today Thanksgiving?"

She nodded and I couldn't help but laugh at myself. I'd thought I was healing well, but it seemed not enough for me to know the days yet.

"Sanderson asked for time off and with everything that happened, I wanted to keep it simple," Eligius announced, motioning for us to sit at the table.

We unwrapped our store-bought Thanksgiving sandwiches in our elegant dining room, and beneath the table I reached over and gave Noric's hand a squeeze. He squeezed my hand back in acknowledgement, but it was weak, like he was afraid he'd hurt me.

A tickling feeling spread over me, as if spiders crawled along my skin. I didn't want Noric to worry about me that way, to think I was so breakable.

We finished our simple Thanksgiving dinner and the reapers returned to their homes. I spent the rest of the holiday weekend and the days following dancing in the barn, while Noric was busy with work. One cloudy morning he came to watch me and the stiffness in his posture sent chills along my flesh again.

"What's wrong?" I asked him.

"Hm?" he said, clearly caught deep in thought. "Oh, I've got an appointment with a repairman tonight." He crossed to where I stood by the barre. "He's the only one qualified to fix the tall clock in the hall. You know, the one from Bavaria. I'm just thinking of how to whisk it to his shop myself, without raising questions."

"Oh."

"Come by after?" Noric asked, laying a kiss on me so quickly he only connected with half my lips. "Around nine, Carpathian time? I'll meet you outside. You should be just about finished practicing then and I think it would be good for you to get out of the house. If you're feeling up to it."

"Oh… wow, you're right," I mused, realizing how close to home I'd stayed since losing Archie and Yvette. "It's been a month since I've left."

I kissed Noric full on the lips. "I'll see you at nine."

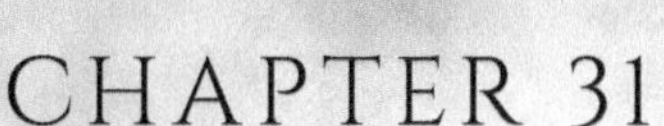

CHAPTER 31

I ARRIVED IN THE CARPATHIANS AT EXACTLY nine o'clock. When I left Orsha's magical shell of warmth, a frigid gust nearly knocked me over and I pulled my jacket tighter around me.

"Noric?" I called into the fierce wind. Having released my hair from its ballerina bun after practice, it whipped about wildly, slapping my face.

Where was he?

"Noric?" I shouted louder this time, pulling strands sticking to my lip gloss. I'd put on a thick coating over a sticky oint- ment because they were chapped to the point of bleeding. It always happened when I danced too much and failed to properly hydrate, especially in the cold, dry months.

Scanning the petite castle, I found no lights on inside, making Noric's residence look even more formidable. It was a sheer tower of gray rock against a black sky, topped with menacing gargoyles. For the first time, I realized how it might look like a picture from someone's nightmare. A gibbous moon provided my only light; the sky was too clouded to make out the usual cover of stars that seemed to cocoon Noric's land like a snug, heavenly blanket.

This mountain, part home to me, had turned wrong somehow. Either the landscape before me or my presence in it.

My heart stuttered at the thought.

"Noric?" I called, soft and tentative this time.

The howl of a gray wolf pierced the night and I whipped my head in the direction of the sound. It was a long way off, as best I could tell. Orsha looked too, and her eyes glowed a brighter red in acknowledgement. *Would the wolves remember me?* I wondered. Could Noric be down in the valley with them? Perhaps they'd been playing together and he'd lost track of time?

No, he would never.

Perhaps one was injured and he'd gotten stuck in the valley, trying to care for it and —

Out of thin air, Noric appeared on the mountain slope astride Orphneaus. Beside him, Sevastian descended upon Alastor's back. I hadn't been expecting company and started a little.

"Noric."

His name came from my lips in a breathy rush and I ran to him as he dismounted. I didn't know why I'd gotten so spooked, but something about the night felt foreboding.

"Where were you?" I asked, clinging to his jacket.

Bewilderingly, Noric held up his hand and took a step backwards. Away from me. His face was fixed with an almost stern expression. I stopped abruptly, blinking in confusion. Side-eying Sevastian, I tried to guess what he was doing here and if that was the reason Noric was acting strangely.

"Is something wrong?" I asked, hating the question both for what I did and did not know. *Yes, something is wrong.* But what? My muscles tensed, instinctively preparing for some undesirable, forthcoming event, even though my brain rallied against it.

This is Noric, and I am safe here. Only love and happiness, laughter and pleasure… only that can come from Noric.

Noric nodded to Sevastian and before I even had a chance to do anything laughably fruitless with my coiled muscles, the blonde reaper grabbed me from behind and pinned my arms at my sides. My heart pounded and my stomach sank to my shoes. I swallowed thickly, well and truly panicked now but determined not to show it.

"Get your hands off me," I ordered Sevastian, who ignored me. "Noric, what is going on?"

Noric had been staring at the ground. Slowly and with reluctance, his gaze rose to mine and his voice wavered as he announced, "I'm going to obscure your mind from the memories of us."

I barked a laugh. "Like hell you are."

"Ava, this isn't a joke. It's not a threat, and it's not negotiable. This is what's best for us."

Absolutely not.

There was no point in trying, but I fought to free myself from Sevastian's iron grip. My mind did what my body could not, racing in all directions to figure out what in the world brought Noric to this decision and how to change his mind. Fast.

"This is because of Archibald and Yvette, isn't it?" I asked, unable to keep the desperation from my voice.

Noric rubbed at his forehead like he was trying to rub out pain or to wipe away his own memories.

"I'm doing this for *you,*" he insisted. "For your own good. So you can forget about me and move on with your life. There is no way to make you immortal Ava, and no way for me to die. There is no ending for us that leads anywhere but unto an empire of agony."

He's really going to do this.

My heart raced dangerously fast, hammering against my ribcage like it wanted to break out.

"I can try to turn spectre," I protested, jerking against Sevastian's hold. It was useless, of course. "Or we can see if the vampires can do anything!"

Noric shook his head, resolved. "Even if you possessed the ichor, which you do not, it would be too risky. Less than half survive the transformation. And it's no life, Ava, it's a half life at best."

He really means to wipe my memories. As the idea sank in, I wondered if I might actually have a heart attack. Noric's beauty was intimidating and godlike in the dark of night, with the wind whipping his hair and cloak. I couldn't imagine never seeing him again, never loving him or feeling his love in return.

"Coward!" I screamed. One blink and tears fell. "You're a coward! This isn't for me. You're afraid for *you,* you're afraid to try, afraid to fail."

Panic iced my blood and outside, the cold wind punished me more for each tear soaking my face. How could this be happening so suddenly? The idea that I'd lose everything in the next few seconds and not even care about it, not even know… it was unbearable.

"Ava…" My name on Noric's lips was half-plea, half-warning.

"Don't take my memories, they're mine!" I sobbed. "They belong to *me.* Liar, thief, coward!"

"Sevastian is going to ingrain new ones, better ones," Noric said, trying to soothe me and justify his decision.

"No, I don't want some ingrained life of lies!" I yelled.

Another ominous wolf howl pierced the night, and I wished the pack would fall upon us, divert Noric and save us from what he was doing. But they were too far away.

Noric fisted his hands and stared at me, hardening himself for the task.

No, no, no.

"I love you. Noric, I love you. *Please.*" My words were howls, like the wolves. "Eligius stays away long enough that he curbs the urge to cull me. We can do that too."

"Your father isn't taking you to bed when he returns, either," Sevastian bit out, behind me.

I struggled for something to say.

"I know the pain she's in and it's only going to get worse," Sevastian called out to Noric. "And for you…" he trailed off. "Look at her," he said, shaking me roughly. "The more time you spend with her, the more you love her, the more you'll ache to reap her. And that's not even the worst of what's in store for you. But you can end it in mere seconds, as soon as you obscure her mind."

As he neared, Noric's gray eyes hardened into rocks upon which I'd shatter. There was no comfort there, no mercy. I was falling and those sharp, rigid boulders would break my body upon landing.

He took another step forward. No one was here on this remote mountaintop, no one was coming to save me.

To save me from the man I love.

What an impossible thought.

"I'm sorry," Noric rasped, and now his eyes clouded, his tortured face begging me to understand. "I love you too. And that's why I have to do this. It will all be over in a minute, all your pain will be gone."

"It's my pain, it's for me to decide!" I yelled, tears falling into my mouth.

"I'll whisk you into your room after. You won't remember me telling you this, but I want you to know I'll safely return you to… the place I should never have taken you from to begin with."

Noric clenched his jaw, steeling himself to steal away my love.

"No, don't do this!" I screamed. "Noric, no!"

CHAPTER 32

A BLADE, I THOUGHT WILDLY.

If I could find a weapon, I could cut myself and maybe I'd remember, just like I had when Eligius attempted to obscure me.

Yes, yes!

But no…

My heart sank.

The only weapon within reach was Noric's reaper dagger, and a single prick of that would kill me.

A few feet to my left, Orphneaus let out an eerie, high-pitched neigh as he pawed the ground, and another idea struck me.

If I can reach Orphnaeus, I can fly to the Rotunda, I thought. *He knows the way, and perhaps Eligius didn't think to dissuade Noric's Strider from carrying me there. Then I can beg the gods directly…*

But how could I gain freedom? Sevastian's grip was too strong, and I could never overpower Noric, the idea was laughable.

Oh.

The obvious thought hit me as Noric's jacket blew open, revealing the handle of his dagger once more.

I can't cut myself *on Noric's blade, but I can use it against* him.

The fact that a horseman's weapon could wound themselves—or one another—was always a curious thing to me, but right now I was only grateful for the ability.

With the semblance of a plan, I immediately stopped struggling against Sevastian's hold and allowed myself to fall limp in his arms. Despite witnessing me push my body to the extreme in ballet, the reapers still regarded me as a delicate mortal.

So be it. Noric was very good at seeing through lies when I spoke, but I was a born dancer. If I could only do one thing in this world, it was tell a story with my body.

"I… I…" I whispered, letting my head loll and my eyelids flutter. I fought an instinct to struggle and forced my muscles to relax, to soften. "Dizzy. Help…"

"Stop!" Noric cried, smacking Sevastian's hands from my biceps. "You're squeezing her arms too tight!"

Now that I thought about it, Sevy was cutting off my circulation. When he let go, I slumped to the ground and Noric threw himself onto his knees, cradling me in his arms.

"Noric… I…" Feebly, I reached for him, moving my hands around his chest as if seeking a place to hold onto.

I'm sorry, my love, I thought. *You were doing what you felt you had to, just as I must.*

My finger's brushed against Noric's dagger, tucked into the leather holster strapped around his chest.

To have any chance, I needed to withdraw it and cut him in the same movement. Otherwise, his reflexes would be too quick to stop my attack. Luckily, Noric was bent over me. He was at the perfect angle for me to draw the blade across his torso in one swipe, and his arms were wrapped around me, out of the way.

It was the best position for an attack, *if* I managed to pull the dagger loose in the first place.

If the weapon didn't release, if it got stuck for any reason or if I failed to draw blood, I'd lose the only opportunity I had.

"Dizzy…" I whispered weakly. "Faint…"

One shot, I thought, *make it count.*

I grabbed the handle of the blade and with lightning speed, yanked the dagger free and sliced a cruel gash across Noric's chest, making him gasp.

In the fraction of a second it took for me to wound him, I wasn't sure if Noric could have stopped me. But if he'd had the time, he likely restrained himself because any struggle with the deadly blade in my hand could result in it accidently cutting and killing *me*.

Before Sevy could make sense of what occurred, I whirled around and sliced him too. The cut I gave Sevastian was in reverse, running diagonally from his neck down to his waist. He hissed as he clutched his chest and fell to the ground, mirroring Noric.

I broke out in a cold sweat. I'd brought two reapers to their knees, but they wouldn't stay there long. As I sprinted for Orphnaeus, I let Noric's dagger fall from my grasp. With mere seconds to make my escape, I didn't have time to juggle holding the weapon and mounting the Time Strider.

From the corner of my eye, I saw Noric was already standing halfway when I made it onto his Strider's back. Quickly, I leaned down to Orphnaeus's ear and whispered, "Take me to the Rotunda."

"No!" Noric's shout echoed off the mountaintops.

I didn't think he heard my destination and was only yelling because I was escaping, but I couldn't be sure.

My heart screamed as I flew. *Don't find me. Don't chase me.*

Within seconds the mist parted and I saw my destination, though I couldn't name it and could make out very little in the night. Below me, I caught a glimpse of a small, dark lake, set within dry, brown mountains. Perhaps a few pine trees dotted the hillsides in the distance.

Where was I?

I tried to imprint the landscape in my mind but there were no significant markers. If I were torn from the area now, if Noric caught up and whisked me away, I'd have nothing to use to find my way back. It was all a little underwhelming for the location I'd been wondering about my whole life, but that was likely because it was so dark. I imagined daylight would illuminate the site to full beauty.

"Ava! Ava, where are you? Come back!"

Noric's plea, sent directly to my mind, made my heart stutter. I ignored him and urged Orphnaeus faster.

Up, up, and up we rose, flying higher than I'd ever been before, and my heart pounded at the impossibility of it. Each second it felt like I would lose oxygen, or freeze, or shoot right up into outer space and float, suddenly adrift and unable to make it back to the safety of Earth's atmosphere. My stomach lurched and I tried not to think about it.

I'm finally going to see the Rotunda. Wrapping my arms around Orphnaeus's neck, I held the soft leather reins tightly as well. Just in case.

And still we flew higher.

What if mortals can't make this journey and I die in the process? I hadn't thought about that before. *What if it was for souls only, and my physical body couldn't withstand the atmosphere?* I'd get myself killed before my time.

I locked my legs tighter around Orphnaeus's solid body, though it did nothing to stop me from shaking. At a distance of about ten feet, the air surrounding me swirled and blurred, as if I was in a different, cylindrical pocket of air. It was like a separate channel reaching upwards to… to… some beyond?

Surely, we can't keep going?

We flew higher. It was well past possibility, and yet, we continued to ascend.

I cried out when the scene suddenly changed and Noric's Strider shot us through a circular hole in a room—a *room*.

A room in the sky! *A room. In the sky.*

The Rotunda.

At least, the part of it existing in our dimension, which my mind still didn't fully grasp.

I stared, wide-eyed, because even after everything I'd seen it still felt impossible.

A sparkling, breathtaking material constructed circular walls, shining like some kind of divine relation of quartz or marble. Whatever the material was, I'd never seen it on Earth. The Rotunda seemed about as wide as it was tall, gently curving up into a high, arched ceiling. The floor itself was perfectly flat, making the room look as if someone had taken a circle and sliced it in half. My skin tingled and a strange sensation ran through my body, as if my blood itself were awed, overcome by the holiness. Only two items existed in the curved room, save the central hole from which I'd emerged.

The doors and the Book stood opposite one another.

Glancing around, an image of our manor popped into my head. Our second-story rotunda was a simple, earthy imitation of this magnificence. Perhaps mortals were inspired by a subconscious memory of this place, because I'd seen many historical, political, and other rooms of elegance constructed in a vaguely similar way, especially in governing structures throughout the world.

But they were pale imitations at best, a toddler scribbling a rendering of a Van Gogh painting with crayons and markers.

Orphnaeus landed us equidistant from the doors and the Book. The floor was wide enough for his body, but the gaping hole occupying the middle of the room made me nervous. What would happen if I fell through it? Could I float? Would Orphnaeus fly to catch me?

Hurry, I commanded myself. *Or Noric might figure out what you're doing.*

But I was too curious to head to the doors first. Towering high, they were constructed of the same gleaming substance as the walls, but the outlines indicated their purpose.

Turning away, I sprinted to the Reclamation of Souls Book. I wanted—*needed*—to see it, to see the book that mystified me since I'd learned of its existence. My footsteps echoed ominously in the hollow, airy chamber as I raced around the circular floor.

The Reclamation of Souls book was a heavy, black tome resting on a pedestal. I supposed that meant three items in total occupied the Rotunda, but only two held any magic and therefore, my interest. The book was open and perhaps dated to today, to this moment, but the numbers at the top of the page didn't make sense to me. The names were also written in characters and symbols, comprising no language I'd ever seen or heard.

I blinked, noticing that each name was not written in ink, but they glowed with a dark golden light, as if burning into the page. Yet one by one they blackened, like they'd been seared from a branding iron into human flesh, before fading entirely.

Were the pages of the book made of flesh? I wondered with horror, reaching out to touch one.

But no—despite the massive number of pages, they were light as air. There had to be some magical system to manage them because the book itself couldn't hold more than a few years at a time, judging by its thickness.

Incredible.

Forcing myself to tear away from the object that haunted my dreams since childhood, I again sprinted around the edges of the Rotunda until I stood in front of the two imposing doors. Glancing up, I wondered if maybe there'd be some window or way to see anything beyond, but the ceiling only arched and rounded, without even a skylight at its peak.

I brought my fist to the door, then paused.

How does one demand an audience with the gods?

I hadn't thought that part through. What would sway them? Courage? Humility? Threats? Pleas? Did it depend on the overlord? Was there an appropriate term of address? Eligius had never mentioned any. I scanned my brain for all the earthly religions that had come and gone. So many names for so many gods. Had one of the faiths gotten it right?

Was I the only mortal throughout all of time, ever, to stand here in this sacred, windswept room?

My first, gentle knock sounded pitifully weak, lost to the large chamber. Straightening my spine, I banged harder and cried, "I would like to speak to our makers."

Makers, the room echoed back.

"I am Avalia Thrailkill and I've come to request immortality."

Mortality, the room echoed, missing the first part of the word. I frowned.

Knocking harder, I cried, "I—I can make a bargain."

Bargain.

Once I'd spoken the words, I realized how silly they sounded. But in the myths and legends, mortals were always making bargains with the gods.

I ignored the fact that they never turned out well.

What could I bargain? Service? Dance? Sometimes in the myths of old, the gods favored a mortal for their beauty or their art. Perhaps I could be granted immortality if they wanted to watch me dance for eternity.

Stepping back, I held my breath and tried to calm my pounding heart. Nothing happened. I craned my neck to take in the outline of the tall doors, searching for any small motion to indicate a response, any creak or crack.

Nothing.

Seconds passed, then a full minute. Sobbing in the Rotunda wasn't my plan, but desperate tears leaked and I sniffled pitifully. It was all made worse by the fact that my whimper echoed off the divine walls.

"Please," I whispered. *"I love him."*

The gods were unmoved.

I chewed my lip hard, debating what to do next. Bang some more? Shout? Hurl something at the door? Maybe if I were able to steal Noric's dagger, I could wedge it between...

Suddenly, the floor shook and the walls rumbled. The trembling quickly worsened, and though I'd never experienced one, I imagined it felt like an earthquake. There was nothing to hold onto and I was thrown to the floor before I could even reach out. Any hope I had that this was a good sign quickly faded, and panic shot through me when I looked up to find Orphnaeus was gone.

I blinked, hard. *Gone.*

Where? How?

This was bad and quickly worsening.

The floor shook harder.

Had I angered the gods by entering their sacred Rotunda? Mortals weren't supposed to know anything, and I had the audacity to request far more than knowledge.

I scrambled to find purchase in the smooth, polished floor, but there was nothing to grip. If the shaking didn't stop, I was at risk of falling. My stomach lurched as I realized I was alone in the Rotunda with no way to leave, and the increasing rumbling beneath my feet made it feel as if...

...I was being discarded.

The floor beneath me cracked with a thundering *boom* and I screamed.

No!

Twisting, I tried to hold onto the edge of what was now a broken piece of that glittering, marble-like substance. But the wedge of sparkling stone beneath me tilted so fast that I was tossed from it, over the edge of the hole, and straight down into nothingness.

There was no floor beneath me now and I screamed as I fell to my death. Down through that mystical air shaft, I tumbled so long my scream wore out and reduced itself to a whimper. How much time did I have before I hit the earth? Seconds? I tried recalling how long my flight up to the Rotunda had taken. *Would I hit the ground, or that dark lake beneath the portal?*

It was irrelevant as either would kill me.

No! A furious will to live tore through me and I thrashed, reaching out as if my hands could catch something to hold onto in this column of air.

Astoundingly, my body *slammed* into something.

I was dizzy and ready to release the contents of my stomach as the direction of my fall suddenly reversed, and I was carried upward.

Noric, I realized with amazement.

I was sitting sideways in Orphnaeus's saddle, tightly wrapped in Noric's strong arms.

"I've got you," he cried, as we briefly flew upwards before turning and heading back down again. My heart leapt and I gasped for air as I clung to him.

Oh my God, Noric had just saved my life. Had Orphnaeus returned and led him to me? I banished the image of my slamming into the lake. Everything was okay now, or it would be, as soon as we landed safely back on Earth.

But Noric's next words and his tone sent chills up my spine.

"What have you done, Avalia?" There was admonishment in his voice, but there was pain too. *"What have you done?"*

"I… the floor can repair itself, can't it? The overlords can easily do that."

"You shouldn't have entered the Rotunda. And the *Book*. You touched it, didn't you?" Noric's fingers dug into my flesh as he pulled me tighter. "You've angered them."

Orphnaeus's leathered wings beat the air in wild flight back to Earth. If I wasn't already, I'd have been forced to cling to Noric just to stay on his Strider's back.

"I'm sorry," I yelled. "You were going to steal my memories, wipe my mind! What was I supposed to do?"

"Ava, Ava," Noric moaned, gripping me hard. "You don't understand," Noric gritted out the words in that strange voice—angry and agonized. Like he couldn't decide whether to shout or to soothe me for whatever my rebelliousness had done.

Noric's next words changed my life. Ended it, really.

"Your name has appeared in the Book," he said. "You're scheduled to die in Solebury when the sun rises on the winter solstice."

PART III

TO CRY
IN RAPTURE

CHAPTER 33

I SHOULD HAVE PANICKED BUT THE CLOUDS in my mind momentarily cleared, blown to the wayside as if blasted by that blinding sun, rising on the day of my death and revealing my mortal end.

Today was the eighth of the month. Winter solstice was on December twenty-first this year.

I had thirteen days to live. Noric had just saved my life, but only temporarily. I supposed he'd been fated to find me and catch me, because I already had my destined ending seared into the pages of the Book.

I laughed and it grew louder and longer. Oh, I knew it was hysteria, but my giggles continued until I popped like a balloon, bursting into sobs and deflating against Noric's chest.

I was going to die and I had no one to blame but myself. I was the foolish girl Noric claimed me to be, cutting my own life short. Sure, I wouldn't have done it if he hadn't threatened my memories, but I couldn't be positive I wouldn't have tried someday in the future anyway, like a curious Pandora opening the box.

"Where is the portal to the Rotunda?" I whispered. There was no harm in me knowing everything now. What more could the gods do to me?

"Above Lake Hazar in the Taurus Mountains. Modern day Turkey," Noric replied in a strained voice.

Turkey. I rolled the knowledge around in my head, getting used to it. My guesses had always centered on the poles, or somewhere in Eastern Africa, or a place with significant structures like the pyramids of Egypt. I hadn't expected a lake in Turkey, which, admittedly, I'd never heard of before.

"Why there?" I asked.

Noric shrugged. "Maybe because it's the source of the Tigres River, which joins with the Euphrates. Hazar is the wellspring of the cradle of civilization."

He answered my question distractedly, with obvious tension in his voice. His breathing was far from normal, almost heaving, if he were bloody and broken in the midst of a death match. I was sure his mind raced, and he was likely carrying on more than one conversation with the other horsemen.

I chewed my chapped lip and let the quiet tears slip down my cheeks.

"How—how will I die?" I asked, hoping it wouldn't be one of those mysterious, clouded deaths.

Noric swallowed thickly. "It is a divine death. Either one of us or the overlords are going to reap you directly."

I hadn't realized I was holding out some hope until he dashed it.

"So you do it, or they do?" I whispered.

"Yes it is…" Noric furrowed his brow, like he was trying to read something in the Book. Maybe he was. "Unclear. Much like when our blades create an instant, unknowable cause of death in a mortal, the gods can apply their own divine hand to culling you.

There's no way to escape it unless the Book means that one of us reaps you instead." He took a shuddering breath. "I don't know how it will unfold but it is certain."

We landed outside of Noric's estate, and I had only a moment to note the dark, clouded sky, before he whisked us into his bedroom and placed me directly in his bed.

Taking a large step back and staring hard at the gargoyles making up his bedposts, Noric whispered a string of sentences I couldn't make out. My heart jumped into my throat as I watched his creatures come to life, something that still amazed me. Hard eyes opened and their bodies moved, stone wings flapping as they readjusted position. I stared with an open mouth while Noric continued whispering commands in some language possibly akin to Latin. The creatures listened intently to their master and when he finished speaking, their focus turned to me.

"You will not leave this bed until I return," Noric ordered. The raw pain and fear in his voice scared me. "They will ensure it. I suggest you do not test their strength."

"You can't keep me here, Noric," I protested, fearful and angry myself. "You're not my father, you know."

It was a little childish, but it was the first thing that had popped into my mind, which was too anxious to operate at peak performance.

"No, but he's downstairs right now and in full agreement that we contain you before you go running off and get yourself—and the world—into more trouble."

I sucked in a breath. *My father? Here?*

Wait—*the world?*

"We're meeting to discuss what to do and you're staying put," Noric growled as he pointed to the bed. I knew anger was his defense mechanism, but he was a little scary when he was like this. "Right here, where you can't get into any more trouble."

"I want to be included in any plan," I said, fisting the bedsheets.

"There are five immortals gathered here who don't give a damn about what you want right now." Noric's voice boomed as he spoke. He closed his eyes and took a breath to calm himself. "You're not going to win this one, so don't bother trying." He cocked his head toward his gargoyles. "They will physically restrain you if you try to leave."

Noric took a step, and I scooted to the edge of the bed, but one of the gargoyles on the lower bedposts moved to block me. I turned to look at the larger one, whose widespread wings made up the ominous, gothic headboard. His stone gaze pinned on me with a clear warning. I sighed through my nose.

"You can't do this to me," I said through clenched teeth.

Noric scanned his bed with satisfaction and said coldly, "Looks to me like I can."

He spun on his heel and left. Instead of shouting for him, which I knew wouldn't do any good, I huffed and settled back under the watchful eye of his gargoyles.

TO MY UTTER shock, I fell asleep. The sun had already risen when I awoke, light streaming through the windows telling me it was morning in Romania. I swallowed. Technically, it was still nighttime in New Hope, so I still had thirteen days left to live. By a few hours at least.

Noric loomed in the doorway, watching me.

"I've laid out fresh clothes for you. Wash up and come straight down to meet us." His eyes narrowed. "Do you understand? No running off anywhere?"

He held himself apart, away from me. Afraid, I knew. Now that a very real and very short countdown had been put on my lifespan, his nightmare had come true.

"Noric, I'm not going to return to the Rotunda and cause more trouble," I breathed. "I'm here, I'm… I… don't want to die," I sniffled and shook, feeling pathetic. "Just give me a moment and I'll be right down."

He nodded and I sprang from his bed and into his bathroom. I splashed cold water on my face, used a spare toothbrush to clean my teeth, and found the clothing Noric had provided. It was a simple pair of black pants and a loose gray sweater with a soft white camisole to wear beneath. He knew my preferred palette—black and gray, cream and ivory, pink and red. Classic colors of the ballet.

Will Noric think of me in the future, at any mention of dance? Will my death make it hard for him to compose, or will he throw himself into his art the way Sevastian had?

I collapsed on the bathroom floor, trying to stop the flow of tears before I went downstairs to face everyone. I raged at myself for going to the Rotunda. My death was always inevitable, but I'd brought it about so much sooner. And what had Noric meant about the world? How was that connected?

Needing to find out, I descended Noric's dramatic staircase, finding Eligius and the horsemen standing in the hall, staring at me gravely.

"Oh, Ava!" Embrette cried. I think she meant to hug me but before I could blink, my father had whisked himself to me. As soon as I was in his arms, I lost the battle to hold anything in.

Eligius had saved me, given me a life beyond mortal imagination, and this was how I repaid him? By doing something foolish and getting my name in the Book. I couldn't bear to think about it, it made me hate myself.

"I'm sorry," I sobbed. "I'm sorry, this is all my fault."

"No," Eligius said. "It was happening anyway."

"But what?" I asked, completely confused. *"What's* happening?"

"I will not let you die, daughter, I will *not."* Eligius insisted, with all the power of his reaper voice behind it. If Noric's voice had the magical ability to sound like rough stone, Eligius's reminded me of the terrifying emptiness of space, of an endless black abyss. I wanted to believe his impassioned vow, but I saw nothing different now than any other time he'd tried to find a way to immortalize me.

"Come, sit," Death ordered.

We made our way into Noric's library, the room that rose several stories high with a painted, celestial ceiling, giving it a look of dark whimsy. This room had enchanted me, and I'd thought I'd grow old here, amongst the ancient books and curled into one of his deep chairs with a cup of black tea.

Noric held me as I sat. No, *held* was too weak a word. He lost his battle for control and gripped me as if he could hold me to the Earth, in the same manner I'd tried to grip Archibald and Yvette, and just as hopeless. Still, I nested tighter into his solidness. I knew it was a lie but I felt safe, wrapped in that protective embrace. As if no one could touch me, not even the gods.

Hexley and Embrette took a seat on a couch together, hands tightly clasped. Sevastian stood behind them, holding onto the back of the sofa.

"Do you remember how I told you about this pervasive malaise?" My father asked, and I nodded. "It's been spreading and growing stronger. Even humans can feel it, but for us it's more pronounced."

"And somehow me going to the Rotunda has strengthened it?" I offered, sounding as guilty as I was confused.

"Strengthened and increased its speed," Eligius agreed. "I can feel the change in humanity, and more spontaneous cullings have been added to the Book. Fighting has broken out in several regions, another earthquake of historic magnitude hit near Santiago, and a listeria outbreak is sweeping several major American cities. All previously unscheduled."

"What does it mean?" I asked, afraid I already knew. I'd caused this. I'd angered the gods and they were killing people because of it.

"The end of the world." Sevastian's grim announcement was

both sardonic and casual, as if he might not care at all if it ended. I caught Noric shoot him a warning look and Sevy quickly averted his gaze, effectively cowed.

"Something along those lines," Eligius agreed, stroking his chin with one bony finger.

I didn't think I could feel any worse, but I was wrong. I didn't just cause my own culling, my recklessness might have brought about the apocalypse. Or, at least, sped up the process.

Pandora indeed. Or Eve, with a hunger for knowledge casting us out of our earthly garden. Curious, catalyst. I supposed the two women weren't so dissimilar.

But was it carelessness… or courage that spurred them?

My thoughts must have been written all over my face, because my father protested, "Don't take it all on your shoulders, Lee Lee. This was going to happen regardless. This has happened before, and its righted itself."

"But… how?" I asked.

"With a reset," Sevastian announced, ginning darkly. "Most likely, the system wants a sacrifice. And it already selected the candidate. Or really, she selected herself."

I felt Noric's muscles tense as he restrained himself from rising. That would mean he'd need to let me go, and he didn't want to do that.

Instead, he growled, "Sevastian, if you don't shut your mouth, I'm going to slash you across it so deeply that you won't heal for several hours." Noric was bone-chillingly calm as he made the threat. Promise. It rose the hair on my arms. "I will not repeat myself," he warned.

Sevastian folded his arms and shut his mouth but didn't wipe the petulant look from his face. I didn't blame him for his fury. He always said I'd bring heartache and misery to Noric and now I'd done far worse than that, I'd brought it to the world.

"I don't understand." My words were whispered pleas as I directed my attention back to my father. "Why?"

Eligius shrugged. "We cannot know why and we cannot know to what end. But it is… a feeling we have, as reapers. When the world met this phase in the past, something was needed, required, to change course. Usually it's a wide-scale event, like the grand flood across the land. But the death of a singular, important figure can sometimes do the trick."

"But I'm not important," I pointed out.

My father brought a fisted hand to his mouth and shook his head, stumped. I looked at Hexley and Embrette. Their round, sorrowful eyes confirmed they felt the same—grieved and confused at what was happening.

The grandfather clock in the hall struck the hour and I jumped. Suddenly, I wanted to laugh as I remembered that it was supposed to have recently been repaired. That was Noric's lie that had put this horrible chain of events in motion. Misdirected rage consumed me, made me want to race into the hall and tip that grand old clock over, smashing it to the floor.

If only Archibald and Yvette weren't collected…

If only Noric hadn't felt the need to wipe my mind…

If only I hadn't raced to the Rotunda…

I chewed my lip. *So what if anything had happened differently? What would it have bought me, anyway, but a little more time?*

I clutched Noric tighter and inhaled his otherworldly reaper scent.

But that was the thing… all mortals really had that mattered, was time. More or less of it.

No, no—that wasn't right.

It mattered if they had something of value to spend that time on, and I *did*. I *had*. Noric and my father and the reapers and dance. I wasn't done with this life, but apparently, it was done with me.

Sniffling, I closed my eyes and tried to breathe.

Thirteen days. Well, barely, as I was slated to die the morning of the twenty-first and today was almost over back in Solebury.

"What is it, exactly?" I looked up at Noric. "What does it feel like to you, this malaise?"

He furrowed his brow. "For us, it feels like a stretching garment we wear, like the fabric of the world tearing at its seams. In the same way there is a countdown on your life, it feels as if one has been added to the realm, and the clock is now ticking faster. I can't know the final date, but it's as if a shadow has been cast over the world. One that will darken more each day, until all the light is snuffed out."

I gulped.

There was a pause, and I could tell the reapers were communicating telepathically. My father gave Noric a subtle nod of approval, and he continued.

"You are a part of this, but perhaps not the whole part," Noric said carefully. "There may be other moving pieces. We're keeping an open mind, but it does not matter because the most important thing to us is keeping you alive, and we are going to try."

"How?" I breathed.

My father reached into his robes and pulled out four sheets of paper. He handed one to Hexley and Embrette, one to Sevastian, one to Noric and I, and kept one for himself.

"This is a list I've made of every rumored anomaly across the globe, every whispered glitch in the system, every potential aberration—that is, any creature that might be magical. We'll start here, tracking them all down and seeing what we can find."

"But if you knew about these creatures before, why didn't you talk to them then?" I asked.

"Because none of them are solid enough leads to be worth the investigation," Sevastian answered venomously. "This is no more than mortals possess—conspiracy theories, suspicious allegations against introverted neighbors, local lore and legends. Our plan is the same as it was several months ago, to cast an ever wider, ever weaker net, and we're going to meet the same result."

I looked at my father to refute it, but he only tried, and failed, to offer a sad smile.

"We have to start somewhere," Noric insisted, gritting his teeth. "Everyone, take your list and whisk down the names and places one by one. When you're finished, return to Grimsmere to wait for the others."

"I'm coming with you," I told Noric, lifting my chin. "What more harm could befall me when the gods already marked me for death? If it's all a game to them, they're not going to spoil it before it's over."

I watched his throat dip as he swallowed. "Unfortunately," he said. "I agree. But there's another task we need to do first."

"What's that?" I asked.

Noric gripped my shoulders and said, "As a backup plan—a very last resort, you understand—you need to practice turning spectre."

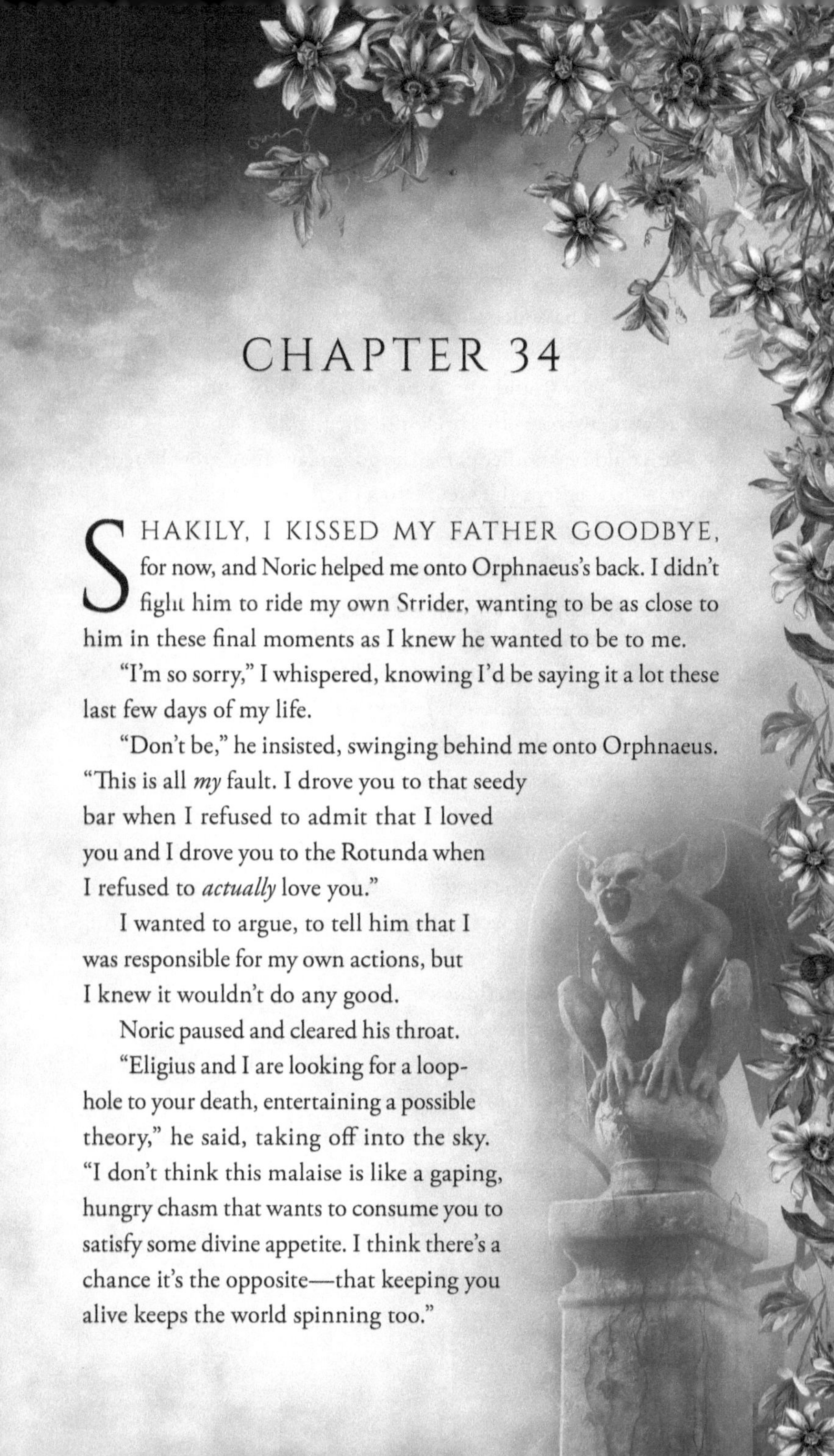

CHAPTER 34

S HAKILY, I KISSED MY FATHER GOODBYE, for now, and Noric helped me onto Orphnaeus's back. I didn't fight him to ride my own Strider, wanting to be as close to him in these final moments as I knew he wanted to be to me.

"I'm so sorry," I whispered, knowing I'd be saying it a lot these last few days of my life.

"Don't be," he insisted, swinging behind me onto Orphnaeus. "This is all *my* fault. I drove you to that seedy bar when I refused to admit that I loved you and I drove you to the Rotunda when I refused to *actually* love you."

I wanted to argue, to tell him that I was responsible for my own actions, but I knew it wouldn't do any good.

Noric paused and cleared his throat.

"Eligius and I are looking for a loophole to your death, entertaining a possible theory," he said, taking off into the sky. "I don't think this malaise is like a gaping, hungry chasm that wants to consume you to satisfy some divine appetite. I think there's a chance it's the opposite—that keeping you alive keeps the world spinning too."

"I think your feelings for me are clouding your judgement."

"As does Sevastian," Noric agreed. "Who finds no logic in the idea."

I didn't want to hope, but my heart clung to the possibility that my life could have deeper meaning, that sustaining it might be the goal. Like Sevastian, however, I didn't see the reasoning either.

"But… why would my name be in the Book then?" I pointed out as we flew westward, back into the night.

"It could be another game the gods play. They grow bored, as mortals do. Perhaps they set forth a challenge for us."

"Or perhaps they're like animals who play with their food before eating it, like a cat toying with a mouse."

Was it a dangerous insult to voice if there was any truth to Noric's statement, if the gods were listening and watching? But once again, it didn't matter when there was nothing more they could do to me. "Although I suppose I'm more like a cat right now, because you know what they say about cats and curiosity."

Behind me, Noric's body stiffened. "That's just the thing," he said urgently. "Everyone only knows half the expression. In full it's *curiosity killed the cat, but satisfaction brought it back.* If the gods do want you dead, maybe we could find a loophole where you effectively die, saving the world, but in a manner where we can bring you back." Behind me, Noric released a frustrated growl. "I've been trying to think of something temporary. Imagine a situation where a person drowns or their heart stops, but they are later resuscitated. If something like that exists on a soul level, only…" Noric shook his head. "Such a thing does not exist, and even if it did it would be impossible with the gods involved in your death. The closest we have ever come is the creation of spectres."

I now understood why we were flying instead of whisking. Noric wanted time to think, and being in the air astride Orphnaeus helped him do that.

"Where are we going?"

"The old lunatic asylum," he replied.

"I don't think they call them that any longer," I pointed out.

"No, it's actually the name. The Trans-Allegheny Lunatic Asylum in West Virginia is riddled with ghosts. It will be a good place to talk to them and practice what they've learned."

I knew many of the unlucky mortals conscripted to asylums were perfectly sane, but I also knew the horrific treatments they received might have changed that. Whatever ghosts we were speaking with, I hoped they retained their minds enough to teach me… something. But I doubted it because I'd plagued Archie and Yvette with questions growing up, and the biggest factor in turning phantom was chance, and I had no control over that.

We landed in the dead of night in Weston, just outside the imposing, historic building. Long wings reached out on either side, a clocktower rose from its center, and small hills guarded the asylum's back. The air was bone-chillingly cold, but that wasn't why I shivered. Even looking at the hospital repelled me, as I was sure it had unleashed countless atrocities over the decades.

Noric took my hand. "I don't want you to be a ghost." His nostrils flared and his eyes flashed dangerously. "But I won't let them take you," he vowed, voice rumbling like an avalanche.

I didn't want to turn spectre either—forever beside Noric but never able to truly touch him, to love him? It was a solution that invited another type of torture. But I held onto Noric while he whisked us inside.

Immediately, that dank, old building smell filled my nose. It was coupled with something sharp—astringent cleaners attempting to cover up dust and dirt and pain. The dark, eerie hall and paint-chipped ceiling looked like something out of a horror film. I stayed close to Noric because this place looked like it would suck me into a void of darkness if I strayed too far.

Sensing my nervousness, Noric explained, "Originally, the asylum was constructed to house only a small number of women and it began with good intentions, but you know where those lead. And this was indeed a hell," he remarked, as we shuffled down the hall. "Dissatisfied husbands could commit their wives for something as simple as self-pleasuring or even reading novels. None of the unfortunate victims confined here deserved to be treated that way, and even by the preposterous definition of the time very few were insane."

We spied our first ghost running down the hallway. He screamed gibberish at the top of his lungs, wailing and tearing at his long hair and completely oblivious to us.

"Well, not that one," Noric noted, grimacing.

Great, I thought, discouraged. *How am I supposed to learn anything when —*

"I know you," a disembodied female voice said, and I jumped just a little.

She was hiding herself better than the last, so I let my eyes relax, let them go a bit cross-eyed, and her spectral image came into view. Like all ghosts, once I had her in my sights, I didn't have to concentrate any longer as I wasn't likely to *un-see* her.

"I don't believe I've had the pleasure of meeting you before," Noric said, giving a small, polite bow—another of his manners forged in another time and place.

"You can call me Nurse Agnes. I don't know what business you have here but if the overlords sent you, I'm sure we can work out some kind of a deal. I'm good at deals," she said with a wink. There didn't seem to be sexual innuendo to it; Nurse Agnes delivered her statement with pride more than anything else.

Noric waved his hand and assured her, "No, that is not why we're here. I came here to see if you can help her."

"Ah," Agnes said, appraising me with her sharp eyebrows raised high. "I understand. Follow me."

The ghostly nurse had an unusual accent, part Southern twang, part Trans-Atlantic, and her manner of speaking was confident and feisty. I wasn't sure if women in her day or in her position held such authority, but she'd certainly grown into it over her non-corporeal decades.

Noric and I followed as Nurse Agnes led us into what must have been the offices of the asylum prior to its closure. She hovered over a seat behind the desk, and Noric and I sat in the two chairs facing it.

"Let's cut to the meat of the matter," Nurse Agnes said. "You're here because we're just bursting with spectres and you want us to help your girlfriend become one of us."

Noric nodded, but I blinked in surprise. Were we that obvious? *There could be other reasons we were here,* I thought angrily. I could be a student of history—which I was. Technically. And maybe I just happened to know a reaper and he brought me here in the middle of the night for a... a... history lesson.

"Yes. Her name is in the Book and I can't circumvent it, although I'm trying. The gods are reaping her, personally. As a back-up plan, I'm hoping she can become a phantom."

Agnes started to reply as a blood-curdling scream pierced the air—though it didn't distract her at all. But when the screams continued and she caught the look on my face, she paused and explained, "That's just the good doctor receiving a dose of his own medicine." Her lips curled into a pleasant smile. "Eternally. We stay out of Ward F and the ghosts there generally stay within their designated area. They have what they want in there more than anything they desire out here."

"A... doctor?" I asked.

"Oh, several," she said, cheerfully. "And a few troublesome guards and other staff. You see, the inmates have taken over the asylum, as it were, finding bliss in their vengeance instead of the Above."

Noric squeezed my hand. We'd expected several patients to be anchored or to return here, not doctors. "So many deserve justice, but so few see it delivered," he said, skeptically. "It's lucky for you that such a number of mortals needing punishment found themselves as ghosts."

"Well," the nurse said, tightly. "We gave them a little push, as it were. Helped them remain in this realm for the retribution they'd earned."

Noric stiffened and I realized that whatever he knew of the phantom realm, ghosts targeting others to tether wasn't something he'd seen before. At least, not on this scale.

"How?" I begged, squeezing Noric's hand in return. "How did you help them do it?"

"With enough anger, anything's possible," Agnes replied, leaning back in her chair. "I wouldn't call it helping though, we forced them to stay." Her ghostly eyes gleamed as she spoke. Whatever was being done to patients in the past, I was sure Nurse Agnes was both against it and helpless to stop it. "We weren't successful every time, but for a number of those wicked souls we were able to rip them from the clutches of Elysia and harness them to the earth, right here in the hospital."

"But *how?*" Noric repeated.

Agnes folded her hands beneath her chin and rested it there. "Those with ties to this institution are prone to glitches, as luck would have it. Or perhaps the widescale horrors created the rift." She eyed Noric suspiciously before speaking next. "Sometimes we lurk. To you or your familiars it feels like the soul is returning to the Above. When they're beyond your reach but before they've completed the journey, we attempt to rip them aside. Sometimes we're successful. Sometimes not."

I knew from Eligius that ghosts slipped through the cracks *after* he'd done his part, but I'd never heard of other ghosts getting their hooks in them somehow.

"Can you do it for me?" I begged. "If I fail to tether myself, can you, uh, hook me?"

Nurse Agnes gave me a sympathetic look. "No," she said. "I'm guessing someone like you would not only risk turning the overlord's gaze in our direction—something we've long avoided—but it takes the collective strength of many of us to do it, and the emotion we use is our rage." It was strange the way Agnes spoke of emotion, as a sort of currency, a power. "I have no emotion to spare you," she said, matter-of-factly. "Not to mention, to turn spectre the mortal's death has to be susceptible to a glitch in the first place, and no one has control over that."

I sank back into my chair, defeated. As much as I wanted to shout that love would tether me here, there was a low probability the right set of conditions existed, and the gods would never allow it anyway.

Still, it was all we had to try.

"But you'll teach her what you can?" Noric asked in a strained voice. "Show her how you yourself managed to stay? And show me how you hold others?"

"For a price," Nurse Agnes agreed, folding her arms.

Noric leveled his gaze at her. "What do you want?"

"There's a few humans who once worked here still plaguing the material world. They don't deserve their lives."

"You want me to reap them," Noric said.

Nurse Anges shook her head. "I want you to use your powers to make the remainder of their lives a living hell. When their time comes, we'll do our best to collect those we can."

"Deal," Noric easily agreed.

The ghostly nurse rattled off a short list of names and Noric promised that he and the other reapers would make their lives miserable until the time of their death. He even said he'd notify Agnes when that time came, so that she wouldn't need to keep watch for the moment.

Finally, Agnes called the other ghosts to her office—the benevolent ones not in Ward F.

About a dozen phantoms crowded the room, and we moved into one of the larger wards for more space. Over the decades, the hospital must have seen tens of thousands of staff and patients working or living within its walls, but even so, the number of ghosts was unusually high, and that didn't include the more violent spectres elsewhere.

Me—the mortal girl the high reaper was desperate to save—was someone they all wanted to meet, and each ghost was eager to teach me how they'd done it.

The more I learned, however, the less sure I felt, because there was no one true method.

"It's a sideways push," some would say.

Others argued, "No, no, it's a hunkering *down*."

"It's the moment the reaping occurs," one female spirit insisted.

And another would shake his head and swear, "It's only several seconds after that you can do it."

There was little I learned that Yvette and Archie hadn't already said whenever I pelted them with questions. But I attempted the vague task of imagining I *pushed* my soul away from an imaginary force and in the direction I wanted. Meanwhile, Noric listened intently to explanations on how the inmates hooked the guilty men and women they wanted to anchor.

Whenever I stole a glance at him, I could tell it wasn't a productive conversation. The more the ghosts talked the more it sounded like a special set of circumstances surrounded their hospital at its height, a script with a unique clustering of glitches.

The sun was near rising by the time we finished and Noric whisked us back outside and to Orphnaeus. Our hearts were heavy and there was no point in denying it. The chances of me being able to become a ghost were as likely as finding one specific pebble on a mountain range.

"Stay in Elysia," Noric ordered, gripping my shoulders. Desperation made him more dangerous looking than ever, tall and powerful and wild. "If you die and can't hold to the earth, don't jump when you're in the Above. You won't remember me if you leap and it's unlikely I'd find or remember you, that's not how it works. Stay and I will find a way to die, I *swear* it. I will join you."

"Even Sevastian couldn't," I protested weakly. "And what if you're Eliminated? What if that's what happens to a reaper after their time is done? There's no way to know."

"I will find a way to storm the heavens and come to you god dammit!" he roared, eyes wet with tears. "I won't let you go."

"If they were going to let us be together, they would have done so already," I whispered.

"There is hope, Avalia, there's still hope." Noric crushed me to him. "I can't lose you, I've only just found you." His face twisted in a deep, wretched agony that broke my heart. "It took thousands of years to find you and they're trying to take you away."

I tried to speak but I couldn't without sobbing, so I pressed my lips together and buried my head into Noric's jacket and against his chest. He stiffened and my stomach flipped. Pulling back, I looked up to find that faraway look in those steel eyes.

"What's happening?" I asked.

He averted his gaze, but it made no difference. "A last-minute change in the book. Wildfires ripping through southern Australia. Many are dying," he mumbled.

I closed my eyes like I could close out the truth, but we both knew.

The world wants a sacrifice and I've been selected.

We flew back to Grimsmere and Noric whisked us into the library. Sevastian had already arrived and was sitting on the chesterfield sofa. I wasn't surprised, sure he'd gone through his list in a perfunctory manner and had quickly returned once the task was completed with minimal effort. Hexley, Embrette, and my father were still out searching. Noric and I hadn't even begun to visit our list of names yet.

I didn't resent Sevastian for his unenthusiastic participation. The blonde reaper looked worse than usual, with purple-black circles beneath his eyes. His unsteady gait and the open bottle told me he'd found his way into our wine cellar.

"Did you uncover anything useful?" Noric hurried to ask the question to which we already knew the answer.

"You're grasping at straws," Sevastian said, shaking his head and holding up his empty glass. "Limp, flimsy blades of grass by the riverbed, and they will not save you from the current any more than a leaf would help a drowning man stay afloat."

You still have hope of becoming a ghost, I consoled myself. *You can try to anchor and Noric can try to hold you.* I glanced at him, sure from the dark look in his eye he was going to pummel Sevastian.

Instead, Noric froze, and what little color he had drained from his face.

Then he *roared*.

It was the sound of mountains rumbling, loud enough to shake the books on our shelves. My chest tightened and my stomach lurched at his wild, animalistic fury. By the time I blinked, my father had appeared in the room, and Noric had me in his arms so tightly I had difficulty breathing.

"No!" he yelled. "I will not allow it."

Allow what? What could possibly be wrong? I was already slated to die, so there was nothing left to take from me.

Chills broke out all over my flesh. Unless the overlords moved up the date of my death. Could they do that?

"Lee Lee," Eligius said, his voice grieved. "There's been a change in the Book. You are not returning to Elysia." He took a breath. "You've been designated for Elimination."

Oh.

Oh god. It was so much worse than dying just a bit sooner.

It was my soul being utterly annihilated.

It was ceasing to exist in any form.

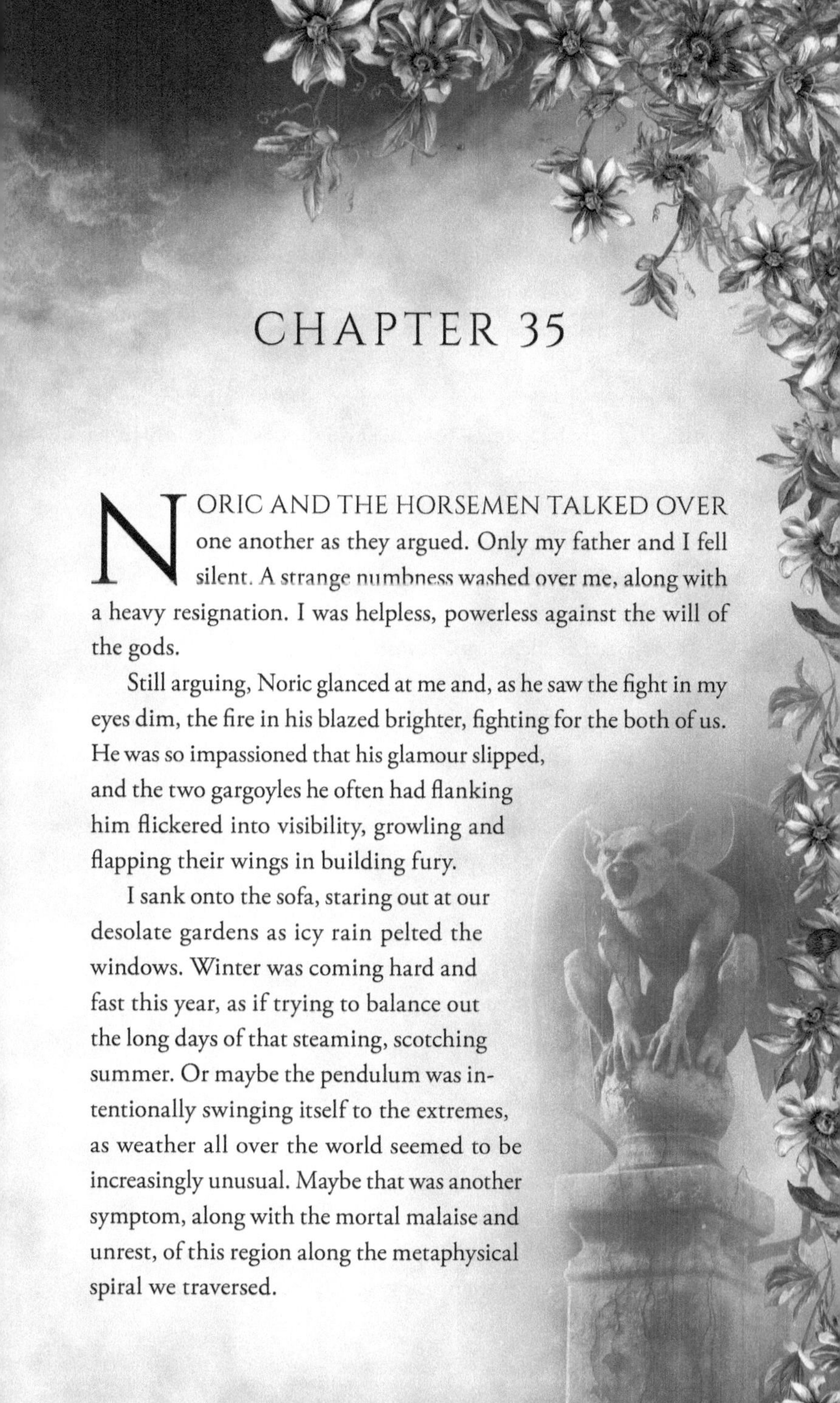

CHAPTER 35

NORIC AND THE HORSEMEN TALKED OVER one another as they argued. Only my father and I fell silent. A strange numbness washed over me, along with a heavy resignation. I was helpless, powerless against the will of the gods.

Still arguing, Noric glanced at me and, as he saw the fight in my eyes dim, the fire in his blazed brighter, fighting for the both of us. He was so impassioned that his glamour slipped, and the two gargoyles he often had flanking him flickered into visibility, growling and flapping their wings in building fury.

I sank onto the sofa, staring out at our desolate gardens as icy rain pelted the windows. Winter was coming hard and fast this year, as if trying to balance out the long days of that steaming, scotching summer. Or maybe the pendulum was intentionally swinging itself to the extremes, as weather all over the world seemed to be increasingly unusual. Maybe that was another symptom, along with the mortal malaise and unrest, of this region along the metaphysical spiral we traversed.

So what could I do against all that? My whole life I'd been fighting to be something else. It was always impossible and now, the gods had conspired to ensure that I was cut off from what little happiness remained, should I have lived a full mortal life with Noric. What good would raging against any of it do?

In my final moments, I wanted only to love Noric, to soak up as much of us as I could.

Sevastian, drink in hand, swayed on his feet. He handled all of this if it were happening to him, and I supposed it was making him relive his personal horror. *No, worse.* He helplessly watched his brother fall into the same torment.

The rain lashing our windows turned to hail and some of those icy bits were large and hard enough they broke a nearby pane, and I jumped.

Everyone fell silent until Sevastian spoke.

"The world is hungry, Ava. And it wants to eat you."

Noric lunged forward and swung, his powerful fist connecting with Sevastian's nose in a gory crunch.

"Stop, please!" I shouted, springing to my feet.

Eligius was already between Noric and Sevastian, holding out his hands to keep them apart.

"This solves nothing," my father growled his warning. "I will not have either of you wasting precious time or energy on anything that does not involve saving my daughter. Do you understand me?"

I shivered. He'd used his reaper voice, and its fathomless depths shook me to my core.

Noric clenched his jaw as he took deep, steadying breaths. Then he stalked over to me and I could practically feel his frustration at allowing himself to be distracted by fighting.

"I'm sorry," he said, pulling me into his embrace and tucking my head against his broad chest. I ran my hands along his muscular arms and breathed his wild reaper scent, hating that I was quickly losing opportunities to enjoy these small, precious things.

I could almost handle death—folding one hand of cards and being dealt another. But being dealt out of the game completely… I could hardly wrap my head around the thought. I wasn't evil, wasn't a vile soul or any kind of horror that demanded utter destruction. Was I? Had entering the Rotunda been that bad?

No, it couldn't be, since I wasn't slated for Elimination until now. Why?

Maybe the gods were watching and didn't want to allow a chance for me to turn spectre. Preventing it, maybe they removed my existence in any form.

Sevastian was right.

The world is hungry and it wants to eat me.

"Ava, let's go through your father's list during the day," Noric said, suddenly all-business, as if retreating into order would help. "At night we'll return here and research for more information, more leads."

Research what and why? I wanted to protest. *If you've had millennia to uncover truths about the nature of immortality and gotten nowhere, what good did it do to scrutinize more books or to track down ever dwindling and desperate leads?*

But in my last moments alive, I wanted to do whatever I could to make Noric happy, and he wanted to do whatever he could to save me.

"Okay," I whispered.

With his hands on my waist, he whisked us to our first destination. There was no time for Striders now.

From there, I spent the next few days following Noric to the ends of the earth. Literally. I trailed a few steps behind as he'd urgently pull me faster, further… We met with an Indian podiatrist in Mumbai who was rumored to possess mystical powers. There was some truth to the whispers, as it turned out he practiced podomancy on the side, and he was the real deal. Somehow, the doctor could read a person's fate from studying the lines in their feet. But he knew nothing of the realm beyond, the true nature of the universe, or the immortal reapers serving it. Begrudgingly, Noric allowed him to examine my own feet, and when the man began stammering and looking for an upside, it was clear that he'd seen death written somewhere on my sole.

Noric only scowled when I made the pun as we left.

Frustrated, he whisked us to the next name on our list, and the next. Sometimes there was a spark, a kernel of something magical, and sometimes not. But it was never enough to rival anything close to a reaper's knowledge or power. I had a ticking clock over my head, a countdown that only granted me mere days to exist. When the reality hit, it was often so hard I'd double over, clutching my stomach.

We whisked to a nightclub in Moscow where it was rumored that vampires possessed a den beneath the dance floor. And while we found a secret VIP room for those who cosplayed, none of the participants were beyond human. They drank blood in their play, and without an aberration's ability to process it, I wasn't even sure their human lives would last very long with such unsanitary practices.

Each night, we gathered in the library of Grimsmere, reporting our findings to one another and losing more hope. The horsemen grew increasingly despondent and snappish with each other, all except my father. He sat in his armchair with his fisted hand pressed against his lips, deep in thought.

I was tearing my loved ones apart and this was only the beginning. What would happen after my death? Would Noric mourn for eternity, as Sevastian did? I'd spoiled their happiness, soured their lives, and that grief would last forever.

My gut twisted.

I'd ruined the world too, but dying would make that right, while there was nothing that would repair the damage I'd done to the immortals. My father, Noric, Hexley and Embrette. Maybe even Sevastian would grieve me.

Maybe they'd all have been better off if I'd never come into their lives.

"I feel like I might pass out from fear at any moment," I whispered to Noric, glancing at the eighteenth-century French clock on the mantle. I'd loved it as a child—ornate, gold, and sculpted with happy little cherubs frolicking amongst the clouds. Now its cruel hands were just a reminder of my countdown. "I almost want you to wipe my mind so that I forget this is happening. But I don't mean it. I—I want to face my end, knowing." Trying to be light-hearted, I said, "And the only time I've been obscured it didn't fully take."

"Well, that one time it worked, of course," Noric said. There was the edge of resentment in his voice for some reason. "When Eligius allowed Vasilios to taste you for the ichor."

"No," I argued. "My father has never obscured me since that first attempt."

"Then how else would he know you're not able to turn ikavorn?"

I shrugged and Noric furrowed his brow. Not removing his keen gaze from my face, he called across the room, "Eligius. You obscured Ava after Vasilios tasted her, correct?"

My father, who'd rested his forehead against his hand in that way he did whenever he was in deep thought, looked up and said, "No, I had Vasilios scent her. It is enough."

Noric stopped breathing. "Are you saying no ikavorn has tasted Avalia to be sure?"

My father's dark eyes saddened and he held up his hands. "Noric. It makes no difference."

"It *might,*" Noric argued. He shot to his feet, spread his arms wide, chest thrust forward. "It might make all the difference in the world!"

"What are you saying?" I asked, quickly popping up to join him.

"Your father only had Vasilios come close and smell your blood. Ava, he could be mistaken. He didn't taste you. There's much we don't know about their kind."

I looked at Hexley and Embrette for confirmation.

"That's not how it works," Hexley's face was pained. "But I suppose it couldn't hurt to try…"

"You're desperate," Sevastian said, sneering.

"Of course I'm desperate!" Noric shouted. "And you of all people should understand that."

Sevastian closed his mouth.

I sighed. He'd only been trying to help and moreover, I agreed with Sevastian. If my father said it made no difference, I knew he wasn't wrong.

But it wasn't as if there were better options.

"Noric, a mortal is more likely to die than to survive the transformation. And even if Ava could become ikavorn, you'd be forbidden from interacting with her," Embrette said gently. "Not to mention, as an aberration you'd have a powerful desire to cull her."

I groaned. When put that way, it wasn't much of an option at all.

Noric spun toward my father and as they stared at one another, I knew they were communicating telepathically to save time. Still, the conversation went on quite a while before my father gave an almost-imperceptible nod.

"Come on," Noric ordered, pulling me by my hand. "We're going to New Orleans. Right now."

"Slow down a minute," I pled, yanking back on my arm. "Even if it worked, what good will turning me into an aberration do now? If the gods want me to die it doesn't solve the problem."

"Maybe this is all just one of their games. They love to test people, toy with them," Noric argued, biting his words through bared teeth. "Perhaps it's like a riddle and if we solve it, they'll let you live."

From a glance around the room, I could tell that Noric's theory didn't have a lot of support.

"Vasilios runs a transitory bar in New Orleans—"

I shook my head rapidly and said, "Stop. What is a transitory bar?"

"Are you familiar with card shuffling?" Noric asked.

"Yes?" I said, cocking a brow.

"I haven't yet explained every hitch in the script," Eligius announced.

"New Orleans has crap for coding," Noric said with a wave of his hand. "It's the home to many glitches, magical portals, time loops. All sorts of anomalies. When a building disappears and reappears within the mortal realm, the humans christened the occurrence as card shuffling. It's usually an establishment from another time, appearing on a street and disappearing by morning." Noric grabbed my biceps and declared, "Perhaps, Ava, what we do in the space *between* realities won't be too closely monitored. Vampires tend to scatter like birds on the wind, but Vasilios haunts this bar because it does the traveling for him."

Dumbfounded, I tried to wrap my head around the concept as I agreed, "Okay, let's go to the transitory bar."

"Yes, now," Noric said, kissing the top of my head possessively.

Perhaps he was right, and I could escape the watchful eye of the gods there. But would it stop the world from ending if it hungered for my death as the chosen sacrifice?

"Noric," I protested softly. "What if you're only half-right? What if I'm able to live as an aberration, but I'm not dead enough to satisfy the overlords? What if the world continues to crumble?"

"I don't give a shit about saving the world, I care about saving you," he swore roughly.

"They seem pretty connected," I pointed out. "What would remain of any of us, if the gods rendered destruction to their hearts' content? A wasteland for scavengers? Or nothing at all?"

It was even more difficult to picture the world itself ceasing to exist than to imagine a space between realities, and a cosmic horror beyond even my personal Elimination.

Noric clenched his jaw. "I don't know. But we have to try."

My father watched us carefully and when I glanced at him for reassurance, he gave another solemn nod as permission.

"Let's go," Noric repeated, checking his daggers to ensure they were securely in place.

"Wait," Sevastian said. He yanked Noric close and pressed their foreheads together, reaching around to hold his brother in place with one hand on the back of his head.

"I love you," Sevastian said. "And I don't want you to be like me."

Noric, who hadn't pulled away but hadn't embraced his brother either, sighed deeply through his nose. Closing his eyes, he said, "I know." He opened his eyes and finally put his hand on the back of Sevastian's head in return. "But I am like you. It's too late, and I wouldn't change it if I could. Despite your pain, I have envied you, envied that you found someone to love. I never thought it would happen to me and I don't regret any of it now that it has."

Sevastian pursed his lips, wanting to argue and knowing it did no good. Noric might not regret our love, but Sevastian mourned our situation enough for both of them.

I said goodbye, and Noric whisked us to a dark and deserted road somewhere in New Orleans. I didn't know much beyond Bourbon and Canal Streets, and this didn't look like either, but we weren't too far from the hubbub. There were no people or cars here, though at this late hour I didn't expect any. As we walked, we passed shops and houses on either side of the road. The whole scene felt eerie, but nothing looked blatantly out of place until we arrived at our obvious destination.

Between the more modern structures stood a bar with architecture dating to the late eighteen or early nineteen hundreds. There were far older structures in this historic city, of course, but this establishment, abnormally wedged where it was, did not look as if it belonged. Not just for the abrupt variance in its façade, but for the strangest feeling emoting from the building itself.

Warm light glowed within the bar, the only light on this dark street. I realized one of the reasons the road felt so creepy was that it was unnatural for no other structure to have a light of some kind, either through the windows or outside on the porch. As we neared, there was a pungent scent of horse urine on the night air, but that could be from any time period in New Orleans.

"This bar is often here when the cards shuffle, but not always. It likes the city though, so it doesn't tend to stray far when it pops up on other streets."

Noticing my trepidation, Noric said, "Think of it like a sector prone to anomalies, like the Bermuda Triangle."

"Right. And what happens to people who get caught there under the wrong circumstances?" I asked, a bit sarcastically.

"I won't let anything happen to you," Noric swore.

I let out a low laugh, because we were indeed hoping something would happen to me. We were hoping a vampire-like creature would bite me, kill me, and turn me into an aberration to plague the system.

Noric clasped my hand and led us into the old tavern.

There wasn't a single patron but there was a bartender standing behind a wooden counter, polishing a glass and eyeing us. He had a long brown ponytail and wore a dark apron that didn't fit our time period, nor did any of the glassware, wooden chairs, or tables. Were I a normal human, I might have thought I'd stumbled upon a historical bar attempting to keep its appearance authentic to the time period.

As we approached the server asked, "What can I get you?"

Something about his manner of speaking made it clear he was familiar with modern times, even if he was currently employed in a pocket outside of it.

"Your master," Noric said, cutting to the point. "We both know what the other is and I will not have my time wasted pretending otherwise. I want Vasilios to taste her, to see if she possesses the ichor. He has scented her before, but we want to be sure. This is Avalia Thrailkill, Death's adoptive daughter. If you harm one hair on her head you'll make her father quite upset, and me, and I will quickly do something about it." As Noric spoke, he opened his jacket and flashed his reaper's dagger, making the threat clear. "I don't care what deal you've worked out with the overlords, in case my being here doesn't make that apparent enough."

The man, who'd listened silently throughout, simply nodded and marched through a door and into a back room in the establishment. He seemed neither afraid nor very interested in us. Maybe his blasé attitude was what made him a good guard, because I did not believe his only function was to pour drinks.

I kept waiting for something interesting to happen, but nothing did. For my first encounter with a vampire, it was rather unremarkable.

A few seconds later the man reappeared and behind him, more than half a dozen aberrations funneled into the bar. With them, they carried the undercurrent of a threat that I'd been subconsciously fearing.

CHAPTER 36

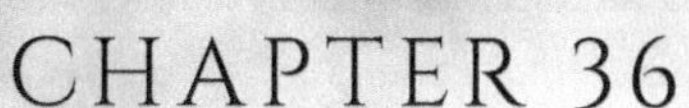

VASILIOS AND THE VAMPIRES WERE EVERYTHING
the guard was not. Richly dressed in long black jackets
and lacy red dresses, this gathering more closely aligned
with how I expected their kind to appear. None here would have
been out of place on the streets of New Orleans, and perhaps that
was the intention.

Their power, however, was unmistakable. It radiated from
the group, permeating the air like the con-
tinual hum of a low-level threat—one
that could increase in volume at any moment. Whatever these beings truly were,
however they were created, it went far
deeper than the portrayals of the undead
in media.

The ikavorn sprawled onto chairs
to our left and right while the man I assumed to be Vasilios stood at the opposite
end of the room and faced us.

His hair was a short, dirty blonde, his
eyes were a deep brown, and he possessed pale
skin that was surprisingly dewy and fresh.
Physically, he appeared somewhere in his
mid-twenties, which was so much younger

than I'd anticipated. Vasilios was somewhat on the thinner side, spry, and at best average-looking, which went against everything I'd thought about vampires. Though I had to admit there was a puckish appeal to his energy and an intriguing quality in his sharp eyes.

Those eyes seemed to look everywhere and nowhere at once. It was as if he simultaneously took in the entire room while homing in on us specifically, like some kind of supernatural bird of prey.

His greeting was an immediate warning.

"You may well turn the gods' eyes here and get all of us culled with this blatant violation. I've scented Eligius's daughter before," he remarked flatly. "What is your purpose in repeating it?"

"Not to scent her, but," Noric gritted his teeth. "To taste her. To be sure. Her name has appeared in the Book and—" Noric's voice cut off abruptly. He took a breath and finished, "As you can imagine, her father and I will be very pleased to keep her alive. *Indebted*, you could say."

Vasilios's eyes danced. "I don't make mistakes, but I'm not going to look a gift horse in the mouth," he declared. He spoke languidly, as if we discussed which scones to serve at teatime and not my life in the balance.

My immortal soul.

Noric's hands tightened on my shoulders and his protective energy enveloped me. He was poised, strained, ready to attack. Whatever the reaper equivalent was to a cat raising its hackles, that's what I felt from Noric in that moment.

Vasilios crooked one finger at me. The ikavorn on our left and right practically licked their lips, and their eyes gleamed to watch what was about to unfold. But beneath the enthusiasm ran an undercurrent of anxious tension. Like Noric, their bodies stiffened, readying for a potential fight.

Which was the *last* thing I wanted. Noric was by far the most powerful entity in the room, yet we needed Vasilios more than he needed us.

Noric's eyes hardened. "One taste," he commanded. "If she is harmed in any way, I will break the treaty and kill everyone in this room. Do you understand me, aberration?"

"What would be the point in harming her?" Vasilios asked, offering a lazy sigh. "She's going to die soon anyway, as she's not of the blood."

Noric flinched at the casual proclamation of my death, but he laid a kiss on my forehead and said, "Come right back to me when it's done. Do you understand me?"

"Yes," I said, with as much confidence as I could muster. Then I swallowed hard and, alone, I crossed the distance between Noric and Vasilios. The haunting flicker of torchlights along the bar's brick walls gave me the sensation of being in a horror movie.

The kind where a foolish girl puts herself in danger.

If Noric were a dog, he would have been snarling while I walked further away from him. Instead, it was as if his gargoyles spoke through him. He made a threatening sound I could only describe as rumbling stones, warning the ikavorn that a mountain of destruction was forthcoming if anything happened to me.

Please, let me be of the blood, I willed.

I expected Vasilios to grab me and taste me while I faced him, chest to chest, as if in some kind of embrace. That was the way it always happened in the movies.

I should have known by now that popular depictions of any immortal creatures were wildly inaccurate… and that Vasilios wanted to twist the knife in Noric's chest.

As soon as I reached him, Vasilios roughly seized and turned me around to face the other direction. Noric snarled some more but held himself back. The others tittered and giggled.

Vasilios's movements turned sensual as he bent my head to the left and gently brushed my hair from my neck with exaggerated care. His hands were cold, but no more than I'd felt from some mortals, and his nails were slightly long, but not so much as to be distinctive.

I was kind of let down by my first encounter with these vampire-like creatures, but the strength in which Vasilios had spun me told me there was a lot hidden beneath the surface.

Head bent far to the side, I locked eyes with Noric while I suffered Vasilios's indulgent stroking.

Please let me have the ichor.

"You know, if she were to possess the ever-essence *and* on the off chance she survived the transformation, I'd have to kill one of my own kind to allow space for her creation," Vasilios announced. "That is the deal we struck with the overlords."

"I'm aware of the general terms of your existence," Noric bit out. "Though if you'd ever care to enlighten us as to how they came about, the horsemen and I would love to chat."

Vasilios only chuckled.

The master of this vampire den leaned down slowly, drawing it out, and I could feel his breath on me before he bit. Noric's eyes flashed and I immediately knew Vasilios had smirked or done something to taunt. But I soon didn't have time to think of anything else, as I felt the sudden sting of his bite. I gasped when fangs pierced me, but a moment later I relaxed into the strangest sensation washing over me.

This is how they subdue their prey, I thought, while I still could. As Vasilios drained me, I dreamily succumbed to it. Fighting back was far from my mind. It felt like a sedative entered my bloodstream, like a soothing, pleasant drug that gave me the sensation of floating in a realm where no earthly concerns could reach me.

But Noric's voice did.

"Enough!" he shouted. "If you suck one more drop of her blood, I will spill all of yours."

Vasilios released me, but I was only aware of the fact because Noric had caught and whisked me back to his side of the room. With his reaper magic, it happened in a flash.

"Exquisite," I heard the head vampire sigh.

"Does she have the ever-essence?" Noric demanded, using his sleeve to stanch the puncture wound on my neck.

"She tastes like truffles," Vasilios continued, ignoring Noric. "A rare, white truffle one can only enjoy in small doses, before the flavor overwhelms."

"Answer the question!" Noric yelled.

"No, that's not right at all," Vasilios pondered. His raised hands and reached out, as if trying to grasp the information he sought. "There's nothing sharp or pungent about it."

"Answer the question, aberration." Noric's low voice was a warning.

Vasilios's pale face lit, like moonlight shining across its surface. "Ambrosia," he declared, voice as dreamy as I still felt. But the room was slowly coming into sharper focus, so I knew I was shaking off whatever he'd injected into my blood.

"Ah, I remember the taste, before humans wiped it from existence," Vasilios crooned, closing his eyes and smiling. Then, just as quickly, his eyes snapped open. "She wants more," he drawled. "They always do."

The ikavorn was wrong. What I'd experienced with Noric was a thousand times more seductive than anything he could ever do.

I'd heard Noric play. I'd tasted my reaper's kiss and felt his caress. I'd flown across the sky on his Strider and right into the storm.

I put more weight onto my feet as I leaned away from Noric and announced coolly, "I don't."

Vasilios frowned, then arched a brow.

"Is she of the blood?" Noric shouted the question loudly enough that a few tittering vampires in our audience jumped and immediately quieted.

Vasilios's frown deepened and, emotionless, he declared, "She is not."

"You're lying," Noric accused, squeezing me tightly to him. "Tell me the truth or I'll kill you all."

Vasilios arched a brow. "And why would I lie?"

Noric fisted his hands and I could feel the anger vibrating from his body. "Immortalize her," he cried. "Immortalize her, *try!*"

"She does not possess the ichor so it will not achieve the result you seek, and it would only kill her sooner," Vasilios announced. "There's still time, there's always time, for her name to be moved up in the Book. Would you rather she die today?"

My ears pricked. The ikavorn knew about reapers and the Reclamation of Souls book. So what else did they know? Why were they so protected by the overlords? Could I strike a similar deal?

The gaggle of vampires around us began laughing.

"I want to taste the truffles," a short female ikavorn said, her voice a hiss.

"Ambrosia," another corrected.

"Let's drain her," said an excited male. "And spare her the wait for death."

I felt Noric's muscles coil, and his rage moved like a living thing, expanding to encompass the room. The leering vampires did not notice, but Vasilios did.

"It would be a kindness," a redheaded male agreed.

"There's not a single kind bone in your body," a blonde female taunted. "The day anyone would call you kind is the day I let you stick your favorite bone in me." She leaned down and ran a seductive hand over the bare chest of the redheaded vampire. "Right where you've always wanted."

A male with long, dark hair eyed me and said slowly, "Speaking of sticking things in places, I think this girl is a virgin. Before she dies, we should show her all the pleasures of life."

"That *would* be a kindness," another voice agreed.

I barely had time to be horrified at the implication. Those words sealed the ikavorn's fate—and maybe mine too. There was a fraction of a second in which I registered the emptiness beside me, and then I felt the cage of Vasilios's arms around my chest. All in the blink of an eye.

I gasped when I saw our audience of eight vampires sprawled onto the chairs and the floor, blood seeping from their lifeless bodies. Noric brandished his dagger, ready to reap Vasilios too. His breathing was ragged—not from any exertion but from fury.

Oh my god.

They were all dead; he'd culled the den of ikavorn.

With a sinking stomach I realized that I was Vasilios's only defense from him joining his deceased flock.

Once more, the head vampire bent and exposed my neck to his bite. I imagined he could kill me before Noric could reach me, or at least, make it a close enough call that Noric didn't want to risk it. Already robbed of more blood than Vasilios was supposed to drink, it wouldn't take much to drain me.

He wouldn't even need to do that, I thought, breaking out in a cold sweat. One bite and Vasilios could probably tear out my throat. Maybe one punch of a supernatural fist and he could pull my heart from my chest. There were endless ways Vasilios could kill me.

Right? I actually wasn't sure the extent of his power and realized I had a lot to learn. Maybe the reapers did too, which wasn't an encouraging thought.

"Look what you have done," Vasilios scolded angrily. "You better hope no one is watching the transitory places or *you'll* be the one the gods punish. If I don't kill her first and teach you a lesson."

Noric froze, head cocked. I knew he braced to feel my name move up in the Book, from December twenty-first to today. He lowered his dagger and bared his teeth, not wanting any action to cause that to happen.

An awful, pungent smell reached my nose and I gagged. *Dead ikavorn.* It was as if a malodorous gas suddenly released from the bodies beside us. Vasilios and Noric stared hard at one another, locked in unbroken combat as if the sudden scent of decay didn't assault their noses. Maybe it hadn't. Maybe they just turned off their sense of smell.

Vasilios's demeanor changed as his face lit with pleasure. "I've faced countless stalemates in my life but this *is* one of the more interesting," he taunted.

Noric cocked a one-sided grin, utterly full of hate. "Is it? I think it's rather dull. She is *Death's daughter,*" he reminded. "Even if you managed to harm her and escape, the grand reaper himself would find and end you."

For some reason, that made Vasilios smile and close his eyes briefly.

When he re-opened them, he countered, "Oh, but I don't mean what's happening between *us.*" He stroked my neck sensually and I shivered in disgust. Noric's eyes flashed with that steely hate once more. "I mean what's happening outside."

I watched curiously and Noric drew a sharp breath. *What could possibly make this situation worse? More vampires drawing near, ready to overtake us?*

"The cards are about to shuffle again. Do you know what happens when a mortal gets stuck in the space *between* time and space?"

They die? I guessed, gulping. Or perhaps they were just lost until the cards shuffled again? Whatever it was, it couldn't be good, and we didn't have time for delays.

"When? How long?" Noric bit out his demand.

Vasilios paused, but not to torment us. He seemed distracted, detached from what was happening and lost in his own thoughts. "You truly love her, don't you?" He sounded amazed by his own declaration. His stroking of my hair and neck suddenly didn't feel like taunting but... envy?

"Why did he choose you?" Vasilios asked rhetorically. Then, with a sigh, he declared, "Soon now. And every second you delay increases your chances of missing the opportunity to leave."

Noric cursed.

"Take her," Vasilios said, magnanimously, "and go. If you depart now, I will not *personally* consider the treaty breached. Indeed, I will thank you for ridding me of this tiresome den of fools and for opening space for a fresh following to be crafted."

Noric snorted. "And for sparing your life."

For some reason, this made Vasilios laugh, yet there was no mirth in it. Then he bowed his head and concurred, "And I will thank you for sparing my life."

Noric and Vasilios came to an agreement with their eyes, and the next thing I knew, I was in Noric's powerful arms and blinking at my new surroundings. In a flash, he'd whisked us out of the ikavorn den and back onto the streets of New Orleans.

Noric supported my weight while I sucked in great gulps of air. There was still no light and the strange darkness enveloped us. I couldn't see anyone else—human or otherwise—on the quiet road. Clouds covered the sky and an eerie feeling permeated the air. It reminded me of the so-called *backrooms,* yet it was too crowded and completed to be one of them. Shops and residences lined the street, as real as anything else in this world. Perhaps *backstage* would have been a better term, as it felt like a place of movement and transition, a holding area for something to happen. Everything around us seemed in place, except for the turn-of-the-century bar serving as a vampire's lair. I was still gasping for breath as I turned to look for it and…

…it was gone.

I blinked at the jarring sight. One second the bar was *there,* it existed, and the next, it was if it never was.

"Son of a bitch," Noric spat, snarling and baring his teeth. I covered my mouth as a cry escaped. We'd had, *what?* Seconds before the cards shuffled again?

"What would have happened if I'd have been caught in the reshuffling?" I asked, never taking my eyes from the space the bar had recently occupied. Now, an unassuming tea shop and an abandoned, boarded-up building squashed together to fill the area. "Would I have died?"

"Possibly," Noric said, rage still roughening his voice. "The shuffling works in mysterious ways, but it doesn't usually happen until closer to dawn. You could have gotten lost in the in-between and died naturally, before the shift even had a chance to spit you out again. Your body would be lost to this realm."

Gently guiding my head to the side, Noric examined my neck and declared, "You need sleep. I know you don't want to lose time, but you're weak. We'll accomplish nothing until you recover."

I didn't protest. He was right—Vasilios drank more than a mere taste and the loss of blood had weakened me. My reaper, on the other hand, practically vibrated with power.

"Did it feel good?" I asked. "Reaping the aberrations?"

"Better than you can imagine," Noric confessed. "From the moment we entered their den, I wanted to cull them. The satisfaction was…" he licked his lips. "Elite."

That knowledge made my disappointment sting a little less. Even if I possessed the ichor, how would we be together? It was as hopeless as turning spectre, and, for the first time, I felt a little grateful to simply be human.

Noric whisked us to a lobby I recognized as the Hotel Monteleone for its iconic carousel bar. We approached the front desk and he secured us a suite—the largest in the hotel—without any reaper magic. Noric paid the four-figure sum like a mortal and escorted me to a set of rooms bigger than most apartments. I wondered if, with our youthful appearance, cash payment, and suspicious lack of luggage, the staff thought we were using the accommodations for a dalliance.

Overtired, the thought made me giggle.

Noric looked down at me with worry swirling in those stone eyes.

Suddenly, I didn't feel like laughing. I felt very serious. Breathless. Nervous. My heart beat a little bit faster and those ethereal, Glasswing butterflies took flight.

Noric's lips turned down in a small frown, picking up on the change in me.

We stood in the living room of the FJ Monteleone suite, stuffed with creamy, upholstered furniture and fresh with the immaculate scent of newly-cleaned quarters. Noric stilled as he waited for me to speak.

"The ikavorn were right about one thing," I whispered. "I am a virgin. And I don't want to die without experiencing the physical act of love." Blushing a little, I concluded, "With you."

Noric eyes darkened and he arched a brow as if to ask *now?* I quickly shook my head and said, "Sleep, first. We can... make arrangements tomorrow. It must be near dawn."

He rubbed my biceps and said, "I've paid for two nights here, just in case. I'll put the Do Not Disturb sign on the door and we can sleep in."

I stripped down to my underwear, crawled into the plush hotel bed, and nestled beneath the pillowy bedding.

Despite my terror about my final days and my profound disappointment in possessing no ever-essence, Vasilios had drunk deeply from me and I couldn't fight the exhaustion.

I fell asleep the moment Noric returned.

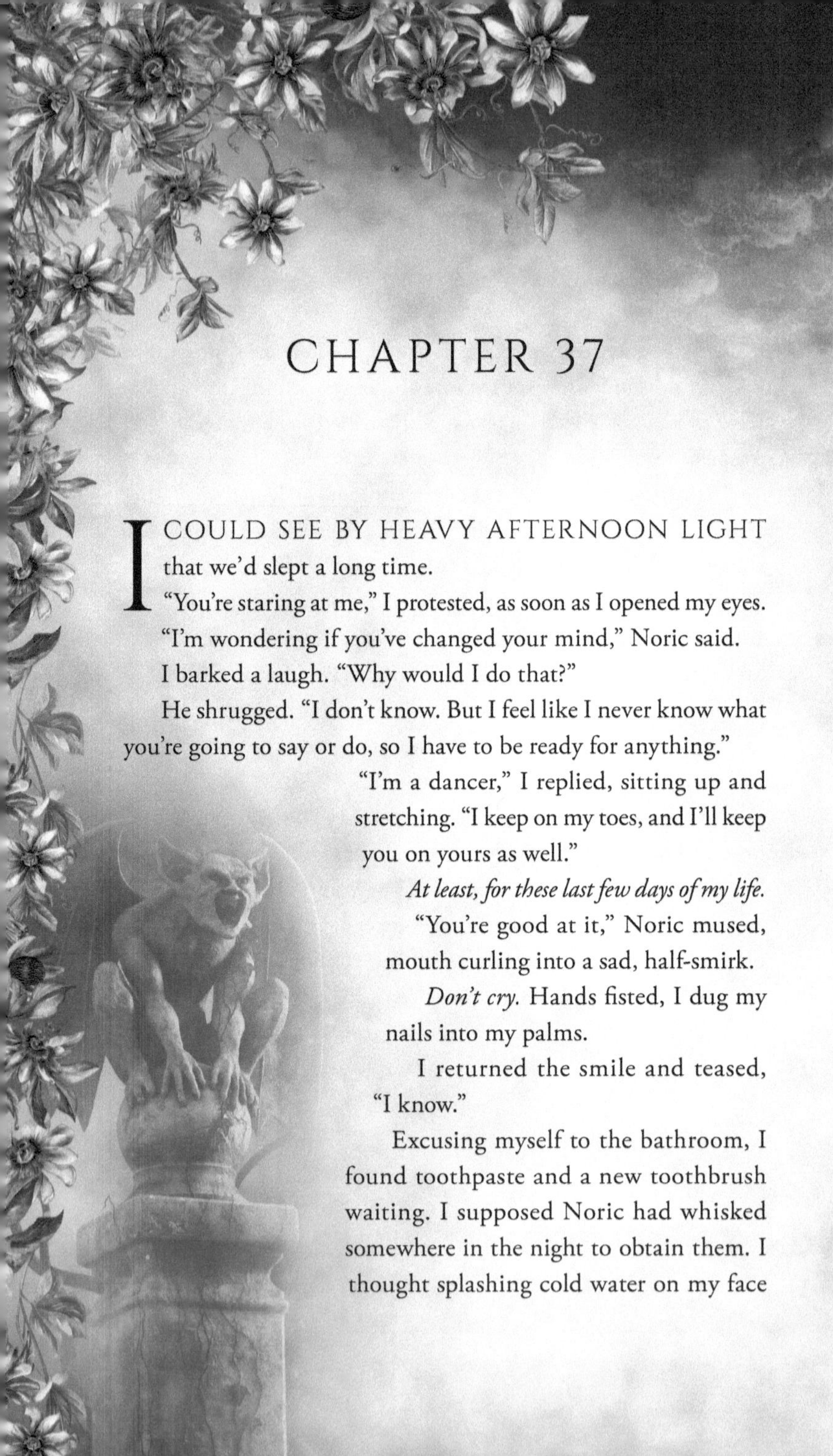

CHAPTER 37

I COULD SEE BY HEAVY AFTERNOON LIGHT that we'd slept a long time.

"You're staring at me," I protested, as soon as I opened my eyes.

"I'm wondering if you've changed your mind," Noric said.

I barked a laugh. "Why would I do that?"

He shrugged. "I don't know. But I feel like I never know what you're going to say or do, so I have to be ready for anything."

"I'm a dancer," I replied, sitting up and stretching. "I keep on my toes, and I'll keep you on yours as well."

At least, for these last few days of my life.

"You're good at it," Noric mused, mouth curling into a sad, half-smirk.

Don't cry. Hands fisted, I dug my nails into my palms.

I returned the smile and teased, "I know."

Excusing myself to the bathroom, I found toothpaste and a new toothbrush waiting. I supposed Noric had whisked somewhere in the night to obtain them. I thought splashing cold water on my face might help stave off the thoughts of my impending Elimination, but it did not.

Well, I had more distracting ideas in mind anyway.

There was a delicious tension in the air when I exited the bathroom.

"Here?" Noric asked, and I shook my head. I wondered what it would have been like to have sex with him under normal circumstances, instead of us both being distracted by my annihilation in mere days.

"Where would you like to go? Tell me anywhere and I'll make it happen. Do you want a suite in Paris? Hong Kong? The Caribbean?" he asked frantically, searching my face for some glimmer of agreement. Noric continued before I could speak. "Something more isolated? I know of endless cabins, manors, treehouses, if you wish. Where do you want to go? The Serengeti or a Scottish isle or—"

I laid a finger gently over Noric's lips.

"I want to go to your home," I whispered. "Just there. To your bed." Sharing a small smile, I added, "I think a hidden castle in the Carpathians, guarded by gargoyles who come to life at your command, is magical enough for my first time."

Noric smiled back, though it did not touch his eyes. Without another word, he wrapped his arms around me, kissed my forehead, and whisked us away.

The next moment I found myself standing in Noric's darkly-colored bedroom, brightened by the moonlight spilling in through large windows overlooking the vast mountain range peaking and sloping before us. Beside us, his towering bed with its gargoyle statues was made as neatly as ever.

The setting was perfect and Noric was perfect… but me? I glanced down at my dirty clothes and asked, "Can I use your shower first?"

"Of course," Noric said. "Do you want a drink?"

"No," I quickly answered. "I don't want anything to cloud my thoughts in these..." I swallowed, then continued firmly, "in these last moments. But especially not this one. I want to experience and remember all of it."

Not that I will have much time for memories.

Noric nodded. "Do what you need. I'll be waiting."

Alone in Noric's bathroom, I tied my hair into a knot atop my head to keep it dry as I showered, then hastily washed the dirt from the past evening off my body. Time being of the essence now, I didn't want to linger. On the other hand, the skittish butterflies in my stomach felt as if they moved in unison, madly pitching themselves to one side of my belly as if their combined weight could pull me toward the shower wall and pin me there. Because as soon as I moved...

This is Noric, I chided myself. I shouldn't be frightened because *it's Noric.*

On the other hand, he was the only man in the world who could make me this nervous. I ached to be perfect for him and I felt so utterly flawed for this kind of activity. Stepping out of the shower, I studied myself in the mirror and found all my usual imperfections to critique in a harsh new light with impending intimacy. Nothing about me was voluptuous. My breasts weren't full or tempting; I possessed a dancer's chest. My hips weren't wide and sensuous; those too were built for dancing. My ribs were visible, their cage as skeletal as a reaper's true form. My rear was cute and pert—my best feature when it came to particular areas of the body men enjoyed—but it was nothing special, and Noric was beyond special.

And oh, my feet. I cringed as I looked down, curling my toes self-consciously. They were as blistered and cracked as any dancer's feet, and no amount of lotion would reverse the abuse they'd endured over the years. Hastily, I ripped off the two now-soaked bandages I'd been wearing and tossed them into the trash.

Noric, who'd been pacing outside the door, suddenly shouted through it.

"If you don't come out soon, I'm going to come in and we'll have sex in the shower. If I can make it that far. The floor might have to do."

I laughed at the desperation in his voice and opened the door ajar.

Noric shoved something at me, "I brought you a dress," he said.

Relieved at the way he thought of everything, I grabbed the garment from his outstretched hand. It was a silky black slip with spaghetti straps, but as I searched the dress, I realized that was all he provided.

"No underwear?" I asked through the door. My voice came out a little high-pitched.

I heard Noric's low laugh. "You ask too much of me. I'm a reaper, not a saint."

I laughed and tried not to cry.

You're perfect.

After dressing, I slipped out the door and Noric immediately grabbed me. He wasted no time moving me to the bed and gently laying me down. I couldn't help but sigh, partially relieved. I had a tendency to get lost in my own head, overthinking. It was one of the reasons I loved dancing so much—it quieted my mind. Without giving me time to stew, I was forced to focus on the pleasure of the moment.

Noric laid gentle kisses on the tops of my thighs to coax them apart. The dress I'd just donned was rendered almost irrelevant as he slid it upwards. It wasn't as if Noric hadn't already seen me—I'd boldly shown myself to him that day in the classroom. But this was different. This was a prelude to sex, something I'd never done before. And despite wanting to do it with Noric more than any other man—or immortal being—it still terrified me.

Noric moved his lips down between the curve of my thighs, to the line where I'd clamped them tightly shut.

"It's okay," he whispered. "I'll stop if you say so."

Nodding, I whispered, "I know."

But it still felt reassuring to hear.

"I want to make you feel good," he said, staring up at me with heat in his gaze. Noric's hair, dark in the candlelight, fell carelessly across his forehead, partially obscuring his eyes from my angle. Seeing Noric look up at me from between my legs and knowing what he intended to do, what his dark stare communicated, made me feel lightheaded.

Huskily, he asked, "Can I kiss you where it will feel best?"

Unable to speak, I only nodded again and allowed Noric to pry my legs wider apart. The image of his face between my thighs was pure sin. I'd asked for this, and the wetness there told me my body had readied itself, but I was so nervous about the act itself. Part of me wished I'd gotten it over with long ago, because building it up like this only made it monumental. Yet the other part of me was glad I'd never shared it with anyone else, because no one could compare to my reaper.

Noric inhaled deeply, making my cheeks *burn*. He laid one kiss directly on my core, a prelude, a promise—then his tongue slipped into me and I slipped into rapture. I lost all sense of time and space as his mouth explored me; everything melted away. What happened next felt akin to the magic of Time Striders, something like bending the laws of physics. Yet this was a magic anyone could do.

I wondered, though, in a haze of bliss, if Noric did it better than anyone else, having ages of practice?

He slipped two fingers inside me, curling and stroking until it was almost too much pressure… but then his warm, soft tongue would replace the fingers and I'd melt into the plush bedding once more.

"*Noric,*" I pled his name as my pleasure rose.

With his tongue occupied, Noric sent his voice into my head.

"*Yes, Ava,*" he coaxed, and I gasped at the profound intimacy. Noric had never spoken to me in my mind except when I'd taken off on Orphnaeus, and that had been shouting in fear and fury. *"Let go. Let it take you."*

That was exactly what it felt like as I came—as if I'd been flying upward on a Time Strider and we tipped into a swan dive, tumbling down from the uppermost limits of the sky, spiraling in a rush back to the earth. I fought for breath as I fell. I'd done this part before, but it was never like *this*.

A moment later, Noric guided my legs wider and wedged himself between them. Riveted, I stared at his erection as he lowered himself. Noric was big, hard, and beautiful. Seeing him rigid, hot lust spread throughout my whole body.

Watching me intently, he smirked a little and asked, "Do you want to feel me inside you, Avalia?"

I could hardly speak in my post-orgasmic state.

"Yes," I breathed.

Noric's impish grin shone down like a crescent moon. He leaned closer and lined himself up at my entrance. "I'll go slow," he promised.

As he sank his first few inches into me, I gasped and he moaned.

"Avalia," Noric whispered, and I opened my eyes to find he looked concerned. "Can you take more?"

Oh. I realized I was clenching my teeth and scrunching my face.

"Yes," I whispered, untensing and wrapping my arms tighter around his back. "I want more."

Noric pushed into me slowly, making me pant with each inch. When he'd finally filled me until he could go no further, he stilled once more. It hurt a little, but the pain was quickly fading.

"God, you feel so good," he rasped, and I shivered as his warm breath caressed my ear. "So hot and tight around me."

"You feel, um… it's a lot," I admitted. "Can you just hold for a moment?"

"I can stop if you want to. I can pull out." Noric's face tensed as he said in a rush, "But *fuck*, Ava, I don't want to."

He sounded so desperate, I gave a breathy laugh. "I don't want you to," I swore, kissing him for reassurance and trying to relax. "Just give me a moment."

After a few seconds, during which it looked like Noric was experiencing more pain than pleasure, he rasped, "Can I move? Ava, love, can I move now?"

I couldn't help but laugh again, seeing my powerful reaper brought to a state of such desperate pleading for my permission simply to unfreeze.

"Yes," I breathed, and Noric moved.

Dear God, how he moved.

"I WANT TO do that all night," I told him, basking in the pleasure of my second climax and the first I'd ever had through sex. Noric held himself above me, staying near but giving me room to catch my breath. "Can you… um… how many times in a night can you… go?" I asked.

"I'm a reaper, love, my stamina is limitless," Noric bragged with casual arrogance as he stroked my face. "But if we continue until morning," he warned, arching a brow, "you'll be sore."

I scrunched my lips in mock-consideration before grinning. I pulled him back to me and ordered, "Then you better make the pleasure worth the pain."

Noric's eyes flashed and with his knee, he wedged my leg wider.

"Wait!" I cried, averting my eyes and biting my lip. "Do you think you could, um, wear that horned mask? You know, the skull headdress in that case downstairs? I don't have much time left and I want to try new things before I—"

There was an absence of Noric's weight and then, in a flash, he stood by the base of the bed, completely naked but for the skull mask.

"Oh," I whispered. I couldn't manage more.

His tight body was glorious, his muscles simultaneously arousing and intimidating—the latter of which only aroused me *more*. My eyes danced upon his long legs, hard chest, and powerful arms. I blinked several times at the menacing figure he made with the horned animal skull. My heart beat faster and my nipples hardened.

I wondered if Noric had grinned at my reaction, but I couldn't tell as the mask obscured his mouth. He was equal parts terrifying and tempting and it released a flurry of butterflies in my stomach.

Noric grabbed my ankles and yanked me to the foot of the bed.

I squealed when I was dragged and again when I was filled.

CHAPTER 38

I FLUTTERED OPEN MY EYES TO SEE NORIC laying next to me and stroking my face, just like the day before. *"Mmm,"* I sighed dreamily. "What time is it?"

"Late," he replied. My heart sank and he must have seen it on my face. I didn't have time left for sleeping in. He hurried to add, "But you needed the rest."

He was right, but I hated that I'd done it. I shifted my body, feeling a most delicious soreness between my legs, a light ache to remind me what we'd done.

What *he'd* done, if I were honest. Noric had been responsible for most of the work.

"How sore are you?" he asked, nuzzling my hair.

"Not sore enough that I don't want to feel you inside me again," I murmured, wrapping my arms around him. "I know it's not right to say this but," I shrugged, "what we did made me feel like I changed in some way. Like I walked into this room a girl and I'm leaving a woman."

"Can you wait?" Noric asked. "Can you wait until I change you again?"

Back into a girl? I thought, confused. *It's too late for that, my love.*

"Change me into what?"

"My wife."

Noric uttered two words that made my breath hitch and left me utterly speechless. Something about hearing *those* words from *Noric's* lips made my heart pound, my stomach flutter, and even caused the area between my legs to tingle.

"Will you marry me?" he asked, searching my face for clues. His words were bold, but his expression was nervous.

Grinning wide, I asked, "Aren't we out of order here? Isn't the wedding supposed to come *before* the bedding?"

"Well, I had to sample you first." He teased me with a wink and a devilish smile on his beautiful lips. "To be sure you were satisfactory."

"And?" I asked, haughtily.

"I learned I better lock you down quickly, before another man gets his hands on you," he declared fervently. "So I ask again, Avalia. Will you marry me?"

Still pretending to be miffed, I smacked him lightly and cried, "Such arrogance. I am happy to have satisfied *you*, sir, but you forget that I have not yet expressed whether or not *you* have pleased *me.*"

"You screamed loud enough last night to wake my gargoyles," Noric said, smug as ever. "I think that expressed all I need to know."

I darted my gaze to the looming statues at the foot and head of his bed, horrified at the idea of being watched. "Not really? Did they truly wake up?"

Noric laughed. "No, that's not how it works. But you did cry out loudly enough that I wouldn't have been surprised if they had."

"If you want to persuade me to marry you," I said, trying to scold him convincingly through my pouting and blushing. "You're not doing a very good job."

In a flash, Noric knelt on the floor and lifted me into a seated position on the bed, directly above him.

"Avalia, there is no one in the world like you. Never has been, never will be. I want you to be my wife. My first, my only. There is… almost nothing in this world I could ever want more."

Noric's eyes were wet as he finished, and I understood. There was only one thing in this world he wanted more, and the overlords wouldn't allow it.

"Will you marry me?" he asked. "Third time's a charm, right?"

I badly wished I had more time. To tease Noric, to plan a wedding—to set him upon three quests to earn the right to my hand. But I only had three days left on this earth, and right now, I wanted nothing more than to be Noric's wife and to have him as my husband.

Well, almost nothing.

"Yes," I replied, crying and laughing. "Yes, Noric. And for a third time, just so you're sure, *yes.*"

Noric kissed me, but when he pulled back, he rolled his neck.

"Today, on the mountain. I'll fetch a priest and your wedding trousseau."

I bit back a grin at the antiquated term, and Noric continued before I had the chance to say anything.

"But first, I must reap. Now," he said through gritted teeth.

I realized he'd been too distracted to reap the last few days and must be in pain.

"A few, at least…" Noric trailed off, and I supposed he was thinking about who and where.

A culling for our wedding. How macabre.

"Tell me what you'd like—flowers and the type of gown. I'll gather everything while I'm out."

He was procuring my wedding dress while reaping, and he'd said it as if offering to pick up milk on the way home from the office.

Well, this is the life I chose, short as it is.

"And our wedding day sacrifice?" I asked, tracing his sensuous lips with my fingertip. "Shall I choose that as well?"

"If it pleases you," Noric said with sincerity.

I hadn't been serious, but I gave it some thought.

"On this day, honor me with three men," I declared, "who do not honor women."

I didn't have to explain; Noric understood completely.

"As my bride commands," he swore, still kneeling and kissing my hand before whisking away.

MY PACE WAS a bit faster than usual as I walked through the biting cold of the mountain slope. We'd chosen a lower portion with no snow and only hard-packed earth, but my silky gown was paltry protection against the frigid air. I hurried because when I reached Noric, I'd be enveloped in his magical warmth once more, and every step I took brought me closer to being his wife. Until...

...until the day I died. So, three more days.

Don't, I warned. *Don't think about that or you'll cry and ruin your makeup and your wedding.*

I'd flown my own Time Strider to the spot we'd chosen, wanting to surprise my bridegroom with a first look at me. As much as I could surprise him, since he'd been the one to hastily source the dress. I'd described to Noric what I liked and he whisked away to find it in a wedding shop or a designer studio or... I wasn't even sure where he'd grabbed it, but I knew he'd left behind a stack of cash beyond whatever it cost.

While I soaked in his generous tub overlooking the snow-capped mountains, Noric also bought us two platinum rings and a bouquet. The arrangement contained loosely bundled black baccara roses, burgundy ranunculus, and blackstone lilies. The edges dripped with gorgeous amaranth. I hadn't known the names of all those flowers, but I told Noric what I wanted and he brought that for me too, describing each bloom when he returned.

The gown was simple and stunning nonetheless—a silken slip dress with an organza layer on top, delicately beaded at the edges of the small train and along the neckline of the bodice. My veil did not cover my face, it only draped over my unbound hair and halfway down my back. I wore no jewelry—it seemed a bit too much to add, given the short time we had to assemble everything.

As for his own wedding attire, I'd asked Noric to remain as I'd come to know him best—wearing one of his all-black reaper ensembles.

Perhaps I hadn't thought that through properly, because the menacing cloak only seemed to frighten the trembling priest even more. There to wed us, it was an event that would soon be obscured from his mind. Noric had acquired the obviously reluctant, heavily religious man with god-only-knew-what methods of persuasion.

At least it's not storming, I thought, suppressing a smile. If lightning flashed and illuminated Noric's skeletal form, the gray-haired officiant might have run off screaming.

The old priest was all we had obtained when it came to the law. Noric had secured no official paperwork. There would never exist a record of our vows. I wasn't sure if our union was even legal in Romania, let alone anywhere else in the world.

But it was binding to *us*.

Dear God, he is gorgeous, I thought as I walked. Was it any surprise I'd fallen in love with a reaper, given my upbringing? As terrible as it all turned out, it felt, in some way, like this was always meant to be.

Noric's hair was slicked back, darkening it. Dressed in his black reaper clothing he looked astoundingly powerful and dangerous, especially while towering over the trembling officiant beside him. He stared at me, enraptured, as I walked the short path I'd given myself.

"You look like a goddess," Noric said, eyes dancing all over me. Before I could return the compliment, he quickly added, "Please tell the priest you're marrying me of your own free will. He's set on risking his life to protect you from me if he doesn't hear it from your own mouth." Noric shrugged, "And even when you tell him, I'm assuming he'll dismiss you a lost cause, participating in your own damnation."

I tried not to laugh—really I did. But the fact that I was marrying Noric, coupled with the whole unlikely scene, just made me giddy.

Looking meaningfully at the wizened priest, I said, "I fear it's too late, Father, as I already participated in my own damnation many times last night, and in many different positions." The priest's eyes widened in horror while Noric's lips curled into a diabolical grin. "Might as well bless this union, as, should a child be born of such rabid, unholy fornication, his or her soul might otherwise be damned too."

"Child," the priest exclaimed, committed to saving me. His accent was thick, but his English was clear enough. "You know not what you say. He has entranced you."

"Oh no," Noric protested, eyes twinkling. He took my hand and brushed a soft kiss onto my knuckles. "I swear to the gods that it is she who has bewitched me."

I gave the priest a sympathetic smile but said, "You heard the man. Actually, he's not so much a man as a demon. And he all but called me a witch, so… best do as he says or who knows what evil we'll unleash."

Technically, three mortals have already been sacrificed in the name of this union, I thought, but wouldn't say unless the priest needed more prodding.

Noric gave a stern look to the old man, and I wondered what baseless threats he'd made to convince the resolute believer to marry us. Perhaps Noric had sworn to render destruction upon his entire village. I'd have to ask him later.

Whatever the case, the elderly priest gritted his teeth and conducted an abbreviated wedding ceremony, wincing all the while.

Noric and I barely noticed. He stared at me as if I was the only thing that mattered in all his years of reaping. I tried to memorize him like this—black cloak stark against the dead, wintry landscape. It blew gently behind him with the soft breeze he allowed to penetrate our bubble.

We said our vows, slid the platinum rings onto each other's fingers, and shared a matrimonial kiss that left me as breathless as our first.

When our wedding concluded, I only had time to blink before Noric had whisked away the priest, obscured the man's memory, and returned to stand before me. Like a bird of prey, he swooped down to claim my mouth and before I knew it, I was on my back with my dress around my waist.

Enveloped in the bubble of his warmth, Noric and I consummated our union on the mountaintop, right on the spot where we'd just wed.

I CURLED UP in the supple brown leather chair in Noric's celestial library. I liked this seat especially, as it faced the snowy mountains. Sipping the cup of strong Earl Gray tea Noric had made, I gazed at those peaks and valleys.

I was a Thrailkill, both through adoption and by marriage, but not by blood. Calling me *Thrailkill*, loaning me the name, did not make me a true immortal.

Glancing at Noric on the leather chair opposite me, I steeled myself to say what I had to.

"When the time comes, I want you to be the one to reap me."

Noric's gray eyes swirled with that ocean of agony only an immortal's could contain.

"Don't," he begged hoarsely. "Don't say that."

"What else should I say?" I pled softly. "Who else? What is the alternative? Would you leave me to writhe in psychic pain?"

"Never," he swore, standing beside me so quickly he must have whisked himself there. Face twisted, he took my hands in his. "But I cannot reap you, I *cannot.*"

"Please, Noric," I begged. "I don't want anyone else to do it. I want the last person to touch me in this world—to touch my body or my soul—to be you."

His tortured cry was one no human could ever make, and I whimpered at its sound. It was not at all similar to the ecstasy-infused music he played for me at his full capacity, but the wretched despair it contained pierced me in a supernatural manner.

"Sevastian was right all along," I said, unable to stop my tears. "There is no happy end for us and now I have condemned you to his eternal misery. You cannot die. I cannot live."

"I'll take it," Noric swore. "I'll take the pain forever to have known you. I wouldn't change it."

"I would," I whispered.

"Don't say that!" he shouted, grabbing my face with his hands once more. "Don't you dare say that. I told you—I will decide how much pain I can endure and what is worth it, and you *are.*"

We'd reversed. *Oh, how we'd reversed.*

If I could go back in time, I'd ask Noric to obscure me before we even fell in love. Not because I feared the death I now faced, though I did. But because I would do anything to spare Noric, just as he had wanted to spare me. Those haunting gray eyes had transformed, now they were as haunt*ed* as Sevastian's. They'd hardened into the stone of ancient ruins, a labyrinth of secrets concealing ghosts. I'd done that to him, and I couldn't undo it. Worse, I asked for more still.

"Would you really let another be the last to touch me?" I whispered, voice cracking. "To reap me?"

"No," he swore. "Never."

"Then it has to be you."

A cry tore through Noric's throat and he pushed himself up and whisked to the other side of the room. With his back to me he stood in front of the decadent, burled-walnut bar built into a tower of bookshelves. Atop sat an array of crystal decanters filled with amber liquids that I knew from experience burned going down. Noric poured one of them into a stout, thick glass with some unknown coat of arms etched onto the side. He tossed the drink down in one swig. I could see the tension coiling muscles along his broad, strong back as he stood frozen with indecision. Then he quickly poured and drank another. As soon as it left his lips, Noric threw the glass across the room and I jumped a little as it smashed against his wall. Before I could stop him, he picked up the entire bottle and threw that as well.

"Noric!" I cried, lunging at him. I grabbed his arm, knowing he could easily wrest himself free but hoping I soothed his fury. "Breaking things isn't helping."

"I'd break the goddamn world if I could. If I can't have you, they shouldn't have any of it."

"It still wouldn't change my fate." Clutching his shirt, I begged, "Please. It has to be you. I guess… let me writhe in psychic pain for a second or two—just to be sure. But show me mercy and end my agony. Release me, Noric, when the time comes."

His face crumpled in utter anguish. His eyes were screwed tight, his nostrils flared, and agony wrecked his features like he was the one in psychic pain.

"*Please,*" I whispered.

"I…" Noric struggled to speak. "I… A honeymoon," he declared desperately, eyes popping wide as he avoided answering. "We're married now, we should have a honeymoon. Where would you like to go? Anywhere in the world, Ava, just tell me."

Noric looked at me with such raw longing at that moment, it shattered my heart. Helpless to save my life, he was desperate to do anything else that may be within his power. He looked as if my giving him an order he could fulfill would bring him some small measure of satisfaction, however minuscule and temporary.

But I didn't want to go anywhere new and glamorous, didn't want to spend my last days on earth somewhere unfamiliar. I wanted to die where I'd lived, and with those I loved around me. Archibald and Yvette were gone, but my father and his horsemen would be there, at my end.

"Take me home, Noric," I said softly, cupping his face with my hands. "Please. I just want to go home. Take me to Grimsmere."

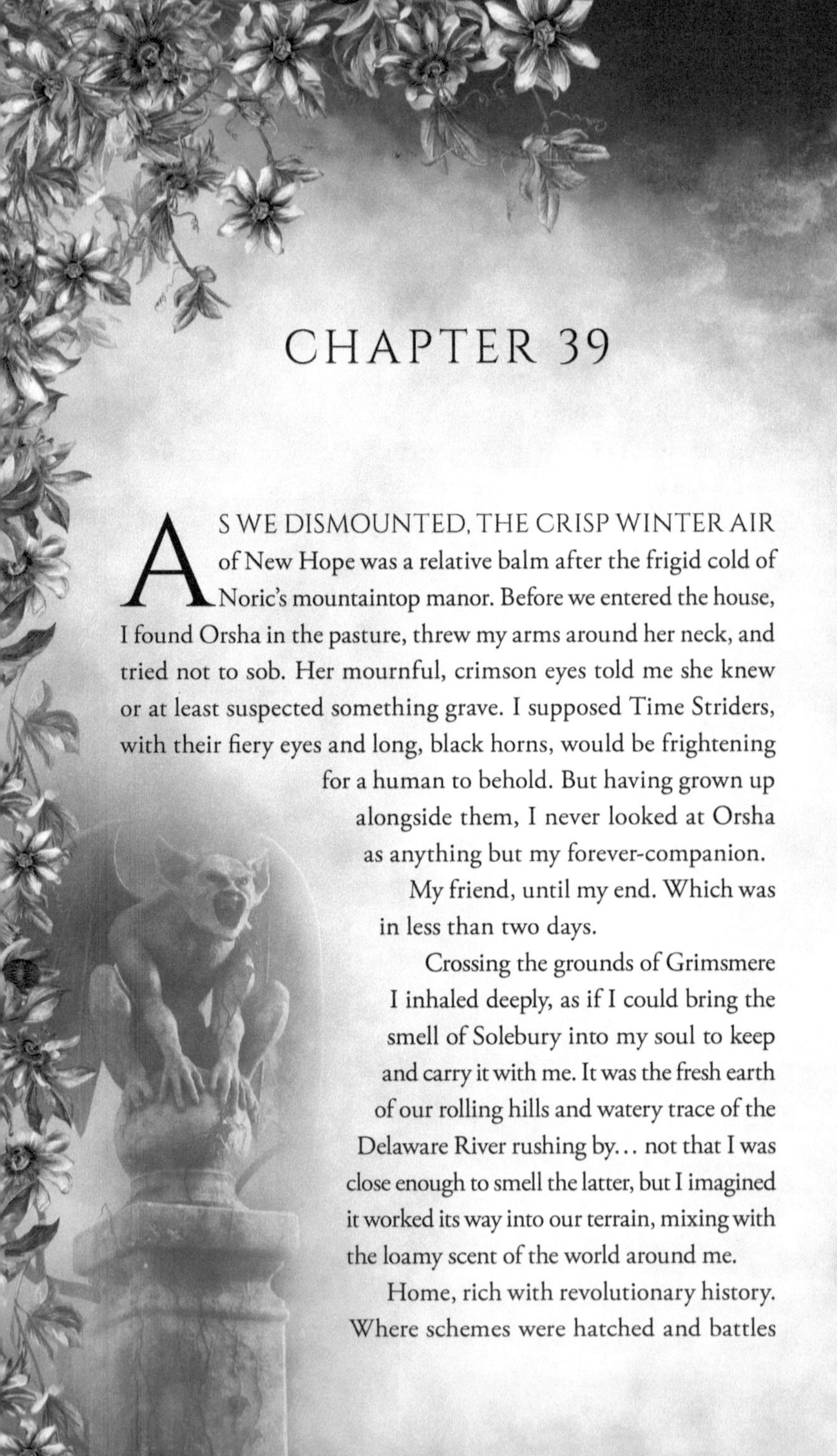

CHAPTER 39

S WE DISMOUNTED, THE CRISP WINTER AIR of New Hope was a relative balm after the frigid cold of Noric's mountaintop manor. Before we entered the house, I found Orsha in the pasture, threw my arms around her neck, and tried not to sob. Her mournful, crimson eyes told me she knew or at least suspected something grave. I supposed Time Striders, with their fiery eyes and long, black horns, would be frightening for a human to behold. But having grown up alongside them, I never looked at Orsha as anything but my forever-companion.

My friend, until my end. Which was in less than two days.

Crossing the grounds of Grimsmere I inhaled deeply, as if I could bring the smell of Solebury into my soul to keep and carry it with me. It was the fresh earth of our rolling hills and watery trace of the Delaware River rushing by… not that I was close enough to smell the latter, but I imagined it worked its way into our terrain, mixing with the loamy scent of the world around me.

Home, rich with revolutionary history. Where schemes were hatched and battles fought leading to the birth of this nation. It was a land of change, of endings and beginnings. I supposed it was fitting to witness mine.

I wished my Elimination would have been ordered in warmer months, but if I couldn't enjoy our gardens, the breathtaking array of holiday lights entwined around our majestic willows, stately swamp oaks, and strung to the highest turrets of Grimsmere was the next best thing. The holidays were always magical here, and my last was no exception. Sanderson always lit fires in several hearths, each trimmed with fragrant pine or cedar garlands Olga collected from the grounds. If her mind needed another task, she'd decorate them with red velvet bows and dried oranges. Even Eligius always contributed, baking something with nutmeg or cinnamon or ginger, and he didn't need any magic to carry the warm smells throughout the rooms nearest the kitchen. As an impatient child, I always bit into his yuletide muffins before they cooled and I'd burn my tongue each time.

Perhaps I'd done the same now—bitten into something I shouldn't and suffered the worst of burns.

I swallowed thickly. Being raised by Death and two ghosts was an unusual upbringing, but I'd had the happiest of childhoods.

Squeezing Noric's hand I thought, *except for a bit of loneliness*. Which I'd finally banished, only to face Elimination before I'd had much time to enjoy my newfound friends or my love.

Don't cry, I warned, biting down hard on my trembling lip.

Before me, Grimsmere was resplendent with warm white lights and behind me, a section of our woods had been trimmed with multi-colored ones. Perhaps knowing how much I enjoyed it, Eligius must have ordered it done, despite what was to become of me. Or perhaps he hadn't told Sanderson. What could he say, truly?

My heart swelled, taking in the magical, and final, view of Christmas at Grimsmere.

Noric and I entered the house through the solarium at the back, but we both came to an immediate halt when we saw Eligius—who was not alone.

Vasilios stood very close to Death.

They'd clearly been talking, and we'd interrupted them.

"What is he doing here?" Noric demanded, tightening his grip on my hand, as if he'd need to pull me into a run or whisk me away.

Eligius was slow to reply and in the hesitation, Vasilios said, "Giving you what I can't have."

He tore his gaze from Eligius and looked at us with… longing? I couldn't have been more confused. Everything felt like it was happening in slow motion and my mind couldn't wrap around the *why* of it.

"You will want to thank me someday." Vasilios's voice was as thick and dense as molasses. Not at all puckish. He turned back to Eligius and stared deeply at my father, who furrowed a concerned brow while a weighty tension filled the room.

"But I won't be here to hear it."

Four things happened at once.

"Stop!" Eligius cried out, as Vasilios used his supernatural speed to practically teleport across the room and to my father's scythe. To my astonishment, Vasilios touched the blade and reaped himself, falling into a pile of ruddy dust. That same second, Noric pushed me behind him.

And I *screamed*.

"What the—what just happened?"

I could barely get the words from my mouth as I panted for air. A millennia-old ikavorn had just killed himself before my eyes. He'd been so ancient he'd turned to dust. What could make him do such a thing? What in the world was happening?

My father froze. He faced the pile of red-brown dust that had been Vasilios, but his eyes were closed as if he couldn't bear to look at it.

Several stunningly perplexing seconds passed before Noric took control of the situation.

"I'll ask Sanderson to collect him within an urn. We can arrange a funeral." He spoke very gently. "Will you tell us what transpired to bring this on?"

Noric's request jarred Death out of his reverie, but he only spoke to himself at first, whispering, "Yes." Eligius closed his eyes and shook his head again, pulled back into his own thoughts.

Finally, he turned to us and said, "Vasilios..." he broke off, then began again. "Vasilios has imparted the most miraculous knowledge. Information that can help us." His voice grew low as he added, "But it came at a price."

Eligius looked at me strangely, perhaps sadly. "He gifted us hope I can scarcely believe."

My heart skipped a beat. I didn't dare hope. I didn't want to.

No, I did. But I was terrified to allow it. My whole life I'd thought I had nothing to fear, and now it was more than I could bear—the fear of losing Noric and the fear of Elimination.

Eligius's gaze landed on my ringed finger, then moved to Noric's matching platinum. Death said nothing, but understanding lit his face.

"I will meet you by the fire in the medieval hall," Eligius ordered. "We haven't much time, and it is a long tale I must tell." He looked again at the dust. "But first, I will collect what remains of Vasilios, and then I will join you."

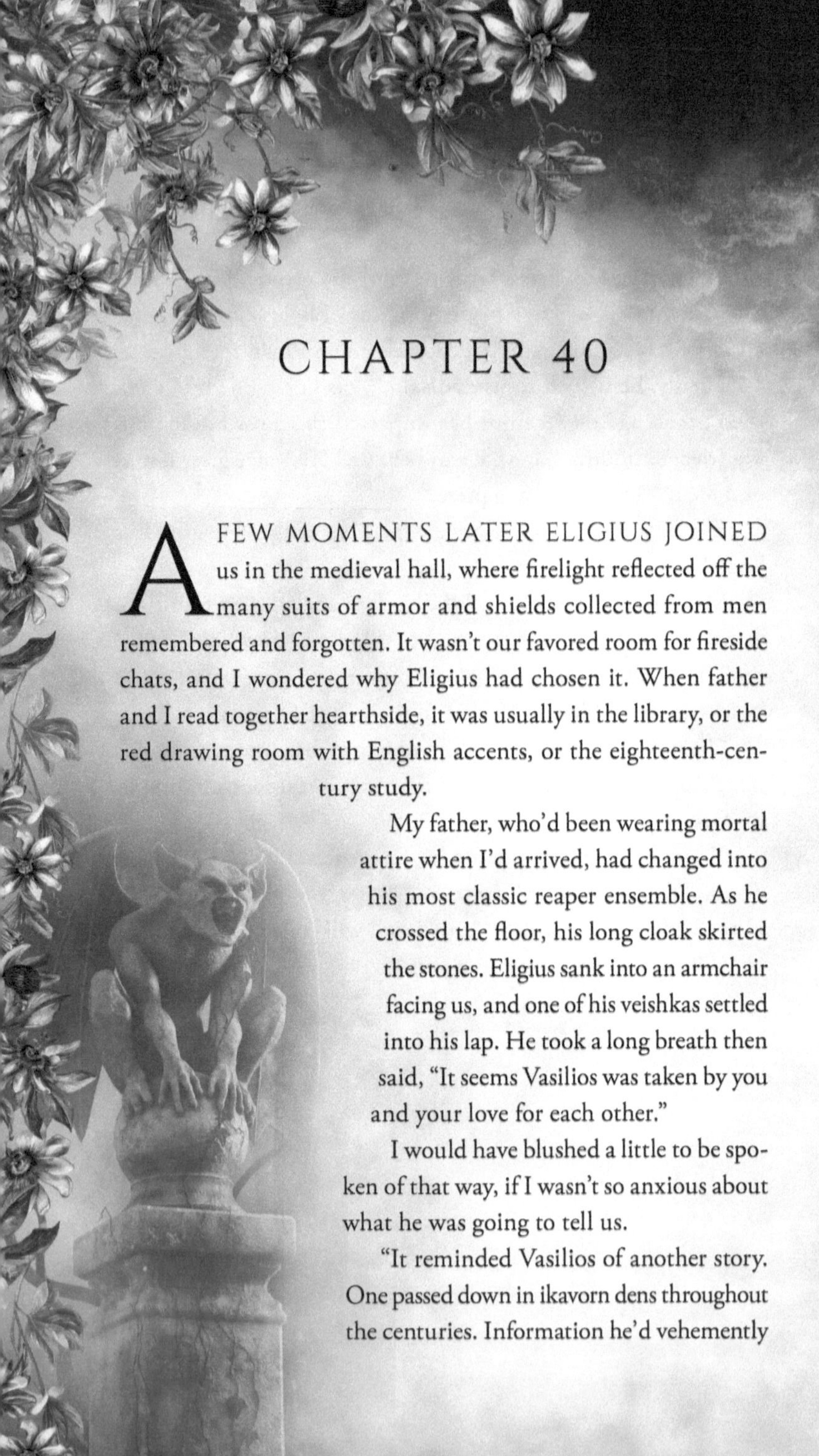

CHAPTER 40

A FEW MOMENTS LATER ELIGIUS JOINED us in the medieval hall, where firelight reflected off the many suits of armor and shields collected from men remembered and forgotten. It wasn't our favored room for fireside chats, and I wondered why Eligius had chosen it. When father and I read together hearthside, it was usually in the library, or the red drawing room with English accents, or the eighteenth-century study.

My father, who'd been wearing mortal attire when I'd arrived, had changed into his most classic reaper ensemble. As he crossed the floor, his long cloak skirted the stones. Eligius sank into an armchair facing us, and one of his veishkas settled into his lap. He took a long breath then said, "It seems Vasilios was taken by you and your love for each other."

I would have blushed a little to be spoken of that way, if I wasn't so anxious about what he was going to tell us.

"It reminded Vasilios of another story. One passed down in ikavorn dens throughout the centuries. Information he'd vehemently denied having, when I last sought him out. He came here to share it with us." Eligius had a funny look on his face, one I'd never seen before. Dazed or nostalgic as he stared at the fire. Quickly he looked back at us and said, "Vasilios and I have been… chatting… for more than a day and we haven't much time left. Let me share the good news, but first, I must tell you the tale he's told me."

Noric and I settled back in our armchairs, but he didn't let go of my hand.

"A very long time ago, two were kicked out of the Above, a male and a female. Lovers," Eligius said. "For the purpose of this tale, we'll call them Adam and Eve. As Vasilios tells it, no one knew what crime they committed. Various stories were whispered about their *original sin,* as it were."

Eligius stroked his chin and mused, "It could be that none are allowed to love in their ranks, and they broke the rules. It could be that they belonged to others and carried on an illicit liaison. It could be something much worse, but whatever the transgression, it had something to do with loving one another. Adam and Eve were cast out of Elysia and sent here, to the Below, for a short life as punishment before facing Elimination. Two rules were added to make the sentence more severe and the game more interesting. One, the lovers did not pass the River Lethe and retained all their knowledge, with the caveat that if either of them ever told any mortals the truth, the other would be instantly Eliminated. Over time, Adam and Eve found a way to share hints and insinuations, but neither could reveal the full story of their excommunication or the workings of the Above. The second rule was that if Adam or Eve ever came within a thousand paces of one another, they'd both be Eliminated."

I exchanged a look with Noric, who'd moved forward to sit on the literal edge of his seat. I imagined it had been a long time since he'd learned anything new about the realms, however questionable this information might be.

"But what the overlords did not know was that Adam and Eve had already smuggled out knowledge, in the form of pages torn from books and copies hastily created. If you were to think of this world as a game, these pages would contain some of the programming information behind it. Cheat codes."

I laid a hand on my racing heart. Noric's concerned look told me he'd noticed, so I forced a smile to ensure he didn't worry.

"Using the stolen knowledge and with some experimentation and practice," my father continued, "Adam was able to transform himself and achieve immortality—with caveats. There was something unique about certain types of blood. Not as in type A positive and the like, but something else he taught himself to know," Eligius explained. "Adam was attempting to find a way around the overlord's second rule, that he'd be Eliminated if he got close to Eve. It seems he did not achieve exactly what he wanted but morphed into something else instead."

I gasped. "He became ikavorn, the first vampire," I said, connecting the story to Vasilios's visit.

Eligius nodded.

"Eve was sent to another continent. The lovers had no Time Striders and the means to easily travel toward one another did not exist in ancient times. Nor did they want to get too close and risk Elimination. Isolated and with a different set of half-complete information, Eve worked through her pages and achieved a means of manipulating the realm—what we'd call casting spells and crafting magic."

Squeezing my hand with excitement, Noric asked, "She became a... witch?"

Eligius smiled and nodded.

"Eve used what she learned to shape the world around her. It was only a fraction of what the overlords do, but just as real. In teaching her skills to other women, she found a way to skirt the rules by sharing adjacent knowledge. Women only—men were much too dangerous for her to integrate, especially in those days. This event might be what created the story of the forbidden fruit, the plucking of an apple or pomegranate from the tree of knowledge."

Open-mouthed and perfectly still, I pondered this incredible new idea. More importantly, could it help us? Was there some magic we could do?

"It seems the overlords weren't terribly concerned, as the more Eve's knowledge spread, the more it was corrupted, like a game of whisper down the lane," Eligius explained. "The further such spells moved from the source, the more incorrect they became. This led to an abundance of misinformation, and finding an accurate incantation or true witch today is as rare as finding a needle in a haystack," Eligius said. "With her pages pertaining more to molding the realm itself and not as focused on human design, Eve was not able to turn as indestructible as Adam. But she achieved a supernatural longevity and did not age as a normal mortal."

"What happened to them?" Noric asked the same burning question I had.

"No one knows," Eligius replied, steepling his fingertips. "It could be that they met in a final embrace and were Eliminated for it. It could be that they were forgiven, after serving their sentence. It could be that the knowledge they spread and the creation of other vampires and witches was used as a bargaining chip or blackmail of the gods. Because we know the ikavorn made a deal with the overlords at some point—the agreement never to create one without destroying another, and the deal to be left alone from reapers, just as they swore to give us the same wide berth in return."

"What about the witches?" I asked. "Do they have a deal too?"

Eligius shrugged. "I am uncertain. Their power diluted naturally, through the parroting of so many false spells. Perhaps there is no need to cap their number as true casters are buried under a pile of pretenders and they are even more discrete than vampires."

"How is this possible?" Noric mused, slack-jawed.

Eligius smiled wryly. "When they were excommunicated, the overlords shielded them from our sight."

Noric and I exchanged a glance, half-awed, half-disbelieving.

"It is Vasilios's belief that Adam was the first vampire, and Eve, the first witch," my father said. "They *both* stole knowledge from the gods, but you know how it is." He shrugged. "Women take the blame when the tale is told by men. What happened in the end is unknown, but if the couple found a way to reunite, I suspect another tale came from the event as well. Perhaps the story of Adam giving Eve a rib for her creation was rather, in the end, the immortal kiss the vampire bestowed upon his witch."

I drew in a long breath and let it out slowly. *Reapers, Vampires, Witches.* The world was full of more magic than I'd known... or rather, this strange combination of science-magic I barely grasped. I listened as the fire crackled and a log split, falling from the grill and sending embers to dance in the air before dying out and disappearing.

"Whatever became of the couple this much Vasilios insists—the drama amused the gods quite a bit. As they play with our world, he believes the overlords enjoy instigating similar versions of forbidden, thwarted, and tragic love. That these stories are reworked, retold, and repeated. Often."

"Like the Hessian and the Harlot," I whispered. It was my favorite local lore, a tragedy of star-crossed lovers, and not just because we tended their forgotten graves.

Eligius nodded.

"But *why?*" I exclaimed. "Why torture us like this? Is it really all just a sick game?"

"What makes the world go 'round?" Eligius asked sagely, and from his dark stare I could tell he wanted an answer.

"Money," I replied with a scoff, recalling the oft-used expression and feeling cynical. "They say money makes the world go 'round."

"That's part of it," he agreed, leaning in as if he expected me to guess again. I searched my brain for a better answer but didn't know what to say.

That wasn't true. I wanted to reply "love," but it felt like a hopelessly naïve idea.

"Want. Desire," Eligius answered for me. "Yearning makes the world spin. For money, fame, love. Anything and everything." Holding my gaze to ensure I was paying attention, he continued, "It is possible, I believe, that this desire creates an energy that sustains the system. That there is no positive or negative, there is only *want* and the energy it produces. Perhaps that is why this storyline is stimulated so often. I believe it worth considering, that the universe only exists... because it *wants* to."

I blinked several times and shook my head, trying to comprehend my father's theory. "Are you saying the universe is... what? Sentient? And hungry? That it feeds off our fantasies?"

Eligius shrugged. "It could be a symbiotic relationship. Our want sustains it; it sustains us." He waved his hand dismissively. "Or I could be so far off the mark that I'm not even in a nearby realm of accuracy. It is just something to consider, in light of this new information."

"So it is like the movies," I grumbled. "Only it's not artificial intelligence and it's not a physical source..." I frowned. "It's the world itself and our mental energy nourishing it?"

"I don't know, but given the growing malaise, it's worth considering how each component influences another," my father replied.

While I was busy trying to reassemble my mind after having it blown apart, Noric had only one question.

"This is all fascinating," he said with impatience, "but what does it have to do with Ava's life?"

"I'm getting there," Eligius replied, leaning back again in his armchair and stroking his veishka. "And you must brace yourself for this part."

I knit my brow, confused, because Death had directed the command to Noric specifically, not me.

"Adam and Eve's original pages have been lost to history. Vasilios's copies are weak, spotty, and mostly concerning the creation of ikavorn."

Convenient, I thought angrily, and not sure I fully believed it.

Though he said nothing, I could feel Noric's frustration—and his desperation. Eligius sensed it as well, as he hurried to finish.

"One critical piece of information contained within these pages, however, pertains to *us.* I believe it is one of the reasons we have been forbidden from mingling."

Noric snapped to attention, spine straightening. Eligius stared at both of us with those black eyes that had seen civilization dawn and blossom as he decreed, "There is a way for us to die. We can be killed, under the right circumstances." He paused and took a breath, as if hardly believing it himself. "And for the first time in our existence, I now possess the instructions for the process."

My mouth fell, both shocked at this news and confused as to what Eligius was really getting at.

On the other hand, Noric's entire body relaxed. He sank in his chair and exhaled with relief, as if he'd just dipped into a hot spring. His eyes were hooded and a small smile ghosted his lips as he said, "You can kill me when she dies."

"What?" I cried, shooing up in my seat. *"No.* That's not what this means. Eligius, tell me that's not the point of all this?" My heart pounded a frantic beat as I searched my father's pale face for answers. This *couldn't* be the news he wanted to impart, or the point of this whole story. Could it? "Why did Vasilios finally tell you all this in the first place? It can't just be because our love intrigued him. And why did he reap himself right in front of us?"

"Because you are my daughter," Eligius whispered. "And you don't just remind him of the story I told you... you remind him of himself." He paused overlong before continuing, and his shoulders slumped. "As he sees it—the tale of a lesser creature in love with a greater one. An impossible love."

What could be an impossible love for a vampire? I wondered. *A mortal who did not possess the ever-essence? Did he hold humans in such high regard?*

"Vasilios guarded this information with his life, because sharing it is a bridge that, once crossed…" Eligius trailed off. "Well. There is no retreat. The overlords would have culled him for what he's done, even though I believe there is a chance they *wanted* him to do it."

I didn't fully comprehend where my father was headed, but my stomach sank at the unfairness of it all. If he was right, the overlords were crueler and more capricious than I'd thought.

"Instead of waiting for them, Vasilios claimed the only power left to him and reaped himself before they could."

Death smiled, but unlike Noric's, it wasn't a happy one at all. "You see, what I have learned is that like ikavorn, we are to keep the same number. It is a rule even older than theirs, coded into our creation."

At those words, the air in the room shifted so much that I could *feel* it, but I didn't know why. Noric and Eligius stared at one another in heavy silence that stretched on for several unbearably weighty seconds.

Then Noric reached into my lap, took my hand, and squeezed it. Grief plumed in his eyes, storm clouds in the gray. Why? This mind-bending conversation was supposed to contain *hopeful* news.

"I don't understand," I whispered.

I looked back and forth between the two immortals, not at all comprehending what was happening. Finally, Eligius gave Noric a slight nod and he turned his body to face me. Noric ran his free hand beneath my hair and cupped me between my neck and my head, as if holding me upright.

"Your father is going to die," Noric said. "So that you can take his place."

CHAPTER 41

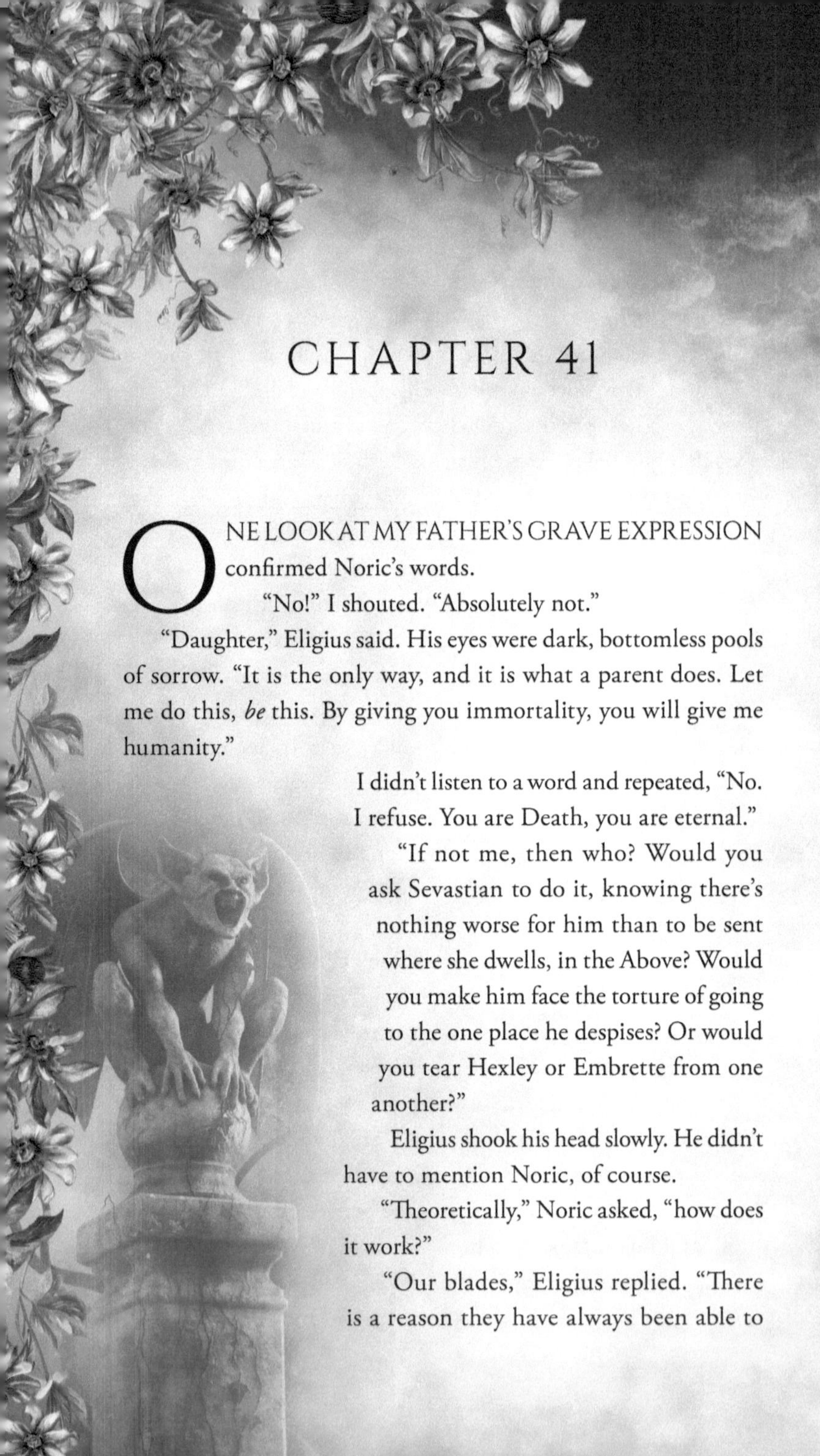

ONE LOOK AT MY FATHER'S GRAVE EXPRESSION confirmed Noric's words.

"No!" I shouted. "Absolutely not."

"Daughter," Eligius said. His eyes were dark, bottomless pools of sorrow. "It is the only way, and it is what a parent does. Let me do this, *be* this. By giving you immortality, you will give me humanity."

I didn't listen to a word and repeated, "No. I refuse. You are Death, you are eternal."

"If not me, then who? Would you ask Sevastian to do it, knowing there's nothing worse for him than to be sent where she dwells, in the Above? Would you make him face the torture of going to the one place he despises? Or would you tear Hexley or Embrette from one another?"

Eligius shook his head slowly. He didn't have to mention Noric, of course.

"Theoretically," Noric asked, "how does it work?"

"Our blades," Eligius replied. "There is a reason they have always been able to wound but not cull us. We speak an incantation that invokes a charged circle around us, a sort of channel to the Above. The tone of this chant is key. Once the circle is cast, only a reaper can cull another reaper, and only with one of our weapons. According to the pages I have from Vasilios, a single slice from one of your blades to another horseman's flesh will kill, as long as the wound is given within this circle. For me, however, it will take one cut from each of you."

Noric was in a delayed state of shock, eyes wider than I'd ever seen as he digested the astonishing news. He did not move or even breathe for several long seconds, and I could tell he was struggling with the idea of his possible mortality. The mechanics of it seemed logical, however. If a reaper's blade caused injury to a reaper *outside* a magical circle, wielding it within one…

My chest tightened. "There will be no cuts at all," I gritted out, "because you're not dying for me. Did Vasilios know Adam or any of the earliest ikavorn to verify these supposed pages? How do we even know if any of this is true?"

"Because Vasilios never *wanted* it to be true, but he told me anyway," Eligius replied cryptically. "Told me what he's hidden all these years," he whispered to himself, staring into space.

Why would Vasilios care if the information was true? I wondered. *So what if reapers could die and have another take their place and…*

Oh.

And I'm Eligius's daughter. One he'd do anything for.

I sucked in a breath, slowly realizing that though they were made to stay apart… somehow, from afar, Vasilios might have fallen in love with my father.

But it was unclear if Eligius returned the feeling.

Clasping his hands, Death continued in a firmer voice, "While his information may be incorrect, it is clear to me that Vasilios *believes* it to be accurate information, handed down from one ikavorn to the next."

"But how would she take your place?" Noric asked, finally finding his voice. His eyes were clouded with confusion, but I could see the hope blossoming there too. "What exactly happens if… when we die? How would Ava become Death?" With a quick glance at me, he hastened to add, "Theoretically."

"It is theoretical indeed, as I do not know any of this with certainty," Eligius agreed. "The text claims that a black mist will appear, and souls within the circle can sort of *push* themselves into the position, perhaps similar to the manner in which spirits push to the side and refuse the Above. But it has to be a person's choice to claim the role—the mist will not choose the reaper." My father drummed his fingers on the armrest, just once. "Another aspect I am unsure of is if, being Death, the rule is different for me, and the information Vasilios has does not address it. Should it require a more hierarchical ascension, than it is you, Noric, who will have to push into the role I vacate, and Avalia will then seize yours."

Nearly shouting, I cried, "I'm not seizing anything. I refuse, and if it is my choice, you cannot make me." The hysteria I'd bottled up over the past few weeks wouldn't be held back any longer, and emotions shot out of me with the force of a volcanic eruption. Warm tears spilled over my cheeks as I sprang to my feet, as I insisted, "If a push is required or some other action on my part, than I will refuse to do it. Don't you understand, I won't let you die for me! You're *Death*. You always were and always will be. Not me, *please*. I'm just Ava. Just a human girl."

Noric studied me like I was a puzzle with a missing piece. I lifted my chin at him because I knew there was no way he could force me to do it.

Eligius covered his eyes with one pale, slim hand, and sighed deeply. "Okay, Lee Lee. Okay. You're right in that regard. I can't make you if you won't do it."

Noric swore beneath his breath, shot to his feet, and grabbed me. "Ava, *no*. You will do as your father says, you will do as I say. Do you understand me? You will do as you're told."

"I would think you'd know by now," Eligius said, cocking a sad smirk, "that she does not. Will not."

"Ava, no," Noric repeated, fingers encircling my arms so tightly I thought I might bruise. *"No*. You will not die. I won't let you, not if there's another way."

I held Noric's face and said, "Find a different one. Because it won't be this way."

MOMENTS LATER, ELIGIUS summoned the horsemen to Grimsmere, sat them down in the armory hall, and repeated the story. Sevastian's face was the picture of shock—*and* horror. I knew he was thinking that, however painful his life on earth, it would be worse for him to be condemned to a land where Zosime dwelled, happily ever after with her true love. Hexley and Embrette clasped each other's hands tightly, as if they could be torn from one another any minute.

Backing up his tale, Eligius withdrew the papers Vasilios had provided—two weathered documents, tattered around the edges. I conceded that they were old, but that didn't prove anything. The horsemen nearly grappled to be the first to read the texts, and once they reviewed them quickly, they spent the next hour re-reading slowly, dissecting every word.

It wasn't long before they inevitably decided to try the incantation, testing the validity by at least casting this supposed circle. I knew they would soon enough, but I protested it anyway, and Noric insisted that I remain in the house while they went to the woods to experiment. Witnessing something else forbidden was probably unwise, he'd said, given the trouble I'd already gotten into. So I anxiously paced the hall and bit my nails until my father and the horsemen returned.

Their speechlessness upon entering the house told me everything.

Sevastian collapsed onto the sofa with a blank, horrified stare. Hexley poured himself a drink with shaky hands, and then one for Embrette as well. My father and Noric both looked sallow, grim.

"It works?" I breathed, hoping somehow to be wrong.

"There's at least… a way to cast a circle that's seemingly… charged," Noric answered slowly, still in a state of shock. "Similar to the mists when you fly with a Strider."

I was rapidly shaking my head before he'd even finished. "Good to know, but it means nothing right now. No one is dying for me."

The reapers didn't say anything and I kept talking, fearing that if I didn't fill the silence they might speak telepathically and leave me out.

"Why doesn't Vasilios want the role?" I demanded. "Death is far more powerful than any vampire, even an ancient one."

"And it's a role with far more responsibility than any ikavorn will ever know," Eligius answered. "He is not compelled to serve any god or master but himself, and that suits Vasilios. Why would he assume the work of a reaper when he already has power without service?" Eligius closed his eyes and corrected, *"Had."*

Everyone in the room froze in unison, and the tension in the air caressed my neck like an icy, phantom breath. I hated being a step behind.

"What is it now?" I asked. "What's happening?"

"War," Noric said. "War will be declared. Names have appeared in the book for an upcoming assault… many innocents."

He didn't say where and I couldn't bear to know. I slapped my hand over my mouth, but it was too late. Bile rose, and I ran to the bathroom to vomit what little I ate. Noric was immediately behind me, holding my hair away from my face. When I finished, I rinsed my mouth out and straightened.

Looking at his reflection in the mirror, I declared, "I have to die. Don't you see? I caused this to happen, they want me."

I stormed out of the bathroom before Noric could argue, but he caught up to me in seconds, grabbing my waist and spinning me around. There was no breaking his steel grip.

"If you die, I will follow you," Noric vowed. "I will invoke this circle and ask Sevastian to push his sword into my heart."

"No don't, please," I begged, holding Noric's face. "Then I would die twice. Because as long as you live, some part of me lives too. Please. Carry my memory and find happiness again. I—I want that for you. Wouldn't you want the same for me, if the situation were reversed?" Tears slipped down my cheeks and my nose ran. "And what good would it do when I am Eliminated, and you'll most likely be sent to the Above?"

Noric's eyes flashed angrily. Then he roared, pulled away from me, and stormed out of the house. I started to follow but my father laid a hand on my shoulder.

"Let him go," he said.

"You won't let him cull himself, will you?" I asked, panicked. "I mean, if it's even possible? Once I'm gone, please don't let him die."

"I will not allow it," Eligius assured me, and I relaxed.

I NEVER REALIZED how quickly the sun moved across the sky, until I was willing it not to. Too soon it dipped below the horizon, and hope seemed to set with it.

We'd searched all day, and we failed. Noric translated the incantation into English for me, but not having the original words made it almost useless. The reapers read the pages until they'd memorized them, then ransacked our library and others as well.

At my father's command, Noric whisked himself directly into the heavily guarded depths of the Vatican archives and pulled out any books he thought might have some clues or connection to the spell, to vampires, to Adam and Eve. Some of the texts were so old, simply handling them threatened the integrity of the pages and I was sure exposing them to the air couldn't be good. Eligius sent Hexley and Embrette to seek out scrolls and clay tablets from ancient libraries in Egypt, Turkey, and Morocco. Lastly, Death ordered Sevastian to pilfer grimoires from private collections across Europe. We cross-referenced anything we could find, looking to further illuminate Vasilios's pages, searching for any hints that might expand upon the knowledge the reapers had waited millennia to receive...

...and would still be studying long after I was gone.

I had to admit there was a keen thrill running through me at being able to possess, on a whim, any book or any artifact I desired. If I wasn't about to die and Noric was still my professor, I would have insisted we *borrow* these old books for more rigorous study. Of course, I would have to spend years brushing up on several ancient tongues first. Outside of modern English and basic Russian and French—the major languages of ballet—I wasn't much use in deciphering the pages.

It was dark in Solebury when I realized I needed sleep. We were still in our library with piles of priceless, *temporarily-stolen* tomes and documents from the secret libraries of the world. I'd only managed to nibble some bread Sanderson brought, and I was too distracted to even notice what kind. Noric offered to stay with me until I fell asleep in my bed, but I didn't want to leave everyone and insisted I sleep on the couch while they continued to research.

Falling asleep was difficult, and only the idea of being too tired to miss my last day on earth forced me to get rest. The last thing

I remembered was wondering what everyone would speak about while I slept and worrying they would scheme to change my mind.

But when I awoke, Noric was beside me with hollowed, grief-stricken eyes, telling me he'd accepted my refusal.

"Don't say it," I croaked. "I know. It's my last day alive."

Tears were already streaming down my face.

I don't want to go. I'm not ready.

"We researched all day yesterday and we can do it again today, but… we've been talking while you were sleeping—"

I braced. They were going to fight me on my decision. "I knew it."

"-And we thought it might be good for you do something else… something else before…" Noric's voice cracked and it took him a few seconds to continue. "There's a gala in Los Angeles, a secret party the night before the solstice. A ball. I thought maybe…" Noric looked down and had to work his mouth a few times before he could speak again. I watched his throat dip as he swallowed. "Would you like to attend? I thought you might like to spend your last night dancing before returning here, to Grimsmere to…"

To die. He didn't say it.

I thought the offer over, drawing my knees to my chest and chewing my lip. What would I like to do, in my final hours? Not many people had the blessing and the curse to know when their end was coming.

Yes, dance, I thought. *Dance and then return to Grimsmere, my home. Make love with Noric one last time. And then… let him reap me.*

I tried to speak, but all I got out was, "Yes. Ball. Thank you."

Every cell in my body was urging me to run and stay far away. But I would return for my scheduled Elimination because there was no point in trying to escape it. The gods would simply drag me back to where I was doomed and kill me themselves. They might even punish the world some more if I tried to avoid my fate, and I couldn't do that.

But I also would return because I wanted to retain what little control I had, and that meant that I would rather Noric be the one to reap me.

So no, I would not run.

I would dance, and then I would die.

CHAPTER 42

LIKE OUR WEDDING, NORIC HAD PROCURED my attire for the affair. Tonight's dress was a little too short—a frequent issue with clothing at my height—but I didn't mind because I didn't want to wear high heels anyway. If I wore my red pointe shoes, the gown's hem hit perfectly along my ankle, so I laced up the footwear that always made me feel the most comfortable.

This was the outfit I was going to die in, I realized with a jolt.

If I'd ever thought about it though, pointe shoes would have been what I'd choose to wear at my end. And the dress was fit for a runway.

Would I be buried in it?

I involuntarily clutched my throat. All this time to prepare, and I hadn't even discussed with my father what I wanted him to do with my corpse. I'd have to let him know that a burial in our graveyard was probably best. Going into the earth of Grimsmere suited me more than being cremated and thrown to the wind or kept in an urn somewhere.

With macabre fascination I stroked the rich, red satin of my gown. The color made it impossible not to think about dripping blood, but such images never frightened me. The dress was such a work of art, it seemed a shame to go into the earth with me, never to be seen or worn again.

I left the opera-length gloves on the bed and hoped I didn't look out of place without them. I didn't want anything to obstruct my hands from touching Noric on my last night alive.

Diamonds are a lady's swords, my dear, and pearls, her shield.

Yvette's voice echoed in my mind. Any hope I had of seeing her or Archie again was lost with my Elimination.

To honor her memory, I selected my pearl earrings and a delicate diamond necklace to wear. Not that anything or anyone could help battle against what was coming for me.

Noric was waiting in our hall as I descended the stairs, and he was so handsome that my heart sputtered before remembering how to work again—then racing to prove it. *Mine,* my aching heart screamed from my very first look at him. *This man, this reaper, is all mine.*

Noric's unusual height and preternaturally fit body made him stand out wherever he was, but it was his sculpted face where mortals found their eyes returning again and again, and I was no exception. He looked ridiculously perfect in an all-black tuxedo. It wasn't traditional though, which made me worry less about my lack of gloves. Wherever we were going, the dress code had to be flexible.

I skipped the last step, ran to Noric, and kissed him deeply. *Don't cry and ruin the night,* I scolded myself, digging my fingers into his shoulders. But I knew I wouldn't be able to help it when my time came closer.

As Noric and I broke apart, my father, Embrette, Hexley, and Sevastian stood in the hall with us.

"You'll have her home before sunrise," Eligius ordered Noric. It sounded like something a father would say to a boy taking his teenage daughter out on a simple date. I gave a pained laugh, wanting to pretend that I was a young, regular human, and his words were no more than a reminder to an eager boyfriend to have me home by curfew.

Embrette laid a hand on my shoulder. I had to bite my lip to keep from sobbing, but I couldn't slow my panting.

Don't faint and ruin your last night on earth.

"We'll all be here when you return," she said softly, giving me a reassuring squeeze.

Be here to say goodbye.

She didn't say that part, but I knew.

Flying upon Orphnaeus, Noric took us on a more unhurried route to Los Angeles. As the end of my life barreled toward me, as it sped nearer and faster, we conversely slowed down, savoring every minute. I tried to remember the endless sky of stars, the caress of the wind on my face, and Noric's strong arms around me. I wanted to be as close to him as possible, though I simultaneously wished I had flown one last time with Orsha. I would be sure to say goodbye to her when we returned.

I swallowed back a lump in my throat. There were so many things I wanted to do at my end, and not enough time to do them all.

At our slower pace, we arrived above LA in a few minutes. The night was clear, cloudless, and the lights of the sprawling city stretched out in every direction below, ending at the dark ocean on one side. Although I was well-traveled, I wasn't intimately familiar with Los Angeles, and I didn't know exactly where we landed when Noric brought us down to an ornate mansion. The lawn was bordered by tall hedges and thick walls, and we settled into a shadowed corner of the grounds.

Noric helped me dismount, as it was tricky with the many layers of my dress, but he kept me in a bridal carry as he walked toward the brick pathway.

I cocked an eyebrow and he explained, "I won't let you get your slippers dirty."

"Aren't you going to whisk us inside?" I whispered, when he finally stood me on the path and relinquished invisibility, joining a few other guests on their way to the front doors.

Noric winked and said, "Let's cause a little trouble. Do it the fun way."

I wondered if he might summon Embrette for a moment, so that she could use her power of obliging to persuade the guards to let us pass. There looked to be two or even three checkpoints ahead, each confirming a guest's identity. But instead, Noric simply took my hand and pushed his way past each guard like he owned the place. Inevitably, the guard would turn and try pull us back, and Noric would quickly wipe their minds. Then, as the burly men stood blinking in confusion, Noric would ask with mock concern, "Sir? Sir, are you quite alright?"

I'd have to stifle my giggles as I watched each of the guards stammer, too embarrassed to admit they'd blacked out for a few seconds. Noric would crease his brow and ask with exaggerated politeness, "Sir? Do you need me to send someone to check on you?"

The shamed guards would quickly wave us along, not wanting the witnesses of their misstep to linger any longer than necessary.

"Sevastian's rubbed off on you over the years, hasn't he?" I teased Noric as we walked up a small set of stairs.

"Who's to say I'm not the one who's rubbed off on him?" he shot back.

I snorted. "He takes his shenanigans a lot further than you do."

"Are you not impressed?" Noric joked. "We're crashing one of the most exclusive parties in the world and doing it the slow way, so I hope I'm catching up to him with this stunt."

Noric winked as he spoke, and I guessed that he'd been trying to be playful one last time, since it would have been much easier to whisk us directly inside. Or perhaps this memory was one he made for himself, since he would be the only one remaining to remember it.

Don't cry. Don't you dare.

A liveried butler escorted us into the house and to a massive ballroom at the rear. It was appointed in a gilded, French style, with multiple crystal chandeliers and gold mirrors. Rich, brocade curtains were pinned back to reveal arched, double doors. Along another opulent wall, upholstered chairs were lined for guests to take a break. The lights had been dimmed, though several shone along one side of the room where a small orchestra played upon a stage.

I imagined this was a gathering of society's upper crust, so high as to be untouchable, unknowable to the masses. I thought I'd spy a politician or an actress, but as I looked around I didn't recognize any of the faces, and I supposed they preferred to keep it that way. Work and fame were for the needy, and this well-heeled crowd wanted for nothing—other than to be entertained for the evening.

I sighed with relief to notice that I blended perfectly with the women, who wore a colorful array of dresses in various styles. This was not a tight-laced ball one would attend in Prague or Vienna. It was neither new money—straining to assert itself, to declare that it belonged; nor was it old money—strictly adhering to traditions as if clinging to manners would help them hold onto an ever-dwindling pot the younger generations failed to refill. No, this lot was eternally rich; ever was, ever would be, and it followed its own rules.

Had I more time on earth, I would have liked to infiltrate their secret little society. I wondered if they all knew one another and if Noric and I would be rooted out. I released a breathy laugh because whatever these mortals thought of themselves, they were just that—mortals who'd leapt and got lucky.

Enjoy it now, I wanted to say. *For there's no telling where your next leap will land you.*

We'd come to dance, and Noric and I wasted no time getting started. The music was classical, and though I wasn't familiar with each piece the orchestra played, I knew a fair amount from ballet and others from Noric.

And I could always find my feet, could forever rely upon that. No matter the song, no matter the style of music thrown at me, it was as if my body knew how to hold it, play with it, and respond with the right movement. I was born to dance and I did, from one tune to the next. My heart swelled when I heard the first notes of *Emperor Waltz* and we twirled through it. Noric danced better than he ever had before. He was always capable—that wasn't the issue. But his passion when we moved together was never really for the act of dancing itself, but rather his enthusiasm to hold and lift and please *me*.

Tonight, however, he gave it his all, and it was perfect.

All around me, guests toasted the holidays or themselves or whatever excited them. Glasses clinked and they threw back their heads with laughter. They flirted and stole kisses. They jumped up for a dance or threw themselves into a chair, giddy and breathless. I didn't know who these people were, but I began to envy them. Not for their money or their power, but for the length of their mortal lives and their passage to Elysia. The bitter irony did not escape me that I had set myself apart from other mortals for most of my life, and now I'd do anything to change positions with any one of them. All I wanted was to *live,* to be with Noric.

But I wouldn't do it at the cost of my father's immortality.

Hours passed and we spun and spun; my impending Elimination kept me from wasting a second. I couldn't stomach any of the gourmet food from trays the servers carried, but I managed a few sips of Champagne.

Time ticked on. Cruel, merciless, hateful time. Every being was subject to its ruthless rule, and every minute of my countdown forced me further onto my knees.

I was sweating and wisps of my hair had fallen when Noric and I finally stopped for a moment. He looked ready to speak, and I knew the awful thing he'd say. It had to be getting toward sunrise in Solebury; it was past midnight here.

"Another dance," I pled. "Another dance, Noric. This is not a ballet. When I *stop* dancing, it is time to die."

"Another dance," he agreed, voice cracking. "But you want to return home, don't you, Ava? You want to see home again."

"Yes, yes," I said breathlessly, and the tears I'd been holding back all evening slipped down my cheeks. "In the end. But let this not be the end, not yet. Another dance, Noric. One more."

When the orchestra struck up those unmistakable first notes, a half-laugh, half-cry tore through my throat. It was Tchaikovsky's *Sleeping Beauty Waltz*. Even those who weren't a part of the ballet world knew some of the melody, which had been incorporated for the popular song, *Once Upon a Dream*.

Noric took my hand and led me into the dizzying twirls of a Viennese Waltz. Tears streamed freely down my face as we spun. Like the song, I knew Noric in my soul, as if from a dream. I squeezed his hand, remembering first laying eyes upon him at my dinner table. Kissing him in the storm upon his Strider. Picnicking and frolicking in the castle ruins.

Making love in his large, gothic bed.

I'd danced to this waltz so many times, alone in my barn. Never did I imagine, in my youth, that I'd one day be dancing it with a reaper whom I loved madly.

Who was going to kill me in an hour or so.

Perhaps I'd pretend that I wasn't being Eliminated from the universe, but rather slumbering like Aurora, and that one day true love's kiss would awaken me. I chewed my lip to keep myself from breaking down in sobs in the middle of the ballroom. *Yes, when Noric slices his blade over my heart, I'll pretend I'm just going into a deep sleep.*

When the song ended, I threw myself against Noric and nuzzled my head into his chest, weeping all over his pristine black tux. It had to be well past midnight in Los Angeles, so the sun would be rising in Solebury within the hour.

"Okay, okay," I whispered. "I'm ready."

I wasn't. I was so far from ready. But what choice did I have?

The world is hungry and it wants to consume me.

Noric gripped me tightly and his chest shook as he tried not to cry.

"I'll be with you until the end, Avalia."

The only reply I could manage was a whimper. I was starting to feel lightheaded, and I did not want to black out in my final moments.

Noric pulled me into a shadowed corner of the ballroom and lifted my chin. He tried wiping away some of my tears with his thumb, but that only made me cry harder. He swooped down and kissed me and I melted into it.

"I love you, Ava," Noric swore when he pulled back. "Remember that, hold onto that."

"I will," I promised. There wasn't much time to hold onto anything, but I would keep that thought in my mind, even as he reaped me. "I love you more than anything, Noric."

Noric paused and scrutinized my face, wanting to memorize it, I supposed. I let the salty tears fall freely, licking away the ones that passed to my lips, and offered him a weak smile. Weeping wasn't how I wanted him to remember me.

He nodded, almost to himself, then pulled me close to whisk us home.

I didn't know in which room of the house he would reap me. I wondered if I'd left enough time for me to feel him naked and pressed against me, inside me, and hoped that he'd chosen my bedroom. We hadn't discussed the logistics and my panicking mind was losing its ability to function. But the important thing was that I died at Grimsmere.

In a flash, the elegant ballroom disappeared and —

I blinked as I focused.

Noric hadn't whisked us into the manor directly and we weren't alone. We were on the lawn to the left of Grimsmere and my father, Hexley, Embrette, and Sevastian stood in a loose circle around us. The air was still and frosty. A bright moon—either full or nearly—shone through a few wispy clouds. Strangely, two of Noric's larger gargoyles were here too.

My blood ran cold. Something was happening, something *wrong*.

Sevastian was gripping one of his swords, Embrette held onto her small blade, and Hexley had brandished his curved steel. Releasing me, Noric withdrew his own dagger.

"Seize her," Noric told his gargoyles. "Don't release her until I give the command."

My stomach dropped so suddenly it was like I'd free-fallen from a great height.

I didn't understand what they were doing but I was sure of one thing.

I'd been horrifyingly tricked.

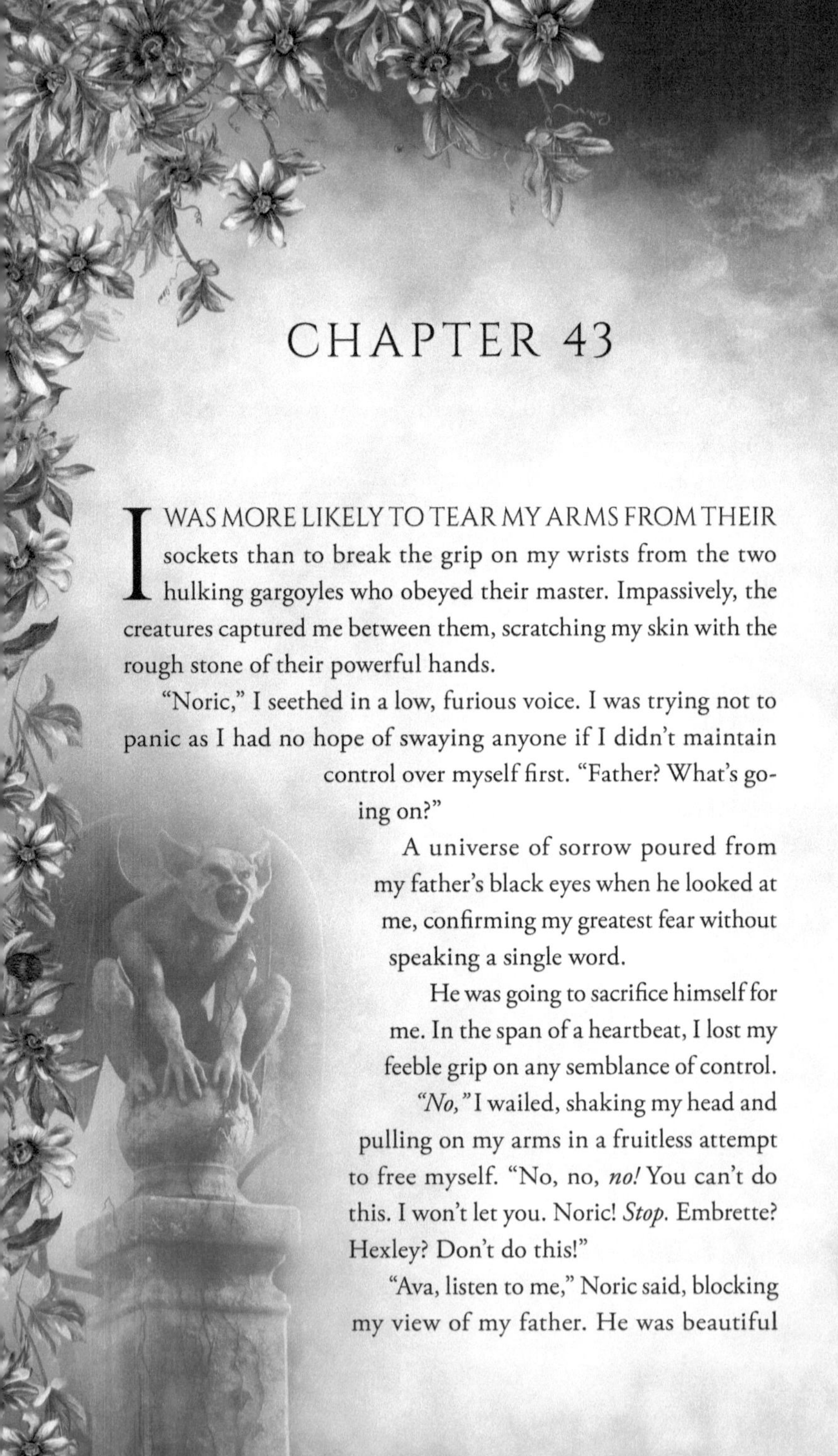

CHAPTER 43

I WAS MORE LIKELY TO TEAR MY ARMS FROM THEIR sockets than to break the grip on my wrists from the two hulking gargoyles who obeyed their master. Impassively, the creatures captured me between them, scratching my skin with the rough stone of their powerful hands.

"Noric," I seethed in a low, furious voice. I was trying not to panic as I had no hope of swaying anyone if I didn't maintain control over myself first. "Father? What's going on?"

A universe of sorrow poured from my father's black eyes when he looked at me, confirming my greatest fear without speaking a single word.

He was going to sacrifice himself for me. In the span of a heartbeat, I lost my feeble grip on any semblance of control.

"No," I wailed, shaking my head and pulling on my arms in a fruitless attempt to free myself. "No, no, *no!* You can't do this. I won't let you. Noric! *Stop.* Embrette? Hexley? Don't do this!"

"Ava, listen to me," Noric said, blocking my view of my father. He was beautiful and terrible and I hated and loved him. "It's as I said. A sacrifice is needed and a recalibration, of sorts, seems to be required. Your father will vacate his role, and you will claim it. That is what the world needs to right itself. Think of it like a repair or an upgrade to the system. *You* are the patch to be applied."

"I'm not anything!" I screamed, trying to shake Noric away as he kissed my forehead. In my heart, I knew they were wrong. *Death always was and always will be.* This was so very wrong, but I didn't know how to convince everyone what I understood in my bones. Who knew how long they were silently communicating this plan to one another?

The pity in their eyes was unbearable. They'd ambushed me; I never stood a chance.

Noric ignored me, stepped back, and began to chant. I'd never heard a sound like their collective reaper voices before, and I finally understood why they were so distinct. My father's hollow echo evoked the vastness of the universe and Noric's rumble was that rough sound of mountains clashing. Embrette possessed the high-pitched noise of insect wings beating and Hexley released a menacing purr-growl like a beast of prey. Finally, Sevastian joined in, whose note reminded me of the haunting resonance of whales.

Together, their voices combined to evoke a divine note that keyed us into the Above. I gasped as the night air swirled, encircling our group in this spell, collecting the five of us and Noric's gargoyles within a channel whose power reverberated in my spirit.

I wondered how many times they'd practiced this casting while I was sleeping. They seemed quietly enthralled by their new power but no longer rendered speechless. I, however, was too frightened of losing my father to be in total awe of the magic.

Beyond the enchantment, the winter woods of Grimsmere were lethally quiet, the cold mountain at our back as silent as the grave. It was the kind of hush that foretold; a pregnant pause during which the earth holds its breath before a catastrophe unfolds.

Once the circle was cast, the reapers stopped chanting and I found my voice again.

"Get off me!" I yelled, breaking the sacred silence and kicking at my cumbersome gown. "Get your gargoyles off me!"

"Ava, we have to do this to save you," Noric insisted. "It's your father's choice. Not yours. Not ours. His and his alone."

I began shouting incoherently. A soft, icy breeze caressed my face, cooling the tears as they soaked my cheeks, but more hot streaks fell in their wake. I was lightheaded and manic and howling hysterically enough that I thought my cries might reach the river. I didn't belong in this scene. The reapers and the realm around us were somber, solemn, and I was shrieking chaos piercing and slashing their reverence.

"Are there any neighbors nearby?" Hexley asked, nervously looking left and right.

"I still can't glamour either," Embrette said in a worried voice. "The spell is preventing it, and this is putting out an energy that's bound to attract attention."

"Our powers do not function properly within this channel we have opened. We must hurry," Eligius said. "I am ready."

That explained why I felt the bite of cold wind. With the casting preventing it, the horsemen had no power to banish the cold December in Solebury.

Eligius pulled me into an embrace, although Noric's gargoyles still held my arms. "I love you, Ava. I cannot think of a better way to end my reign on Earth than to give you my role. Whether I watch over you from Elysia or am Eliminated, know that I love you and that everything I do is for you."

"No, father, listen to me!" I pled, but he did not. Were they all so blinded by their desire to save me that they couldn't see this wasn't *right*?

Or was I the one in denial?

How could I explain when it was just something I *felt*?

Or had my desire to save my father confused me?

Eligius turned to his horsemen, shrugging off his cloak and letting it fall onto the grass. He looked so brave, so gallant. As if he prepared to dance and not to die. Death met his end as regal as a king entering a ballroom, expecting to be greeted by noble kinsmen and courtiers.

"You know what to do. One slice from each of you." Eligius opened the neck of his dark shirt and pulled it wide, baring the pale expanse of his chest. I pled and thrashed but it did no good. Eligius calmly offered his reapers his own flesh as a canvas. Their blades would be the brushes to paint the picture of death into his body.

The circling wind around us picked up speed and the pulse of the spell grew deeper, as if sentient, as if it knew what they intended. Eligius nodded to Sevastian, who stood nearest. My heart pounded a rapid thump upon my ribcage, faster than a mortal hand could beat a drum. The blonde reaper stepped forward and my father nodded again for encouragement.

Sevastian sliced Eligius's chest and I howled as if the lethal sword cut my own skin.

"No, no, no, stop!" I cried, but my words did nothing to hold the horsemen back. They didn't heed my orders, my desires. They obeyed Death, who'd been their king, their commander for as long as they could remember. And they *wanted* to do this; each of them thought it was the right thing.

It wasn't.

I could feel that in my heart, my bones, my soul. But I couldn't convince them.

Embrette approached Eligius and embraced him. Heads bent together, I had no idea what they whispered to one another before she backed up and drew her tiny, lethal blade across his chest.

Eligius winced and swayed on his feet. Two cuts wept blood down the white-gray flesh of his slim torso.

"Stop, please!" I screamed, thrashing against the gargoyles and kicking my ridiculous, luminous skirts. My father was dying and I was in a ballgown, restrained by monsters. My captors were as cold and uncaring as the stone from which they were made. Beneath their punishing grip I could feel the skin of my arms scraping to the point I'd soon bleed, if I wasn't already. It was my own fault for struggling, but nothing could make me stop.

Hexley came next, raising his sword with its sinister curve. When he hesitated like Sevastian, my father again nodded his encouragement.

Gritting his teeth, Hexley only managed to nick Eligius's chest.

But it was enough that my father fell to his knees. My screaming reached heights I'd never thought possible and still everyone paid me as much attention as if I wasn't there at all. Several of Eligius's veishkas appeared, fluttering wildly around the circle in sheer panic.

Noric approached my father.

"No, Noric, please, listen to me! Father, no, don't let him! Noric, please, if you love me, don't do this!"

Wailing and blubbering, tears and mucus ran down my chin and dripped onto my chest and dress. My heart couldn't take the pain of losing my father. Didn't they see that they were killing me anyway?

I was so dizzy that stars danced before my eyes, but as I blinked and focused I realized they were snowflakes. In the clearing around us, the dark, bare branches of trees reached up in supplication as if they yearned for the dusting coating their boughs. My stomach roiled at the scent of freshly fallen snow, something I used to enjoy but would now forever pair with death. In the distance I saw both the warm, white holiday lights on the house and the colorful, cheerful ones upon the trees. It was December, the end of the year and the end of my life no matter what happened. I felt the cold as an entirely external thing; it did not penetrate me, did not cool my sweaty skin. My despair generated its own heat, stronger than any reaper's magic, and it burned my body from the inside out.

"Remember, I don't know if there's a hierarchy." Clenching his teeth against the pain, Eligius struggled to speak. "If the role I vacate requires an experienced reaper, claim it, and ensure Avalia takes the one you'll open."

This couldn't be happening. Eligius was Death, no other. *Death.* Infallible, eternal. He was my father—the man who reached out his hand to me when I was only four years old. I had been alone on the wooden floor, as if I waited there for him to take me away. I loved Death from the moment he offered me that bony hand. How could I not? Who knew what horrible fate had awaited me, lost in the foothills of the Julian Alps, a young girl without parents? He saved me and gave me a life beyond mortal imagination.

"Father, I love you. Don't die, please," I begged. "I love you!"

For a moment, Eligius held Noric's eyes with his dark command, willing his reaper not to falter. Though he was on his knees, there was no doubt that Death was in control. My father slid his gaze to me one last time.

I would be the last thing he ever saw.

"Avalia, in all my millennia of walking this Earth, nothing has compared to the love I have for you, daughter," Eligius said. White snow glittered on his shining black hair and dark reaper shirt. "You are the most magnificent thing I've ever beheld. Raising you, knowing you, loving you, is the only thing I've done that has truly mattered."

"No!" I wailed, slipping into hysteria. The snowflakes and tears on my lashes blurred my eyes, making it hard to see my father, and I wanted nothing more in the world than to hold him with my gaze. My eyes and my tongue were the only things left to me, and I used my mouth to repeat, "*I love you, I love you, I love you.*"

The magical wind around us swirled faster. A putrid sea poured into my mouth, the salt of my sweat, tears, and mucus overpowering my tongue.

"No," I wailed.

Noric raised his dagger, the glint of its steel in the moonlight an absolute horror to behold.

"Please, no. If you love me, you won't do this!"

I lost Archie and Yvette. I can't lose Eligius.

"Not him too," I cried. "You cannot love me if you kill my father!"

I thought my heart would give out in that moment.

Noric squeezed his eyes tight, then roared.

He spun on his heel to face Sevastian.

"She takes my place," he yelled over the din of the swirling magic. "Raise your sword, cut me."

What?

Oh god, no. Not that either.

"Noric, no!" I cried, and the horsemen echoed my protest.

"Noric," my father's voice was strained, guttural. "I command you to stop." He reached up, but wounded so deeply, Eligius couldn't muster the strength to rise from his knees, let alone to intervene.

"You would do the same Sevastian, you understand," Noric's command was a plea. "I will not let Ava face Elimination."

My stomach dropped and I thought I might wretch. However furious I was for his deception and for this plan, I would never want Noric dead. He raced across the clearing and took my face in his hands. I wailed and thrashed because he still hadn't commanded his gargoyles to release me. With my arms stretched and pinned by their steel grip, I couldn't reach out to hold Noric, to stop him.

"I love you more than I love myself. I will not let your soul cease to be," he swore.

"Please, no," I sobbed. "Don't do this."

Noric kissed me all over my face and especially my lips, over and over, hard and urgent. But he couldn't give me a true, deep kiss, because I wouldn't stop begging him throughout.

"Even if my soul is annihilated, my love for you lives on. That cannot be destroyed," he swore, tears streaking his beautiful face.

Beside me, his gargoyles growled menacingly in displeasure, but they did not let me go or stop their master.

Noric turned to his reaper family to say hasty goodbyes, but I barely heard them through my screaming protests. Mimicking my father's earlier offering, Noric opened his shirt to reveal his pale, hard chest to Sevastian.

It was happening all over again, this time with the man I loved. My father cried out, but he wasn't healed enough to physically stop Noric. As the second-in-command, Sevastian followed Noric's order and raised his sword once more.

Noric held my eyes and said, "Always remember that I love you."

Sevastian clenched his teeth and took aim.

I had no power to stop him. Constrained by the gargoyles, I couldn't even command my own arms to fight.

There was nothing left for me to use, except my voice. I scrambled for some notion of a divine vibration, the way the reapers invoked something miraculous to create this circle. But there was nothing magical about me. I could only use the voice I had and hope it was enough. Grasping at anything, I thought about the emotional strength the ghosts leveraged when anchoring themselves or when tethering other souls. There was power in that *wanting*, as father had theorized.

Taking a deep breath, I channeled everything into my lungs— my love for Noric, for my father, for my friends and for life and… hope. All the hope inside me that one wild cry, filled with all of that want, could do *something*.

I released the longest, loudest, most earsplitting scream possible. It rang out, startling the reapers and even myself. The forest echoed with my wail, maybe even shook with it.

When it ended, a deafening silence followed.

One heartbeat. Two.

The reapers were stunned while I struggled to breathe, choking on the tears pouring into my throat.

No.

Looking at their faces, I could see that it hadn't been enough to change anything.

All I'd managed was to buy a couple of seconds. For the span of a few heartbeats, the grounds were silent.

I'd failed.

My scream hadn't been enough to reach the horsemen, to pierce through their resolve and make them stop.

But it penetrated something else.

In that temporary fracture, a word carried on the breeze and into our circle of death.

One word.

The only word in the universe that had the power to stop this nightmare.

Not so much a word as a name.

Not so much spoken as it was croaked.

"Sevastian?"

CHAPTER 44

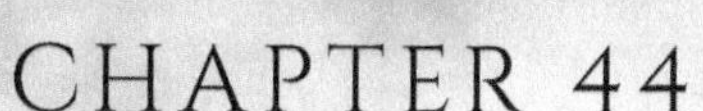

I T WASN'T A STATEMENT, BUT IT WASN'T QUITE a question either. Rather, that one word fell from her lips somewhere between hope and disbelief and without a proper term to describe its quality.

And Olga uttered it.

The sound of his name caused Sevastian to freeze, which, in turn, caused everyone to halt.

My mouth dropped as our housekeeper approached, lured by the raucous magic, lured by my scream, lured by… *Sevastian?* She stared at him as if she knew what he was, as if she saw a god. She wore her long white nightdress and her white hair fell in wiry waves halfway down her back. Olga didn't hobble, but at her age she was unable to walk swiftly across the grass. As she shuffled into the enchanted circle, I flicked my gaze back and forth between her and the blonde reaper. Surprised and confused, so did everyone else.

The color had drained from Sevastian's already-pale face. If Olga saw a god, he looked like he'd seen a ghost. But what kind of ghost could put a reaper on the verge of fainting?

What was in a name that astonished Sevastian to this extent? Was it the tone?

Sevastian's mouth opened and shut several times in a failed attempt to speak. Olga breached our circle by the time he succeeded. Just as Olga's one word stunned Sevastian, his one word shocked the rest of us.

"Zosime?"

Zosime? Zosime?

No, he couldn't mean…

Olga reached the pale, wide-eyed Sevastian and laid her knobby hand on his cheek. Sevastian's chest rose and fell with ragged breaths. I wondered again if he might collapse.

"Zosime?" he whispered, wildly searching Olga's face. "Is it really you?"

"I remember." Her voice cracked as she spoke; the declaration torn from her throat as if brutally yanked free. Tears streamed down her face. "I have been searching for you for more lifetimes than I can count and each time I leapt, I lost you, lost the memory of you. I tried to hold onto it, Sevastian, oh I tried! But I couldn't. Not until now. This—her—what is this?" she asked, waving at the circle. "Her scream, this magic you've evoked… it… it… jogged my memory. *I remember.*"

"This cannot be," Sevastian said, but he was clutching Olga with desperation, even as his words denied it. "How is it possible? It's you, you're here. But you—spurned me. The gods—"

"Showed you a lie!" she sobbed, bringing one shaking hand to her mouth. "An illusion! Games, Sevastian, oh, their games. The test was never for me, it was for *you*." Olga covered her eyes, gasping and whimpering before she could continue.

I stole a glance at everyone and found they were doing the same. It was as if we all wanted to be sure what we were seeing now wasn't some kind of deception.

Olga… was Zosime?

"They held me back and brought the illusion forward. It wasn't real! She pretended to be me, said the things to push you away. They wanted to see if you'd see through it, or if you'd believe their lie. They made me watch, Sevastian! I was shouting but you couldn't hear me. Screaming and shrieking for all I was worth… like her," Olga said, dipping her head in my direction. "Like her scream."

I sucked in a breath. When I was four and I'd sliced my palm, creating that physical reminder… when I'd imprinted the memory deeper in my mind than Death's obscuring could reach… had my scream done something similar, triggering Zosime's memories of her own?

Despite what was unfolding before me, my mind struggled to accept it. I blinked at our old housemaid with her gnarled hands, feeble mind, and wiry white hair, trying to picture the young Greek slave Sevastian had rescued three thousand years ago. It was hard to see either that girl or her soul's true form in the singular picture Sevastian had painted. Where had she been all this time?

Still tightly bound by Noric's gargoyles, I couldn't move, but I was too shocked to muster a step anyway. I glanced at Eligius, who was caught in the same stunned silence as the rest of us.

Sevy's knees gave out and his face crumpled in agony.

"I failed," he moaned, tears streaming down his cheeks as he looked around helplessly. "I failed you, and they parted us. *I* parted us. All this time, I was the one who parted us."

"But I did not give up, my love, and you couldn't have known." Zosime's other hand grabbed his face to steady it, to make him look up at her. "I demanded the gods to give me a chance to find you again. And, if I succeeded in remembering you, then they had to let us be together in Elysia. To send you there with me. You know how they love their mortal bargains, especially in those days. Since there isn't any rule against leaping as one pleases, and they didn't believe I'd ever win, they granted my wish. But *oh,* Sevastian, they were right," Zosime moaned and her whole body trembled. "I tried to look for you in a hundred lifetimes all over the earth, but always I'd forget as soon as I returned here. Sometimes, as a child especially… there were glimmers of you in my dreams. But I thought they were just the fantasies of girlhood and they were fleeting—gone with the sun's rise. But each time when I died, I remember everything all over again, and I'd weep and I'd rage and I'd leap to find you, again and again."

Oh my god. I couldn't imagine Zosime's pain, and being condemned to experience it repeatedly, each time worse than the last.

"Zosime," Sevastian moaned her name. Then he sprung to his feet so fast he might have whisked himself there and kissed her deeply. In the midst of the falling snow and the swirling magic, the blonde reaper kissed our elderly housekeeper. I thought it might change her, and that I'd be able to see the Zosime of Greece or her true form in the Above, but she remained the withered, white-haired Olga.

Sevastian couldn't have cared. Even when he was able to tear his mouth from her, he couldn't tear away his gaze.

"We were both in hells of different making, and I put us there," Sevastian rasped. Disgusted and horrified with himself, he looked as if he wanted to climb out of his own skin. "I should have seen you with my heart and not my eyes. No! I saw you with my fears, and I created millennia of misery for us both."

"No, my love!" Zosime insisted, forcefully shaking her head. "It was a rigged game, an impossible trick they played on you. You couldn't have known. And it doesn't matter anymore. We've *won,* I've found you and I *remember.* I have searched the world and I have finally found you."

"And what have I done in all this time?" Sevastian wept. "What have I done to earn you?"

Zosime's sigh was full of love and admiration. "You endured."

Sevastian didn't look convinced. The rest of us stood immobilized and gaping in our enchanted ring, spectators to a reunion that had been denied for thousands of years.

"If you hadn't rescued me, if you hadn't risked your role for love in the first place, none of this would be possible," Zosime insisted. "I don't imagine you've had an easy life since the day I died."

You don't know yet, I thought. *How much he's yearned for you. How faithful his heart has been.*

"Sometimes I'd leap and live a life of relative peace. I was always a little empty, always searching for something I couldn't name, but I wasn't in agony. While you… you were doomed to never know peace, to always remember."

Sevastian clutched Zosime's hands, stroked her face, and twined their fingers together in her hair. It didn't matter that she was in another form, he would never let her go. Snowflakes fell upon the couple, dusting them with sparkles.

Looking around the circle, Sevastian said, "I don't know what the gods intended, but Zosime, I can die. Here and now, I can return to Elysia with you."

Oh God. A chill ran up my spine as his words set in. Sevastian was offering—no, insisting—he be the one to relinquish his role.

"*Sevastian,*" Embrette whimpered, clutching her heart. Hexley and Noric exchanged tense looks, at war with themselves as they tried not to interfere. Then everyone turned to my father, who, in the midst of the reunion had found the strength to stand. Eligius's eyes fluttered shut and he bowed his head, accepting Sevastian's decision.

Oh my god.

Sevastian let his gaze slide over his sister and his brothers. At Eligius, who was like a father.

"I go willingly, happily," he told them, breathlessly. "You have no idea how happily. Let me go."

No one protested—no one would dare, knowing Sevy's heart as we did. Even if I wasn't there to take the role, they wouldn't prohibit him from vacating it when his Zosime stood before him. But the pain the horsemen felt to lose one of their own after thousands of years together was something I couldn't even begin to comprehend. I swear in that magical circle it became tangible, a desperate grieving in the air.

Sevastian turned to me. "The sun waits for no one, not even an immortal," he said, reminding us that dawn wasn't far off.

"Let her go," Noric brusquely ordered his gargoyles, and they immediately freed my arms. I'd been so stunned by Zosime's appearance, I'd forgotten I was restrained. Sevastian stood before me, and I remained too shocked to even rub my sore and scratched wrists.

"Your coming into our lives was a blessing I could not have conceived until now. You have my deepest apologies and gratitude," he said. "Thank you, Avalia."

"You're welcome," I whispered feebly, unsure what else to say and not wanting to misstep in what would be his final moments on Earth.

"You'll make an excellent horseman," Sevy pronounced. His eyes were full of tears, but they were joyous. "You were born to reap." He looked back at Noric. "And you were born to love each other."

Once again, words failed me, and I could only utter a soft, "Thank you."

"I could not have asked for better immortal companions," Sevastian said to his reaper family. "I love you all. I will miss you. And I'm sorry I haven't been myself the last few years."

Hexley made a scoffing sound in his throat. "Only the last few thousand."

Sevastian grinned and, one by one, he hugged Hexley, Embrette, Noric, and my father. Then he returned to Zosime and met Noric's eyes.

"Set me free, brother."

The blonde reaper wrapped Zosime in the tightest embrace. She was transformed—not into a different body or even a younger version of herself, but into a woman with the sharpest of minds and the strongest of wills.

"It will be over in a few seconds, my love," Sevy said, stroking her face. "Do not be afraid."

"I have died a hundred times," she reminded him, smiling. "I am not afraid. I daresay I am more prepared to die than you are."

Sevastian laughed like I'd never seen before—deep and free, head thrown back. He was transformed too.

"As it was since the beginning," he agreed, pulling her tight and kissing her forehead.

Directing his attention back to Noric, he ordered, "I don't want to take any chances. Use my blade. Strike us through, all the way."

Noric retrieved Sevastian's sword from where it lain forgotten in the snow-coated grass. He approached the tightly locked couple and cupped the back of Sevastian's head, pulling it close to his own and pressing their foreheads together. From the silence, I knew they were saying goodbye telepathically.

"Until it's my time and we meet again in Elysia," Noric swore in an impassioned voice.

"We will see each other again someday," Sevastian vowed.

Noric stepped back and firmed his grip on Sevastian's sword. With several deep breaths, he slowly took aim. Head bent, Noric closed his eyes but did not move for a few seconds. Then, resolved, he snapped his head up to look at Sevastian.

"We will see each other again someday." Noric struggled to grit out the words.

Sevastian gave a tight nod and whispered something to Zosime I couldn't hear. Her once-cloudy eyes shone with pure love as they kept their gazes and bodies locked.

For a moment we all paused, and Noric took one last deep breath. Then, thrusting with all his reaper strength, he pierced both Zosime and Sevastian, skewering them together on Sevastian's sword and killing them instantly.

I couldn't help but cry out, and I wasn't alone.

Oh my god. They're gone.

They'd just been reaped, right before me.

Despite Sevastian's lifeless body, I almost didn't believe it. But at the moment of his death, his drasyg had flashed into view. Those serpentine dragons undulated for a brief second as they flew around us, then disappeared.

Embrette let out a whimper and began shaking. Hexley wrapped her in his arms.

"We'll miss him forever," Hexley said in a hoarse voice. "But he's finally happy now."

"I know, I know," Embrette whispered, tucking her head into his chest.

Noric withdrew Sevastian's sword, gritting his teeth and losing the fight against the tears in his eyes. Gently, he lowered Sevastian and Zosime's bodies onto the grass. There was no time to mourn as the sky had visibly lightened from black to gray. Not only was my death minutes away, but the magic around us was growing and changing in an alarming way.

"Oh my god," Hexley said, stunned. "It worked. Oh my god, there's a vacant reaper role. We actually did it. I can *feel* it. Embrette, can you feel it?"

She lifted her head, eyes wide, and nodded.

The energy that had been swirling around us morphed into something beyond the spell, beyond control—and where Sevastian once stood, a black cloud formed. It was a strange vapor, more than shadow, less than smoke. The magical wind around us blew harder, emitting a powerful new sensation, and the shadow-cloud called to me.

Just as Eligius had said, this was Sevastian's reaper role, and I could take it as easily as stepping forward and accepting it.

"Ava," Noric rasped my name. This time, the tears wetting his eyes were hopeful, thankful. "It's there for you."

Outside our circle, a strange storm gathered. Despite the lightly falling snow, thunder crackled and a flash of lightning illuminated the clearing.

"Ava," my father's voice was a warning. He'd returned to his feet and his wounds were almost fully healed. "This energy is powerful. It's putting out a signal other beings will feel."

"Here, take Sevastian's sword," Noric urged, pressing the grip into my hand. "And claim the power. Just step into the darkness and claim it for yourself."

The nebulous, throbbing cloud of dark energy pulsated harder the closer I came. It wanted me—or at least, it wanted someone. My heart felt a strange tug, like the pull I experienced when I danced to Noric's music.

But when I reached the edges of the shadowy cloud, I stopped and turned around, denying its lure.

"No," I whispered. "I refuse."

CHAPTER 45

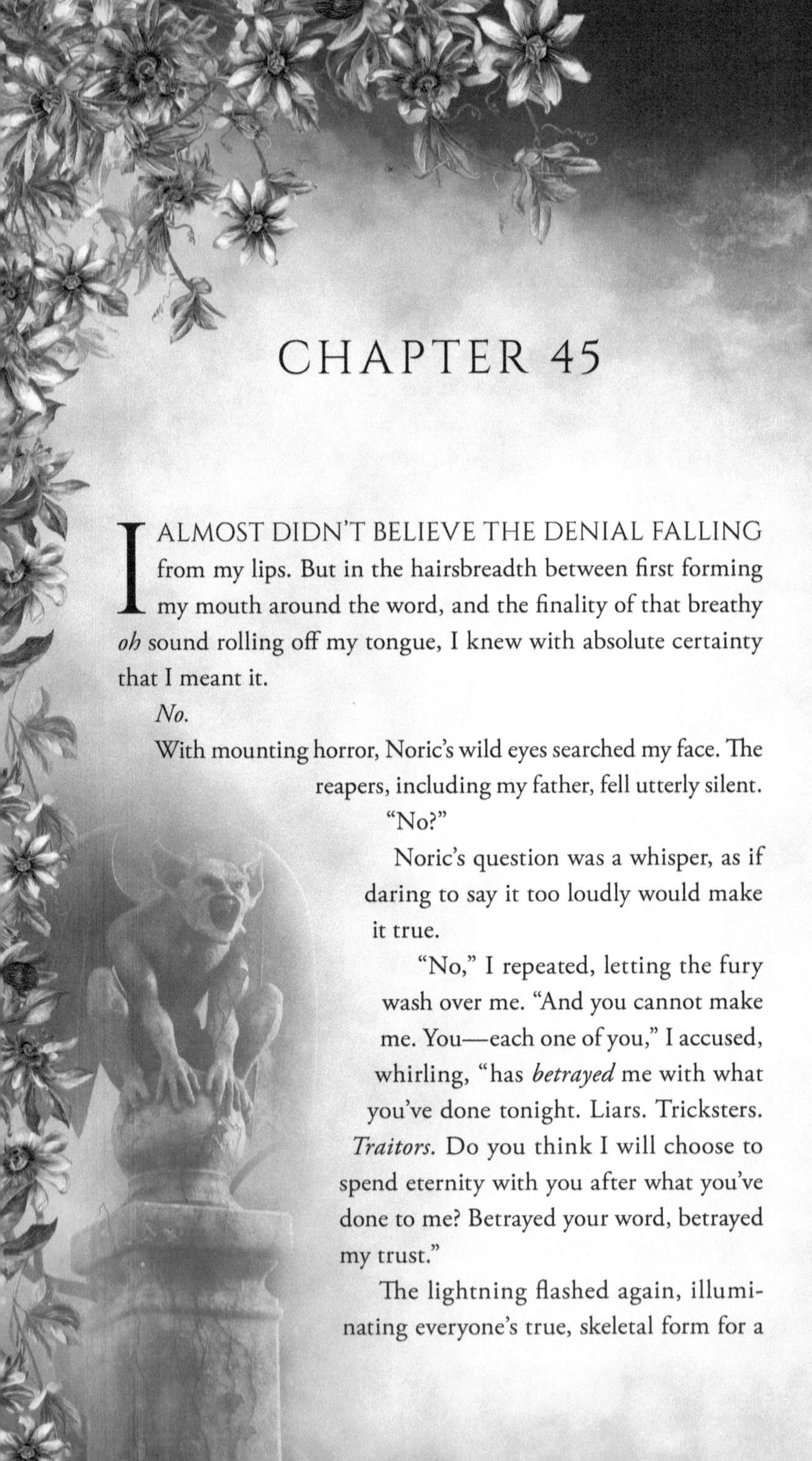

I ALMOST DIDN'T BELIEVE THE DENIAL FALLING from my lips. But in the hairsbreadth between first forming my mouth around the word, and the finality of that breathy *oh* sound rolling off my tongue, I knew with absolute certainty that I meant it.

No.

With mounting horror, Noric's wild eyes searched my face. The reapers, including my father, fell utterly silent.

"No?"

Noric's question was a whisper, as if daring to say it too loudly would make it true.

"No," I repeated, letting the fury wash over me. "And you cannot make me. You—each one of you," I accused, whirling, "has *betrayed* me with what you've done tonight. Liars. Tricksters. *Traitors.* Do you think I will choose to spend eternity with you after what you've done to me? Betrayed your word, betrayed my trust."

The lightning flashed again, illuminating everyone's true, skeletal form for a moment. I hurled my words at everyone but returned my gaze to Noric again and again. His betrayal hurt far more than the others. I could almost forgive my father, could understand that I *didn't* understand the unknowable depths of love a parent had for a child, the kind that would drive them to any self-sacrificing end. But Noric and I had started on such unequal ground to begin with, and for him to leverage his power over me to bring me to an end of his choosing and not my own… it made something inside me buck and howl. To live eternally exposed to this pain… it was unendurable.

Raising Sevastian's sword, I twirled in a slow circle, creating a perimeter around myself. Ice crystals dusted my hair and the voluminous skirts of my scarlet gown. "Stand back, all of you."

No one moved—likely confused about my intentions more than threatened by the blade. The sky lightened as daybreak drew nearer. At the ball, I'd danced longer than expected, and the reunion between Sevastian and Zosime was an unanticipated delay.

Dawn, and my death, weren't far off.

"Ava, if you don't take Sevastian's position, you'll have no true power over that blade," Noric said cautiously, with a hint of hope in his voice that the power would persuade me. "You can harm us, but you can't kill us. Not even in this channel."

He was right, but as I held the sword, I remembered Sevastian's tale of Zosime in her stone tower. Quickly changing course, I swung the blade upward and loosely cupped my left hand around it, watching Noric's face fall in horror.

"Maybe not you, but it has the power to kill me."

One squeeze of my hand and I'm dead, I thought with macabre fascination. Like Sleeping Beauty pricking her finger on the spinning wheel—only I wouldn't fall into slumber, I'd vanish into Elimination.

What was it about the idea that mesmerized me? How many times, over the years, had I danced to a deadly finale in ballet?

Strange, that I'd always felt a pull to it. My lifelong proximity only enhanced my fascination. The sharp edge of Sevastian's supernatural steel glinted, luring me like the night itself. Was Noric right… did I have a death wish?

"Ava…" he groaned my name, voice wracked with pain. Noric raised his arms wide, both preventing others from coming toward me and showing that he had no intention of doing anything that would cause me to touch the blade.

With his head cocked, Hexley's muscles tensed and he announced ominously, "Others are coming."

Embrette clutched his hand. Her voice was strained as she said, "I hear them too."

One look in my father's despairing eyes confirmed it.

"No, *no!*" Noric screamed, whirling. His hands flew to his hair and he tore at it. Still clutching the strands he paused, then howled as I assumed he heard others in the distance as well. "Ava, please. They're drawn to the power. They don't yet know why, but they will."

I could hear nothing but I didn't doubt it as the vibrating magic around us thrummed in my blood.

"Fight them off," my father ordered, turning to Hexley and Embrette. "Use your powers to dissuade them. If that doesn't work, wound, but do not reap them, if you can avoid it."

"I'll hold them off for you," Embrette cried. She tied her hair back and called, "Take the power, Ava!"

"Take the power," Hexley echoed, looking at me pleadingly.

The next instant they were gone, with a trail of ronemins and butterfae briefly appearing, then disappearing in their wake.

"If you die, I will die with you," Noric swore, chest heaving. "I will order Hexley to kill me."

"That's blackmail," I spat, turning to look at my father who seemed in agreement with this plan and likely formulating his own leverage if it didn't work.

"You're right," Noric said in a rush. "It's a terrible thing to do. But Ava, I'm desperate and we don't have time and I *can't* live without you. I'll do anything you say." Noric threw himself onto his knees at my feet. "Tell me, command me, anything you say and I'll make it happen."

I heard the unmistakable grunts and shouts of fighting in the nearby trees. Too close. The pull of this reaper vacancy must have been greater than Hexley or Embrette's ability to oblige or dissuade anyone.

"Ava, love, please," Noric begged, fisting and unfisting his hands. "I'm so sorry for betraying your trust. Ava, *please.*"

"They're coming in greater numbers," my father warned. "Not just mortals but ikavorn and ghosts and… other things."

Thunder rumbled and clouds thickened the sky. Though they darkened our clearing, their formation couldn't stop the dawn. Noric clung to my legs and my hips, but he didn't dare attempt to tear the sword from my hands. I might cut myself in the struggle and what good would it do anyway? He still couldn't force me to take the reaper role.

"If you ever want to trust me again then you *have* to take his place," Noric pled. "If you don't, I'll never get the chance to earn back your trust. If you die, you'll die hating me. The only way I can atone is if you claim the power. Take the role, Ava, *please,* take the role."

He had a valid point. I'd punish us both eternally if I didn't allow him an opportunity to make amends.

"*Lee Lee,*" my father held my gaze, desperate. "Please. You must hurry. This is the way, this is what the universe wants."

I'd never heard Eligius beg before. My name was so strained through his lips, it was barely a sound. His eyes were as black as ever, as dark as a moonless, starless night.

But I found nights of any kind to be a balm to my haunted soul.

"Cataclysmic events are happening, unscripted," Eligius said. His gaze became unfocused, pained. "More names are appearing in the Book the longer you wait."

"It's you, Ava," Noric cried. "The universe wants you. Not to die but to ascend."

I sucked in a breath, still so unspeakably angry at his betrayal. I brought the blade of the sword to Noric's neck, resting it there. It couldn't kill him, but it could harm him, and that would hinder any hope he had of being able to grab me, to plead or persuade me in any way.

Noric's eyes fluttered and he tilted his head to the side, baring more of his long, pale neck and offering me a clean strike. He was even more impossibly beautiful in such despairing supplication. Noric kneeled at my feet, not like a knight awaiting anointment from his queen but bearing the wretched look of the condemned accepting the death blow. Lightning flashed again, showing his skeletal nature, and Noric's eyes alternated between gray human irises, and the large, dark hollows within a white skull.

Either way, he was impossibly, hauntingly striking.

I was so angry that he'd deceived me that I wanted to rake my nails down his perfect cheeks, to make him bleed as he'd made my heart bleed.

Yet I was so in love with him that any spoken word to convey the depth of my feelings was as pitiful as a raindrop in an ocean.

My heart beat for Noric alone, and I could sooner destroy the world than I could deny that truth.

"Swear it," I growled my demand. "Swear it on your life and on my life that you will never again betray me or threaten my father's life or your own."

"I swear it, Ava." Noric's pledge was manic, a plea of promise and regret. *"I swear it, Ava. I swear it,"* he repeated, falling into a breathy, desperate whisper. Suddenly, his eyes blew wide and he cried, "Please, love, hurry. They're here, too many have come!"

I didn't want the blood of so many innocents on my hands— either those nearby, lured by the power, or those faraway, dying in unscripted disasters. If the world was truly speeding toward a collapse, I wanted to do whatever I could to stop it.

And, seeing beyond my fury, I knew I didn't truly ever want to be parted from Noric.

I took a breath and turned to the nebulous energy hovering in the air behind me. It was a translucent cloud of black, pulsating and undulating.

Beckoning.

I choose a life of death, instead of the death of life.

Letting my head fall back, I moved like I'd danced to Noric's divine music, stepping into the darkness and letting it envelop me. It did not claim me—oh no. Eligius was right about that. It was all my choice, my doing.

I take you, I told the magnetizing cloud of energy. It swirled around me with an almost tangible anticipation as it sought a master, a mistress. *I claim you. I take you into me.*

I'd thought I'd claim the sword and the drasyg too, but I was wrong. Sevastian's familiars had already disappeared into the ether and now his sword followed, leaving room for the creation of new beasts and blades.

I heard the caw of birds before I saw them. Darker and larger than ravens, their wings were tipped with a purplish-blue iridescence, perhaps similar to my eyes. The creatures' elongated necks did not match the length of a swan's, but they surpassed that of any crow, giving them a horrific beauty. Their talons were unnaturally long and the slight curve of their beaks ended in a point sharper than any mortal blade.

As I transformed, my heart picked up so much speed I thought it might explode. The beat was pressing the limits of what a human could withstand, and my breath came in rapid punches, trying to keep up.

The magical circle the horsemen first invoked to cast the spell suddenly burst and blew outwards as it dissipated. But the birds circled in its place, caws increasing to a chilling volume. A reaper's familiar was borne of some aspect of the reaper themselves, I remembered, because something about these creatures reminded me of the fluidity and grace of a dancer as they moved.

The wind gusted more fiercely and the birds flew at a supernatural speed. An earth-shattering sound, like that of a mountain cracking, split the sky. Lightning flashed in an intricate web, splintering the firmament like fractures in the heavens. Yet not a single drop of rain fell in this strange storm.

My rushing heart pushed beyond mortal limits, yet my body did not break.

The birds tightened their circle around me, so that I could not only hear but feel the flapping of their wings. I was not the least bit frightened. I was those birds and they were me. The wind whipped my hair, black and beating the air just like their wings. Two shining blades appeared in the air, levitating. Their sudden existence didn't startle me; I knew my weapons as I knew my own limbs. They were longer than Noric's daggers, but shorter than Sevastian's swords. The slight curve was not of any typical mortal design, but a strange blade all my own, arcing more than a sabre yet not as rounded as Hexley's weapons. Perhaps my blades matched my bird's unusual beaks.

I felt my father and his horsemen gaping as they watched, for the first time, a reaper come into power. And *oh,* that power raced through my veins like a divine drug.

Reaching out, I gripped my weapons and brought them to me. My heart rate decreased, matching the deceleration of my birds. My familiars—I'd need to name them. One settled upon each of my shoulders, their weight a comfort, while the remainder rested upon the snowy grass at my feet. I would bear no mortal child, but I'd birthed an immortal flock. The last of the lightning plumed across the sky and I knew my face flashed with it, illuminating the truth of its new, skeletal nature. Then one final, deafening clap of thunder bellowed, an energy exploded all around me, and the wind and the world quieted.

Through the trees, I noticed the first of the sun's rays.

Noric stared at me, enraptured, still as one of his gargoyles. Were it not for the awe and adoration, the love and relief in his eyes, I might have thought he'd turned to stone, while I'd turned into…

…the world. I could feel it coursing through me, I was connected to all of it now. The Reclamation of Souls book, the Rotunda in the sky, the humans slated to die.

Avalia the mortal was gone. I'd become eternal.

A reaper, a horseman.

In death, I was born.

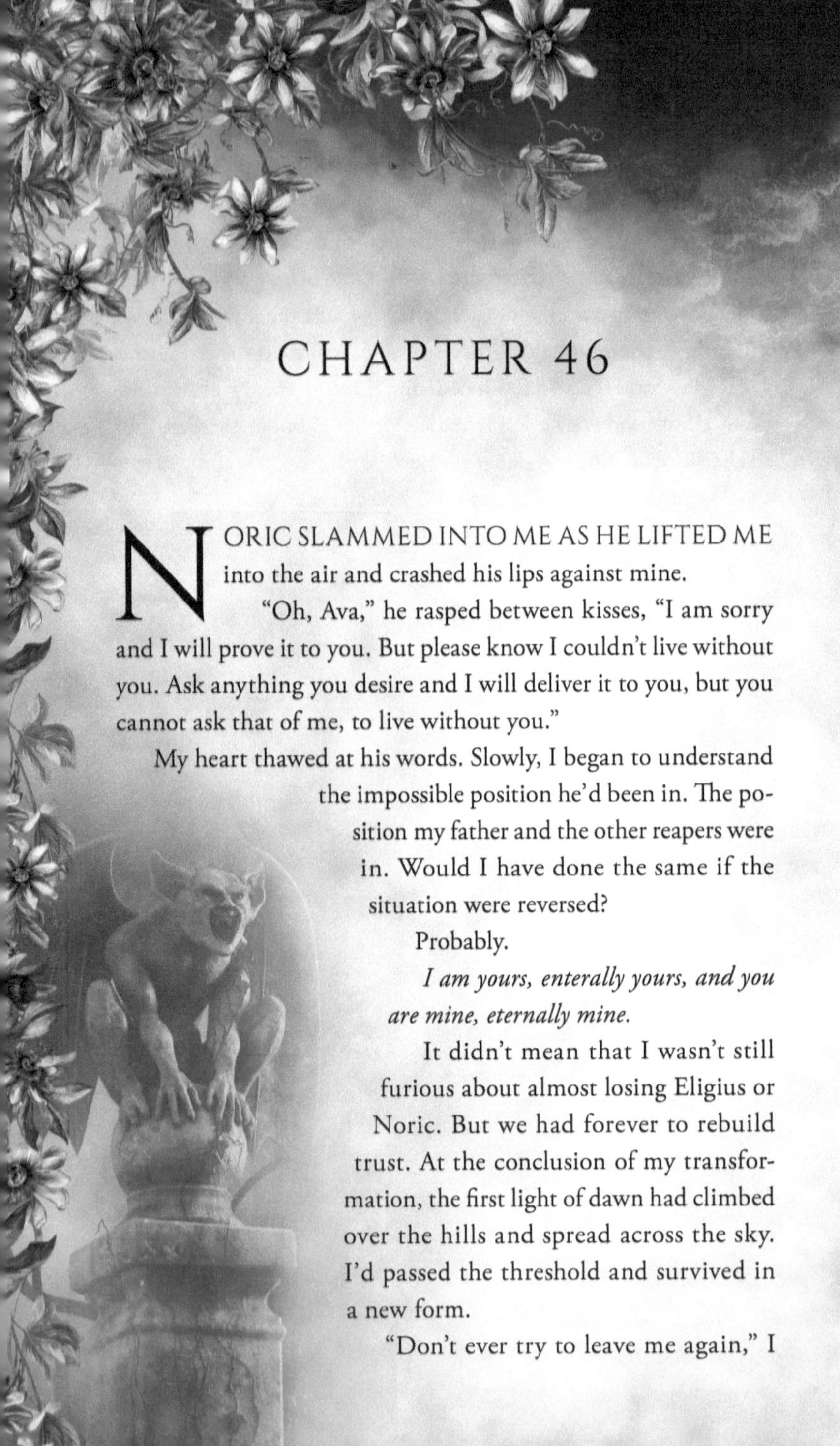

CHAPTER 46

NORIC SLAMMED INTO ME AS HE LIFTED ME into the air and crashed his lips against mine.

"Oh, Ava," he rasped between kisses, "I am sorry and I will prove it to you. But please know I couldn't live without you. Ask anything you desire and I will deliver it to you, but you cannot ask that of me, to live without you."

My heart thawed at his words. Slowly, I began to understand the impossible position he'd been in. The position my father and the other reapers were in. Would I have done the same if the situation were reversed?

Probably.

I am yours, enterally yours, and you are mine, eternally mine.

It didn't mean that I wasn't still furious about almost losing Eligius or Noric. But we had forever to rebuild trust. At the conclusion of my transformation, the first light of dawn had climbed over the hills and spread across the sky. I'd passed the threshold and survived in a new form.

"Don't ever try to leave me again," I

whisper-shouted. "I would rather not exist than to inhabit a world where you don't. Promise me!"

"Never," Noric swore.

He released me to allow my father to embrace me.

"And don't you ever try to leave me again, either," I commanded Eligius as he stroked my hair. "You should know by now I'm never letting you go. It's not for my own good, no life without you could be good."

"My daughter," he whispered, hugging me tighter. "Forever." With a breathy laugh, Eligius added, "Yes, I should know by now that it's as I told Noric. You will have your way."

I laughed. How often had I thought the same of him? "Well, I *am* your daughter. Would you have expected anything less?"

Hexley and Embrette threw their arms around me next. Everyone was laughing and crying, grieving the loss of Sevastian and celebrating my rebirth.

"You are one of us," Embrette cooed, throwing her arms around me again. "A sister."

My father's face was the picture of profound relief, and I was equally relieved to see the light back in his black eyes, a candle's flame illuminating a dark room.

"I *told* you it wasn't right," I said. "I *knew* you weren't meant to die."

You are Death. You are eternal.

And now you are not just my father but also my... boss?

That was going to be weird.

"Everything is going to be good again, I can feel it," Embrette said, smiling. "It's just a spark but... we're going to enter a new age."

Hexley's voice was strong and sure as he echoed, "I can feel it too."

I looked around the misty forest. A light snow continued to fall upon the hillside, dusting the pine trees in sparkles. A blue jay darted past, flying from our manor into the wood. The holiday lights twinkled upon our turrets, as enchanting as ever. All felt right within me and the world, but I couldn't compare it to the past the same way the reapers could. I had died, as the Book ordained, and perhaps I had fulfilled the wishes of the gods too.

Noric stood tightly behind me, not letting me go beyond his reach as he ran his fingers through my hair.

"Perhaps. Perhaps it had to happen like this," Eligius mused. "How do you feel?"

"Powerful. As powerful as the whole world," I answered. "Connected to it on a level I couldn't access before. It's a bit overwhelming."

Noric chuckled in my ear. His hands found my hips. "You'll get used to it."

I knew that with an eternity to practice, he was right.

You have some groveling to do, I admonished him telepathically, wanting to test out my abilities and thrilling at them. *I haven't forgotten.*

Put me through my paces for years, Ava, love. Noric's voice replied directly in my mind, and I jumped a little at my success. *I will bear the harshest punishment from you with the same enthusiasm as if you were to bestow upon me your tenderest affection. You live, and I will live on that happiness forever.*

I tried to think up some terrible penance for Noric, but it would have to wait. I wanted another kind of satisfaction from him more urgently. Hopefully as soon as the sun set and he whisked us to his manor.

I suddenly realized I could whisk myself now.

At the thought I willed it, magically moving myself to the other side of the clearing. I was so shocked it knocked me off balance and I fell into the snow.

I laughed, and my family laughed with me.

"I think I need a shower and something else to wear," I announced. Reaper robes hadn't magically appeared on me, and I still wore the scarlet ball gown.

Finding my feet, I whisked myself back to everyone and, though I swayed, I managed to remain upright this time.

Examining my hands and arms, it seemed nothing on my body was different, and yet everything had changed. If I let in the cold, I could feel it bite, but the bubble of my reaper magic kept me warm without effort. An eerie, gnawing feeling also emanated from somewhere deep inside me. It was barely a tingle, yet I was sure I wasn't imagining it.

My father and Noric exchanged a look, as if they knew.

"You'll need to reap of your own choosing soon enough," Noric announced. "But let's start with the Book first. Tomorrow."

"Today," my father said, kissing my forehead, "I think we all should take a well-deserved break to celebrate the solstice."

FOR THE REST of the day, I vibrated with excitement. My life had been chained to a countdown before and now it came with no limitations. I could dance *forever*. I could love Noric *eternally*. I would never be parted from my father or my new family.

Except, one day, if we chose to relinquish our roles. The reapers only had mere days to process this mind-blowing information, and I knew it would take a long time to really sink in.

They were no longer the same cursed beings some would argue them to be.

Upon leaving the clearing, the first thing I did was to whisk myself up to my bedroom. I tried to shower, but it took longer than usual because Noric insisted on helping me. Whenever I was squeaky clean, he'd manage to make me sticky once more and we'd start all over. I even made it to the bedroom once, only to find myself bent over the bed. We had to return to the shower and repeat the whole process yet again, as somehow that session even tangled my wet hair.

No one said anything when we finally came downstairs to share steaming cups of Sanderson's treasured, mulled wine. The very first sip warmed my *soul.* It tasted like the holidays at Grimsmere. Like a fire in the hearth and snow on the hillside and the scent of the icy river rushing by.

That evening, I had my father alone for a moment as we sipped our holiday wine, and I asked him something I'd been debating how to handle delicately.

"Eligius, did a part of you *want* to give up your role, to follow Vasilios into Elysia? If that is where ikavorn and reapers go?" Softly, I whispered, "Did you… love him?"

I didn't want to invade my father's privacy, but I was unsure what exactly had transpired the day Noric and I found them together. I knew it was more than *chatting,* at least. But did Vasilios strike some kind of calculated deal for the information? Or was it more mutual, more desperate?

"I did not know him enough to love him," Eligius replied, stroking his lips with the backs of his knuckles. "But I admired him, from afar. I suppose, over the years, he did the same, and more than I knew." Eligius templed his fingers, as he often did when thinking. "But if the ikavorn are Eliminated or returned to Elysia, I have no more knowledge of that than I do of what becomes of ghosts." He looked at me sternly and swore, "Know that I did not want to die for the possibility of following him. I have only loved one mortal in this world, and it is you, daughter."

Eligius leaned back in his chair and smiled. *"But,* if anyone could find a way of skirting the rules, if Zosime's story gives us any hope… Well, I would bet on Vasilios to circumvent the system." Eligius released a soft sound through his nose, somewhere between a sigh and a laugh. His gaze grew unfocused, as if he stared at something faraway; eyes dark tunnels to some unknown end. "If we should ever meet again, and in forms where I am not so forcefully compelled to cull him, *well.* Let's just say in that case… I'd very much like to see where it goes."

I smiled and I laid a hand on my father's, hopeful for us all. I had lost Archibald and Yvette, but I would never lose my loved ones again, and now I had a new brother and sister to share in our traditions. As far as children were concerned, I only felt immense relief that that would never be something I had to worry about. Our family was perfect. I could see it now, how we fit together so well. Hexley and Embrette. Noric and I. It was as if the missing puzzle piece had been found and set into place… and it was me.

I still had trouble believing it though.

That night, Sanderson whipped up what he called a *simple* Carbonera pasta—though it was still better than any I'd tasted this side of the Atlantic—and we shared a solstice supper while making plans for the week… and the rest of our lives.

Noric and I agreed to spend the warmer months at Grimsmere, and the holidays too, of course. In the wintertime we'd hole up in his manor, watching the snow fall over the Carpathians and listening to the wolves howl at night. I'd continue studying history, and he'd install a barre for me in one of the spare rooms, so that I could dance there as well. I couldn't *wait* to dance to Noric's playing at his fullest, without the risk of dying. We'd whisk back and forth with the seasons, a customized Hades and Persephone plan, where I could keep my master of death with me in either location.

I looked forward to curling up in Noric's celestial library and reading books, with cup after cup of strong, dark tea, and I was as excited to hike with him in the woods beyond Grimsmere as I was to explore more remote and far-flung destinations around the world.

I was endlessly grateful to never lose my father.

I was overjoyed to hold Hexley and Embrette close to me—something beyond friends and deeper than a mortal family.

All of it was *perfect.*

CONNECTING TO MY new power had easily made it the most amazing day of my life, but when the sun rose the following day, it was time.

The date was December twenty-second; the day after the winter solstice and two days before Christmas Eve.

I'd reaped with my father before and I was no stranger to both the gift and the grief. But it was different, being the one to deliver it myself. Everyone agreed that I should start with the Book, so I did. Soon, however, the craving to cull my own would burn inside me like a fire I needed to cool, and I knew I'd need to choose my first victims within a few days, before the ache grew unbearable.

My desire to reap, however, did not surpass man's own.

Today, the mortals had decided to deliver death to one another in bombastic fashion. From a distance, I surveyed the concrete buildings. The war Noric predicted was de-escalating, but an attack would take place now anyway, bolstered by black market weapons. Two waves in rapid succession were forthcoming, and both sides would suffer severe casualties. I had not written these humans' names in the Reclamation of Souls book, nor had I decided to march them into battle, but I would do my job, collecting their last breaths and ferrying their souls back to the Above.

Noric pressed himself behind me and lightly held my biceps.

"Reap, my love," he whispered in my ear. "The power is yours to unleash."

"All of them? Shall I reap them all?"

"Do you want me to help?" he asked.

"Yes. No." Was it better if I did it alone, or reckless to refuse assistance my first time? "I'll reap the first wave of fighters," I decided. "You come in for the second strike."

Behind me, I felt Noric nod his head.

My heart pounded despite having witnessed the process my entire life. What if something was flawed in my technique and I created inadvertent spectres? Was that possible? I didn't know, since the glitch was a stubborn mystery to begin with.

There was no more time to think as the first shot fired and I whisked to reap the victim. I hadn't even a second to process it before a bomb exploded and I collected the next three souls in rapid succession. From there, it was like muscle memory, though I'd never personally culled before. I knew Noric was watching me and I strived to perform well, to make him proud. The next several minutes were a blur as I culled through the crumbling streets and within the run-down buildings. My power surged through me and it was *satisfied*. Not quite like reaping of my own choosing, but there was a pleasure, however perverse, in doing what I was made to do.

Before I knew it, the first wave of the skirmish was over and the second had begun. I only realized it when I noticed Noric no longer stood in the distance but had joined me in the fray.

He was glorious on the battlefield—rushing, turning, and slashing faster than a mortal eye could follow. Not that Noric allowed the humans to see him at all. But I couldn't take my eyes off him, and the flash of his black cloak whipping in his wake. He was irrefutably unbeatable, a terrifying apex predator.

As am I, I realized, kicking myself back into action. *A dark lady of death.* No ballet had ever ended like this, but I moved with dancer's grace as I pivoted and spun. My magic pulled me to the right person at the right time, and I sliced and ferried, bringing souls back to the Above. I'd trained my whole life for this, even if I didn't know it. I wasn't heartless, but it wasn't a horror. The release of the soul and its return to Elysia was a gift I bestowed.

The shots slowed and the air grew quieter as the men picked each other off. When the last one lay dying on the road, I'd flown to him so fast that I nearly slammed into Noric, who'd done the same. He grinned, stepped back, and spread his hand in offering.

I knelt to reap the last soul.

"You were glorious, my love," he pronounced, looking down at me with that diabolical smirk.

Before I knew what I was doing, I had jumped up, wrapped my legs around Noric's waist, and kissed him deeply. Catching him by surprise, his body shook as he tried not to laugh.

"It felt… right," I told him when I settled back on my feet. I hadn't let go and had to tilt my head to look up at him. "But it hasn't sated the craving."

"No," he said, darkly. "You will have to get used to choosing your own victims every few days. You will try, I am sure, to select carefully. But after many years…" Noric shook his head and trailed off. Then he looked over the destruction around us and said, "They won't all be this easy."

"I know," I said, softly. "I have reaped alongside Eligius."

And I did know. The unspeakable pain. The children, the spouses, the loved ones left alive to mourn. Young ones named in the Book were unquestionably the hardest. It would be so much easier if we could reassure the living. But the mortals didn't know what we knew, and we couldn't tell them.

"Blood," Noric murmured, lifting his hand and wiping my cheek.

"Oh," I said, blushing and wondering what a mess I might be.

"Happens to the best of us." He flashed a half-grin. "Let's return home and clean up. Your birds can take care of the rest of your work for today."

I still needed to name my familiars, but I had plenty of time to decide.

Noric took my hand and together, we whisked back to Grimsmere.

EPILOGUE

OVER THE NEXT FEW MONTHS, the rise in fighting reversed, for now, and the world began to slowly heal. A time of energy and excitement sprouted—tentative buds on a tree. The air hummed with possibility in a way it hadn't in *years,* and people moved faster, smiled more. I understood that another malaise would someday come; everything moved in cycles as we traveled along a golden spiral. But this cycle was just beginning.

I still struggled to comprehend my place in it.

If it was as Eligius theorized and the world's software required an update, if the coding needed a patch… it was hard to believe it had been *me.* Maybe Sevastian was the real sacrifice required, and I was just the beneficiary. Plus there was always more than one solution to repair a bug. Perhaps another could have been applied, and the system would still function, albeit not as smoothly. Maybe I was best suited for the role, because as it looked now, things were working out beautifully. The world might even be entering a new golden age. Who knew, as the will of the overlords was beyond our understanding?

And I couldn't help but ruminate on Vasilios's idea—that we were pieces in a game, stories to amuse the gods.

History doesn't repeat, but it rhymes.

Perhaps it should be that *stories* don't repeat, they rhyme. They echo. They are reshaped and retold. The gods plant the archetypal seeds, and we grow into different versions. *We* are the stories.

When I thought about my decision to breach the Rotunda, and how it triggered a chain of events, I pictured myself as a tale of myth—an inquisitive Eve, a curious little Pandora-patch. My mind raced in a million directions as I considered what was planned by the overlords and where I'd deviated from whatever script they'd tried to write. How much was free will and how much was predestined? Was my father always meant to adopt me? Was I always fated to touch the Book? Did my relationship with Noric play into all this?

Whenever my brain felt ready to burst with possibilities, I considered that maybe I was so far from the truth it was laughable.

But sometimes in bed, I liked to tease Noric about it, just to watch him lose control. I'd whisper in his ear, "I was made for you, my love, crafted by the gods as Pandora was for Epimetheus and sent to the earth to fit you perfectly inside me." Then I'd straddle him and ask, "Do you want to be inside me now, my love?"

Inevitably he'd ravish me, all while looking as if my words alone had finished him off and swearing that *he* had been made for *me* too.

Spring came quickly, and I was stunned to realize it had only been a year since I'd first met Noric—the year of my life where everything changed. We'd just returned to Grimsmere, to the fresh scent of the Delaware River and the mossy earth of our hillside. The first dandelions dotted the wild lawn beside our house, reminding me of Sevastian and Zosime. I wondered if they found eternal love in the Above and hoped so.

"I'm sorry that I took Sevastian's place," I told Noric one day, as we walked along a path with a stunning view into the valley. "I know you will miss him."

"I will, but I'm not sorry for how it turned out, nor is he, I am sure," Noric said, looking out across the hills. "That was the end of Sevastian and Zosime's story on earth, but ours is just beginning."

I sucked in a deep breath, considering the far-away future.

"I might be okay now that I've turned reaper, or I might still be slated for Elimination someday," I mused softly. "And you might be too. We don't know if Sevastian was an exception for Elysia that Zosime negotiated. I could still cease to exist in any form, if the end ever comes. I might scatter into oblivion."

Noric grabbed me by my waist. That piercing gaze cut through me as he swore, "Then I hope I am designated for Elimination too, and if not, I will find a way to follow you into oblivion."

I smiled. "I don't know what the gods have planned, but I know it's going to be a long time before a reckoning of any kind."

Noric cocked a brow. Even that simple gesture made my knees feel like they might buckle and drew heat between my legs. He was so ridiculously gorgeous that it was almost hard to believe he was real.

"When I was slated to die, you said you didn't care about saving the world—not that I believed you. But I do think you meant it, in the moment," I told him. "But saving me may have saved the world. Not just from the latest malaise, but for quite a long time."

"How's that?" Noric asked, searching my face.

"Do you remember what Eligius theorized about wanting? That it's yearning the overlords encourage, especially the love stories?" Noric nodded and I continued, "If it's our collective desire that keeps it all going, that fuels all of this," I said, waving a hand around me to indicate the green hills and the burgeoning forest, our magical manor and the rushing river below, "if our wanting keeps this all going, then the world will never stop spinning. It will never cease to exist, never end."

Knowing where I was going, Noric's gray eyes danced with amusement.

"Because I will never stop wanting you," I declared.

He licked his lips and teased, "So our love sustains the very universe?"

I grinned and blushed. "Well. Maybe it helps."

He took my chin in his hands. "Mmm," he murmured, leaning down and kissing my left cheek. "I'll remind you of that next time you're angry with me." He kissed my right cheek. "Or if you ever seek to deny me in any way," he said, smirking like the devil himself and laying a firm kiss on my lips, "that laying back in our bed and giving yourself to me might just be necessary to keep the world turning."

I laughed and playfully smacked him.

Noric rose his eyebrows even higher than usual, and one hand started a tantalizing climb beneath my skirt. "In fact," he whispered huskily, "if your theory is correct, the more I make you beg and scream, the better off the world will be."

His fingers slipped beneath my underwear and immediately found the spot that made me buck and fall against him. I didn't have to look up to know there would be a self-satisfied gleam in his eyes. His fingers alternated between circling there and dipping inside me.

"Shall we whisk home for the afternoon and help the world heal?"

"Yes," I breathed. "I need you to take me home right now, Noric…" I trailed off, panting too hard to finish because his fingers hadn't stopped moving.

"As my Lady Death commands," he agreed, whisking us back to the Carpathian manor and right into our gargoyle bed.

Over the course of several hours, Noric loved me so wildly as he made me quiver and scream—so fervently as he worshipped every inch of my body—that I was sure the world would never end.

FIN

The Hessian and the Harlot

AS TOLD BY AVALIA THRAILKILL

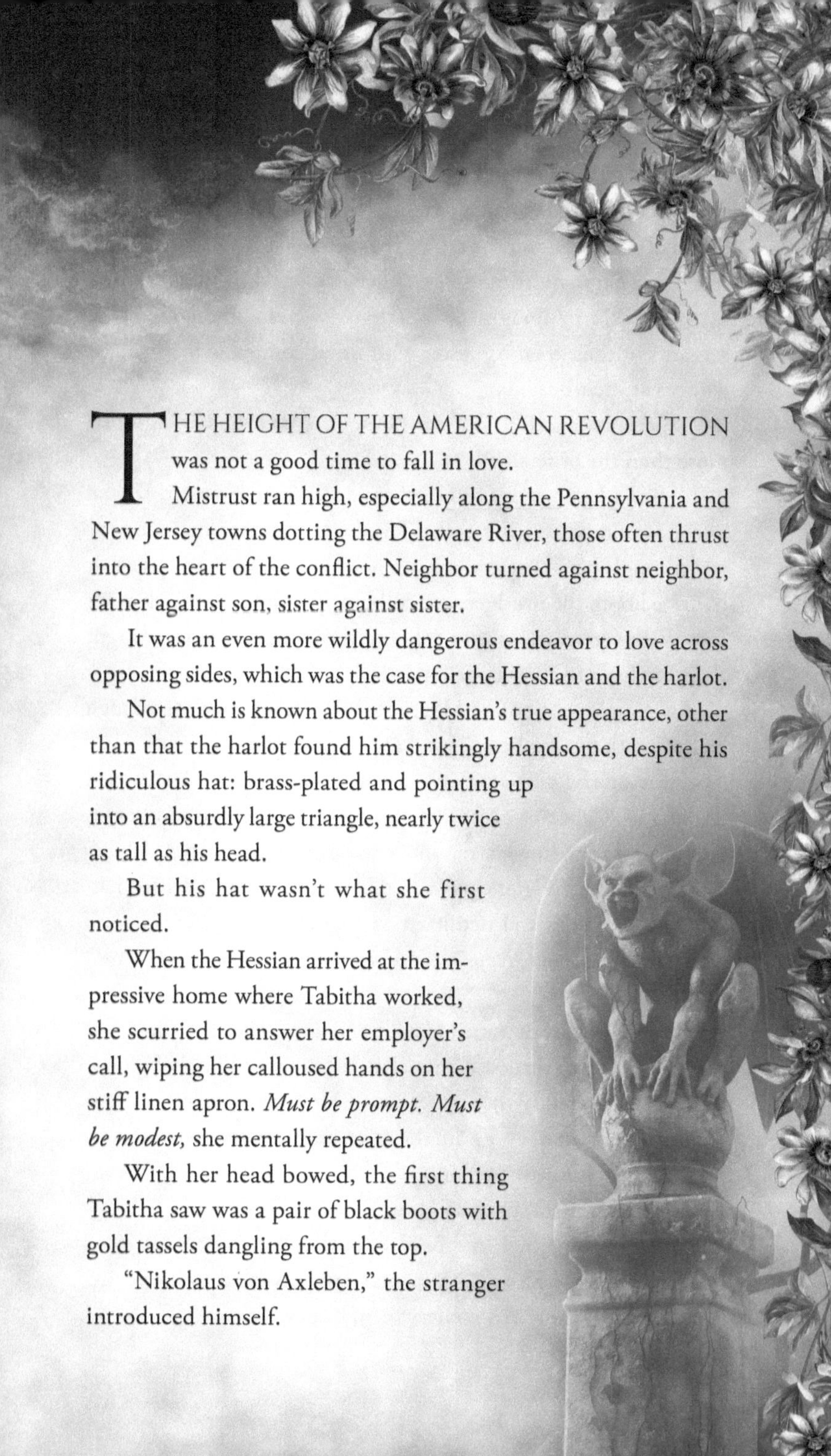

THE HEIGHT OF THE AMERICAN REVOLUTION was not a good time to fall in love.

Mistrust ran high, especially along the Pennsylvania and New Jersey towns dotting the Delaware River, those often thrust into the heart of the conflict. Neighbor turned against neighbor, father against son, sister against sister.

It was an even more wildly dangerous endeavor to love across opposing sides, which was the case for the Hessian and the harlot.

Not much is known about the Hessian's true appearance, other than that the harlot found him strikingly handsome, despite his ridiculous hat: brass-plated and pointing up into an absurdly large triangle, nearly twice as tall as his head.

But his hat wasn't what she first noticed.

When the Hessian arrived at the impressive home where Tabitha worked, she scurried to answer her employer's call, wiping her calloused hands on her stiff linen apron. *Must be prompt. Must be modest,* she mentally repeated.

With her head bowed, the first thing Tabitha saw was a pair of black boots with gold tassels dangling from the top.

"Nikolaus von Axleben," the stranger introduced himself.

His voice, heavy and melodic, reminded her of the time she'd tried alcohol, one evening after serving a dinner party. Half a bottle of port sat upon the table. The drunken men had departed, staggering out to horse or carriage, then heaving their sweaty bodies upstairs, Tabitha imagined, to irritated wives and disinterested servants of their own to pester with unwelcome touches or lewd glances at their bosoms.

Especially men like Chester Pinnock, who leered and groped more than the others.

Tabitha had never imagined the intoxication would feel so sweet, would possess her body like a ballerina marionette, coursing through her veins and setting her limbs to sway in dance. It banished both the drudgery of scrubbing pots and the unrelenting fear that every musket shot echoing through the wood brought the war closer to their doorstep.

Her employer, Bernard Magruder, was already courting enough trouble with his duplicitous and dubious allegiances.

Hearing the deep, melodic tones of Nikolaus's voice carried Tabitha away like that port wine. Lifting her eyes off the floorboards for the first time in what felt like years, she took in von Axleben's handsome face. Wigless, powdered hair poked out under his hat, curled at the sides and tied back. His chest—*was this a man or a beast?* she wondered. *How could a mere mortal be so broad, so tall, so strong?*

Tabitha's heart pounded like it wanted to escape her chest. She was caught in the throes of immediate attraction and Nikolaus was even more riveted by her appearance. How was it that the most beautiful woman to ever walk the earth had been sequestered away to serve in this loyalist's manor?

In that moment, not a single word was spoken for one to know the heart of the other. In rare cases of true love, words are but a bonus, and Tabitha and Nikolaus's eyes revealed every desire, whether they wanted to confess them or not.

Much later that evening, when nothing stirred but the rustling of trees enchanted by night winds, or the odd hoot of an owl in those branches …. later, when Nikolaus's fingertips brushed Tabitha's lips in the cove of springy ferns where they lay… her heart succeeded in its endeavor, breaking free of her chest and finding its rightful place enveloped in his.

Their time together was cut short when Nikolaus was sent to Saratoga, but he promised to return and marry Tabitha. They would stay in Solebury, but if the world wouldn't let them be, if the war never ended, they vowed to run West together.

Nikolaus had no choice but to fight, having been shipped straight from Hesse and conscripted to aid the British. Tabitha secretly and fervently supported the rebellion, though she feared the escalating war. Something about it always felt personally ominous to her.

And Bernard Magruder, her employer, was a shrewd man playing both sides—loyalist on the surface, rebel spy beneath, triple agent below that cover, and even deeper and closer to the truth—a man who acted in his own self-interest, swinging according to each situation. When the dust settled on the last battle, Bernard would assure that he came out on top either way. The man was more than a turncoat, he was a spinning top, and whichever way he fell once set into motion was anybody's guess.

He had not counted on his own slipping up; hadn't thought it possible.

One moonless summer evening, Bernard was ambushed by Washington's men, who'd grown suspicious that their dubious agent was playing both sides. Unable to conclusively prove his devotion to the revolutionists, character witnesses were called.

Tabitha, his serving girl, was amongst them.

If they hung her employer, she'd be out of work and without a roof over her head. Since Nikolaus had been sent to Saratoga, Tabitha had no one else to help her and no way to know when he'd return. *If* he'd return. Because why hadn't he written?

Reluctantly, Tabitha testified on Bernard's behalf.

But it wasn't enough. Her employer was hanged for espionage and as an unexpected result, her own reputation was now called into question.

Tabitha found herself out of work, homeless, and more alarmingly...

...pregnant.

And Nikolaus still hadn't written.

At just this desperate moment when she had nothing, Chester Pinnock, one of the local men who enjoyed groping her at Bernard's many dinner parties, proposed marriage. Tabitha had no choice but to accept, though she wondered if he may have schemed for this exact end, having been the one to encourage her to testify for Bernard in the first place.

Her fate went from bad to worse, when their wedding night was a horror beyond anything Tabitha could have imagined. The monster earned himself a knife in the gut from his bride.

Eight times.

Which may or may not have occurred before the slicing of his genitals, which authorities found in a chamber pot.

Traumatized and terrified, Tabitha hadn't been quick enough to even attempt escape, and she was quickly caught and ordered to a speedy execution. With no alternative, she was forced to reveal her pregnancy, showing evidence of the slight bump in her stomach.

A bump which couldn't have come from her husband.

Harlot, they called her and *harlot* she'd henceforth be known.

Tabitha's hanging was stayed until she delivered her baby, and during that time she received one last blessing.

Tabitha learned that Nikolaus had been wounded at the Battle of Saratoga, but he was still alive. Her Hessian wrote, unknowing her fate, and informing Tabitha that he'd been taken in by peaceful Quakers. Once healed, he would come as fast as he could to Tabitha, to his love.

He was too late.

Tabitha gave birth to her baby and Chester Pinnock's family quickly intervened with their vengeance. Instead of the regulatory hanging, they circumvented the proceedings by kidnapping and publicly burning Tabitha instead. Such cruelty was unheard of for the region at that time, and the scene erupted in chaos.

It was straight into that fiery pandemonium that Nikolaus raced to return. When he saw what happened, he raged, killing as many revolutionaries as he could with his musket, his sword, even his bare hands—until he was shot and killed himself, right beneath the charred corpse of the woman he loved.

To the locals, the mystery of the baby's father had been solved, which was the only satisfaction they desired.

But while the townsfolk couldn't outright refuse, no cemetery truly wanted to take the bodies of the now infamous Hessian and harlot. Eventually, the couple was given space in the graveyard of the small settlement at Devil's Acres. Years later, this land was purchased by Death himself.

Now here, at Grimsmere, those bones have been laid to eternal rest.

Some folk called the orphaned infant a bastard, or traitor spawn, or worse. Some called it a miracle or a blessing, like all life.

But though the graves of the Hessian and the harlot are preserved in our cemetery, no one, not even Eligius, knows what ultimately became of the baby.

ALSO BY ELORA MORGAN